VISIONS OF FEAR

Clive Barker
Philip K. Dick
Gertrude Atherton
E.T.A. Hoffman
Octavia Butler
Richard Matheson
Edgar Pangborn
Mary Wilkins Freeman
Gerald Durrell
Scott Baker
Thomas Ligotti

D0057943

Tor anthologies edited by David G. Hartwell

The Ascent of Wonder
Christmas Forever
Christmas Stars
Northern Stars (with Glenn Grant)

The Dark Descent

The Color of Evil
The Medusa in the Shield
A Fabulous, Formless Darkness

Foundations of Fear

Shadows of Fear
Worlds of Fear
Visions of Fear

VISIONS
OF
FEAR

FOUNDATIONS OF FEAR VOLUME III

EDITED BY

DAVID G. HARTWELL

A TOM DOHERTY ASSOCIATES BOOK
NEW YORK

This is a work of fiction. All the characters and events portrayed in this book are fictitious, and any resemblance to real people or events is purely coincidental.

VISIONS OF FEAR: FOUNDATIONS OF FEAR, VOLUME #3

Cover art by Tom Canty

A Tor Book
Published by Tom Doherty Associates, Inc.
175 Fifth Avenue
New York, N.Y. 10010

Tor® is a registered trademark of Tom Doherty Associates, Inc.

ISBN: 0-812-55001-3

First Tor edition: November 1994

Printed in the United States of America

0 9 8 7 6 5 4 3 2 1

To the editors and anthologists who first gave the genre a canon in the 1920s–1940s;

To the publishers who stuck with it and gave the genre an identity for better or worse;

To the writers who often ignored them all and just wrote powerfully and well;

And finally, to my children, Alison and Geoffrey, without whom I couldn't have completed the book during difficult times.

Acknowledgments

This book continues the revaluation of horror literature I began in *The Dark Descent,* and so to the same people and books given credit there I continue my indebtedness. Discussions with Alfred Bendixen (and of course his books) have proven helpful, and with Robert Hadji, whose wide reading in and out of the genre and considered critical judgement have influenced several of my choices for inclusion herein. The support of those who were enthusiastic enough about *The Dark Descent* to demand that I continue working in this area—particularly Joanna Russ—carried me through a number of rough spots. Certainly the most important acknowledgment is to Kathryn Cramer, not only for discussion, critical commentary, and moral support, but for sharing with me her unfinished writings and researches on horror publishing and the distinctions between category and genre, and on Henry James, as well as her published work surveying influences among horror writers today. At every point her creative insights have been provocative and useful. The critical reconsideration of the evolution of horror in literature begun by Kathryn Cramer, Peter D. Pautz, and myself five years ago has borne a variety of fruits, including all our various anthologies. This is only the most recent.

No acknowledgment would be complete without proper recognition of the support of my publisher, Tor Books, who took a chance. To Tom Doherty, publisher, and Melissa Singer, editor, for patient enthusiasm, my sincere gratitude.

Contents

INTRODUCTION

I   High and Low

There is no delight the equal of dread.

   —Clive Barker, "Dread"

. . . if not the highest, certainly the most exacting
form of literary art.

   —L.P. Hartley on the ghost story

Taken as a whole, the output . . . stands in need of
critical study, not to erect theories upon subterra-
nean surmises, but by using direct observation and
following educated taste . . . to enlarge for all readers the repertory of the well-wrought and the
enjoyable.

   —Jacques Barzun, Introduction to
   *The Penguin Encyclopedia of
   Horror and the Supernatural*

We dislike to predict the future of the horror story.
We believe its powers are not yet exhausted. The
advance of science proves this. It will lead us into
unexplored labyrinths of terror and the human
desire to experience new emotions will always be
with us. . . . Some of the stories now being published in *Weird Tales* will live forever.

   —editorial, *Weird Tales* (vol. 4, no. 2; 1924)

This anthology of horror literature is a companion
volume to *The Dark Descent*, continuing a pano-

rama of examples and an examination of the evolution
of horror as a mode of literary expression from its roots
in stories in the early Romantic period to the rich
varieties of contemporary fiction. In *The Dark Descent*,
it was observed that the short story has, until the 1970s,
been the dominant literary genre of horror throughout
its evolution (horror was in at the origination of the
short story and has evolved with and through it); and
that it is now evident that the horror novel is in a period
of rapid development and proliferation, for the first time
achieving dominance over the shorter forms. So it is a
particularly appropriate historical moment for us to look
back over the growth and spread of horror stories.

Furthermore, a general consideration of literary examples yields several conclusions about the nature of horror. First, that horror is not in the end either a marketing
category or a genre, but a literary mode that has been
used in every genre and category, the creation of an
atmosphere and emotional environment that sparks a
transaction between the reader and the text which yields
the horrific response. Horrific poems and plays and
novels predate the inception of the short story. There
can and have been western horror stories, war horror
stories, ghost stories, adventure stories, mystery stories,
romances—the potential exists in every category.

But by the early twentieth century, horror began to
spread and separate in two directions, in literary fiction
and in popular literature, mirroring the Modernist distinction between high art and low, a distinction that is
rapidly disintegrating today in the post–Modern period,
but remains the foundation of marketing all literature in
the twentieth century. For most of the century, horror
has been considered narrowly as a marketing category or
a popular genre, and dismissed by most serious readers
and critics. In many ways, horror is associated with
ghosts and the supernatural, which in a way stand for
superstition and religion—and one of the great intellec-

tual, cultural and spiritual battles of the past 150 years has been on the part of intellectuals, to rid western civilization of the burdens of Medieval religion and superstition, especially in the wake of the great battles over Darwin and Evolution. The Modernist era, which began in the late nineteenth century, is an era of science.

The death of horror was widely announced by Modernist critics (particularly Edmund Wilson, who devoted two essays to demolishing it), the specialists such as Lovecraft and Blackwood denounced, and the psychological investigations of Henry James, Franz Kafka, Joseph Conrad and D.H. Lawrence enshrined as the next stage in literary evolution, replacing superstition and the supernatural as the electric light had replaced the flame.

Yet it was precisely at that moment, in the 1920s and 1930s, that the first magazines devoted to horror began to appear, that the first major collections and anthologies of horror fiction from the previous hundred years were done, and the horror film came into prominence. Significantly, Lovecraft, in his classic study, *Supernatural Horror in Literature* (1936, revised), in examining the whole history of western literature concluded that over centuries and in a large preponderance of texts, the true sensations of horror occur rarely, and momentarily—in parts of works, not usually whole works. He wrote this during the generation when horror was actually becoming a genre, with an audience and a body of classic texts. A threshold had been reached after a century of literary evolution, in which a parallel evolution of the ghost story and the horror story had created a rich and varied body of tropes, conventions, texts, and passed, and the horror genre was established as a vigorous variety of popular literature, in rich interaction with the main body of the literature of this century ever since. One can speculate that, since the religious and superstitious beliefs had passed from overt currency in the reading public, their transformation into the subtext of horror fiction fulfilled certain desires, if not needs, in the audience and writers. As was noted in *The Dark Descent,* the most popular current of horror fiction for decades has been moral allegories of the power of evil.

The giant of the magazines of horror was *Weird Tales,* founded in 1923 and published until the 1950s (and recently revived). It was there that H.P. Lovecraft, Frank Belknap Long, Robert E. Howard, Clark Ashton Smith and many others flourished. Davis Grubb, Tennessee Williams, Ray Bradbury and many other literary writers also published early work in *Weird Tales,* which was hospitable to all forms of the weird and horrific and supernatural in literature. "Up to the day the first issue of *Weird Tales* was placed on the stands, stories of the sort you read between these covers each month were taboo in the publishing world. . . . Edgar Allan Poe . . . would have searched in vain for a publisher before the advent of this magazine," said the editorial of the first anniversary issue in 1924.

One of the conditions that favors genrification is an accessible category market, and *Weird Tales* provided this, along with a letter column in which the names and addresses of correspondents were published. This allowed readers and writers to get in touch with each other, and they did. The Lovecraft circle was composed of writers, poets and readers, and generated thousands of letters among them over several decades, forming connections that lasted years after Lovecraft's death in 1937, some at least until the death of August Derleth in the 1960s. Some of the early correspondents were involved, as Lovecraft was, in the amateur journalism movement of the teens and twenties, and they generated amateur magazines and small press publications, which flourished from the 1930s to the 1960s—their descendents exist today. The World Fantasy Awards has a separate category award for excellence in fan publishing each year, and there are many nominees. So *Weird*

Tales was seminal not only in creating a genre, but also in creating a field, a subculture of devotees.

In the 1940s and 1950s, the development of the popular form continued and, through a series of historical accidents, came under the protective umbrella of the science fiction field, as did the preponderance of fantasy literature. H.P. Lovecraft and many of his circle published in the science fiction magazines of the 1930s. And the letter-writing subcultures generated by the science fiction magazines interpenetrated with the horror field, creating one body, so that by the late 1930s the active fans commonly identified themselves as fans of the fantasy fiction field.

In 1939, the great science fiction editor, John W. Campbell, Jr., whose magazine, *Astounding Stories,* dominated science fiction, founded a companion magazine, *Unknown,* devoted to fantasy and horror, and to modernizing the style and atmosphere of the fiction. Campbell, who had written an influential science fiction horror story in 1938, encouraged his major science fiction writers to work for his new magazine, and in the five years of its existence, *Unknown* confirmed a bond between horror and science fiction that has not been broken, a bonding that yielded the flowering of SF horror movies in the fifties and encouraged a majority of the important horror writers for the next fifty years. Shirley Jackson once told me in conversation that she had a complete run of *Unknown.* "It's the best," she said. Several of Jackson's stories first appeared in the 1950s in *The Magazine of Fantasy and Science Fiction* (as did, for instance, one of the earliest translations of Jorge Luis Borges). Since the 1930s, a majority of the horror stories in the English language have first appeared in genre magazines.

In times when censorship or conventions operated to deter authors from dealing specifically with certain human situations, the occult provided a reservoir of images which could be used to convey symbolically what could not be presented literally.

—Glen St John Barclay, *Anatomy of Horror*

Meanwhile, from the 1890s onward, to a large extent under the influence of Henry James, writers such as Walter de la Mare, Edith Wharton and others devoted significant portions of their careers to the literary ghost story. "In a certain sense, all of his stories are ghost stories—evocations of a tenuous past; and his most distinguished minor work is quite badly cast in this rather vulgar, popular form. 'The "ghost story,"' he wrote in one of his prefaces, 'as we for convenience call it, has ever been for me the most possible form of the fairy tale.' But at a deeper level than he consciously sought in doing his intended stories of terror (he called, we remember, even 'The Turn of the Screw' a 'potboiler'), James was forever closing in on the real subject that haunted him always: the necrophilia that has always so oddly been an essential part of American romance," says critic Leslie Fiedler.

At the time of his death, Henry James was writing *The Sense of the Past,* a supernatural novel in which a character named Ralph becomes obsessed with a portrait and is translated into the past as a ghost from the future. The supernatural and ghosts were major strains in the work of this great and influential writer throughout his career and, under the pressure of his Modernist admirers, have often been ignored or banished from consideration by being considered only as psychological metaphors during most of the twentieth century. Virginia Woolf, for example, in defending the ghost stories, says the ghosts "have their origin within us. They are present whenever the significant overflows our powers of expressing it; whenever the ordinary appears ringed by the strange. . . . Can it be that we are afraid? . . . We are afraid of something unnamed, of something, perhaps, in ourselves." True, of course, but a defense of the meta-phorical level of the text at the expense of the literal surface—which is often intentionally difficult to figure out.

Since the Modernists considered the supernatural a regressive and outmoded element in fiction, the contemporaries and followers of James who were strongly influenced by the literal level of his supernaturalism have been to a large extent banished from the literary canon. Most of them are women writers. A few, such as Edith Wharton, still have critical support, but not on the whole for their supernatural works. Those whose best work was largely in the supernatural, such as Violet Hunt and Gertrude Atherton, Harriet Prescott Spofford and Mary Wilkins Freeman, have been consigned to literary history and biographical criticism, marginalized. In the recent volume, *Horror: 100 Best Books* (1988—covering literature from Shakespeare to Ramsey Campbell), five women writers were chosen for the list, omitting novelists such as Ann Radcliffe, Emily Brontë and Anne Rice, and every short story collection by a woman—except Marjorie Bowen's and Lisa Tuttle's.

Horror, often cast as ghost story, was an especially useful mode for many woman writers, allowing them a freedom to explore the concerns of feminism symbolically and nonrhetorically with powerful effect. Alfred Bendixen, in the introduction to his excellent anthology, *Haunted Women* (1985), says: "Supernatural fiction opened doors for American women writers, allowing them to move into otherwise forbidden regions. It permitted them to acknowledge the needs and fears of women, enabling them to examine such 'unladylike' subjects as sexuality, bad marriages and repression." He goes on to identify stories rescued from virtual oblivion and observe that "most of the stories . . . come from the 1890s and early 1900s—a period when the feminist ghostly tale attracted the talents of the finest women writers in America and resulted in some of their most powerful and intriguing work." Alan Ryan, in his excellent anthology, *Haunting Women* (1988), adds the work of Ellen Glasgow, May Sinclair, Jean Rhys and Isak Dinesen, extending the list into the present with works by Hortense Calisher, Muriel Spark, Ruth Rendell and others. "One recurring theme," says Ryan, ". . . is a female character's fear of a domineering man, who may be father, husband or lover."

Richard Dalby, in the preface to his *Victorian Ghost Stories by Eminent Women Writers* (1988—from Charlotte Brontë to Willa Cather), claims that "over the past 150 years Britain has led the world in the art of the classic ghost story, and it is no exaggeration to state that at least fifty percent of quality examples in the genre were by women writers." And in the introduction to that same volume, Jennifer Uglow observes, "although—perhaps because—they were written as unpretentious entertainments, ghost stories seemed to give their writers a license to experiment, to push the boundaries of fiction a little further. . . . Again and again we find that the machinery of this most conventional genre frees, rather than restricts, the women who use it."

An investigation of the horror fiction of the nineteenth and early twentieth centuries reveals that a preponderance of the supernatural fiction was written by women and that, buried in the works of a number of women writers whose fiction has been ignored or excluded from the literary canon, there exist significant landmarks in the evolution of horror. Harriet Prescott Spofford, for instance, is emerging as one of the major links between Poe and the later body of American women writers. Gertrude Atherton's "The Bell in the Fog" is both an homage to and critique of Henry James—and perhaps an influence on *The Sense of the Past*. It is provocative to wonder, since women were marginalized in English and American society, and since popular women writers were the most common producers of supernatural fiction, ghostly or horrific, whether supernatural fiction was not in part made marginal because of its association with women and feminine concerns. Just as James (except for "The Turn of the Screw") was forgotten as a writer of supernatural fiction for most of the Modernist era (although it was an important strain throughout his career), so were most of the women who wrote in that mode in the age of electricity. But the flame still burns, can illuminate, can heat the emotions.

In the contemporary period, much of the most popular horror is read by women (more than sixty percent of the adult audience is women in their thirties and forties, according to the most recent Gallup Poll surveys of reading). Best-selling horror most often addresses the traditional concerns of women (children, houses, the supernatural), as well as portraying vividly the place of women and their treatment in society.

Intriguingly, the same Gallup Poll indicates that in the teenage readership, an insignificant percentage ("0%") of girls read horror. The teenage audience is almost exclusively male. Perhaps this is because a very large amount of genre horror fiction (that is published in much smaller numbers of copies than best-selling horrific fiction) is extremely graphic and characteristically features extensive violence, often sexual abuse, torture or mutilation of women alive, who then return for supernatural vengeance and hurt men. One wonders if this is characteristic of boys' concerns.

L.P. Hartley, in the introduction to Cynthia Asquith's anthology, *The Third Ghost Book* (1955), remarked, "Even the most impassioned devotee of the ghost story would admit that the taste for it is slightly abnormal, a survival, perhaps, from adolescence, a disease of deficiency suffered by those whose lives and imaginations do not react satisfactorily to normal experience and require an extra thrill." And a more recent comment: "Our fiction is not merely in flight from the physical data of the actual world . . . it is, bewilderingly and embarrassingly, a gothic fiction, nonrealistic and negative, sadist and melodramatic—a literature of darkness and the grotesque in a land of light and affirmation. . . . Our classic [American] literature is a literature of horror for boys." So says Leslie Fiedler in his classic study, *Love and Death in the American Novel*. Still, one suspects that the subject of who reads horror, and why, and at what age, has been muddied by the establishment of genre and category marketing, and is more complex than has been illuminated by market research and interpretation to date.

II   The Sublime Transaction

The sublime provided a theory of terror in literature and the other arts.

—Carl Woodring, *The Penguin Encyclopedia of Horror and the Supernatural*

. . . confident skepticism is required by the genre that exploits the supernatural. To feel the unease aimed at in the ghost story, one must start by being certain that there is no such thing as a ghost.

—Jacques Barzun, Introduction to *The Penguin Encyclopedia of Horror and the Supernatural*

Supernatural horror, in all its bizarre constructions, enables a reader to taste a selection of treats at odds with his well-being. Admittedly, this is not an indulgence likely to find universal favor. True macabrists are as rare as poets and form a secret society unto themselves, if only because their memberships elsewhere were cancelled, some of them from the moment of birth. But those who have sampled these joys marginal to stable existence, once they have gotten a good whiff of other worlds, will not be able to stay away for long. They will loiter in moonlight, eyeing the entranceways to cemetaries, waiting for some terribly propitious moment to crash the gates.

—Thomas Ligotti, "Professor Nobody's
 Little Lectures on Supernatural Horror"

The transaction between reader and text that creates the horrific is complex and to a certain extent subjective. Although the horrifying event may be quite overt, a death, a ghost, a monster, it is not the event itself but the style and atmosphere surrounding it that create horror, an atmosphere that suggests a greater awe and fear, wider and deeper than the event itself. "Because these ideas find proper expression in heightened language, the practiced reader of tales in our genre comes to feel not merely the shiver of fear, but the shiver of aesthetic seizure. In a superior story, there is a sentence, a word, a thing described, which is the high point of the preparation of the resolution. Here disquiet and vision unite to strike a powerful blow," said Jacques Barzun. M. R. James said that the core of the ghost story is "those things that can hardly be put into words and that sound rather foolish if they are not properly expressed." It is useful to examine literary history and criticism to illuminate some of the sources of horror's power.

We do know, from our study of history, that there was a time in our culture when the sublime was the goal of art, the Romantic era. Poetry, drama, prose fiction, painting strove to embody it. Horror was one of its components. Carl Woodring, summarizing the subject in *The Penguin Encyclopedia of Horror and the Supernatural,* says: "As did the scholars of tragedy, [Edmund] Burke and others who analyzed the sublime asked why such awesomeness gave pleasure when it might be expected to evoke only fear or abhorrence. Immanuel Kant, in his *Critique of Judgment* (1790), explained: "Whereas the beautiful is limited, the sublime is limitless, so that the mind in the presence of the sublime, attempting to imagine what it cannot, has pain in the failure but pleasure in contemplating the immensity of the attempt." Kant noted that the sublime could be mathematical—"whereby the mind imagines a magnitude by comparison with which everything in experience is small —or it could be dynamic—whereby power or might, as in hurricanes or volcanoes, can be pleasurable rather than frightening if we are safe from the threat of destruction."

One response to this aesthetic was the rise of Gothic fiction in England and America, and in Germany, "the fantastic." Jacques Barzun gives an eloquent summary of this period in his essay, "Romanticism," in the aforementioned Penguin *Encyclopedia.* "What is not in doubt is the influence of this literature. It established a taste for the uncanny that has survived all the temporary realisms and naturalisms and is once again in high favor, not simply in the form of tales of horror and fantasy, but also as an ingredient of the 'straight' novel." He goes on to discuss at length the fantastic, the Symbolist aspect of Romanticism, tracing its crucial import in the works of major literary figures in England, France and America. Here, if anywhere, is the genesis of horror fiction.

If the short story of the supernatural is often considered as an "inferior" literary genre, this is to a great extent due to the works of those authors to whom preternatural was synonymous with horror of the worst kind. To many writers the supernatural was merely a pretext for describing such things as they would never have dared to mention in terms of reality. To others the short story of the supernatural was but an outlet for unpleasant neurotic tendencies, and they chose unconsciously the most hideous symbols. . . . It is indeed a difficult task to rehabilitate the pure tale of horror and even harder, perhaps, for a lover of weird fiction, for pure horror has done much to discredit it.

—Peter Penzoldt, *The Supernatural in Fiction*

Now that we have an historical and aesthetic background for the origins of horror literature, let us return to the nature of its power. Horror comes from material on the edge of repression, according to the French critic, Julia Kristeva, material we cannot confront directly because it is so threatening to our minds and emotional balances, material to which we can gain access only through literary indirection, through metaphor and symbol. Horror conjoins the cosmic or transcendental and the deeply personal. Individual reactions to horror fiction vary widely, since in some readers' minds the material is entirely repressed and therefore the emotional response entirely inaccessible.

But as Freud remarked in his essay on the uncanny, horror shares with humor the aspect of recognition— even if an individual does not respond with the intended emotional response, he or she recognizes that that material is supposed to be humorous or horrific. Indeed, one common response to horror that does not horrify is laughter. Note again the M.R. James comment above.

The experience of seeing an audience of teenage boys at the movies laugh uproariously at a brutal and grotesque horror film is not uncommon. I have taught horror literature to young students who confess some emotional disturbance late in the course as the authentic reaction of fear and awe begins to replace the dark humor that was previously their reaction to most horror.

Boris Karloff remarked, in discussing his preferred term for the genre, "horror carries with it a connotation of revulsion which has nothing to do with clean terror." Material on the edge of repression is often dismissed as dirty, pornographic. It is not unusual to see condemnations of genre horror on cultural or moral grounds. One need only look at the recent fuss over Bret Easton Ellis' novel, *American Psycho* (1990), to see these issues in the foreground in the mainstream. Certain horror material is banned in Britain.

And I have spoken to writers, such as David Morrell, who confess to laughing aloud during the process of composition when writing a particularly horrific scene —which I interpret as an essential psychological distancing device for individuals aware of confronting dangerous material. L.P. Hartley, in the introduction to his first collection, *Night Fears* (1924), said: "To put these down on paper gives relief. . . . It is a kind of insurance against the future. When we have imagined the worst that can happen, and embodied it in a story, we feel we have stolen a march on fate, inoculated ourselves, as it were, against disaster." Peter Penzoldt, in his book, *The Supernatural in Fiction,* concurs: ". . . the weird tale is primarily a means of overcoming certain fears in the most agreeable fashion. These fears are represented by the skillful author as pure fantasy, though in fact they are only too firmly founded in some repression. . . . Thus a healthy-minded even if very imaginative person will benefit more from the reading of weird fiction than a neurotic, to whom it will only be able to give a momentary relief."

There is a fine border between the horrific and the absurdly fantastic that generates much fruitful tension in the literature, and indeed deflates the effect when handled indelicately. Those who never read horror for pleasure, but feel the need to condemn those who do, like to point to the worst examples as representative of the genre. Others laugh. But the stories that have gained reputations for quality in the literature have for most readers generated that aesthetic seizure which is the hallmark of sublime horror.

III   Category, Genre, Mode

The modern imagination has indeed been well trained by psychiatry and avant-garde novels to accept the weird and horrible. Often, these works are themselves beyond rational comprehension. But stories of the supernatural—even the subtlest —are accessible to the common reader; they make fewer demands on the intellect than on the sensibility.

> —Jacques Barzun, Introduction to
> *The Penguin Encyclopedia of Horror
> and the Supernatural*

Genres are essentially literary institutions, or social contracts between a writer and a specific public, whose function is to specify the proper use of a particular cultural artifact.

> —Frederic Jameson, *Magical Narratives*

A category is a contract between a publisher and a distribution system.

> —Kathryn Cramer, unpublished dissertation

. . . one thing we know is real: horror. It is so real, in fact, that we cannot quite be sure that it couldn't exist without us. Yes, it needs our imaginations and our awareness, but it does not ask or require our consent to use them. Indeed, both at the individual and collective levels, horror operates with an eerie autonomy.

> —Thomas Ligotti,
> "Professor Nobody's Little Lectures on Supernatural Horror"

Sir Walter Scott, to whom some attribute the creation of the first supernatural story in English, said, "The supernatural . . . is peculiarly subject to be exhausted by coarse handling and repeated pressure. It is also of a character which is extremely difficult to sustain and of which a very small proportion may be said to be better than the whole." This observation, while true, has certainly created an enduring environment in which critics can, if they choose, judge the literature by its worst examples. The most recent announcement of the death of horror literature occurs in Walter Kendrick's *The Thrill of Fear* (1991), which demise Kendrick attributes to the genrification of the literature as exemplified by the founding of *Weird Tales*: "*Weird Tales* helped to create the notion of an entertainment cult by publishing stories that only a few readers would like, hoping they would like them fiercely. There was nothing new to cultism, but it came fresh to horror. Now initiates learned to adore a sensation, not a person or a creed, and the ephemeral embarked on its strange journey from worthlessness to great price. . . . By about 1930, scary entertainment had amassed its full inventory of effects. It had recognized its history, begun to establish a canon and even started rebelling against the stultification canons bring. Horrid stories would continue to flourish; they would spawn a score of sub-types, including science-fiction and fantasy tales. . . ." But three lines later he ends his discussion of literature, and his chapter, by declaring that by 1940, films had taken over from literature the job of scary entertainment. Thus evolution marches on and literature is no longer the fittest. It seems to me very like saying that lyric poetry is alive and well in pop music.

That an intelligent critic could find nothing worthwhile to say about horror in literature beyond the creation of the genre is astonishing in one sense (it betrays a certain ignorance), but in other ways not surprising. Once horror became a genre (as, under the influence of Dickens in the mid-nineteenth century, had the ghost story told at Christmas), it became in the hands of many writers a commercial exercise first and foremost. One might, upon superficial examination, not perceive the serious aesthetic debates raging among many of the better writers, from those of the Lovecraft circle, to Campbell's new vision in *Unknown,* to today's discussions among Stephen King, Peter Straub, Ramsey Campbell, David Morrell, Karl Edward Wagner and others on such topics as violence, formal innovation, appropriate style (regardless of current literary fashion) and many others. That money and popularity was a serious consideration for Poe and Dickens, as well as King and Straub, does not devalue them aesthetically. Never mind that Henry James was distraught that he was not more popular and commercial, and expressed outrage at "those damned scribbling women" who outsold him—even his so-called "potboilers."

The curious lie concealed in James' last phrase (which he used to describe "The Turn of the Screw"), and in the public protestations of many writers before and since, up to Stephen King, today, is illuminated by Julia Briggs. In her *Night Visitors,* she states her opinion, based upon wide reading and study, that the supernatural horror story "appealed to serious writers largely because it invited a concern with the profoundest issues: the relationship between life and death, the body and the soul, man and his universe and the philosophical conditions of that universe, the nature of evil. . . . It could be made to embody symbolically hopes and fears too deep and too important to be expressed more directly." She then goes on to say, "The fact that authors often disclaimed any serious intention . . . may paradoxically support this view. The revealing nature of fantastic and imaginative writing has encouraged its exponents to cover their tracks, either by self-deprecation or other forms of retraction. The assertion of the author's detachment from his work may reasonably arouse the suspicion that he is less detached than he supposes."

To further complicate the matter, the marketing of literature in the twentieth century has become a matter of categories established by publishers upon analogy with the genre magazines. Whereas a piece of genre horror implies a contract between the writer and the audience, the marketing category of horror implies that the publisher will provide to the distribution system a certain quantity of product to fill certain display slots. Such material may or may not fulfill the genre contract. If it does not, it will be packaged to invoke its similarity to genre material and will be indistinguishable to the distribution system from material that does. As we discussed above, horror itself may exist in any genre as a literary mode, and, as a mode, is in the end an enemy of categorization and genrification. It is in part the purpose of this anthology to bring together works of fiction from within the horror genre together with works ordinarily labelled otherwise in contemporary publishing, from science fiction to thriller to "literature" (which is itself today a marketing category).

I have previously discussed, in the introduction to *The Dark Descent,* my observations that horror literature occurs in three main currents: the moral allegory, which deals with manifest evil; the investigation of abnormal psychology through metaphor and symbol; the fantastic, which creates a world of radical doubt and dread. Whether one or another of those currents is dominant in an individual work does not exclude the presence or intermingling of the others. Rather than taking the myopic stance that horror means what the marketing system says it does today, I have applied my perceptions of horror to the literature of the past two centuries to find accomplished and significant works that manifest the delights of horror and which mark signposts in the development of horror. Horror literature operates with an "eerie autonomy" not only without regard to the reader, but without regard to the marketing system. Critic Gary Wolfe's observation that "horror is the only genre named for its effect on the reader" should suggest that the normal usage of genre is somewhat suspect here.

IV   Short Forms

Why an ever-widening circle of connoisseurs and innocents seek out and read with delight stories about ghosts and other horrors has been accounted for on divers grounds, most of them presupposing complex motives in our hidden selves. That is what one might expect in an age of reckless psychologizing. It is surely simpler and sounder to adduce historical facts and literary traditions. . . .

> —Jacques Barzun, Introduction to
> *The Penguin Encyclopedia of Horror
> and the Supernatural* .

It is all the more astonishing to find English weird fiction the property of the drama in Elizabethan days, and later see it confined to the Gothic novel. On first reflection this development seems strange because the supernatural appears to flow more easily into the short tale in verse or prose. The human mind cannot leave the solid basis of reality for long, and he who contemplates occult phenomena must sooner or later return to logical thinking

in terms of reality lest his reason be endan-
gered. . . .

—Peter Penzoldt, *The Supernatural in Fiction*

A horror that is effective for thirty pages can
seldom be sustained for three hundred, and there is
no danger of confusing the bare scaffolding of the
ghost story with the rambling mansion of the
Gothic novel.

—Julia Briggs, *Night Visitors*

Commentators on horror agree that the short story
has always been the form of the horror story: "Thus
if it is to be successful the tale of the supernatural must
be short, and it matters little whether we accept it as an
account of facts or as a fascinating work of art," says
Peter Penzoldt. At the same time, most of them have
observed that some of the very best fiction in the history
of horror writing occurs at the novella length. Julia
Briggs, for instance, after having given the usual set of
observations on the dominance of the short form, states:
"There are, however, a number of full-length ghost
stories of great importance. Most of these, written in the
last century, are short in comparison to the standard
Victorian three-volume novel, though their length would
be quite appropriate for a modern novel. More accurately described as long–short stories, or novellas, they
include [Robert Louis Stevenson, Vernon Lee, Oscar
Wilde, Arthur Machen, Henry James]. They are quite
distinct from the broad-canvas full-length novel of the
period not only in being shorter, but also in using what is
essentially a short-story structure, introducing only a few
main characters within a strictly limited series of events.
The greater length and complexity is often the result of a
sophistocated narrative device or viewpoint. In each of
these the angle or angles from which the story is told is of

crucial importance to the total effect, while the action itself remains comparatively simple."

Only in a collection of this size could one gather a significant selection of novellas, and I have included a number of them to emphasize the importance of that length. I have excluded familiar masterpieces such as Robert Louis Stevenson's "Dr. Jekyll and Mr. Hyde," Henry James' "The Turn of the Screw" and Conrad's "The Heart of Darkness" in favor of significant works such as Daphne Du Maurier's "Don't Look Now" and H.P. Lovecraft's sequel to Poe's *Narrative of Arthur Gordon Pym,* "At the Mountains of Madness," John W. Campbell, Jr.'s "Who Goes There?" (from which the classic horror film, *The Thing,* was made), Gerald Durrell's "The Entrance" and others.

I have included several examples of horror from the science fiction movement by writers such as Robert A. Heinlein, Frederik Pohl and Philip K. Dick, Octavia Butler and George R.R. Martin, wherein horror is the dominant emotional force for the fiction, and a sampling of horror stories by women often excluded from notice in the history and development of horror, such as Gertrude Atherton, Violet Hunt, Harriet Prescott Spofford and Mary Wilkins Freeman. Contemporary masters and classic names in horror are the backbone of the book, Peter Straub and Arthur Machen, Clive Barker and E.T.A. Hoffmann and many others, but for most readers there will be a few literary surprises. Horror literature is a literature of fear and wonder. Here, then, the *Foundations of Fear.*

This is the third of three volumes, published in paperback by Tor Books, that together comprise the entire contents of the large hardcover book, *Foundations of Fear*. The whole work, subtitled "An Exploration of Horror," is a sequel to *The Dark Descent*, the anthology that defies the nature of horror literature for contemporary times. Readers whose interests are piqued by the general introduction and the story notes in this book would do well to go back to *The Dark Descent*, in which similar concerns are addressed.

All of that having been said, the primary purpose of this book is to entertain. The devotee of the weird, horrific and bizarre will find a feast herein, including much unfamiliar material. The general reader will also find a number of surprises and perhaps some unexpected illumination about literary types and literary politics. This work challenges the notion that the supernatural in fiction has in modern times been supplanted by the psychological, the idea that horror is dead.

Horror is one of the dominant literary modes of our time, a vigorous and living body of literature that continues to evolve and thrill us with the mystery and wonder of the unknown. This book explores where it has been and represents some of its finest accomplishments to date. Vampires, ghosts and witches still plague us, along with many less nameable monsters—including, at times, ourselves.

Read on, in fear and wonder.

David G. Hartwell

Clive Barker (b. 1952)

IN THE HILLS, THE CITIES

Clive Barker, originally from Liverpool, now residing in Southern California, was the most exciting new horror writer to enter the horror field in the early 1980s. His six-volume *The Books of Blood* (1984–85) galvanized the attention of horror readers and instantly drew praise from Stephen King, Ramsey Campbell and Peter Straub, establishing Barker as their peer. He immediately turned to the novel form and produced a string of best-sellers, beginning with *The Damnation Game* (1985) and continuing today. He is one of the world's best-known horror writers. His background was in theater, and he became at the same time a filmmaker of considerable popularity, specializing in the horror genre. His major influences are not the literature, but comics and films. His main preoccupations are with the religious and philosophical meanings of sex and violence. He writes quickly and strives for powerful effects over polish and structure—which he frequently achieves. Nowhere more so than in "In The Hills, The Cities." If not his best story, it is certainly his most memorable to date. Barker creates a fantastic, mythic image that relates more closely to the stories of E.T.A. Hoffman than to more recent literature. It is also consistent with the direction his films and novels have taken in the last five years and so perhaps best represents Barker's strengths.

I t wasn't until the first week of the Yugoslavian trip that Mick discovered what a political bigot he'd chosen as a lover. Certainly, he'd been warned. One of the queens at the Baths had told him Judd was to the Right of Attila the Hun, but the man had been one of Judd's ex-affairs, and Mick had presumed there was more spite than perception in the character assassination.

If only he'd listened. Then he wouldn't be driving along an interminable road in a Volkswagen that suddenly seemed the size of a coffin, listening to Judd's views on Soviet expansionism. Jesus, he was so boring. He didn't converse, he lectured, and endlessly. In Italy the sermon had been on the way the Communists had exploited the peasant vote. Now, in Yugoslavia, Judd had really warmed to this theme, and Mick was just about ready to take a hammer to his self-opinionated head.

It wasn't that he disagreed with everything Judd said. Some of the arguments (the ones Mick understood) seemed quite sensible. But then, what did he know? He was a dance teacher. Judd was a journalist, a professional pundit. He felt, like most journalists Mick had encountered, that he was obliged to have an opinion on everything under the sun. Especially politics; that was the best trough to wallow in. You could get your snout, eyes, head and front hooves in that mess of muck and have a fine old time splashing around. It was an inexhaustible subject to devour, a swill with a little of everything in it, because everything, according to Judd, was political. The arts were political. Sex was political. Religion, commerce, gardening, eating, drinking and farting—all political.

Jesus, it was mind-blowingly boring; killingly, love-deadeningly boring.

Worse still, Judd didn't seem to notice how bored Mick had become, or if he noticed, he didn't care. He just rambled on, his arguments getting windier and windier, his sentences lengthening with every mile they drove.

Judd, Mick had decided, was a selfish bastard, and as soon as their honeymoon was over he'd part with the guy.

It was not until their trip, that endless, motiveless caravan through the graveyards of mid-European culture, that Judd realized what a political lightweight he had in Mick. The guy showed precious little interest in the economics or the politics of the countries they passed through. He registered indifference to the full facts behind the Italian situation, and yawned, yes, yawned when he tried (and failed) to debate the Russian threat to world peace. He had to face the bitter truth: Mick was a queen; there was no other word for him; all right, perhaps he didn't mince or wear jewelry to excess, but he was a queen nevertheless, happy to wallow in a dreamworld of early Renaissance frescoes and Yugoslavian icons. The complexities, the contradictions, even the agonies that made those cultures blossom and wither were just tiresome to him. His mind was no deeper than his looks; he was a well-groomed nobody.

Some honeymoon.

The road south from Belgrade to Novi Pazar was, by Yugoslavian standards, a good one. There were fewer potholes than on many of the roads they'd travelled, and it was relatively straight. The town of Novi Pazar lay in the valley of the River Raska, south of the city named after the river. It wasn't an area particularly popular with the tourists. Despite the good road it was still inaccessible, and lacked sophisticated amenities; but Mick was determined to see the monastery at Sopocani, to the west of the town and after some bitter argument, he'd won.

The journey had proved uninspiring. On either side of the road the cultivated fields looked parched and dusty. The summer had been unusually hot, and droughts were affecting many of the villages. Crops had failed, and livestock had been prematurely slaughtered to prevent them dying of malnutrition. There was a defeated look about the few faces they glimpsed at the roadside. Even the children had dour expressions; brows as heavy as the stale heat that hung over the valley.

Now, with the cards on the table after a row at Belgrade, they drove in silence most of the time; but the straight road, like most straight roads, invited dispute. When the driving was easy, the mind rooted for something to keep it engaged. What better than a fight?

"Why the hell do you want to see this damn monastery?" Judd demanded.

It was an unmistakable invitation.

"We've come all this way . . ." Mick tried to keep the tone conversational. He wasn't in the mood for an argument.

"More fucking Virgins, is it?"

Keeping his voice as even as he could, Mick picked up the Guide and read aloud from it: ". . . there, some of the greatest works of Serbian painting can still be seen and enjoyed, including what many commentators agree to be the enduring masterpiece of the Raska school: 'The Dormition of the Virgin.'"

Silence.

Then Judd: "I'm up to here with churches."

"It's a masterpiece."

"They're all masterpieces according to that bloody book."

Mick felt his control slipping.

"Two and a half hours at most—"

"I told you, I don't want to see another church; the smell of the places makes me sick. Stale incense, old sweat and lies . . ."

"It's a short detour; then we can get back on to the road and you can give me another lecture on farming subsidies in the Sandzak."

"I'm just trying to get some decent conversation going instead of this endless tripe about Serbian fucking masterpieces—"

"Stop the car!"

"What?"

"Stop the car!"

Judd pulled the Volkswagen into the side of the road. Mick got out.

The road was hot, but there was a slight breeze. He took a deep breath, and wandered into the middle of the road. Empty of traffic and of pedestrians in both directions. In every direction, empty. The hills shimmered in the heat off the fields. There were wild poppies growing in the ditches. Mick crossed the road, squatted on his haunches and picked one.

Behind him he heard the VW's door slam.

"What did you stop us for?" Judd said. His voice was edgy, still hoping for that argument, begging for it.

Mick stood up, playing with the poppy. It was close to seeding, late in the season. The petals fell from the receptacle as soon as he touched them, little splashes of red fluttering down on to the grey tarmac.

"I asked you a question," Judd said again.

Mick looked around. Judd was standing on the far side of the car, his brows a knitted line of burgeoning anger. But handsome; oh yes; a face that made women weep with frustration that he was gay. A heavy black moustache (perfectly trimmed) and eyes you could watch forever, and never see the same light in them twice. Why in God's name, thought Mick, does a man as fine as that have to be such an insensitive little shit?

Judd returned the look of contemptuous appraisal, staring at the pouting pretty boy across the road. It made him want to puke, seeing the little act Mick was performing for his benefit. It might just have been plausible in a sixteen-year-old virgin. In a twenty-five-year-old, it lacked credibility.

Mick dropped the flower, and untucked his T-shirt from his jeans. A tight stomach, then a slim, smooth chest were revealed as he pulled it off. His hair was ruffled when his head reappeared, and his face wore a broad grin. Judd looked at the torso. Neat, not too muscular. An appendix scar peering over his faded jeans. A gold chain, small but catching the sun, dipped in the hollow of his throat. Without meaning to, he returned Mick's grin, and a kind of peace was made between them.

Mick was unbuckling his belt.

"Want to fuck?" he said, the grin not faltering.

"It's no use," came an answer, though not to that question.

"What isn't?"

"We're not compatible."

"Want a bet?"

Now he was unzipped, and turning away towards the wheat field that bordered the road.

Judd watched as Mick cut a swathe through the swaying sea, his back the color of the grain, so that he was almost camouflaged by it. It was a dangerous game, screwing in the open air—this wasn't San Francisco, or even Hampstead Heath. Nervously, Judd glanced along the road. Still empty in both directions. And Mick was turning, deep in the field, turning and smiling and waving like a swimmer buoyed up in a golden surf. What the hell . . . there was nobody to see, nobody to know. Just the hills, liquid in the heat-haze, their forested backs bent to the business of the earth, and a lost dog, sitting at the edge of the road, waiting for some lost master.

Judd followed Mick's path through the wheat, unbuttoning his shirt as he walked. Field mice ran ahead of him, scurrying through the stalks as the giant came their way, his feet like thunder. Judd saw their panic, and smiled. He meant no harm to them, but then how were they to know that? Maybe he'd put out a hundred lives, mice, beetles, worms, before he reached the spot where Mick was lying, stark bollock naked, on a bed of trampled grain, still grinning.

It was good love they made, good, strong love, equal in pleasure for both; there was a precision to their passion,

sensing the moment when effortless delight became
urgent, when desire became necessity. They locked together, limb around limb, tongue around tongue, in a
knot only orgasm could untie, their backs alternately
scorched and scratched as they rolled around exchanging
blows and kisses. In the thick of it, creaming together,
they heard the phut-phut-phut of a tractor passing by;
but they were past caring.

They made their way back to the Volkswagen with
body-threshed wheat in their hair and their ears, in their
socks and between their toes. Their grins had been
replaced with easy smiles: the truce, if not permanent,
would last a few hours at least.

The car was baking hot, and they had to open all the
windows and doors to let the breeze cool it before they
started towards Novi Pazar. It was four o'clock, and
there was still an hour's driving ahead.

As they got into the car Mick said, "We'll forget the
monastery, eh?"

Judd gaped.

"I thought—"

"I couldn't bear another fucking Virgin—"

They laughed lightly together, then kissed, tasting each
other and themselves, a mingling of saliva, and the
aftertaste of salt semen.

The following day was bright, but not particularly warm.
No blue skies: just an even layer of white cloud. The
morning air was sharp in the lining of the nostrils, like
ether, or peppermint.

Vaslav Jelovsek watched the pigeons in the main
square of Popolac courting death as they skipped and
fluttered ahead of the vehicles that were buzzing around.
Some about military business, some civilian. An air of
sober intention barely suppressed the excitement he felt
on this day, an excitement he knew was shared by every
man, woman and child in Popolac. Shared by the
pigeons too for all he knew. Maybe that was why they

played under the wheels with such dexterity, knowing that on this day of days no harm could come to them.

He scanned the sky again, that same white sky he'd been peering at since dawn. The cloud-layer was low; not ideal for the celebrations. A phrase passed through his mind, an English phrase he'd heard from a friend, "to have your head in the clouds." It meant, he gathered, to be lost in a reverie, in a white, sightless dream. That, he thought wryly, was all the West knew about clouds, that they stood for dreams. It took a vision they lacked to make a truth out of that casual turn of phrase. Here, in these secret hills, wouldn't they create a spectacular reality from those idle words? A living proverb.

A head in the clouds.

Already the first contingent was assembling in the square. There were one or two absentees owing to illness, but the auxiliaries were ready and waiting to take their places. Such eagerness! Such wide smiles when an auxiliary heard his or her name and number called and was taken out of line to join the limb that was already taking shape. On every side, miracles of organization. Everyone with a job to do and a place to go. There was no shouting or pushing: indeed, voices were scarcely raised above an eager whisper. He watched in admiration as the work of positioning and buckling and roping went on.

It was going to be a long and arduous day. Vaslav had been in the square since an hour before dawn, drinking coffee from imported plastic cups, discussing the half-hourly meteorological reports coming in from Pristina and Mitrovica, and watching the starless sky as the grey light of morning crept across it. Now he was drinking his sixth coffee of the day, and it was still barely seven o'clock. Across the square Metzinger looked as tired and as anxious as Vaslav felt.

They'd watched the dawn seep out of the east together. Metzinger and he. But now they had separated, forgetting previous companionship, and would not speak until the contest was over. After all Metzinger was from Podujevo. He had his own city to support in the coming battle. Tomorrow they'd exchange tales of their adventures, but for today they must behave as if they didn't know each other, not even to exchange a smile. For today they had to be utterly partisan, caring only for the victory of their own city over the opposition.

Now the first leg of Popolac was erected, to the mutual satisfaction of Metzinger and Vaslav. All the safety checks had been meticulously made, and the leg left the square, its shadow falling hugely across the face of the Town Hall.

Vaslav sipped his sweet, sweet coffee and allowed himself a little grunt of satisfaction. Such days, such days. Days filled with glory, with snapping flags and high, stomach-turning sights, enough to last a man a lifetime. It was a golden foretaste of Heaven.

Let America have its simple pleasures, its cartoon mice, its candy-coated castles, its cults and its technologies, he wanted none of it. The greatest wonder of the world was here, hidden in the hills.

Ah, such days.

In the main square of Podujevo the scene was no less animated, and no less inspiring. Perhaps there was a muted sense of sadness underlying this year's celebration, but that was understandable. Nita Obrenovic, Podujevo's loved and respected organizer, was no longer living. The previous winter had claimed her at the age of ninety-four, leaving the city bereft of her fierce opinions and her fiercer proportions. For sixty years Nita had worked with the citizens of Podujevo, always planning for the next contest and improving on the designs, her energies spent on making the next creation more ambitious and more lifelike than the last.

Now she was dead, and sorely missed. There was no disorganization in the streets without her, the people were far too disciplined for that, but they were already falling behind schedule, and it was almost seven-twenty-five. Nita's daughter had taken over in her mother's stead, but she lacked Nita's power to galvanize the people into action. She was, in a word, too gentle for the job in hand. It required a leader who was part prophet and part ringmaster, to coax and bully and inspire the citizens into their places. Maybe, after two or three decades, and with a few more contests under her belt, Nita Obrenovic's daughter would make the grade. But for today Podujevo was behindhand; safety-checks were being overlooked; nervous looks replaced the confidence of earlier years.

Nevertheless, at six minutes before eight the first limb of Podujevo made its way out of the city to the assembly point, to wait for its fellow.

By that time the flanks were already lashed together in Popolac, and armed contingents were awaiting orders in the Town Square.

Mick woke promptly at seven, though there was no alarm clock in their simply furnished room at the Hotel Beograd. He lay in his bed and listened to Judd's regular breathing from the twin bed across the room. A dull morning light whimpered through the thin curtains, not encouraging an early departure. After a few minutes' staring at the cracked paintwork on the ceiling, and a while longer at the crudely carved crucifix on the opposite wall, Mick got up and went to the window. It was a dull day, as he had guessed. The sky was overcast, and the roofs of Novi Pazar were grey and featureless in the flat morning light. But beyond the roofs, to the east, he could see the hills. There was sun there. He could see shafts of light catching the blue-green of the forest, inviting a visit to their slopes.

Today maybe they would go south to Kosovska Mitrovica. There was a market there, wasn't there, and a museum? And they could drive down the valley of the

Ibar, following the road beside the river, where the hills rose wild and shining on either side. The hills, yes; today he decided they would see the hills.

It was eight-fifteen.

By nine the main bodies of Popolac and Podujevo were substantially assembled. In their allotted districts the limbs of both cities were ready and waiting to join their expectant torsos.

Vaslav Jelovsek capped his gloved hands over his eyes and surveyed the sky. The cloud-base had risen in the last hour, no doubt of it, and there were breaks in the clouds to the west; even, on occasion, a few glimpses of the sun. It wouldn't be a perfect day for the contest perhaps, but certainly adequate.

Mick and Judd breakfasted late on hemendeks—roughly translated as ham and eggs—and several cups of good black coffee. It was brightening up, even in Novi Pazar, and their ambitions were set high. Kosovska Mitrovica by lunchtime, and maybe a visit to the hill-castle of Zvecan in the afternoon.

About nine-thirty they motored out of Novi Pazar and took the Srbovac road south to the Ibar valley. Not a good road, but the bumps and potholes couldn't spoil the new day.

The road was empty, except for the occasional pedestrian; and in place of the maize and corn fields they'd passed on the previous day the road was flanked by undulating hills, whose sides were thickly and darkly forested. Apart from a few birds, they saw no wildlife. Even their infrequent travelling companions petered out altogether after a few miles, and the occasional farmhouse they drove by appeared locked and shuttered up. Black pigs ran unattended in the yard, with no child to feed them. Washing snapped and billowed on a sagging line, with no washerwoman in sight.

At first this solitary journey through the hills was refreshing in its lack of human contact, but as the morning drew on, an uneasiness grew on them.

"Shouldn't we have seen a signpost to Mitrovica, Mick?"

He peered at the map.

"Maybe . . ."

"—we've taken the wrong road."

"If there'd been a sign, I'd have seen it. I think we should try and get off this road, bear south a bit more—meet the valley closer to Mitrovica than we'd planned."

"How do we get off this bloody road?"

"There've been a couple of turnings . . ."

"Dirt-tracks."

"Well it's either that or going on the way we are."

Judd pursed his lips.

"Cigarette?" he asked.

"Finished them miles back."

In front of them, the hills formed an impenetrable line. There was no sign of life ahead; no frail wisp of chimney smoke, no sound of voice or vehicle.

"All right," said Judd, "we take the next turning. Anything's better than this."

They drove on. The road was deteriorating rapidly, the potholes becoming craters, the hummocks feeling like bodies beneath the wheels.

Then:

"There!"

A turning: a palpable turning. Not a major road, certainly. In fact barely the dirt-track Judd had described the other roads as being, but it was an escape from the endless perspective of the road they were trapped on.

"This is becoming a bloody safari," said Judd as the VW began to bump and grind its way along the doleful little track.

"Where's your sense of adventure?"

"I forgot to pack it."

They were beginning to climb now, as the track wound its way up into the hills. The forest closed over them, blotting out the sky, so a shifting patchwork of light and shadow scooted over the bonnet as they drove. There was birdsong suddenly, vacuous and optimistic, and a smell of new pine and undug earth. A fox crossed the track, up ahead, and watched a long moment as the car grumbled up towards it. Then, with the leisurely stride of a fearless prince, it sauntered away into the trees.

Wherever they were going, Mick thought, this was better than the road they'd left. Soon maybe they'd stop, and walk a while, to find a promontory from which they could see the valley, even Novi Pazar, nestled behind them.

The two men were still an hour's drive from Popolac when the head of the contingent at last marched out of the Town Square and took up its position with the main body.

This last exit left the city completely deserted. Not even the sick or the old were neglected on this day; no one was to be denied the spectacle and the triumph of the contest. Every single citizen, however young or infirm, the blind, the crippled, babes in arms, pregnant women —all made their way up from their proud city to the stamping ground. It was the law that they should attend: but it needed no enforcing. No citizen of either city would have missed the chance to see that sight—to experience the thrill of that contest.

The confrontation had to be total, city against city. This was the way it had always been.

So the cities went up into the hills. By noon they were gathered, the citizens of Popolac and Podujevo, in the secret well of the hills, hidden from civilized eyes, to do ancient and ceremonial battle.

Tens of thousands of hearts beat faster. Tens of thousands of bodies stretched and strained and sweated as the twin cities took their positions. The shadows of the bodies darkened tracts of land the size of small towns; the weight of their feet trampled the grass to a green milk; their movement killed animals, crushed bushes and threw down trees. The earth literally reverberated with their passage, the hills echoing with the booming din of their steps.

In the towering body of Podujevo, a few technical hitches were becoming apparent. A slight flaw in the knitting of the left flank had resulted in a weakness there; and there were consequent problems in the swivelling mechanism of the hips. It was stiffer than it should be, and the movements were not smooth. As a result there was considerable strain being put upon that region of the city. It was being dealt with bravely; after all, the contest was intended to press the contestants to their limits. But breaking point was closer than anyone would have dared to admit. The citizens were not as resilient as they had been in previous contests. A bad decade for crops had produced bodies less well-nourished, spines less supple, wills less resolute. The badly knitted flank might not have caused an accident in itself, but further weakened by the frailty of the competitors it set a scene for death on an unprecedented scale.

They stopped the car.

"Hear that?"

Mick shook his head. His hearing hadn't been good since he was an adolescent. Too many rock shows had blown his eardrums to hell.

Judd got out of the car.

The birds were quieter now. The noise he'd heard as they drove came again. It wasn't simply a noise: it was almost a motion in the earth, a roar that seemed seated in the substance of the hills.

Thunder, was it?

No, too rhythmical. It came again, through the soles of the feet—

Boom.

Mick heard it this time. He leaned out of the car window.

"It's up ahead somewhere. I hear it now."

Judd nodded.

Boom.

The earth-thunder sounded again.

"What the hell is it?" said Mick.

"Whatever it is, I want to see it—"

Judd got back into the Volkswagen, smiling.

"Sounds almost like guns," he said, starting the car. "Big guns."

Through his Russian-made binoculars Vaslav Jelovsek watched the starting-official raise his pistol. He saw the feather of white smoke rise from the barrel, and a second later heard the sound of the shot across the valley.

The contest had begun.

He looked up at twin towers of Popolac and Podujevo. Heads in the clouds—well almost. They practically stretched to touch the sky. It was an awesome sight, a breath-stopping, sleep-stabbing sight. Two cities swaying and writhing and preparing to take their first steps towards each other in this ritual battle.

Of the two, Podujevo seemed the less stable. There was a slight hesitation as the city raised its left leg to begin its march. Nothing serious, just a little difficulty in coordinating hip and thigh muscles. A couple of steps and the city would find its rhythm; a couple more and its inhabitants would be moving as one creature, one perfect giant set to match its grace and power against its mirror-image.

The gunshot had sent flurries of birds up from the trees that banked the hidden valley. They rose up in celebration of the great contest, chattering their excitement as they swooped over the stamping-ground.

"Did you hear a shot?" asked Judd.

Mick nodded.

"Military exercises . . . ?" Judd's smile had broadened. He could see the headlines already—exclusive reports of secret maneuvers in the depths of the Yugoslavian countryside. Russian tanks perhaps, tactical exercises being held out of the West's prying sight. With luck, he would be the carrier of this news.

Boom.

Boom.

There were birds in the air. The thunder was louder now.

It did sound like guns.

"It's over the next ridge . . ." said Judd.

"I don't think we should go any further."

"I have to see."

"I don't. We're not supposed to be here."

"I don't see any signs."

"They'll cart us away; deport us—I don't know—I just think—"

Boom.

"I've got to see."

The words were scarcely out of his mouth when the screaming started.

Podujevo was screaming: a death-cry. Someone buried in the weak flank had died of the strain, and had begun a chain of decay in the system. One man loosed his neighbor and that neighbor loosed his, spreading a cancer of chaos through the body of the city. The coherence of the towering structure deteriorated with terrifying rapidity as the failure of one part of the anatomy put unendurable pressure on the other.

The masterpiece that the good citizens of Podujevo

had constructed of their own flesh and blood tottered and then—a dynamited skyscraper, it began to fall.

The broken flank spewed citizens like a slashed artery spitting blood. Then, with a graceful sloth that made the agonies of the citizens all the more horrible, it bowed towards the earth, all its limbs dissembling as it fell.

The huge head, that had brushed the clouds so recently, was flung back on its thick neck. Ten thousand mouths spoke a single scream for its vast mouth, a wordless, infinitely pitiable appeal to the sky. A howl of loss, a howl of anticipation, a howl of puzzlement. How, that scream demanded, could the day of days end like this, in a welter of falling bodies?

"Did you hear that?"

It was unmistakably human, though almost deafeningly loud. Judd's stomach convulsed. He looked across at Mick, who was as white as a sheet.

Judd stopped the car.

"No," said Mick.

"Listen—for Christ's sake—"

The din of dying moans, appeals and imprecations flooded the air. It was very close.

"We've got to go on now," Mick implored.

Judd shook his head. He was prepared for some military spectacle—all the Russian army massed over the next hill—but that noise in his ears was the noise of human flesh—too human for words. It reminded him of his childhood imaginings of Hell; the endless, unspeakable torments his mother had threatened him with if he failed to embrace Christ. It was a terror he'd forgotten for twenty years. But suddenly, here it was again, freshfaced. Maybe the pit itself gaped just over the next horizon, with his mother standing at its lip, inviting him to taste its punishments.

"If you won't drive, I will."

Mick got out of the car and crossed in front of it,

glancing up the track as he did so. There was a moment's hesitation, no more than a moment's, when his eyes flickered with disbelief, before he turned towards the windscreen, his face even paler than it had been previously, and said: "Jesus Christ . . ." in a voice that was thick with suppressed nausea.

His lover was still sitting behind the wheel, his head in his hands, trying to blot out memories.

"Judd . . ."

Judd looked up, slowly. Mick was staring at him like a wildman, his face shining with a sudden, icy sweat. Judd looked past him. A few meters ahead the track had mysteriously darkened, as a tide edged towards the car, a thick, deep tide of blood. Judd's reason twisted and turned to make any other sense of the sight than that inevitable conclusion. But there was no saner explanation. It was blood, in unendurable abundance, blood without end—

And now, in the breeze, there was the flavor of freshly opened carcasses: the smell out of the depths of the human body, part sweet, part savory.

Mick stumbled back to the passenger's side of the VW and fumbled weakly at the handle. The door opened suddenly and he lurched inside, his eyes glazed.

"Back up," he said.

Judd reached for the ignition. The tide of blood was already sloshing against the front wheels. Ahead, the world had been painted red.

"Drive, for fuck's sake, drive!"

Judd was making no attempt to start the car.

"We must look," he said, without conviction, "we have to."

"We don't have to do anything," said Mick, "but get the hell out of here. It's not our business . . ."

"Plane-crash—"

"There's no smoke."

"Those are human voices."

Mick's instinct was to leave well alone. He could read
about the tragedy in a newspaper—he could see the
pictures tomorrow when they were grey and grainy.
Today it was too fresh, too unpredictable—

Anything could be at the end of that track, bleeding—

"We must—"

Judd started the car, while beside him Mick began to
moan quietly. The VW began to edge forward, nosing
through the river of blood, its wheels spinning in the
queasy, foaming tide.

"No," said Mick, very quietly. "Please, no . . ."

"We must," was Judd's reply. "We must. We must."

Only a few yards away the surviving city of Popolac was
recovering from its first convulsions. It stared, with a
thousand eyes, at the ruins of its ritual enemy, now
spread in a tangle of rope and bodies over the impacted
ground, shattered forever. Popolac staggered back from
the sight, its vast legs flattening the forest that bounded
the stamping-ground, its arms flailing the air. But it kept
its balance, even as a common insanity, woken by the
horror at its feet, surged through its sinews and curdled
its brain. The order went out: the body thrashed and
twisted and turned from the grisly carpet of Podujevo,
and fled into the hills.

As it headed into oblivion, its towering form passed
between the car and the sun, throwing its cold shadow
over the bloody road. Mick saw nothing through his
tears, and Judd, his eyes narrowed against the sight he
feared seeing around the next bend, only dimly registered that something had blotted the light for a minute.
A cloud, perhaps. A flock of birds.

Had he looked up at that moment, just stolen a glance
out towards the north-east, he would have seen Popolac's
head, the vast, swarming head of a maddened city,
disappearing below his line of vision, as it marched into
the hills. He would have known that this territory was

beyond his comprehension; and that there was no healing to be done in this corner of Hell. But he didn't see the city, and he and Mick's last turning-point had passed. From now on, like Popolac and its dead twin, they were lost to sanity, and to all hope of life.

They rounded the bend, and the ruins of Podujevo came into sight.

Their domesticated imaginations had never conceived of a sight so unspeakably brutal.

Perhaps in the battlefields of Europe as many corpses had been heaped together: but had so many of them been women and children, locked together with the corpses of men? There had been piles of dead as high, but ever so many so recently abundant with life? There had been cities laid waste as quickly, but ever an entire city lost to the simple dictate of gravity?

It was a sight beyond sickness. In the face of it the mind slowed to a snail's pace, the forces of reason picked over the evidence with meticulous hands, searching for a flaw in it, a place where it could say:

This is not happening. This is a dream of death; not death itself.

But reason could find no weakness in the wall. This was true. It was death indeed.

Podujevo had fallen.

Thirty-eight thousand, seven hundred and sixty-five citizens were spread on the ground, or rather flung in ungainly, seeping piles. Those who had not died of the fall, or of suffocation, were dying. There would be no survivors from that city except that bundle of onlookers that had traipsed out of their homes to watch the contest. Those few Podujevians, the crippled, the sick, the ancient few, were now staring, like Mick and Judd, at the carnage, trying not to believe.

Judd was first out of the car. The ground beneath his suedes was sticky with coagulating gore. He surveyed the carnage. There was no wreckage: no sign of a plane crash, no fire, no smell of fuel. Just tens of thousands of fresh bodies, all either naked or dressed in an identical grey serge, men, women and children alike. Some of them, he could see, wore leather harnesses, tightly buckled around their upper chests, and snaking out from these contraptions were lengths of rope, miles and miles of it. The closer he looked, the more he saw of the extraordinary system of knots and lashings that still held the bodies together. For some reason these people had been tied together, side by side. Some were yoked on their neighbors' shoulders, straddling them like boys playing at horseback riding. Others were locked arm in arm, knitted together with threads of rope in a wall of muscle and bone. Yet others were trussed in a ball, with their heads tucked between their knees. All were in some way connected up with their fellows, tied together as though in some insane collective bondage game.

Another shot.

Mick looked up.

Across the field a solitary man, dressed in a drab overcoat, was walking amongst the bodies with a revolver, dispatching the dying. It was a pitifully inadequate act of mercy, but he went on nevertheless, choosing the suffering children first. Emptying the revolver, filling it again, emptying it, filling it, emptying it—

Mick let go.

He yelled at the top of his voice over the moans of the injured.

"What is this?"

The man looked up from his appalling duty, his face as deadgrey as his coat.

"Uh?" he grunted, frowning at the two interlopers through his thick spectacles.

"What's happened here?" Mick shouted across at him. It felt good to shout, it felt good to sound angry at the man. Maybe he was to blame. It would be a fine thing, just to have someone to blame.

"Tell us—" Mick said. He could hear the tears throbbing in his voice. "Tell us, for God's sake. Explain."

Grey-coat shook his head. He didn't understand a word this young idiot was saying. It was English he spoke, but that's all he knew. Mick began to walk towards him, feeling all the time the eyes of the dead on him. Eyes like black, shining gems set in broken faces: eyes looking at him upside down, on heads severed from their seating. Eyes in heads that had solid howls for voices. Eyes in heads beyond howls, beyond breath.

Thousands of eyes.

He reached Grey-coat, whose gun was almost empty. He had taken off his spectacles and thrown them aside. He too was weeping, little jerks ran through his big, ungainly body.

At Mick's feet, somebody was reaching for him. He didn't want to look, but the hand touched his shoe and he had no choice but to see its owner. A young man, lying like a flesh swastika, every joint smashed. A child lay under him, her bloody legs poking out like two pink sticks.

He wanted the man's revolver, to stop the hand from touching him. Better still he wanted a machine gun, a flamethrower, anything to wipe the agony away.

As he looked up from the broken body, Mick saw Grey-coat raise the revolver.

"Judd—" he said, but as the word left his lips the muzzle of the revolver was slipped into Grey-coat's mouth and the trigger was pulled.

Grey-coat had saved the last bullet for himself. The back of his head opened like a dropped egg, the shell of his skull flying off. His body went limp and sank to the ground, the revolver still between his lips.

"We must—" began Mick, saying the words to nobody. "We must . . ."

What was the imperative? In this situation, what *must* they do?

"We must—"

Judd was behind him.

"Help—" he said to Mick.

"Yes. We must get help. We must—"

"Go."

Go! That was what they must do. On any pretext, for any fragile, cowardly reason, they must go. Get out of the battlefield, get out of the reach of a dying hand with a wound in place of a body.

"We have to tell the authorities. Find a town. Get help—"

"Priests," said Mick. "They need priests."

It was absurd, to think of giving the Last Rites to so many people. It would take an army of priests, a water cannon filled with holy water, a loudspeaker to pronounce the benedictions.

They turned away, together, from the horror, and wrapped their arms around each other, then picked their way through the carnage to the car.

It was occupied.

Vaslav Jelovsek was sitting behind the wheel, and trying to start the Volkswagen. He turned the ignition key once. Twice. Third time the engine caught and the wheels spun in the crimson mud as he put her into reverse and backed down the track. Vaslav saw the Englishmen running towards the car, cursing him. There was no help for it—he didn't want to steal the vehicle, but he had work to do. He had been a referee, he had been responsible for the contest, and the safety of the contestants. One of the heroic cities had already fallen. He must do everything in his power to prevent Popolac from following its twin. He must chase Popolac, and reason with it. Talk it down out of its terrors with quiet words and promises. If he failed there would be another disaster the equal of the one in front of him, and his conscience was already broken enough.

Mick was still chasing the VW, shouting at Jelovsek. The thief took no notice, concentrating on maneuvering the car back down the narrow, slippery track. Mick was losing the chase rapidly. The car had begun to pick up speed. Furious, but without the breath to speak his fury, Mick stood in the road, hands on his knees, heaving and sobbing.

"Bastard!" said Judd.

Mick looked down the track. Their car had already disappeared.

"Fucker couldn't even drive properly."

"We have . . . we have . . . to catch . . . up . . ." said Mick through gulps of breath.

"How?"

"On foot . . ."

"We haven't even got a map . . . it's in the car."

"Jesus . . . Christ . . . Almighty."

They walked down the track together, away from the field.

After a few meters the tide of blood began to peter out. Just a few congealing rivulets dribbled on towards the main road. Mick and Judd followed the bloody tire-marks to the junction.

The Srbovac road was empty in both directions. The tiremarks showed a left turn. "He's gone deeper into the hills," said Judd, staring along the lovely road towards the blue-green distance. "He's out of his mind!"

"Do we go back the way we came?"

"It'll take us all night on foot."

"We'll hop a lift."

Judd shook his head: his face was slack and his look lost. "Don't you see, Mick, they all knew this was happening. The people in the farms—they got the hell out while those people went crazy up there. There'll be no cars along this road, I'll lay you anything—except maybe a couple of shit-dumb tourists like us—and no tourist would stop for the likes of us."

He was right. They looked like butchers—splattered with blood. Their faces were shining with grease, their eyes maddened.

"We'll have to walk," said Judd, "the way he went."

He pointed along the road. The hills were darker now; the sun had suddenly gone out on their slopes.

Mick shrugged. Either way he could see they had a night on the road ahead of them. But he wanted to walk somewhere—anywhere—as long as he put distance between him and the dead.

In Popolac a kind of peace reigned. Instead of a frenzy of panic there was a numbness, a sheeplike acceptance of the world as it was. Locked in their positions, strapped, roped and harnessed to each other in a living system that allowed for no single voice to be louder than any other, nor any back to labor less than its neighbor's, they let an insane consensus replace the tranquil voice of reason. They were convulsed into one mind, one thought, one ambition. They became, in the space of a few moments, the single-minded giant whose image they had so brilliantly recreated. The illusion of petty individuality was swept away in an irresistible tide of collective feeling—not a mob's passion, but a telepathic surge that dissolved the voices of thousands into one irresistible command.

And the voice said: go!

The voice said: take this horrible sight away, where I need never see it again.

Popolac turned away into the hills, its legs taking strides half a mile long. Each man, woman and child in that seething tower was sightless. They saw only through the eyes of the city. They were thoughtless, but to think the city's thoughts. And they believed themselves deathless, in their lumbering, relentless strength. Vast and mad and deathless.

Two miles along the road Mick and Judd smelt petrol in the air, and a little further along they came upon the VW. It had overturned in the reed-clogged drainage ditch at the side of the road. It had not caught fire.

The driver's door was open, and the body of Vaslav Jelovsek had tumbled out. His face was calm in unconsciousness. There seemed to be no sign of injury, except for a small cut or two on his sober face. They gently pulled the thief out of the wreckage and up out of the filth of the ditch on to the road. He moaned a little as they fussed about him, rolling Mick's sweater up to pillow his head and removing the man's jacket and tie.

Quite suddenly, he opened his eyes.

He stared at them both.

"Are you all right?" Mick asked.

The man said nothing for a moment. He seemed not to understand.

Then:

"English?" he said. His accent was thick, but the question was quite clear.

"Yes."

"I heard your voices. English."

He frowned and winced.

"Are you in pain?" said Judd.

The man seemed to find this amusing.

"Am I in pain?" he repeated, his face screwed up in a mixture of agony and delight. "I shall die," he said, through gritted teeth.

"No," said Mick. "You're all right—"

The man shook his head, his authority absolute.

"I shall die," he said again, the voice full of determination, "I want to die."

Judd crouched closer to him. His voice was weaker by the moment.

"Tell us what to do," he said. The man had closed his eyes. Judd shook him awake, roughly.

"Tell us," he said again, his show of compassion rapidly disappearing. "Tell us what this is all about."

"About?" said the man, his eyes still closed. "It was a fall, that's all. Just a fall . . ."

"What fell?"

"The city. Podujevo. My city."

"What did it fall from?"

"Itself, of course."

The man was explaining nothing; just answering one riddle with another.

"Where were you going?" Mick inquired, trying to sound as unaggressive as possible.

"After Popolac," said the man.

"Popolac?" said Judd.

Mick began to see some sense in the story.

"Popolac is another city. Like Podujevo. Twin cities. They're on the map—"

"Where's the city now?" said Judd.

Vaslav Jelovsek seemed to choose to tell the truth. There was a moment when he hovered between dying with a riddle on his lips, and living long enough to unburden his story. What did it matter if the tale was told now? There could never be another contest: all that was over.

"They came to fight," he said, his voice now very soft, "Popolac and Podujevo. They come every ten years—"

"Fight?" said Judd, "You mean all those people were slaughtered?"

Vaslav shook his head.

"No, no. They fell. I told you."

"Well how do they fight?" Mick said.

"Go into the hills," was the only reply.

Vaslav opened his eyes a little. The faces that loomed over him were exhausted and sick. They had suffered, these innocents. They deserved some explanation.

"As giants," he said. "They fought as giants. They made a body out of their bodies, do you understand? The frame, the muscles, the bone, the eyes, nose, teeth all made of men and women."

"He's delirious," said Judd.

"You go into the hills," the man repeated. "See for yourselves how true it is."

"Even supposing—" Mick began.

Vaslav interrupted him, eager to be finished. "They were good at the game of giants. It took many centuries of practice: every ten years making the figure larger and larger. One always ambitious to be larger than the other. Ropes to tie them all together, flawlessly. Sinews . . . ligaments . . . There was food in its belly . . . there were pipes from the loins, to take away the waste. The best-sighted sat in the eye-sockets, the best voiced in the mouth and throat. You wouldn't believe the engineering of it."

"I don't," said Judd, and stood up.

"It is the body of the state," said Vaslav, so softly his voice was barely above a whisper, "it is the shape of our lives."

There was a silence. Small clouds passed over the road, soundlessly shedding their mass to the air.

"It was a miracle," he said. It was as if he realized the true enormity of the fact for the first time. "It was a miracle."

It was enough. Yes. It was quite enough.

His mouth closed, the words said, and he died.

Mick felt this death more acutely than the thousands they had fled from; or rather this death was the key to unlock the anguish he felt for them all.

Whether the man had chosen to tell a fantastic lie as he died, or whether this story was in some way true, Mick felt useless in the face of it. His imagination was too narrow to encompass the idea. His brain ached with the thought of it, and his compassion cracked under the weight of misery he felt.

They stood on the road, while the clouds scudded by, their vague, grey shadows passing over them towards the enigmatic hills.

It was twilight.

Popolac could stride no further. It felt exhaustion in

every muscle. Here and there in its huge anatomy deaths had occurred; but there was no grieving in the city for its deceased cells. If the dead were in the interior, the corpses were allowed to hang from their harnesses. If they formed the skin of the city they were unbuckled from their positions and released, to plunge into the forest below.

The giant was not capable of pity. It had no ambition but to continue until it ceased.

As the sun slunk out of sight Popolac rested, sitting on a small hillock, nursing its huge head in its huge hands.

The stars were coming out, with their familiar caution. Night was approaching, mercifully bandaging up the wounds of the day, blinding eyes that had seen too much.

Popolac rose to its feet again, and began to move, step by booming step. It would not be long surely, before fatigue overcame it: before it could lie down in the tomb of some lost valley and die.

But for a space yet it must walk on, each step more agonizingly slow than the last, while the night bloomed black around its head.

Mick wanted to bury the car thief, somewhere on the edge of the forest. Judd, however, pointed out that burying a body might seem, in tomorrow's saner light, a little suspicious. And besides, wasn't it absurd to concern themselves with one corpse when there were literally thousands of them lying a few miles from where they stood?

The body was left to lie, therefore, and the car to sink deeper into the ditch.

They began to walk again.

It was cold, and colder by the moment, and they were hungry. But the few houses they passed were all deserted, locked and shuttered, every one.

"What did he mean?" said Mick, as they stood looking at another locked door.

"He was talking metaphor—"

"All that stuff about giants?"

"It was some Trotskyist tripe—" Judd insisted.

"I don't think so."

"I know so. It was his deathbed speech, he'd probably been preparing for years."

"I don't think so," Mick said again, and began walking back towards the road.

"Oh, how's that?" Judd was at his back.

"He wasn't towing some party line."

"Are you saying you think there's some giant around here someplace? For God's sake!"

Mick turned to Judd. His face was difficult to see in the twilight. But his voice was sober with belief.

"Yes. I think he was telling the truth."

"That's absurd. That's ridiculous. No."

Judd hated Mick that moment. Hated his naïvete, his passion to believe any half-witted story if it had a whiff of romance about it. And this? This was the worst, the most preposterous . . .

"No," he said again. "No. No. No."

The sky was porcelain smooth, and the outline of the hills black as pitch.

"I'm fucking freezing," said Mick out of the ink. "Are you staying here or walking with me?"

Judd shouted: "We're not going to find anything this way."

"Well it's a long way back."

"We're just going deeper into the hills."

"Do what you like—I'm walking."

His footsteps receded: the dark encased him.

After a minute, Judd followed.

The night was cloudless and bitter. They walked on, their collars up against the chill, their feet swollen in their shoes. Above them the whole sky had become a parade of stars. A triumph of spilled light, from which the eye could make as many patterns as it had patience for. After a while, they slung their tired arms around each other, for comfort and warmth.

About eleven o'clock, they saw the glow of a window in the distance.

The woman at the door of the stone cottage didn't smile, but she understood their condition, and let them in. There seemed to be no purpose in trying to explain to either the woman or her crippled husband what they had seen. The cottage had no telephone, and there was no sign of a vehicle, so even had they found some way to express themselves, nothing could be done.

With mimes and face-pullings they explained that they were hungry and exhausted. They tried further to explain that they were lost, cursing themselves for leaving their phrasebook in the VW. She didn't seem to understand very much of what they said, but sat them down beside a blazing fire and put a pan of food on the stove to heat.

They ate thick unsalted pea soup and eggs, and occasionally smiled their thanks at the woman. Her husband sat beside the fire, making no attempt to talk, or even look at the visitors.

The food was good. It buoyed their spirits.

They would sleep until morning and then begin the long trek back. By dawn the bodies in the field would be being quantified, identified, parcelled up and dispatched to their families. The air would be full of reassuring noises, cancelling out the moans that still rang in their ears. There would be helicopters, lorry loads of men organizing the clearing-up operations. All the rites and paraphernalia of a civilized disaster.

And in a while, it would be palatable. It would become part of their history: a tragedy, of course, but one they could explain, classify and learn to live with. All would be well, yes, all would be well. Come morning.

The sleep of sheer fatigue came on them suddenly.

They lay where they had fallen, still sitting at the table, their heads on their crossed arms. A litter of empty bowls and bread crusts surrounded them.

They knew nothing. Dreamt nothing. Felt nothing.

Then the thunder began.

In the earth, in the deep earth, a rhythmical tread, as of a titan, that came, by degrees, closer and closer.

The woman woke her husband. She blew out the lamp and went to the door. The night sky was luminous with stars: the hills black on every side.

The thunder still sounded: a full half minute between every boom, but louder now. And louder with every new step.

They stood at the door together, husband and wife, and listened to the night-hills echo back and forth with the sound. There was no lightning to accompany the thunder.

Just the boom—

Boom—

Boom—

It made the ground shake: it threw dust down from the door-lintel, and rattled the window-latches.

Boom—

Boom—

They didn't know what approached, but whatever shape it took, and whatever it intended, there seemed no sense in running from it. Where they stood, in the pitiful shelter of their cottage, was as safe as any nook of the forest. How could they choose, out of a hundred thousand trees, which would be standing when the thunder had passed? Better to wait: and watch.

The wife's eyes were not good, and she doubted what she saw when the blackness of the hill changed shape and reared up to block the stars. But her husband had seen it too: the unimaginably huge head, vaster in the deceiving darkness, looming up and up, dwarfing the hills themselves with ambition.

He fell to his knees, babbling a prayer, his arthritic legs twisted beneath him.

His wife screamed: no words she knew could keep this monster at bay—no prayer, no plea, had power over it.

In the cottage, Mick woke and his outstretched arm, twitching with a sudden cramp, wiped the plate and the lamp off the table.

They smashed.

Judd woke.

The screaming outside had stopped. The woman had disappeared from the doorway into the forest. Any tree, any tree at all, was better than this sight. Her husband still let a string of prayers dribble from his slack mouth, as the great leg of the giant rose to take another step—

Boom—

The cottage shook. Plates danced and smashed off the dresser. A clay pipe rolled from the mantelpiece and shattered in the ashes of the hearth.

The lovers knew the noise that sounded in their substance: that earth-thunder.

Mick reached for Judd, and took him by the shoulder.

"You see," he said, his teeth blue-grey in the darkness of the cottage. "See? See?"

There was a kind of hysteria bubbling behind his words. He ran to the door, stumbling over a chair in the dark. Cursing and bruised he staggered out into the night—

Boom—

The thunder was deafening. This time it broke all the windows in the cottage. In the bedroom one of the roof-joists cracked and flung debris downstairs.

Judd joined his lover at the door. The old man was now face down on the ground, his sick and swollen fingers curled, his begging lips pressed to the damp soil.

Mick was looking up, towards the sky. Judd followed his gaze.

There was a place that showed no stars. It was a

darkness in the shape of a man, a vast, broad human frame, a colossus that soared up to meet heaven. It was not quite a perfect giant. Its outline was not tidy; it seethed and swarmed.

He seemed broader too, this giant, than any real man. His legs were abnormally thick and stumpy, and his arms were not long. The hands, as they clenched and unclenched, seemed oddly jointed and over-delicate for its torso.

Then it raised one huge, flat foot and placed it on the earth, taking a stride towards them.

Boom—

The step brought the roof collapsing in on the cottage. Everything that the car-thief had said was true. Popolac was a city and a giant; and it had gone into the hills . . .

Now their eyes were becoming accustomed to the night light. They could see in ever more horrible detail the way this monster was constructed. It was a masterpiece of human engineering: a man made entirely of men. Or rather, a sexless giant, made of men and women and children. All the citizens of Popolac writhed and strained in the body of this flesh-knitted giant, their muscles stretched to breaking point, their bones close to snapping.

They could see how the architects of Popolac had subtly altered the proportions of the human body; how the thing had been made squatter to lower its center of gravity; how its legs had been made elephantine to bear the weight of the torso; how the head was sunk low on to the wide shoulders, so that the problems of a weak neck had been minimized.

Despite these malformations, it was horribly lifelike. The bodies that were bound together to make its surface were naked but for their harnesses, so that its surface glistened in the starlight, like one vast human torso. Even the muscles were well copied, though simplified. They could see the way the roped bodies pushed and pulled against each other in solid cords of flesh and bone. They could see the intertwined people that made up the body: the backs like turtles packed together to offer the sweep of the pectorals; the lashed and knotted acrobats at the joints of the arms and the legs alike, rolling and unwinding to articulate the city.

But surely the most amazing sight of all was the face.

Cheeks of bodies; cavernous eye-sockets in which heads stared, five bound together for each eyeball; a broad, flat nose and a mouth that opened and closed, as the muscles of the jaw bunched and hollowed rhythmically. And from that mouth, lined with teeth of bald children, the voice of the giant, now only a weak copy of its former powers, spoke a single note of idiot music.

Popolac walked and Popolac sang.

Was there ever a sight in Europe the equal of it?

They watched, Mick and Judd, as it took another step towards them.

The old man had wet his pants. Blubbering and begging, he dragged himself away from the ruined cottage into the surrounding trees, dragging his dead legs after him.

The Englishmen remained where they stood, watching the spectacle as it approached. Neither dread nor horror touched them now, just an awe that rooted them to the spot. They knew this was a sight they could never hope to see again; this was the apex—after this there was only common experience. Better to stay then, though every step brought death nearer, better to stay and see the sight while it was still there to be seen. And if it killed them, this monster, then at least they would have glimpsed a miracle, known this terrible majesty for a brief moment. It seemed a fair exchange.

Popolac was within two steps of the cottage. They could see the complexities of its structure quite clearly. The faces of the citizens were becoming detailed: white, sweat-wet and content in their weariness. Some hung dead from their harnesses, their legs swinging back and forth like the hanged. Others, children particularly, had ceased to obey their training, and had relaxed their positions, so that the form of the body was degenerating, beginning to seethe with the boils of rebellious cells.

Yet it still walked, each step an incalculable effort of coordination and strength.

Boom—

The step that trod the cottage came sooner than they thought.

Mick saw the leg raised; saw the faces of the people in the shin and ankle and foot—they were as big as he was now—all huge men chosen to take the full weight of this great creation. Many were dead. The bottom of the foot, he could see, was a jigsaw of crushed and bloody bodies, pressed to death under the weight of their fellow citizens.

The foot descended with a roar.

In a matter of seconds the cottage was reduced to splinters and dust.

Popolac blotted the sky utterly. It was, for a moment, the whole world, heaven and earth, its presence filled the senses to overflowing. At this proximity one look could not encompass it, the eye had to range backwards and forwards over its mass to take it all in, and even then the mind refused to accept the whole truth.

A whirling fragment of stone, flung off from the cottage as it collapsed, struck Judd full in the face. In his head he heard the killing stroke like a ball hitting a wall: a play-yard death. No pain: no remorse. Out like a light, a tiny, insignificant light; his death-cry lost in the pandemonium, his body hidden in the smoke and darkness. Mick neither saw nor heard Judd die.

He was too busy staring at the foot as it settled for a moment in the ruins of the cottage, while the other leg mustered the will to move.

Mick took his chance. Howling like a banshee, he ran towards the leg, longing to embrace the monster. He stumbled in the wreckage, and stood again, bloodied, to reach for the foot before it was lifted and he was left behind. There was a clamour of agonized breath as the message came to the foot that it must move; Mick saw the muscles of the shin bunch and marry as the leg began to lift. He made one last lunge at the limb as it began to leave the ground, snatching a harness or a rope, or human hair, or flesh itself—anything to catch this passing miracle and be part of it. Better to go with it wherever it was going, serve it in its purpose, whatever that might be; better to die with it than live without it.

He caught the foot, and found a safe purchase on its ankle. Screaming his sheer ecstasy at his success he felt the great leg raised, and glanced down through the swirling dust to the spot where he had stood, already receding as the limb climbed.

The earth was gone from beneath him. He was a hitchhiker with a god: the mere life he had left was nothing to him now, or ever. He would live with this thing, yes, he would live with it—seeing it and seeing it and eating it with his eyes until he died of sheer gluttony.

He screamed and howled and swung on the ropes, drinking up his triumph. Below, far below, he glimpsed Judd's body, curled up pale on the dark ground, irretrievable. Love and life and sanity were gone, gone like the memory of his name, or his sex, or his ambition.

It all meant nothing. Nothing at all.

Boom—

Boom—

Popolac walked, the noise of its steps receding to the east. Popolac walked, the hum of its voice lost in the night.

After a day, birds came, foxes came, flies, butterflies, wasps came. Judd moved, Judd shifted, Judd gave birth. In his belly maggots warmed themselves, in a vixen's den the good flesh of his thigh was fought over. After that, it was quick. The bones yellowing, the bones crumbling: soon, an empty space which he had once filled with breath and onions.

Darkness, light, darkness, light. He interrupted neither with his name.

Philip K. Dick (1928-1982)

FAITH OF OUR FATHERS

Philip K. Dick was a prolific American science fiction writer whose work often strayed into the emotional territory of the horror field, though the monsters of his stories are most often science-fictional or technological. His reputation has grown since his death in 1982 and he is widely regarded as the most important science fiction writer of his generation. The nature of reality was a consistent theme in his work: a recent book on the man and his works is entitled *Only Apparently Real* (1986). There is a vigorous international organization devoted to his writings, The Philip K. Dick Society, and many of his best novels are now being reissued, not in genre but in the prestigious Vintage Contemporaries publishing line. Plays, films (including *Bladerunner*), and an avant garde opera based on his works have appeared in the last decade. He is something of a cult figure. "Faith of Our Fathers" was written in the late 1960s on a commission to produce a novella under the influence of LSD, since Dick had a reputation for experimentation with drugs. The result is this politically and philosophically complex horror story of a future in Southeast Asia, a totalitarian and religious nightmare characteristic of Dick at his best.

On the streets of Hanoi he found himself facing a legless peddler who rode a little wooden cart and called shrilly to every passerby. Chien slowed, listened, but did not stop; business at the Ministry of Cultural Artifacts cropped into his mind and deflected his attention: it was as if he were alone, and none of those on bicycles and scooters and jet-powered motorcycles remained. And likewise it was as if the legless peddler did not exist.

"Comrade," the peddler called however, and pursued him on his cart; a helium battery operated the drive and sent the car scuttling expertly after Chien. "I possess a wide spectrum of time-tested herbal remedies complete with testimonials from thousands of loyal users; advise me of your malady and I can assist."

Chien, pausing, said, "Yes, but I have no malady." Except, he thought, for the chronic one of those employed by the Central Committee, that of career opportunism testing constantly the gates of each official position. Including mine.

"I can cure for example radiation sickness," the peddler chanted, still pursuing him. "Or expand, if necessary, the element of sexual prowess. I can reverse carcinomatous progressions, even the dreaded melanomae, what you would call black cancers." Lifting a tray of bottles, small aluminum cans and assorted powders in plastic jars, the peddler sang, "If a rival persists in trying to usurp your gainful bureaucratic position, I can purvey an ointment which, appearing as a dermal balm, is in actuality a desperately effective toxin. And my prices, comrade, are low. And as a special favor to one so distinguished in bearing as yourself I will accept the postwar inflationary paper dollars reputedly of international exchange but in reality damn near no better than bathroom tissue."

"Go to hell," Chien said, and signaled a passing hovercar taxi; he was already three and one-half minutes late for his first appointment of the day, and his various fat-assed superiors at the Ministry would be making quick mental notations—as would, to an even greater degree, his subordinates.

The peddler said quietly, "But, comrade; you *must* buy from me."

"Why?" Chien demanded. Indignation.

"Because, comrade, I am a war veteran. I fought in the Colossal Final War of National Liberation with the People's Democratic United Front against the Imperialists; I lost my pedal extremities at the battle of San Francisco." His tone was triumphant, now, and sly. *"It is the law.* If you refuse to buy wares offered by a veteran you risk a fine and possible jail sentence—and in addition disgrace."

Wearily, Chien nodded the hovercab on. "Admittedly," he said. "Okay, I must buy from you." He glanced summarily over the meager display of herbal remedies, seeking one at random. "That," he decided, pointing to a paper-wrapped parcel in the rear row.

The peddler laughed. "That, comrade, is a spermatocide, bought by women who for political reasons cannot qualify for The Pill. It would be of shallow use to you, in fact none at all, since you are a gentleman."

"The law," Chien said bitingly, "does not require me to purchase anything useful from you; only that I purchase something. I'll take that." He reached into his padded coat for his billfold, huge with the postwar inflationary bills in which, four times a week, he as a government servant was paid.

"Tell me your problems," the peddler said.

Chien stared at him. Appalled by the invasion of privacy—and done by someone outside the government.

"All right, comrade," the peddler said, seeing his expression. "I will not probe; excuse me. But as a doctor—an herbal healer—it is fitting that I know as much as possible." He pondered, his gaunt features somber. "Do you watch television unusually much?" he asked abruptly.

Taken by surprise, Chien said, "Every evening. Except on Friday when I go to my club to practice the esoteric imported art from the defeated West of steer-roping." It was his only indulgence; other than that he had totally devoted himself to Party activities.

The peddler reached, selected a gray paper packet. "Sixty trade dollars," he stated. "With a full guarantee: if it does not do as promised, return the unused portion for a full and cheery refund."

"And what," Chien said cuttingly, "is it guaranteed to do?"

"It will rest eyes fatigued by the countenance of meaningless official monologues," the peddler said. "A soothing preparation; take it as soon as you find yourself exposed to the usual dry and lengthy sermons which—"

Chien paid the money, accepted the packet, and strode off. Balls, he said to himself. It's a racket, he decided, the ordinance setting up war vets as a privileged class. They prey off us—we, the younger ones—like raptors.

Forgotten, the gray packet remained deposited in his coat pocket, as he entered the imposing postwar Ministry of Cultural Artifacts building, and his own considerable stately office, to begin his workday.

A portly, middle-aged Caucasian male, wearing a brown Hong Kong silk suit, double-breasted with vest, waited in his office. With the unfamiliar Caucasian stood his own immediate superior, Ssu-Ma Tso-pin. Tso-pin introduced the two of them in Cantonese, a dialect which he used badly.

"Mr. Tung Chien, this is Mr. Darius Pethel. Mr. Pethel will be headmaster at the new ideological and cultural establishment of didactic character soon to open at San Fernando, California." He added, "Mr. Pethel has had a rich and full lifetime supporting the people's struggle to unseat imperialist-bloc countries via pedagogic media; therefore this high post."

They shook hands.

"Tea?" Chien asked the two of them; he pressed the switch of his infrared hibachi and in an instant the water in the highly ornamented ceramic pot—of Japanese origin—began to burble. As he seated himself at his desk he saw that trustworthy Miss Hsi had laid out the information poop-sheet (confidential) on Comrade Pethel; he glanced over it, meanwhile pretending to be doing nothing in particular.

"The Absolute Benefactor of the People," Tso-pin said, "has personally met Mr. Pethel and trusts him. This is rare. The school in San Fernando will appear to teach run-of-the-mill Taoist philosophies but will, of course, in actuality maintain for us a channel of communication to the liberal and intellectual youth segment of western U.S. There are many of them still alive, from San Diego to Sacramento; we estimate at least ten thousand. The school will accept two thousand. Enrollment will be mandatory for those we select. Your relationship to Mr. Pethel's programing is grave. Ahem; your tea water is boiling."

"Thank you," Chien murmured, dropping in the bag of Lipton's tea.

Tso-pin continued, "Although Mr. Pethel will supervise the setting up of the courses of instruction presented by the school to its student body, all examination papers will oddly enough be relayed here to your office for your own expert, careful, ideological study. In other words, Mr. Chien, you will determine who among the two thousand students is reliable, which are truly responding to the programing and who is not."

"I will now pour my tea," Chien said, doing so ceremoniously.

"What we have to realize," Pethel rumbled in Cantonese even worse than that of Tso-pin, "is that, once having lost the global war to us, the American youth has developed a talent for dissembling." He spoke the last word in English; not understanding it, Chien turned inquiringly to his superior.

"Lying," Tso-pin explained.

Pethel said, "Mouthing the proper slogans for surface appearance, but on the inside believing them false. Test papers by this group will closely resemble those of genuine—"

"You mean that the test papers of *two thousand* students will be passing through my office?" Chien demanded. He could not believe it. "That's a full-time job in itself; I don't have time for anything remotely resembling that." He was appalled. "To give critical, official approval or denial of the astute variety which you're envisioning—" He gestured. "Screw that," he said, in English.

Blinking at the strong, Western vulgarity, Tso-pin said, "You have a staff. Plus also you can requisition several more from the pool; the Ministry's budget, augmented this year, will permit it. And remember: the Absolute Benefactor of the People has hand-picked Mr. Pethel." His tone, now, had become ominous, but only subtly so. Just enough to penetrate Chien's hysteria, and to wither it into submission. At least temporarily. To underline his point, Tso-pin walked to the far end of the office; he stood before the full-length 3-D portrait of the Absolute Benefactor, and after an interval his proximity triggered the tape-transport mounted behind the portrait; the face of the Benefactor moved, and from it came a familiar homily, in more than familiar accents. "Fight for peace, my sons," it intoned gently, firmly.

"Ha," Chien said, still perturbed, but concealing it. Possibly one of the Ministry's computers could sort the examination papers; a yes-no-maybe structure could be employed, in conjunction with a pre-analysis of the pattern of ideological correctness—and incorrectness. The matter could be made routine. Probably.

Darius Pethel said, "I have with me certain material which I would like you to scrutinize, Mr. Chien." He unzipped an unsightly, old-fashioned, plastic briefcase. "Two examination essays," he said as he passed the documents to Chien. "This will tell us if you're qualified." He then glanced at Tso-pin; their gazes met. "I understand," Pethel said, "that if you are successful in this venture you will be made vice-councilor of the Ministry, and His Greatness the Absolute Benefactor of the People will personally confer Kisterigian's medal on you." Both he and Tso-pin smiled in wary unison.

"The Kisterigian medal," Chien echoed; he accepted the examination papers, glanced over them in a show of leisurely indifference. But within him his heart vibrated in ill-concealed tension. "Why these two? By that I mean, what am I looking for, sir?"

"One of them," Pethel said, "is the work of a dedicated progressive, a loyal Party member of thoroughly researched conviction. The other is by a young *stilyagi* whom we suspect of holding petit bourgeois imperialist degenerate crypto-ideas. It is up to you, sir, to determine which is which."

Thanks a lot, Chien thought. But, nodding, he read the title of the top paper.

DOCTRINES OF THE ABSOLUTE BENEFACTOR ANTICIPATED IN THE POETRY OF BAHA AD-DIN ZUHAYR, OF THIR-TEENTH-CENTURY ARABIA.

Glancing down the initial pages of the essay, Chien saw a quatrain familiar to him; it was called "Death" and he had known it most of his adult, educated life.

> Once he will miss, twice he will miss,
>   He only chooses one of many hours;
> For him nor deep nor hill there is,
>   But all's one level plain he hunts for flowers.

"Powerful," Chien said. "This poem."

"He makes use of the poem," Pethel said, observing Chien's lips moving as he reread the quatrain, "to indicate the age-old wisdom, displayed by the Absolute Benefactor in our current lives, that no individual is safe; everyone is mortal, and only the supra-personal, historically essential cause survives. As it should be. Would you agree with him? With this student, I mean? Or—" Pethel paused. "Is he in fact perhaps satirizing the Absolute Benefactor's promulgations?"

Cagily, Chien said, "Give me a chance to inspect the other paper."

"You need no further information; decide."

Haltingly, Chien said, "I—had never thought of this poem that way." He felt irritable. "Anyhow, it isn't by Baha ad-Din Zuhayr; it's part of the *Thousand and One Nights* anthology. It is, however, thirteenth century; I admit that." He quickly read over the text of the paper accompanying the poem. It appeared to be a routine, uninspired rehash of Party clichés, all of them familiar to him from birth. The blind, imperialist monster who mowed down and snuffed out (mixed metaphor) human aspiration, the calculations of the still extant anti-Party group in eastern United States . . . He felt dully bored, and as uninspired as the student's paper. We must persevere, the paper declared. Wipe out the Pentagon remnants in the Catskills, subdue Tennessee and most especially the pocket of diehard reaction in the red hills of Oklahoma. He sighed.

"I think," Tso-pin said, "we should allow Mr. Chien the opportunity of observing this difficult material at his leisure." To Chien he said, "You have permission to take them home to your condominium, this evening, and adjudge them on your own time." He bowed, half mockingly, half solicitously. In any case, insult or not, he had gotten Chien off the hook, and for that Chien was grateful.

"You are most kind," he murmured, "to allow me to perform this new and highly stimulating labor on my own time. Mikoyan, were he alive today, would approve." You bastard, he said to himself. Meaning both his superior and the Caucasian Pethel. Handing me a hot potato like this, and on my own time. Obviously the CP USA is in trouble; its indoctrination academies aren't managing to do their job with the notoriously mulish, eccentric Yank youths. And you've passed that hot potato on and on until it reaches me.

Thanks for nothing, he thought acidly.

That evening in his small but well-appointed condominium apartment he read over the other of the two examination papers, this one by a Marion Culper, and discovered that it, too, dealt with poetry. Obviously this was speciously a poetry class, and he felt ill. It had always run against his grain, the use of poetry—of any art—for social purposes. Anyhow, comfortable in his special spine-straightening, simulated-leather easy chair, he lit a Cuesta Rey Number One English Market immense corona cigar and began to read.

The writer of the paper, Miss Culper, had selected as her text a portion of a poem of John Dryden, the seventeenth-century English poet, final lines from the well-known "A Song for St. Cecilia's Day."

> . . . So when the last and dreadful hour
> This crumbling pageant shall devour,
> The trumpet shall be heard on high,
> The dead shall live, the living die,
> And Music shall untune the sky.

Well, that's a hell of a thing, Chien thought to himself bitingly. Dryden, we're supposed to believe, anticipated the fall of capitalism? That's what he meant by the "crumbling pageant"? Christ. He leaned over to take hold of his cigar and found that it had gone out. Groping in his pockets for his Japanese-made lighter, he half rose to his feet . . .

Tweeeeeee! the TV set at the far end of the living room said.

Aha, Chien said. We're about to be addressed by the Leader. By the Absolute Benefactor of the People, up there in Peking where he's lived for ninety years now; or is it one hundred? Or, as we sometimes like to think of him, the Ass—

"May the ten thousand blossoms of abject self-assumed poverty flower in your spiritual courtyard," the TV announcer said. With a groan, Chien rose to his feet, bowed the mandatory bow of response; each TV set came equipped with monitoring devices to narrate to the Secpol, the Security Police, whether its owner was bowing and/or watching.

On the screen a clearly defined visage manifested itself, the wide, unlined, healthy features of the one-hundred-and-twenty-year-old leader of CP East, ruler of many—far too many, Chien reflected. Blah to you, he thought, and reseated himself in his simulated-leather easy chair, now facing the TV screen.

"My thoughts," the Absolute Benefactor said in his rich and slow tones, "are on you, my children. And especially on Mr. Tung Chien of Hanoi, who faces a difficult task ahead, a task to enrich the people of Democratic East, plus the American West Coast. We must think in unison about this noble, dedicated man and the chore which he faces, and I have chosen to take several moments of my time to honor him and encourage him. Are you listening, Mr. Chien?"

"Yes, Your Greatness," Chien said, and pondered to himself the odds against the Party Leader singling *him* out this particular evening. The odds caused him to feel uncomradely cynicism; it was unconvincing. Probably this transmission was being beamed to his apartment building alone—or at least this city. It might also be a lip-synch job, done at Hanoi TV, Incorporated. In any case he was required to listen and watch—and absorb. He did so, from a lifetime of practice. Outwardly he appeared to be rigidly attentive. Inwardly he was still mulling over the two test papers, wondering which was which; where did devout Party enthusiasm end and sardonic lampoonery begin? Hard to say . . . which of course explained why they had dumped the task in his lap.

Again he groped in his pockets for his lighter—and found the small gray envelope which the war-veteran peddler had sold him. Gawd, he thought, remembering what it had cost. Money down the drain and what did this herbal remedy do? Nothing. He turned the packet over and saw, on the back, small printed words. Well, he thought, and began to unfold the packet with care. The words had snared him—as of course they were meant to do.

Failing as a Party member and human? Afraid of becoming obsolete and discarded on the ash heap of history by

He read rapidly through the text, ignoring its claims, seeking to find out what he had purchased.

Meanwhile, the Absolute Benefactor droned on.

Snuff. The package contained snuff. Countless tiny black grains, like gunpowder, which sent up an interesting aromatic to tickle his nose. The title of the particular blend was Princes Special, he discovered. And very pleasing, he decided. At one time he had taken snuff— smoked tobacco for a time having been illegal for reasons of health—back during his student days at Peking U; it had been the fad, especially the amatory mixes prepared in Chungking, made from god knew what. Was this that? Almost any aromatic could be added to snuff, from essence of orange to pulverized babycrap . . . or so some seemed, especially an English mixture called High Dry

Toast which had in itself more or less put an end to his yearning for nasal, inhaled tobacco.

On the TV screen the Absolute Benefactor rumbled monotonously on as Chien sniffed cautiously at the powder, read the claims—it cured everything from being late to work to falling in love with a woman of dubious political background. Interesting. But typical of claims—

His doorbell rang.

Rising, he walked to the door, opened it with full knowledge of what he would find. There, sure enough, stood Mou Kuei, the Building Warden, small and hard-eyed and alert to his task; he had his armband and metal helmet on, showing that he meant business. "Mr. Chien, comrade Party worker. I received a call from the television authority. You are failing to watch your screen and are instead fiddling with a packet of doubtful content." He produced a clipboard and ballpoint pen. "Two red marks, and hithertonow you are summarily ordered to repose yourself in a comfortable, stress-free posture before your screen and give the Leader your unexcelled attention. His words, this evening, are directed particularly to you, sir; to you."

"I doubt that," Chien heard himself say.

Blinking, Kuei said, "What do you mean?"

"The Leader rules eight billion comrades. He isn't going to single me out." He felt wrathful; the punctuality of the warden's reprimand irked him.

Kuei said, "But I distinctly heard with my own ears. You were mentioned."

Going over to the TV set, Chien turned the volume up. "But now he's talking about crop failures in People's India; that's of no relevance to me."

"Whatever the Leader expostulates is relevant." Mou Kuei scratched a mark on his clipboard sheet, bowed formally, turned away. "My call to come up here to confront you with your slackness originated at Central. Obviously they regard your attention as important; I must order you to set in motion your automatic transmission recording circuit and replay the earlier portions of the Leader's speech.''

Chien farted. And shut the door.

Back to the TV set, he said to himself. Where our leisure hours are spent. And there lay the two student examination papers; he had that weighing him down, too. And all on my own time, he thought savagely. The hell with them. Up theirs. He strode to the TV set, started to shut it off; at once a red warning light winked on, informing him that he did not have permission to shut off the set—could not in fact end its tirade and image even if he unplugged it. Mandatory speeches, he thought, will kill us all, bury us; if I could be free of the noise of speeches, free of the din of the Party baying as it hounds mankind . . .

There was no known ordinance, however, preventing him from taking snuff while he watched the Leader. So, opening the small gray packet, he shook out a mound of the black granules onto the back of his left hand. He then, professionally, raised his hand to his nostrils and deeply inhaled, drawing the snuff well up into his sinus cavities. Imagine the old superstition, he thought to himself. That the sinus cavities are connected to the brain, and hence an inhalation of snuff directly affects the cerebral cortex. He smiled, seated himself once more, fixed his gaze on the TV screen and the gesticulating individual known so utterly to them all.

The face dwindled away, disappeared. The sound ceased. He faced an emptiness, a vacuum. The screen, white and blank, confronted him and from the speaker a faint hiss sounded.

The frigging snuff, he said to himself. And inhaled greedily at the remainder of the powder on his hand, drawing it up avidly into his nose, his sinuses, and, or so it felt, into his brain; he plunged into the snuff, absorbing it elatedly.

The screen remained blank and then, by degrees, an

image once more formed and established itself. It was not the Leader. Not the Absolute Benefactor of the People, in point of fact not a human figure at all.

He faced a dead mechanical construct, made of solid state circuits, of swiveling pseudopodia, lenses and a squawk-box. And the box began, in a droning din, to harangue him.

Staring fixedly, he thought, *What is this?* Reality? Hallucination, he thought. The peddler came across some of the psychedelic drugs used during the War of Liberation—he's selling the stuff and I've taken some, taken a whole lot!

Making his way unsteadily to the vidphone he dialed the Secpol station nearest his building. "I wish to report a pusher of hallucinogenic drugs," he said into the receiver.

"Your name, sir, and conapt location?" Efficient, brisk and impersonal bureaucrat of the police.

He gave them the information, then haltingly made it back to his simulated-leather easy chair, once again to witness the apparition on the TV screen. This is lethal, he said to himself. It must be some preparation developed in Washington, D.C., or London—stronger and stranger than the LSD-25 which they dumped so effectively into our reservoirs. And I thought it was going to relieve me of the burden of the Leader's speeches . . . this is far worse, this electronic sputtering, swiveling, metal and plastic monstrosity yammering away—this is terrifying.

To have to face *this* the remainder of my life—

It took ten minutes for the Secpol two-man team to come rapping at his door. And by then, in a deteriorating set of stages, the familiar image of the Leader had seeped back into focus on the screen, had supplanted the horrible artificial construct which waved its 'podia and squalled on and on. He let the two cops in shakily, led them to the table on which he had left the remains of the snuff in its packet.

"Psychedelic toxin," he said thickly. "Of short duration. Absorbed into the blood stream directly, through nasal capillaries. I'll give you details as to where I got it, from whom, all that." He took a deep shaky breath; the presence of the police was comforting.

Ballpoint pens ready, the two officers waited. And all the time, in the background, the Leader rattled out his endless speech. As he had done a thousand evenings before in the life of Tung-Chien. But, he thought, it'll never be the same again, at least not for me. Not after inhaling that near-toxic snuff.

He wondered, Is that what they intended?

It seemed odd to him, thinking of a *they*. Peculiar— but somehow correct. For an instant he hesitated, not giving out the details, not telling the police enough to find the man. A peddler, he started to say. I don't know where; can't remember. But he did; he remembered the exact street intersection. So, with unexplainable reluctance, he told them.

"Thank you, Comrade Chien." The boss of the team of police carefully gathered up the remaining snuff— most of it remained—and placed it in his uniform— smart, sharp uniform—pocket. "We'll have it analyzed at the first available moment," the cop said, "and inform you immediately in case counter medical measures are indicated for you. Some of the old wartime psychedelics were eventually fatal, as you have no doubt read."

"I've read," he agreed. That had been specifically what he had been thinking.

"Good luck and thanks for notifying us," both cops said, and departed. The affair, for all their efficiency, did not seem to shake them; obviously such a complaint was routine.

The lab report came swiftly—surprisingly so, in view of the vast state bureaucracy. It reached him by vidphone before the Leader had finished his TV speech.

"It's not a hallucinogen," the Secpol lab technician informed him.

"No?" he said, puzzled and, strangely, not relieved. Not at all.

"On the contrary. It's a phenothiazine, which as you doubtless know is anti-hallucinogenic. A strong dose per gram of admixture, but harmless. Might lower your blood pressure or make you sleepy. Probably stolen from a wartime cache of medical supplies. Left by the retreating barbarians. I wouldn't worry."

Pondering, Chien hung up the vidphone in slow motion. And then walked to the window of his conapt—the window with the fine view of other Hanoi high-rise conapts—to think.

The doorbell rang. Feeling as if he were in a trance, he crossed the carpeted living room to answer it.

The girl standing there, in a tan raincoat with a babushka over her dark, shiny, and very long hair, said in a timid little voice, "Um, Comrade Chien? Tung Chien? Of the Ministry of—"

He led her in, reflexively, and shut the door after her. "You've been monitoring my vidphone," he told her; it was a shot in darkness, but something in him, an unvoiced certitude, told him that she had.

"Did—they take the rest of the snuff?" She glanced about. "Oh, I hope not; it's so hard to get these days."

"Snuff," he said, "is easy to get. Phenothiazine isn't. Is that what you mean?"

The girl raised her head, studied him with large, moon-darkened eyes. "Yes. Mr. Chien—" She hesitated, obviously as uncertain as the Secpol cops had been assured. "Tell me what you saw; it's of great importance for us to be certain."

"I had a choice?" he said acutely.

"Y-yes, very much so. That's what confuses us; that's what is not as we planned. We don't understand; it fits nobody's theory." Her eyes even darker and deeper, she said, "Was it the aquatic horror shape? The thing with slime and teeth, the extraterrestrial life form? Please tell me; we have to know." She breathed irregularly, with effort, the tan raincoat rising and falling; he found himself watching its rhythm.

"A machine," he said.

"Oh!" She ducked her head, nodding vigorously. "Yes, I understand; a mechanical organism in no way resembling a human. Not a simulacrum, something constructed to resemble a man."

He said, "This did not look like a man." He added to himself, And it failed—did not try—to talk like a man.

"You understand that it was not a hallucination."

"I've been officially told that what I took was a phenothiazine. That's all I know." He said as little as possible; he did not want to talk but to hear. Hear what the girl had to say.

"Well, Mr. Chien—" She took a deep, unstable breath. "If it was not a hallucination, then what was it? What does that leave? What is called 'extra-consciousness'—could that be it?"

He did not answer; turning his back, he leisurely picked up the two student test papers, glanced over them, ignoring her. Waiting for her next attempt.

At his shoulder she appeared, smelling of spring rain, smelling of sweetness and agitation, beautiful in the way she smelled, and looked, and, he thought, speaks. So different from the harsh plateau speech patterns we hear on the TV—have heard since I was a baby.

"Some of them," she said huskily, "who take the stelazine—it was stelazine you got, Mr. Chien—see one apparition, some another. But distinct categories have emerged; there is not an infinite variety. Some see what you saw; we call it the Clanker. Some the aquatic horror; that's the Gulper. And then there's the Bird, and the Climbing Tube, and—" She broke off. "But other reactions tell you very little. Tell *us* very little." She hesitated, then plunged on. "Now that this has happened to you, Mr. Chien, we would like you to join our gathering. Join your particular group, those who see what you see. Group Red. We want to know what it *really* is, and—"

She gestured with tapered, wax-smooth fingers. "It can't be *all* those manifestations." Her tone was poignant, nai[u]vely so. He felt his caution relax—a trifle.

He said, "What do you see? You in particular?"

"I'm a part of Group Yellow. I see—a storm. A whining, vicious whirlwind. That roots everything up, crushes condominium apartments built to last a century." She smiled wanly. "The Crusher. Twelve groups in all, Mr. Chien. Twelve absolutely different experiences, all from the same phenothiazine, all of the Leader as he speaks over TV. As *it* speaks, rather." She smiled up at him, lashes long—probably protracted artificially—and gaze engaging, even trusting. As if she thought he knew something or could do something.

"I should make a citizen's arrest of you," he said presently.

"There is no law, not about this. We studied Soviet juridical writings before we—found people to distribute the stelazine. We don't have much of it; we have to be very careful whom we give it to. It seemed to us that you constituted a likely choice . . . a well-known, postwar, dedicated young career man on his way up." From his fingers she took the examination papers. "They're having you pol-read?" she asked.

"'Pol-read'?" He did not know the term.

"Study something said or written to see if it fits the Party's current world view. You in the hierarchy merely call it 'read,' don't you?" Again she smiled. "When you rise one step higher, up with Mr. Tso-pin, you will know that expression." She added somberly, "And with Mr. Pethel. He's very far up. Mr. Chien, there is no ideological school in San Fernando; these are forged exam papers, designed to read back to them a thorough analysis of *your* political ideology. And have you been able to distinguish which paper is orthodox and which is heretical?" Her voice was pixie-like, taunting with amused malice. "Choose the wrong one and your budding career stops dead, cold, in its tracks. Choose the proper one—"

"Do you know which is which?" he demanded.

"Yes." She nodded soberly. "We have listening devices in Mr. Tso-pin's inner offices; we monitored his conversation with Mr. Pethel—who is not Mr. Pethel but the Higher Secpol Inspector Judd Craine. You have possibly heard mention of him; he acted as chief assistant to Judge Vorlawsky at the '98 war crimes trial in Zurich."

With difficulty he said, "I—see." Well, that explained that.

The girl said, "My name is Tanya Lee."

He said nothing; he merely nodded, too stunned for any cerebration.

"Technically, I am a minor clerk," Miss Lee said, "at your Ministry. You have never run into me, however, that I can at least recall. We try to hold posts wherever we can. As far up as possible. My own boss—"

"Should you be telling me this?" He gestured at the TV set, which remained on. "Aren't they picking this up?"

Tanya Lee said, "We introduced a noise factor in the reception of both vid and aud material from this apartment building; it will take them almost an hour to locate the sheathing. So we have"—she examined the tiny wristwatch on her slender wrist—"fifteen more minutes. And still be safe."

"Tell me," he said, "which paper is orthodox."

"Is that what you care about? Really?"

"What," he said, "should I care about?"

"Don't you see, Mr. Chien? You've learned something. The Leader is not the Leader; he is something else, but we can't tell what. Not yet. Mr. Chien, with all due respect, have you ever had your drinking water analyzed? I know it sounds paranoiac, but have you?"

"No," he said. "Of course not." Knowing what she was going to say.

Miss Lee said briskly, "Our tests show that it's saturated with hallucinogens. It is, has been, will continue to be. Not the ones used during the war; not the disorienting ones, but a synthetic quasi-ergot derivative called Datrox-3. You drink it here in the building from the time you get up; you drink it in restaurants and other apartments that you visit. You drink it at the Ministry; it's all piped from a central, common source." Her tone was bleak and ferocious. "We solved that problem; we knew, as soon as we discovered it, that any good phenothiazine would counter it. What we did not know, of course, was this—a *variety* of authentic experiences; that makes no sense, rationally. It's the hallucination which should differ from person to person, and the reality experience which should be ubiquitous—it's all turned around. We can't even construct an ad hoc theory which accounts for that, and god knows we've tried. Twelve mutually exclusive hallucinations—that would be easily understood. But not one hallucination and twelve realities." She ceased talking, then, and studied the two test papers, her forehead wrinkling. "The one with the Arabic poem is orthodox," she stated. "If you tell them that they'll trust you and give you a higher post. You'll be another notch up in the hierarchy of Party officialdom." Smiling—her teeth were perfect and lovely—she finished, "Look what you received back for your investment this morning. Your career is underwritten for a time. And by us."

He said, "I don't believe you." Instinctively, his caution operated within him, always, the caution of a lifetime lived among the hatchet men of the Hanoi branch of the CP East. They knew an infinitude of ways by which to ax a rival out of contention—some of which he himself had employed; some of which he had seen done to himself and to others. This could be a novel way, one unfamiliar to him. It could always be.

"Tonight," Miss Lee said, "in the speech the Leader singled you out. Didn't this strike you as strange? You, of all people? A minor officeholder in a meager ministry—"

"Admitted," he said. "It struck me that way; yes."

"That was legitimate. His Greatness is grooming an elite cadre of younger men, postwar men, he hopes will infuse new life into the hidebound, moribund hierarchy of old fogies and Party hacks. His Greatness singled you out for the same reason that we singled you out; if pursued properly, your career could lead you all the way to the top. At least for a time . . . as we know. That's how it goes."

He thought, So virtually everyone has faith in me. Except myself; and certainly not after this, the experience with the anti-hallucinatory snuff. It had shaken years of confidence, and no doubt rightly so. However, he was beginning to regain his poise; he felt it seeping back, a little at first, then with a rush.

Going to the vidphone, he lifted the receiver and began, for the second time that night, to dial the number of the Hanoi Security Police.

"Turning me in," Miss Lee said, "would be the second most regressive decision you could make. I'll tell them that you brought me here to bribe me; you thought, because of my job at the Ministry, I would know which examination paper to select."

He said, "And what would be my first most regressive decision?"

"Not taking a further dose of phenothiazine," Miss Lee said evenly.

Hanging up the phone, Tung Chien thought to himself, I don't understand what's happening to me. Two forces, the Party and His Greatness on one hand—this girl with her alleged group on the other. One wants me to rise as far as possible in the Party hierarchy; the other— *What did Tanya Lee want?* Underneath the words, inside the membrane of an almost trivial contempt for the Party, the Leader, the ethical standards of the People's Democratic United Front—what was she after in regard to him?

He said curiously, "Are you anti-Party?"

"No."

"But—" He gestured. "That's all there is: Party and anti-Party. You must be Party, then." Bewildered, he stared at her; with composure she returned the stare. "You have an organization," he said, "and you meet. What do you intend to destroy? The regular function of government? Are you like the treasonable college students of the United States during the Vietnam War who stopped troop trains, demonstrated—"

Wearily Miss Lee said, "It wasn't like that. But forget it; that's not the issue. What we want to know is this: who or what is leading us? We must penetrate far enough to enlist someone, some rising young Party theoretician, who could conceivably be invited to a tête-à-tête with the Leader—you see?" Her voice lifted; she consulted her watch, obviously anxious to get away: the fifteen minutes were almost up. "Very few persons actually see the Leader, as you know. I mean really see him."

"Seclusion," he said. "Due to his advanced age."

"We have hope," Miss Lee said, "that if you pass the phony test which they have arranged for you—and with my help you have—you will be invited to one of the stag parties which the Leader has from time to time, which of course the 'papes don't report. Now do you see?" Her voice rose shrilly, in a frenzy of despair. "Then we would know; if you could go in there under the influence of the anti-hallucinogenic drug, could see him face to face as actually is—"

Thinking aloud, he said, "And end my career of public service. If not my life."

"You owe us something," Tanya Lee snapped, her cheeks white. "If I hadn't told you which exam paper to choose you would have picked the wrong one and your dedicated public service career would be over anyhow;

you would have failed—failed at a test you didn't even realize you were taking!"

He said mildly, "I had a fifty-fifty chance."

"No." She shook her head fiercely. "The heretical one is faked up with a lot of Party jargon; they deliberately constructed the two texts to trap you. They *wanted* you to fail!"

Once more he examined the two papers, feeling confused. Was she right? Possibly. Probably. It rang true, knowing the Party functionaries as he did, and Tso-pin, his superior, in particular. He felt weary then. Defeated. After a time he said to the girl, "What you're trying to get out of me is a quid pro quo. You did something for me—you got, or claim you got—the answer to this Party inquiry. But you've already done your part. What's to keep me from tossing you out of here on your head? I don't have to do a goddam thing." He heard his voice, toneless, sounding the poverty of empathic emotionality so usual in Party circles.

Miss Lee said, "There will be other tests, as you continue to ascend. And we will monitor for you with them too." She was calm, at ease; obviously she had forseen his reaction.

"How long do I have to think it over?" he said.

"I'm leaving now. We're in no rush; you're not about to receive an invitation to the Leader's Yellow River villa in the next week or even month." Going to the door, opening it, she paused. "As you're given covert rating tests we'll be in contact, supplying the answers—so you'll see one or more of us on those occasions. Probably it won't be me; it'll be that disabled war veteran who'll sell you the correct response sheets as you leave the Ministry building." She smiled a brief, snuffed-out-candle smile. "But one of these days, no doubt unexpectedly, you'll get an ornate, official, very formal invitation to the villa, and when you go you'll be heavily sedated with stelazine . . . possibly our last dose of our dwindling supply. Good night." The door shut after her; she had gone.

My god, he thought. They can blackmail me. For what I've done. And she didn't even bother to mention it; in view of what they're involved with it was not worth mentioning.

But blackmail for what? He had already told the Secpol squad that he had been given a drug which had proved to be a phenothiazine. *Then they know,* he realized. They'll watch me; they're alert. Technically I haven't broken a law, but—they'll be watching, all right.

However, they always watched anyhow. He relaxed slightly, thinking that. He had, over the years, become virtually accustomed to it, as had everyone.

I will see the Absolute Benefactor of the People as he is, he said to himself. Which possibly no one else has done. What will it be? Which of the subclasses of non-hallucination? Classes which I do not even know about . . . a view which may totally overthrow me. How am I going to be able to get through the evening, to keep my poise, if it's like the shape I saw on the TV screen? The Crusher, the Clanker, the Bird, the Climbing Tube, the Gulper—or worse.

He wondered what some of the other views consisted of . . . and then gave up that line of speculation; it was unprofitable. And too anxiety-inducing.

The next morning Mr. Tso-pin and Mr. Darius Pethel met him in his office, both of them calm but expectant. Wordlessly, he handed them one of the two "exam papers." The orthodox one, with its short and heart-smothering Arabian poem.

"This one," Chien said tightly, "is the product of a dedicated Party member or candidate for membership. The other—" He slapped the remaining sheets. "Reactionary garbage." He felt anger. "In spite of a superficial—"

"All right, Mr. Chien," Pethel said, nodding. "We

don't have to explore each and every ramification; your analysis is correct. You heard the mention regarding you in the Leader's speech last night on TV?"

"I certainly did," Chien said.

"So you have undoubtedly inferred," Pethel said, "that there is a good deal involved in what we are attempting here. The Leader has his eye on you; that's clear. As a matter of fact, he has communicated to myself regarding you." He opened his bulging briefcase and rummaged. "Lost the goddam thing. Anyhow—" He glanced at Tso-pin, who nodded slightly. "His Greatness would like to have you appear for dinner at the Yangtze River Ranch next Thursday night. Mrs. Fletcher in particular appreciates—"

Chien said, "'Mrs. Fletcher'? Who is 'Mrs. Fletcher'?"

After a pause Tso-pin said dryly, "The Absolute Benefactor's wife. His name—which you of course had never heard—is Thomas Fletcher."

"He's a Caucasian," Pethel explained. "Originally from the New Zealand Communist Party; he participated in the difficult takeover there. This news is not in the strict sense secret, but on the other hand it hasn't been noised about." He hesitated, toying with his watchchain. "Probably it would be better if you forgot about that. Of course, as soon as you meet him, see him face to face, you'll realize that, realize that he's a Cauc. As I am. As many of us are."

"Race," Tso-pin pointed out, "has nothing to do with loyalty to the Leader and the Party. As witness Mr. Pethel, here."

But His Greatness, Chien thought, jolted. He did not appear, on the TV screen, to be occidental. "On TV—" he began.

"The image," Tso-pin interrupted, "is subjected to a variegated assortment of skillful refinements. For ideological purposes. Most persons holding higher offices are aware of this." He eyed Chien with hard criticism.

So everyone agrees, Chien thought. What we see every

night is not real. The question is, How unreal? Partially? Or—completely?

"I will be prepared," he said tautly. And he thought, There has been a slip-up. They weren't prepared for me—the people that Tanya Lee represents—to gain entry so soon. Where's the anti-hallucinogen? Can they get it to me or not? Probably not on such short notice.

He felt, strangely, relief. He would be going into the presence of His Greatness in a position to see him as a human being, see him as he—and everybody else—saw him on TV. It would be a most stimulating and cheerful dinner party, with some of the most influential Party members in Asia. I think we can do without the phenothiazines, he said to himself. And his sense of relief grew.

"Here it is, finally," Pethel said suddenly, producing a white envelope from his briefcase. "Your card of admission. You will be flown by Sino-rocket to the Leader's villa Thursday morning; there the protocol officer will brief you on your expected behavior. It will be formal dress, white tie and tails, but the atmosphere will be cordial. There are always a great number of toasts." He added, "I have attended two such stag get-togethers. Mr. Tso-pin"—he smiled creakily—"has not been honored in such a fashion. But as they say, all things come to him who waits. Ben Franklin said that."

Tso-pin said, "It has come for Mr. Chien rather prematurely, I would say." He shrugged philosophically. "But my opinion has never at any time been asked."

"One thing," Pethel said to Chien. "It is possible that when you see His Greatness in person you will be in some regards disappointed. Be alert that you do not let this make itself apparent, if you should so feel. We have, always, tended—been trained—to regard him as more than a man. But at table he is"—he gestured—"a forked radish. In certain respects like ourselves. He may for instance indulge in moderately human oral-aggressive and -passive activity; he possibly may tell an off-color joke or drink too much . . . To be candid, no one ever knows in advance how these things will work out, but they do generally hold forth until late the following morning. So it would be wise to accept the dosage of amphetamines which the protocol officer will offer you."

"Oh?" Chien said. This was news to him, and interesting.

"For stamina. And to balance the liquor. His Greatness has amazing staying power; he often is still on his feet and raring to go after everyone else has collapsed."

"A remarkable man," Tso-pin chimed in. "I think his—indulgences only show that he is a fine fellow. And fully in the round; he is like the ideal Renaissance man; as, for example, Lorenzo de' Medici."

"That does come to mind," Pethel said; he studied Chien with such intensity that some of last night's chill returned. Am I being led into one trap after another? Chien wondered. That girl—was she in fact an agent of the Secpol probing me, trying to ferret out a disloyal, anti-Party streak in me?

I think, he decided, I will make sure that the legless peddler of herbal remedies does not snare me when I leave work; I'll take a totally different route back to my conapt.

He was successful. That day he avoided the peddler and the same the next, and so on until Thursday.

On Thursday morning the peddler scooted from beneath a parked truck and blocked his way, confronting him.

"My medication?" the peddler demanded. "It helped? I know it did; the formula goes back to the Sung Dynasty—I can tell it did. Right?"

Chien said, "Let me go."

"Would you be kind enough to answer?" The tone was not the expected, customary whining of a street peddler operating in a marginal fashion, and that tone came across to Chien; he heard loud and clear . . . as the Imperialist puppet troops of long ago phrased it.

"I know what you gave me," Chien said. "And I don't want any more. If I change my mind I can pick it up at a pharmacy. Thanks." He started on, but the cart, with the legless occupant, pursued him.

"Miss Lee was talking to me," the peddler said loudly.

"Hmm," Chien said, and automatically increased his pace; he spotted a hovercab and began signaling for it.

"It's tonight you're going to the stag dinner at the Yangtze River villa," the peddler said, panting for breath in his effort to keep up. "Take the medication—now!" He held out a flat packet, imploringly. "Please, Party Member Chien; for your own sake, for all of us. So we can tell what it is we're up against. Good lord, it may be non-terran; that's our most basic fear. Don't you understand, Chien? What's your goddam career compared with that? If we can't find out—"

The cab bumped to a halt on the pavement; its door slid open. Chien started to board it.

The packet sailed past him, landed on the entrance sill of the cab, then slid into the gutter, damp from earlier rain.

"Please," the peddler said. "And it won't cost you anything; today it's free. Just take it, use it before the stag dinner. And don't use the amphetamines; they're a thalamic stimulant, contra-indicated whenever an adrenal suppressant such as a phenothiazine is—"

The door of the cab closed after Chien. He seated himself.

"Where to, comrade?" the robot drive-mechanism inquired.

He gave the ident tag number of his conapt.

"That half-wit of a peddler managed to infiltrate his seedy wares into my clean interior," the cab said. "Notice; it reposes by your foot."

He saw the packet—no more than an ordinary-

looking envelope. I guess, he thought, this is how drugs
come to you; all of a sudden they're lying there. For a
moment he sat, and then he picked it up.

As before, there was a written enclosure above and
beyond the medication, but this time, he saw, it was
handwritten. A feminine script: from Miss Lee:

> We were surprised at the suddenness. But thank
> heaven we were ready. Where were you Tuesday
> and Wednesday? Anyhow, here it is, and good luck.
> I will approach you later in the week; I don't want
> you to try to find me.

He ignited the note, burned it up in the cab's disposal
ashtray.

And kept the dark granules.

All this time, he thought. Hallucinogens in our water
supply. Year after year. Decades. And not in wartime but
in peacetime. And not to the enemy camp but here in our
own. The evil bastards, he said to himself. Maybe I ought
to take this; maybe I ought to find out what he or it is and
let Tanya's group know.

I will, he decided. And—he was curious.

A bad emotion, he knew. Curiosity was, especially in
Party activities, often a terminal state careerwise.

A state which, at the moment, gripped him thoroughly. He wondered if it would last through the evening, if,
when it came right down to it, he would actually take the
inhalant.

Time would tell. Tell that and everything else. We are
blooming flowers, he thought, on the plain, which he
picks. As the Arabic poem had put it. He tried to
remember the rest of the poem but could not.

That probably was just as well.

The villa protocol officer, a Japanese named Kimo
Okubara, tall and husky, obviously a quondam wrestler,
surveyed him with innate hostility, even after he pre-

sented his engraved invitation and had successfully managed to prove his identity.

"Surprise you bother to come," Okubara muttered. "Why not stay home and watch on TV? Nobody miss you. We got along fine without up to right now."

Chien said tightly, "I've already watched on TV." And anyhow the stag dinners were rarely televised; they were too bawdy.

Okubara's crew double-checked him for weapons, including the possibility of an anal suppository, and then gave him his clothes back. They did not find the phenothiazine, however. Because he had already taken it. The effects of such a drug, he knew, lasted approximately four hours; that would be more than enough. And, as Tanya had said, it was a major dose; he felt sluggish and inept and dizzy, and his tongue moved in spasms of pseudo Parkinsonism—an unpleasant side effect which he had failed to anticipate.

A girl, nude from the waist up, with long coppery hair down her shoulders and back, walked by. Interesting.

Coming the other way, a girl nude from the bottom up made her appearance. Interesting, too. Both girls looked vacant and bored, and totally self-possessed.

"You go in like that too," Okubara informed Chien.

Startled, Chien said, "I understood white tie and tails."

"Joke," Okubara said. "At your expense. Only girls wear nude; you even get so you enjoy, unless you homosexual."

Well, Chien thought, I guess I had better like it. He wandered on with the other guests—they, like him, wore white tie and tails or, if women, floor-length gowns—and felt ill at ease, despite the tranquilizing effect of the stelazine. Why am I here? he asked himself. The ambiguity of his situation did not escape him. He was here to advance his career in the Party apparatus, to obtain the intimate and personal nod of approval from His Greatness . . . and in addition he was here to decipher

His Greatness as a fraud; he did not know what variety of fraud, but there it was: fraud against the Party, against all the peace-loving democratic people of Terra. Ironic, he thought. And continued to mingle.

A girl with small, bright, illuminated breasts approached him for a match; he absentmindedly got out his lighter. "What makes your breasts glow?" he asked her. "Radioactive injections?"

She shrugged, said nothing, passed on, leaving him alone. Evidently he had responded in the incorrect way.

Maybe it's a wartime mutation, he pondered.

"Drink, sir." A servant graciously held out a tray; he accepted a martini—which was the current fad among the higher Party classes in People's China—and sipped the ice-cold dry flavor. Good English gin, he said to himself. Or possibly the original Holland compound; juniper or whatever they added. Not bad. He strolled on, feeling better; in actuality he found the atmosphere here a pleasant one. The people here were self-assured; they had been successful and now they could relax. It evidently was a myth that proximity to His Greatness produced neurotic anxiety: he saw no evidence here, at least, and felt little himself.

A heavy-set elderly man, bald, halted him by the simple means of holding his drink glass against Chien's chest. "That frably little one who asked you for a match," the elderly man said, and sniggered. "The quig with the Christmas-tree breasts—that was a boy, in drag." He giggled. "You have to be cautious around here."

"Where, if anywhere," Chien said, "do I find authentic women? In the white ties and tails?"

"Darn near," the elderly man said, and departed with a throng of hyperactive guests, leaving Chien alone with his martini.

A handsome, tall woman, well dressed, standing near Chien, suddenly put her hand on his arm; he felt her fingers tense and she said, "Here he comes. His Greatness. This is the first time for me; I'm a little scared. Does my hair look all right?"

"Fine," Chien said reflexively, and followed her gaze, seeking a glimpse—his first—of the Absolute Benefactor.

What crossed the room toward the table in the center was not a man.

And it was not, Chien realized, a mechanical construct either; it was not what he had seen on TV. That evidently was simply a device for speechmaking, as Mussolini had once used an artificial arm to salute long and tedious processions.

God, he thought, and felt ill. Was this what Tanya Lee had called the "aquatic horror" shape? It had no shape. Nor pseudopodia, either flesh or metal. It was, in a sense, not there at all; when he managed to look directly at it, the shape vanished; he saw through it, saw the people on the far side—but not it. Yet if he turned his head, caught it out of a sidelong glance, he could determine its boundaries.

It was terrible; it blasted him with its awfulness. As it moved it drained the life from each person in turn; it ate the people who had assembled, passed on, ate again, ate more with an endless appetite. It hated; he felt its hate. It loathed; he felt its loathing for everyone present—in fact he shared its loathing. All at once he and everyone else in the big villa were each a twisted slug, and over the fallen slug-carcasses the creature savored, lingered, but all the time coming directly toward him—or was that an illusion? If this is a hallucination, Chien thought, it is the worst I have ever had; if it is not, then it is evil reality; it's an evil thing that kills and injures. He saw the trail of stepped-on, mashed men and women remnants behind it; he saw them trying to reassemble, to operate their crippled bodies; he heard them attempting speech.

I know who you are, Tung Chien thought to himself. You, the supreme head of the worldwide Party structure.

You, who destroy whatever living object you touch; I see that Arabic poem, the searching for the flowers of life to eat them—I see you astride the plain which to you is Earth, plain without hills, without valleys. You go anywhere, appear any time, devour anything; you engineer life and then guzzle it, and you enjoy that.

He thought, You are God.

"Mr. Chien," the voice said, but it came from inside his head, not from the mouthless spirit that fashioned itself directly before him. "It is good to meet you again. You know nothing. Go away. I have no interest in you. Why should I care about slime? Slime; I am mired in it, I must excrete it, and I choose to. I could break you; I can break even myself. Sharp stones are under me; I spread sharp pointed things upon the mire. I make the hiding places, the deep places, boil like a pot; to me the sea is like a pot of ointment. The flakes of my flesh are joined to everything. You are me. I am you. It makes no difference, just as it makes no difference whether the creature with ignited breasts is a girl or boy; you could learn to enjoy either." It laughed.

He could not believe it was speaking to him; he could not imagine—it was too terrible—that it had picked him out.

"I have picked everybody out," it said. "No one is too small; each falls and dies and I am there to watch. I don't need to do anything but watch; it is automatic; it was arranged that way." And then it ceased talking to him; it disjoined itself. But he still saw it; he felt its manifold presence. It was a globe which hung in the room, with fifty thousand eyes, with a million eyes—billions: an eye for each living thing as it waited for each thing to fall, and then stepped on the living thing as it lay in a broken state. Because of this it had created the things, and he knew; he understood. What had seemed in the Arabic poem to be death was not death but god; or rather God was death, it was one force, one hunter, one cannibal thing, and it missed again and again but, having all eternity, it could afford to miss. Both poems, he realized; the Dryden one too. The crumbling; that is our world and you are doing it. Warping it to come out that way; bending us.

But at least, he thought, I still have my dignity. With dignity he set down his drink glass, turned, walked toward the doors of the room. He passed through the doors. He walked down a long carpeted hall. A villa servant dressed in purple opened a door for him; he found himself standing out in the night darkness, on a veranda, alone.

Not alone.

It had followed after him. Or it had already been here before him; yes, it had been expecting. It was not really through with him.

"Here I go," he said, and made a dive for the railing; it was six stories down, and there below gleamed the river, and death, real death, not what the Arabic poem had seen.

As he tumbled over, it put an extension of itself on his shoulder.

"Why?" he said. But, in fact, he paused. Wondering. Not understanding, not at all.

"Don't fall on my account," it said. He could not see it because it had moved behind him. But the piece of it on his shoulder—it had begun to look to him like a human hand.

And then it laughed.

"What's funny?" he demanded, as he teetered on the railing, held back by its pseudo-hand.

"You're doing my task for me," it said. "You aren't waiting; don't you have time to wait? I'll select you out from among the others; you don't need to speed the process up."

"What if I do?" he said. "Out of revulsion for you?"

It laughed. And didn't answer.

"You won't even say," he said.

Again no answer. He started to slide back, onto the veranda. And at once the pressure of its pseudo-hand lifted.

"You founded the Party?" he asked.

"I founded everything. I founded the anti-Party and the Party that isn't a Party, and those who are for it and those who are against, those that you call Yankee Imperialists, those in the camp of reaction, and so on endlessly. I founded it all. As if they were blades of grass."

"And you're here to enjoy it?" he said.

"What I want," it said, "is for you to see me, as I am, as you have seen me, and then trust me."

"What?" he said, quavering. "Trust you to what?"

It said, "Do you believe in me?"

"Yes," he said. "I can see you."

"Then go back to your job at the Ministry. Tell Tanya Lee that you saw an overworked, overweight, elderly man who drinks too much and likes to pinch girls' rear ends."

"Oh, Christ," he said.

"As you live on, unable to stop, I will torment you," it said. "I will deprive you, item by item, of everything you possess or want. And then when you are crushed to death I will unfold a mystery."

"What's the mystery?"

"The dead shall live, the living die. I kill what lives; I save what has died. And I will tell you this: *there are things worse than I.* But you won't meet them because by then I will have killed you. Now walk back into the dining room and prepare for dinner. Don't question what I'm doing; I did it long before there was a Tung Chien and I will do it long after."

He hit it as hard as he could.

And experienced violent pain in his head.

And darkness, with the sense of falling.

After that, darkness again. He thought, I will get you. I will see that you die too. That you suffer; you're going to suffer, just like us, exactly in every way we do. I'll dedicate my life to that; I'll confront you again, and I'll nail you; I swear to god I'll nail you up somewhere. And it will hurt. As much as I hurt now.

He shut his eyes.

Roughly, he was shaken. And heard Mr. Kimo Okubara's voice. "Get to your feet, common drunk. Come on!"

Without opening his eyes he said, "Get me a cab."

"Cab already waiting. You go home. Disgrace. Make a violent scene out of yourself."

Getting shakily to his feet, he opened his eyes, examined himself. Our Leader whom we follow, he thought, is the One True God. And the enemy whom we fight and have fought is God too. They are right; he is everywhere. But I didn't understand what that meant. Staring at the protocol officer, he thought, You are God too. So there is no getting away, probably not even by jumping. As I started, instinctively, to do. He shuddered.

"Mix drinks with drugs," Okubara said witheringly. "Ruin career. I see it happen many times. Get lost."

Unsteadily, he walked toward the great central door of the Yangtze River villa; two servants, dressed like medieval knights, with crested plumes, ceremoniously opened the door for him and one of them said, "Good night, sir."

"Up yours," Chien said, and passed out into the night.

At a quarter to three in the morning, as he sat sleepless in the living room of his conapt, smoking one Cuesta Rey Astoria after another, a knock sounded at the door.

When he opened it he found himself facing Tanya Lee in her trenchcoat, her face pinched with cold. Her eyes blazed, questioningly.

"Don't look at me like that," he said roughly. His cigar had gone out; he relit it. "I've been looked at enough," he said.

"You saw it," she said.

He nodded.

She seated herself on the arm of the couch and after a time she said, "Want to tell me about it?"

"Go as far from here as possible," he said. "Go a long way." And then he remembered; no way was long enough. He remembered reading that too. "Forget it," he said; rising to his feet, he walked clumsily into the kitchen to start up the coffee.

Following after him, Tanya said, "Was—it that bad?"

"We can't win," he said. "You can't win; I don't mean me. I'm not in this; I just want to do my job at the Ministry and forget about it. Forget the whole damned thing."

"Is it non-terrestrial?"

"Yes." He nodded.

"Is it hostile to us?"

"Yes," he said. "No. Both. Mostly hostile."

"Then we have to—"

"Go home," he said, "and go to bed." He looked her over carefully; he had sat a long time and he had done a great deal of thinking. About a lot of things. "Are you married?" he said.

"No. Not now. I used to be."

He said, "Stay with me tonight. The rest of tonight, anyhow. Until the sun comes up." He added, "The night part is awful."

"I'll stay," Tanya said, unbuckling the belt of her raincoat, "but I have to have some answers."

"What did Dryden mean," Chien said, "about music untuning the sky? I don't get that. What does music do to the sky?"

"All the celestial order of the universe ends," she said as she hung her raincoat up in the closet of the bedroom; under it she wore an orange striped sweater and stretch-pants.

He said, "And that's bad."

Pausing, she reflected. "I don't know. I guess so."

"It's a lot of power," he said, "to assign to music."

"Well, you know that old Pythagorean business about the 'music of the spheres.'" Matter-of-factly she seated herself on the bed and removed her slipperlike shoes.

"Do you believe in that?" he said. "Or do you believe in God?"

"'God'!" She laughed. "That went out with the donkey steam engine. What are you talking about? God, or god?" She came over close beside him, peering into his face.

"Don't look at me so closely," he said sharply, drawing back. "I don't ever want to be looked at again." He moved away, irritably.

"I think," Tanya said, "that if there is a God He has very little interest in human affairs. That's my theory, anyhow. I mean, He doesn't seem to care if evil triumphs or people and animals get hurt and die. I frankly don't see Him anywhere around. And the Party has always denied any form of—"

"Did you ever see Him?" he asked. "When you were a child?"

"Oh, sure, as a child. But I also believed—"

"Did it ever occur to you," Chien said, "that good and evil are names for the same thing? That God could be both good and evil at the same time?"

"I'll fix you a drink," Tanya said, and padded barefoot into the kitchen.

Chien said, "The Crusher. The Clanker. The Gulper and the Bird and the Climbing Tube—plus other names, forms, I don't know. I had a hallucination. At the stag dinner. A big one. A terrible one."

"But the stelazine—"

"It brought on a worse one," he said.

"Is there any way," Tanya said somberly, "that we can fight this thing you saw? This apparition you call a hallucination but which very obviously was not?"

He said, "Believe in it."

"What will that do?"

"Nothing," he said wearily. "Nothing at all. I'm tired; I don't want a drink—let's just go to bed."

"Okay." She padded back into the bedroom, began pulling her striped sweater over her head. "We'll discuss it more thoroughly later."

"A hallucination," Chien said, "is merciful. I wish I had it; I want mine back. I want to be before your peddler got to me with that phenothiazine."

"Just come to bed. It'll be toasty. All warm and nice."

He removed his tie, his shirt—and saw, on his right shoulder, the mark, the stigma, which it had left when it stopped him from jumping. Livid marks which looked as if they would never go away. He put his pajama top on, then; it hid the marks.

"Anyhow," Tanya said as he got into the bed beside her, "your career is immeasurably advanced. Aren't you glad about that?"

"Sure," he said, nodding sightlessly in the darkness. "Very glad."

"Come over against me," Tanya said, putting her arms around him. "And forget everything else. At least for now."

He tugged her against him, then, doing what she asked and what he wanted to do. She was neat; she was swiftly active; she was successful and she did her part. They did not bother to speak until at last she said, "Oh!" And then she relaxed.

"I wish," he said, "that we could go on forever."

"We did," Tanya said. "It's outside of time; it's boundless, like an ocean. It's the way we were in Cambrian times, before we migrated up onto the land; it's the ancient primary waters. This is the only time we get to go back, when this is done. That's why it means so much. And in those days we weren't separate; it was like a big jelly, like those blobs that float up on the beach."

"Float up," he said, "and are left there to die."

"Could you get me a towel?" Tanya asked. "Or a washcloth? I need it."

He padded into the bathroom for a towel. There—he was naked, now—he once more saw his shoulder, saw where it had seized hold of him and held on, dragged him back, possibly to toy with him a little more.

The marks, unaccountably, were bleeding.

He sponged the blood away. More oozed forth at once and seeing that, he wondered how much time he had left. Probably only hours.

Returning to bed, he said, "Could you continue?"

"Sure. If you have any energy left; it's up to you." She lay gazing up at him unwinkingly, barely visible in the dim nocturnal light.

"I have," he said. And hugged her to him.

Gertrude Atherton (1857–1948)

THE BELL IN THE FOG

Gertrude Atherton dedicated her first and best collection of ghost stories, *The Bell in the Fog and Other Stories* (1905), "To the Master, Henry James." The title story of the collection is both an homage to James and an extraordinary critique. Ralph, the central character who becomes obsessed with a painting, is a portrait of the James whom Atherton knew, and the stamp of emulation is everywhere in the piece. But in the end, the portrayal is not entirely sympathetic. One wonders what James made of this piece. An intriguing fact is that Henry James began writing in 1900 upon the request of William Dean Howells a long story about an "international ghost," that he wrote in part and then abandoned when he had difficulty with the plot. In 1915, he took it up again but died before completing *The Sense of the Past*, which was published as a fragment posthumously (1917). Ralph, the central character, becomes obsessed with a century-old painting, and travels back to the past as a "ghost" from the future, who sits for that very portrait. Whatever the case, "The Bell in the Fog" is an effective supernatural piece by a feminist writer who later became James' literary enemy.

I

The great author had realized one of the dreams of his ambitious youth, the possession of an ancestral hall in England. It was not so much the good American's reverence for ancestors that inspired the longing to consort with the ghosts of an ancient line, as artistic appreciation of the mellowness, the dignity, the aristocratic aloofness of walls that have sheltered, and furniture that has embraced, generations and generations of the dead. To mere wealth, only his astute and incomparably modern brain yielded respect; his ego raised its goose-flesh at the sight of rooms furnished with a single check, conciliatory as the taste might be. The dumping of the old interiors of Europe into the glistening shells of the United States not only roused him almost to passionate protest, but offended his patriotism—which he classified among his unworked ideals. The average American was not an artist, therefore he had no excuse for even the affectation of cosmopolitanism. Heaven knew he was national enough in everything else, from his accent to his lack of repose; let his surroundings be in keeping.

Orth had left the United States soon after his first successes, and, his art being too great to be confounded with locality, he had long since ceased to be spoken of as an American author. All civilized Europe furnished stages for his puppets, and, if never picturesque nor impassioned, his originality was as overwhelming as his style. His subtleties might not always be understood—indeed, as a rule, they were not—but the musical mystery of his language and the penetrating charm of his lofty and cultivated mind induced raptures in the initiated, forever denied to those who failed to appreciate him.

His following was not a large one, but it was very distinguished. The aristocracies of the earth gave to it; and not to understand and admire Ralph Orth was deliberately to relegate one's self to the ranks. But the elect are few, and they frequently subscribe to the circulating libraries; on the Continent, they buy the Tauchnitz edition; and had not Mr. Orth inherited a sufficiency of ancestral dollars to enable him to keep rooms in Jermyn Street, and the wardrobe of an Englishman of leisure, he might have been forced to consider the tastes of the middle-class at a desk in Hampstead. But, as it mercifully was, the fashionable and exclusive sets of London knew and sought him. He was too wary to become a fad, and too sophisticated to grate or bore; consequently, his popularity continued evenly from year to year, and long since he had come to be regarded as one of them. He was not keenly addicted to sport, but he could handle a gun, and all men respected his dignity and breeding. They cared less for his books than women did, perhaps because patience is not a characteristic of their sex. I am alluding, however, in this instance, to men-of-the-world. A group of young literary men—and one or two women—put him on a pedestal and kissed the earth before it. Naturally, they imitated him, and as this flattered him, and he had a kindly heart deep among the cere-cloths of his formalities, he sooner or later wrote "appreciations" of them all, which nobody living could understand, but which owing to the subtitle and signature answered every purpose.

With all this, however, he was not utterly content. From the 12th of August until late in the winter—when he did not go to Homburg and the Riviera—he visited the best houses in England, slept in state chambers, and meditated in historic parks; but the country was his one passion, and he longed for his own acres.

He was turning fifty when his great-aunt died and made him her heir: "as a poor reward for his immortal services to literature," read the will of this phenomenally appreciative relative. The estate was a large one. There was a rush for his books; new editions were announced.

He smiled with cynicism, not unmixed with sadness; but he was very grateful for the money, and as soon as his fastidious taste would permit he bought him a country-seat.

The place gratified all his ideals and dreams—for he had romanced about his sometime English possession as he had never dreamed of woman. It had once been the property of the Church, and the ruin of cloister and chapel above the ancient wood was sharp against the low pale sky. Even the house itself was Tudor, but wealth from generation to generation had kept it in repair; and the lawns were as velvety, the hedges as rigid, the trees as aged as any in his own works. It was not a castle nor a great property, but it was quite perfect; and for a long while he felt like a bridegroom on a succession of honeymoons. He often laid his hand against the rough ivied walls in a lingering caress.

After a time, he returned the hospitalities of his friends, and his invitations, given with the exclusiveness of his great distinction, were never refused. Americans visiting England eagerly sought for letters to him; and if they were sometimes benumbed by that cold and formal presence, and awed by the silences of Chillingsworth— the few who entered there—they thrilled in anticipation of verbal triumphs, and forthwith bought an entire set of his books. It was characteristic that they dared not ask him for his autograph.

Although women invariably described him as "brilliant," a few men affirmed that he was gentle and lovable, and any one of them was well content to spend weeks at Chillingsworth with no other companion. But, on the whole, he was rather a lonely man.

It occurred to him how lonely he was one gay June morning when the sunlight was streaming through his narrow windows, illuminating tapestries and armor, the family portraits of the young profligate from whom he had made this splendid purchase, dusting its gold on the black wood of wainscot and floor. He was in the gallery at the moment, studying one of his two favorite portraits, a gallant little lad in the green costume of Robin Hood. The boy's expression was imperious and radiant, and he had that perfect beauty which in any disposition appealed so powerfully to the author. But as Orth stared today at the brilliant youth, of whose life he knew nothing, he suddenly became aware of a human stirring at the foundations of his aesthetic pleasure.

"I wish he were alive and here," he thought, with a sigh. "What a jolly little companion he would be! And this fine old mansion would make a far more complementary setting for him than for me."

He turned away abruptly, only to find himself face to face with the portrait of a little girl who was quite unlike the boy, yet so perfect in her own way, and so unmistakably painted by the same hand, that he had long since concluded they had been brother and sister. She was angelically fair, and, young as she was—she could not have been more than six years old—her dark-blue eyes had a beauty of mind which must have been remarkable twenty years later. Her pouting mouth was like a little scarlet serpent, her skin almost transparent, her pale hair fell waving—not curled with the orthodoxy of childhood —about her tender bare shoulders. She wore a long white frock, and clasped tightly against her breast a doll far more gorgeously arrayed than herself. Behind her were the ruins and the woods of Chillingsworth.

Orth had studied this portrait many times, for the sake of an art which he understood almost as well as his own; but today he saw only the lovely child. He forgot even the boy in the intensity of this new and personal absorption.

"Did she live to grow up, I wonder?" he thought. "She should have made a remarkable, even a famous woman, with those eyes and that brow, but—could the spirit within that ethereal frame stand the enlightenments of maturity? Would not that mind—purged, perhaps, in a long probation from the dross of other existences—flee in disgust from the commonplace problems of a woman's life? Such perfect beings should die while they are still perfect. Still, it is possible that this little girl, whoever she was, was idealized by the artist, who painted into her his own dream of exquisite childhood."

Again he turned away impatiently. "I believe I am rather fond of children," he admitted. "I catch myself watching them on the street when they are pretty enough. Well, who does not like them?" he added, with some defiance.

He went back to his work; he was chiselling a story which was to be the foremost excuse of a magazine as yet unborn. At the end of half an hour he threw down his wondrous instrument—which looked not unlike an ordinary pen—and making no attempt to disobey the desire that possessed him, went back to the gallery. The dark splendid boy, the angelic little girl were all he saw—even of the several children in that roll call of the past—and they seemed to look straight down his eyes into depths where the fragmentary ghosts of unrecorded ancestors gave faint musical response.

"The dead's kindly recognition of the dead," he thought. "But I wish these children were alive."

For a week he haunted the gallery, and the children haunted him. Then he became impatient and angry. "I am mooning like a barren woman," he exclaimed. "I must take the briefest way of getting those youngsters off my mind."

With the help of his secretary, he ransacked the library, and finally brought to light the gallery catalogue which had been named in the inventory. He discovered that his children were the Viscount Tancred and the Lady Blanche Mortlake, son and daughter of the second Earl of Teignmouth. Little wiser than before, he sat down at once and wrote to the present earl, asking for some account of the lives of the children. He awaited the answer with more restlessness than he usually permitted himself, and took long walks, ostentatiously avoiding the gallery.

"I believe those youngsters have obsessed me," he thought, more than once. "They certainly are beautiful enough, and the last time I looked at them in that waning light they were fairly alive. Would that they were, and scampering about this park."

Lord Teignmouth, who was intensely grateful to him, answered promptly.

"I am afraid," he wrote, "that I don't know much about my ancestors—those who didn't do something or other; but I have a vague rememberance of having been told by an aunt of mine, who lives on the family traditions—she isn't married—that the little chap was drowned in the river, and that the little girl died too—I mean when she *was* a little girl—wasted away, or something—I'm such a beastly idiot about expressing myself, that I wouldn't dare to write to you at all if you weren't really great. That is actually all I can tell you, and I am afraid the painter was their only biographer."

The author was gratified that the girl had died young, but grieved for the boy. Although he had avoided the gallery of late, his practised imagination had evoked from the throngs of history the high-handed and brilliant, surely adventurous career of the third Earl of Teignmouth. He had pondered upon the deep delights of directing such a mind and character, and had caught himself envying the dust that was older still. When he read of the lad's early death, in spite of his regret that such promise should have come to naught, he admitted to a secret thrill of satisfaction that the boy had so soon ceased to belong to anyone. Then he smiled with both sadness and humor.

"What an old fool I am!" he admitted. "I believe I not only wish those children were alive, but that they were my own."

The frank admission proved fatal. He made straight for the gallery. The boy, after the interval of separation, seemed more spiritedly alive than ever, the little girl to suggest, with her faint appealing smile, that she would like to be taken up and cuddled.

"I must try another way," he thought, desperately, after that long communion. "I must write them out of me."

He went back to the library and locked up the *tour de force* which had ceased to command his classic faculty. At once, he began to write the story of the brief lives of the children, much to the amazement of that faculty, which was little accustomed to the simplicities. Nevertheless, before he had written three chapters, he knew that he was at work upon a masterpiece—and more: he was experiencing a pleasure so keen that once and again his hand trembled, and he saw the page through a mist. Although his characters had always been objective to himself and his more patient readers, none knew better than he—a man of no delusions—that they were so remote and exclusive as barely to escape being mere mentalities; they were never the pulsing living creations of the more full-blooded genius. But he had been content to have it so. His creations might find and leave him cold, but he had known his highest satisfaction in chiselling the statuettes, extracting subtle and elevating harmonies, while combining words as no man of his tongue had combined them before.

But the children were not statuettes. He had loved and brooded over them long ere he had thought to tuck them into his pen, and on its first stroke they danced out alive. The old mansion echoed with their laughter, with their delightful and original pranks. Mr. Orth knew nothing of children, therefore all the pranks he invented were as original as his faculty. The little girl clung to his hand or knee as they both followed the adventurous course of their common idol, the boy. When Orth realized how alive they were, he opened each room of his home to them in turn, that evermore he might have sacred and poignant memories with all parts of the stately mansion

where he must dwell alone to the end. He selected their
bedrooms, and hovered over them—not through infan-
tile disorders, which were beyond even his imagination
—but through those painful intervals incident upon the
enterprising spirit of the boy and the devoted obedience
of the girl to fraternal command. He ignored the second
Lord Teignmouth; he was himself their father, and he
admired himself extravagantly for the first time; art had
chastened him long since. Oddly enough, the children
had no mother, not even the memory of one.

He wrote the book more slowly than was his wont, and
spent delightful hours pondering upon the chapter of the
morrow. He looked forward to the conclusion with a sort
of terror, and made up his mind that when the inevitable
last word was written he should start at once for Homburg. Incalculable times a day he went to the gallery, for
he no longer had any desire to write the children out of
his mind, and his eyes hungered for them. They were his
now. It was with an effort that he sometimes humorously
reminded himself that another man had fathered them,
and that their little skeletons were under the choir of the
chapel. Not even for peace of mind would he have
descended into the vaults of the lords of Chillingsworth
and looked upon the marble effigies of his children.
Nevertheless, when in a superhumorous mood, he dwelt
upon his high satisfaction in having been enabled by his
great-aunt to purchase all that was left of them.

For two months he lived in his fool's paradise, and
then he knew that the book must end. He nerved himself
to nurse the little girl through her wasting illness, and
when he clasped her hands, his own shook, his knees
trembled. Desolation settled upon the house, and he
wished he had left one corner of it to which he could
retreat unhaunted by the child's presence. He took long
tramps, avoiding the river with a sensation next to panic.
It was two days before he got back to his table, and then
he had made up his mind to let the boy live. To kill him
off, too, was more than his augmented stock of human

nature could endure. After all, the lad's death had been purely accidental, wanton. It was just that he should live—with one of the author's inimitable suggestions of future greatness; but, at the end, the parting was almost as bitter as the other. Orth knew then how men feel when their sons go forth to encounter the world and ask no more of the old companionship.

The author's boxes were packed. He sent the manuscript to his publisher an hour after it was finished—he could not have given it a final reading to have saved it from failure—directed his secretary to examine the proof under a microscope, and left the next morning for Homburg. There, in inmost circles, he forgot his children. He visited in several of the great houses of the Continent until November; then returned to London to find his book the literary topic of the day. His secretary handed him the reviews; and for once in a way he read the finalities of the nameless. He found himself hailed as a genius, and compared in astonished phrases to the prodigiously clever talent which the world for twenty years had isolated under the name of Ralph Orth. This pleased him, for every writer is human enough to wish to be hailed as a genius, and immediately. Many are, and many wait; it depends upon the fashion of the moment, and the needs and bias of those who write of writers. Orth had waited twenty years; but his past was bedecked with the headstones of geniuses long since forgotten. He was gratified to come thus publicly into his estate, but soon reminded himself that all the adulation of which a belated world was capable could not give him one thrill of the pleasure which the companionship of that book had given him, while creating. It was the keenest pleasure in his memory, and when a man is fifty and has written many books, that is saying a great deal.

He allowed what society was in town to lavish honors upon him for something over a month, then cancelled all his engagements and went down to Chillingsworth.

His estate was in Hertfordshire, that county of gentle hills and tangled lanes, of ancient oaks and wide wild heaths, of historic houses, and dark woods, and green fields innumerable—a Wordsworthian shire, steeped in the deepest peace of England. As Orth drove towards his own gates he had the typical English sunset to gaze upon, a red streak with a church spire against it. His woods were silent. In the fields, the cows stood as if conscious of their part. The ivy on his old gray towers had been young with his children.

He spent a haunted night, but the next day stranger happenings began.

II

He rose early, and went for one of his long walks. England seems to cry out to be walked upon, and Orth, like others of the transplanted, experienced to the full the country's gift of foot-restlessness and mental calm. Calm flees, however, when the ego is rampant, and today, as upon others too recent, Orth's soul was as restless as his feet. He had walked for two hours when he entered the wood of his neighbor's estate, a domain seldom honored by him, as it, too, had been bought by an American—a flighty hunting widow, who displeased the fastidious taste of the author. He heard children's voices, and turned with the quick prompting of retreat.

As he did so, he came face-to-face, on the narrow path, with a little girl. For the moment he was possessed by the most hideous sensation which can visit a man's being— abject terror. He believed that body and soul were disintegrating. The child before him was his child, the original of a portrait in which the artist, dead two centuries ago, had missed exact fidelity, after all. The difference, even his rolling vision took note, lay in the warm pure living whiteness and the deeper spiritual suggestion of the child in his path. Fortunately for his self-respect, the surrender lasted but a moment. The little girl spoke.

"You look real sick," she said. "Shall I lead you home?"

The voice was soft and sweet, but the intonation, the vernacular, were American, and not of the highest class. The shock was, if possible, more agonizing than the other, but this time Orth rose to the occasion.

"Who are you?" he demanded, with asperity. "What is your name? Where do you live?"

The child smiled, an angelic smile, although she was evidently amused. "I never had so many questions asked me all at once," she said. "But I don't mind, and I'm glad you're not sick. I'm Mrs. Jennie Root's little girl—my father's dead. My name is Blanche—you *are* sick! No?— and I live in Rome, New York State. We've come over here to visit pa's relations."

Orth took the child's hand in his. It was very warm and soft.

"Take me to your mother," he said, firmly; "now, at once. You can return and play afterwards. And as I wouldn't have you disappointed for the world, I'll send to town today for a beautiful doll."

The little girl, whose face had fallen, flashed her delight, but walked with great dignity beside him. He groaned in his depths as he saw they were pointing for the widow's house, but made up his mind that he would know the history of the child and of all her ancestors, if he had to sit down at table with his obnoxious neighbor. To his surprise, however, the child did not lead him into the park, but towards one of the old stone houses of the tenantry.

"Pa's great-great-great-grandfather lived there," she remarked, with all the American's pride of ancestry. Orth did not smile, however. Only the warm clasp of the hand in his, the soft thrilling voice of his still mysterious companion, prevented him from feeling as if moving through the mazes of one of his own famous ghost stories.

The child ushered him into the dining-room, where an old man was seated at the table reading his Bible. The room was at least eight hundred years old. The ceiling was supported by the trunk of a tree, black, and probably petrified. The windows had still their diamond panes, separated, no doubt, by the original lead. Beyond was a large kitchen in which were several women. The old man, who looked patriarchal enough to have laid the foundations of his dwelling, glanced up and regarded the visitor without hospitality. His expression softened as his eyes moved to the child.

"Who 'ave ye brought?" he asked. He removed his spectacles. "Ah!" He rose, and offered the author a chair. At the same moment, the women entered the room.

"Of course you've fallen in love with Blanche, sir," said one of them. "Everybody does."

"Yes, that is it. Quite so." Confusion still prevailing among his faculties, he clung to the naked truth. "This little girl has interested and startled me because she bears a precise resemblance to one of the portraits in Chillingsworth—painted about two hundred years ago. Such extraordinary likenesses do not occur without reason, as a rule, and, as I admired my portrait so deeply that I have written a story about it, you will not think it unnatural if I am more than curious to discover the reason for this resemblance. The little girl tells me that her ancestors lived in this very house, and as my little girl lived next door, so to speak, there undoubtedly is a natural reason for the resemblance."

His host closed the Bible, put his spectacles in his pocket, and hobbled out of the house.

"He'll never talk of family secrets," said an elderly woman, who introduced herself as the old man's daughter, and had placed bread and milk before the guest. "There are secrets in every family, and we have ours, but he'll never tell those old tales. All I can tell you is that an ancestor of little Blanche went to wreck and ruin because of some fine lady's doings, and killed himself. The story is that his boys turned out bad. One of them saw his crime, and never got over the shock; he was foolish like, after. The mother was a poor scared sort of creature, and hadn't much influence over the other boy. There seemed to be blight on all the man's descendants, until one of them went to America. Since then, they haven't prospered, exactly, but they've done better, and they don't drink so heavy."

"They haven't done so well," remarked a worn patient-looking woman. Orth typed her as belonging to the small middle-class of an interior town of the eastern United States.

"You are not the child's mother?"

"Yes, sir. Everybody is surprised; you needn't apologize. She doesn't look like any of us, although her brothers and sisters are good enough for anybody to be proud of. But we all think she strayed in by mistake, for she looks like any lady's child, and, of course, we're only middle-class."

Orth gasped. It was the first time he had ever heard a native American use the term middle-class with a personal application. For the moment, he forgot the child. His analytical mind raked in the new specimen. He questioned, and learned that the woman's husband had kept a hat store in Rome, New York; that her boys were clerks, her girls in stores, or type-writing. They kept her and little Blanche—who had come after her other children were well grown—in comfort; and they were all very happy together. The boys broke out, occasionally; but, on the whole, were the best in the world, and her girls were worthy of far better than they had. All were robust, except Blanche. "She coming so late, when I was no longer young, makes her delicate," she remarked, with a slight blush, the signal of her chaste Americanism; "but I guess she'll get along all right. She couldn't have better care if she was a queen's child."

Orth, who had gratefully consumed the bread and milk, rose. "Is that really all you can tell me?" he asked.

"That's all," replied the daughter of the house. "And you couldn't pry open father's mouth."

Orth shook hands cordially with all of them, for he could be charming when he chose. He offered to escort the little girl back to her playmates in the wood, and she took prompt possession of his hand. As he was leaving, he turned suddenly to Mrs. Root. "Why did you call her Blanche?" he asked.

"She was so white and dainty, she just looked it."

Orth took the next train for London, and from Lord Teignmouth obtained the address of the aunt who lived on the family traditions, and a cordial note of introduction to her. He then spent an hour anticipating, in a toy shop, the whims and pleasures of a child—an incident of paternity which his book-children had not inspired. He bought the finest doll, piano, French dishes, cooking apparatus, and playhouse in the shop, and signed a check for thirty pounds with a sensation of positive rapture. Then he took the train for Lancashire, where the Lady Mildred Mortlake lived in another ancestral home.

Possibly there are few imaginative writers who have not a leaning, secret or avowed, to the occult. The creative gift is in very close relationship with the Great Force behind the universe; for aught we know, may be an atom thereof. It is not strange, therefore, that the lesser and closer of the unseen forces should send their vibrations to it occasionally; or, at all events, that the imagination should incline its ear to the most mysterious and picturesque of all beliefs. Orth frankly dallied with the old dogma. He formulated no personal faith of any sort, but his creative faculty, that ego within an ego, had made more than one excursion into the invisible and brought back literary treasure.

The Lady Mildred received with sweetness and warmth the generous contributor to the family sieve, and listened with fluttering interest to all he had not told the world

—she had read the book—and to the strange, American-
ized sequel.

"I am all at sea," concluded Orth. "What had my little
girl to do with the tragedy? What relation was she to the
lady who drove the young man to destruction—?"

"The closest," interrupted Lady Mildred. "She was
herself!"

Orth stared at her. Again he had a confused sense of
disintegration. Lady Mildred, gratified by the success of
her bolt, proceeded less dramatically:

"Wally was up here just after I read your book, and I
discovered he had given you the wrong history of the
picture. Not that he knew it. It is a story we have left
untold as often as possible, and I tell it to you only
because you would probably become a monomaniac if I
didn't. Blanche Mortlake—that Blanche—there had
been several of her name, but there has not been one
since—did not die in childhood, but lived to be twenty-
four. She was an angelic child, but little angels sometimes grow up into very naughty girls. I believe she was
delicate as a child, which probably gave her that spiritual
look. Perhaps she was spoiled and flattered, until her
poor little soul was stifled, which is likely. At all events,
she was the coquette of her day—she seemed to care for
nothing but breaking hearts; and she did not stop when
she married, either. She hated her husband, and became
reckless. She had no children. So far, the tale is not an
uncommon one; but the worst, and what makes the
ugliest stain in our annals, is to come.

"She was alone one summer at Chillingsworth—
where she had taken temporary refuge from her husband
—and she amused herself—some say, fell in love—with
a young man of the yeomanry, a tenant of the next estate.
His name was Root. He, so it comes down to us, was a
magnificent specimen of his kind, and in those days the
yeomanry gave us our great soldiers. His beauty of face
was quite as remarkable as his physique; he led all the
rural youth in sport, and was a bit above his class in

every way. He had a wife in no way remarkable, and two little boys, but was always more with his friends than his family. Where he and Blanche Mortlake met I don't know—in the woods, probably, although it has been said that he had the run of the house. But, at all events, he was wild about her, and she pretended to be about him. Perhaps she was, for women have stooped before and since. Some women can be stormed by a fine man in any circumstances; but, although I am a woman of the world, and not easy to shock, there are some things I tolerate so hardly that it is all I can do to bring myself to believe in them; and stooping is one. Well, they were the scandal of the county for months, and then, either because she had tired of her new toy, or his grammar grated after the first glamour, or because she feared her husband, who was returning from the Continent, she broke off with him and returned to town. He followed her, and forced his way into her house. It is said she melted, but made him swear never to attempt to see her again. He returned to his home, and killed himself. A few months later she took her own life. That is all I know."

"It is quite enough for me," said Orth.

The next night, as his train travelled over the great wastes of Lancashire, a thousand chimneys were spouting forth columns of fire. Where the sky was not red it was black. The place looked like hell. Another time Orth's imagination would have gathered immediate inspiration from this wildest region of England. The fair and peaceful counties of the south had nothing to compare in infernal grandeur with these acres of flaming columns. The chimneys were invisible in the lower darkness of the night; the fires might have leaped straight from the angry caldron of the earth.

But Orth was in a subjective world, searching for all he had ever heard of occultism. He recalled that the sinful dead are doomed, according to this belief, to linger for vast reaches of time in that borderland which is close to earth, eventually sent back to work out their final salvation; that they work it out among the descendants of the people they have wronged; that suicide is held by the devotees of occultism to be a cardinal sin, abhorred and execrated.

Authors are far closer to the truths enfolded in mystery than ordinary people, because of that very audacity of imagination which irritates their plodding critics. As only those who dare to make mistakes succeed greatly, only those who shake free the wings of their imagination brush, once in a way, the secrets of the great pale world. If such writers go wrong, it is not for the mere brains to tell them so.

Upon Orth's return to Chillingsworth, he called at once upon the child, and found her happy among his gifts. She put her arms about his neck, and covered his serene unlined face with soft kisses. This completed the conquest. Orth from that moment adored her as a child, irrespective of the psychological problem.

Gradually he managed to monopolize her. From long walks it was but a step to take her home for luncheon. The hours of her visits lengthened. He had a room fitted up as a nursery and filled with the wonders of toyland. He took her to London to see the pantomimes; two days before Christmas, to buy presents for her relatives; and together they strung them upon the most wonderful Christmas tree that the old hall of Chillingsworth had ever embraced. She had a donkey-cart, and a trained nurse, disguised as a maid, to wait upon her. Before a month had passed she was living in state at Chillingsworth and paying daily visits to her mother. Mrs. Root was deeply flattered, and apparently well content. Orth told her plainly that he should make the child independent, and educate her, meanwhile. Mrs. Root intended to spend six months in England, and Orth was in no hurry to alarm her by broaching his ultimate design.

He reformed Blanche's accent and vocabulary, and read to her out of books which would have addled the brains of most little maids of six; but she seemed to enjoy them, although she seldom made a comment. He was always ready to play games with her, but she was a gentle little thing, and, moreover, tired easily. She preferred to sit in the depths of a big chair, toasting her bare toes at the log-fire in the hall, while her friend read or talked to her. Although she was thoughtful, and, when left to herself, given to dreaming, his patient observation could detect nothing uncanny about her. Moreover, she had a quick sense of humor, she was easily amused, and could laugh as merrily as any child in the world. He was resigning all hope of further development on the shadowy side when one day he took her to the picture-gallery.

It was the first warm day of summer. The gallery was not heated, and he had not dared to take his frail visitor into its chilly spaces during the winter and spring. Although he had wished to see the effect of the picture on the child, he had shrunk from the bare possibility of the very developments the mental part of him craved; the other was warmed and satisfied for the first time, and held itself aloof from disturbance. But one day the sun streamed through the old windows, and, obeying a sudden impulse, he led Blanche to the gallery.

It was some time before he approached the child of his earlier love. Again he hesitated. He pointed out many other fine pictures, and Blanche smiled appreciatively at his remarks, that were wise in criticism and interesting in matter. He never knew just how much she understood, but the very fact that there were depths in the child beyond his probing riveted his chains.

Suddenly he wheeled about and waved his hand to her prototype. "What do you think of that?" he asked. "You remember, I told you of the likeness the day I met you."

She looked indifferently at the picture, but he noticed that her color changed oddly; its pure white tone gave place to an equally delicate gray.

"I have seen it before," she said. "I came in here one day to look at it. And I have been quite often since. You never forbade me," she added, looking at him appealingly, but dropping her eyes quickly. "And I like the little girl—and the boy—very much."

"Do you? Why?"

"I don't know"—a formula in which she had taken refuge before. Still her candid eyes were lowered; but she was quite calm. Orth, instead of questioning, merely fixed his eyes upon her, and waited. In a moment she stirred uneasily, but she did not laugh nervously, as another child would have done. He had never seen her self-possession ruffled, and he had begun to doubt he ever should. She was full of human warmth and affection. She seemed made for love, and every creature who came within her ken adored her, from the author himself down to the litter of puppies presented to her by the stable-boy a few weeks since; but her serenity would hardly be enhanced by death.

She raised her eyes finally, but not to his. She looked at the portrait.

"Did you know that there was another picture behind?" she asked.

"No," replied Orth, turning cold. "How did you know it?"

"One day I touched a spring in the frame, and this picture came forward. Shall I show you?"

"Yes!" And crossing curiosity and the involuntary shrinking from impending phenomena was a sensation of aesthetic disgust that *he* should be treated to a secret spring.

The little girl touched hers, and that other Blanche sprang aside so quickly that she might have been impelled by a sharp blow from behind. Orth narrowed his eyes and stared at what she revealed. He felt that his own Blanche was watching him, and set his features, although his breath was short.

There was the Lady Blanche Mortlake in the splendor of her young womanhood, beyond a doubt. Gone were all traces of her spiritual childhood, except, perhaps, in the shadows of the mouth; but more than fulfilled were the promises of her mind. Assuredly, the woman had been as brilliant and gifted as she had been restless and passionate. She wore her very pearls with arrogance, her very hands were tense with eager life, her whole being breathed mutiny.

Orth turned abruptly to Blanche, who had transferred her attention to the picture.

"What a tragedy is there!" he exclaimed, with a fierce attempt at lightness. "Think of a woman having all that pent up within her two centuries ago! And at the mercy of a stupid family, no doubt, and a still stupider husband. No wonder—Today, a woman like that might not be a model for all the virtues, but she certainly would use her gifts and become famous, the while living her life too fully to have any place in it for yeomen and such, or even for the trivial business of breaking hearts." He put his finger under Blanche's chin, and raised her face, but he could not compel her gaze. "You are the exact image of that little girl," he said, "except that you are even purer and finer. She had no chance, none whatever. You live in the woman's age. Your opportunities will be infinite. I shall see to it that they are. What you wish to be you shall be. There will be no pent-up energies here to burst out into disaster for yourself and others. You shall be trained to self-control—that is, if you ever develop self-will, dear child—every faculty shall be educated, every school of life you desire knowledge through shall be opened to you. You shall become that finest flower of civilization, a woman who knows how to use her independence."

She raised her eyes slowly, and gave him a look which stirred the roots of sensation—a long look of unspeakable melancholy. Her chest rose once; then she set her lips tightly, and dropped her eyes.

"What do you mean?" he cried, roughly, for his soul

was chattering. "Is—it—do you—?" He dared not go too far, and concluded lamely, "You mean you fear that your mother will not give you to me when she goes—you have divined that I wish to adopt you? Answer me, will you?"

But she only lowered her head and turned away, and he, fearing to frighten or repel her, apologized for his abruptness, restored the outer picture to its place, and led her from the gallery.

He sent her at once to the nursery, and when she came down to luncheon and took her place at his right hand, she was as natural and childlike as ever. For some days he restrained his curiosity, but one evening, as they were sitting before the fire in the hall listening to the storm, and just after he had told her the story of the erl-king, he took her on his knee and asked her gently if she would not tell him what had been in her thoughts when he had drawn her brilliant future. Again her face turned gray, and she dropped her eyes.

"I cannot," she said. "I—perhaps—I don't know."

"Was it what I suggested?"

She shook her head, then looked at him with a shrinking appeal which forced him to drop the subject.

He went the next day alone to the gallery, and looked long at the portrait of the woman. She stirred no response in him. Nor could he feel that the woman of Blanche's future would stir the man in him. The paternal was all he had to give, but that was hers forever.

He went out into the park and found Blanche digging in her garden, very dirty and absorbed. The next afternoon, however, entering the hall noiselessly, he saw her sitting in her big chair, gazing out into nothing visible, her whole face settled in melancholy. He asked her if she were ill, and she recalled herself at once, but confessed to feeling tired. Soon after this he noticed that she lingered longer in the comfortable depths of her chair, and seldom went out, except with himself. She insisted that she was quite well, but after he had surprised her again looking as sad as if she had renounced every joy of childhood, he summoned from London a doctor renowned for his success with children.

The scientist questioned and examined her. When she had left the room he shrugged his shoulders.

"She might have been born with ten years of life in her, or she might grow up into a buxom woman," he said. "I confess I cannot tell. She appears to be sound enough, but I have no X rays in my eyes, and for all I know she may be on the verge of decay. She certainly has the look of those who die young. I have never seen so spiritual a child. But I can put my finger on nothing. Keep her out-of-doors, don't give her sweets, and don't let her catch anything if you can help it."

Orth and the child spent the long warm days of summer under the trees of the park, or driving in the quiet lanes. Guests were unbidden, and his pen was idle. All that was human in him had gone out to Blanche. He loved her, and she was a perpetual delight to him. The rest of the world received the large measure of his indifference. There was no further change in her, and apprehension slept and let him sleep. He had persuaded Mrs. Root to remain in England for a year. He sent her theatre tickets every week, and placed a horse and phaeton at her disposal. She was enjoying herself and seeing less and less of Blanche. He took the child to Bournemouth for a fortnight, and again to Scotland, both of which outings benefited as much as they pleased her. She had begun to tyrannize over him amiably, and she carried herself quite royally. But she was always sweet and truthful, and these qualities, combined with that something in the depths of her mind which defied his explorations, held him captive. She was devoted to him, and cared for no other companion, although she was demonstrative to her mother when they met.

It was in the tenth month of this idyl of the lonely man

and the lonely child that Mrs. Root flurriedly entered the library of Chillingsworth, where Orth happened to be alone.

"Oh, sir," she exclaimed, "I must go home. My daughter Grace writes me—she should have done it before—that the boys are not behaving as well as they should—she didn't tell me, as I was having such a good time she just hated to worry me—heaven knows I've had enough worry—but now I must go—I just couldn't stay—boys are an awful responsibility—girls ain't a circumstance to them, although mine are a handful sometimes."

Orth had written about too many women to interrupt the flow. He let her talk until she paused to recuperate her forces. Then he said quietly:

"I am sorry this has come so suddenly, for it forces me to broach a subject at once which I would rather have postponed until the idea had taken possession of you by degrees—"

"I know what it is you want to say, sir," she broke in, "and I've reproached myself that I haven't warned you before, but I didn't like to be the one to speak first. You want Blanche—of course, I couldn't help seeing that; but I can't let her go, sir, indeed, I can't."

"Yes," he said, firmly, "I want to adopt Blanche, and I hardly think you can refuse, for you must know how greatly it will be to her advantage. She is a wonderful child; you have never been blind to that; she should have every opportunity, not only of money, but of association. If I adopt her legally, I shall, of course, make her my heir, and—there is no reason why she should not grow up as great a lady as any in England."

The poor woman turned white, and burst into tears. "I've sat up nights and nights, struggling," she said, when she could speak. "That, and missing her. I couldn't stand in her light, and I let her stay. I know I oughtn't to, now—I mean, stand in her light—but, sir, she is dearer than all the others put together."

"Then live here in England—at least, for some years longer. I will gladly relieve your children of your support, and you can see Blanche as often as you choose."

"I can't do that, sir. After all, she is only one, and there arc six others. I can't desert them. They all need me, if only to keep them together—three girls unmarried and out in the world, and three boys just a little inclined to be wild. There is another point, sir—I don't exactly know how to say it."

"Well?" asked Orth, kindly. This American woman thought him the ideal gentleman, although the mistress of the estate on which she visited called him a boor and a snob.

"It is—well—you must know—you can imagine—that her brothers and sisters just worship Blanche. They save their dimes to buy her everything she wants—or used to want. Heaven knows what will satisfy her now, although I can't see that she's one bit spoiled. But she's just like a religion to them; they're not much on church. I'll tell you, sir, what I couldn't say to anyone else, not even to these relations who've been so kind to me—but there's wildness, just a streak, in all my children, and I believe, I know, it's Blanche that keeps them straight. My girls get bitter, sometimes; work all the week and little fun, not caring for common men and no chance to marry gentlemen; and sometimes they break out and talk dreadful; then, when they're over it, they say they'll live for Blanche—they've said it over and over, and they mean it. Every sacrifice they've made for her—and they've made many—has done them good. It isn't that Blanche ever says a word of the preachy sort, or has anything of the Sunday-school child about her, or even tries to smooth them down when they're excited. It's just herself. The only thing she ever does is sometimes to draw herself up and look scornful, and that nearly kills them. Little as she is, they're crazy about having her respect. I've grown superstitious about her. Until she came I used to get frightened, terribly, sometimes, and I

believe she came for that. So—you see! I know Blanche
is too fine for us and ought to have the best; but, then,
they are to be considered, too. They have their rights,
and they've got much more good than bad in them. I
don't know! I don't know! It's kept me awake many
nights."

Orth rose abruptly. "Perhaps you will take some
further time to think it over," he said. "You can stay a
few weeks longer—the matter cannot be so pressing as
that."

The woman rose. "I've thought this," she said; "let
Blanche decide. I believe she knows more than any of us.
I believe that whichever way she decided would be right.
I won't say anything to her, so you won't think I'm
working on her feelings; and I can trust you. But she'll
know."

"Why do you think that?" asked Orth, sharply. "There
is nothing uncanny about the child. She is not yet seven
years old. Why should you place such a responsibility
upon her?"

"Do you think she's like other children?"

"I know nothing of other children."

"I do, sir. I've raised six. And I've seen hundreds of
others. I never was one to be a fool about my own, but
Blanche isn't like any other child living—I'm certain of
it."

"What *do* you think?"

And the woman answered, according to her lights: "I
think she's an angel, and came to us because we needed
her."

"And I think she is Blanche Mortlake working out the
last of her salvation," thought the author; but he made
no reply, and was alone in a moment.

It was several days before he spoke to Blanche, and
then, one morning, when she was sitting on her mat on
the lawn with the light full upon her, he told her abruptly
that her mother must return home.

To his surprise, but unutterable delight, she burst into tears and flung herself into his arms.

"You need not leave me," he said, when he could find his own voice. "You can stay here always and be my little girl. It all rests with you."

"I can't stay," she sobbed. "I can't!"

"And that is what made you so sad once or twice?" he asked, with a double eagerness.

She made no reply.

"Oh!" he said, passionately, "give me your confidence, Blanche. You are the only breathing thing that I love."

"If I could I would," she said. "But I don't know—not quite."

"How much do you know?"

But she sobbed again and would not answer. He dared not risk too much. After all, the physical barrier between the past and the present was very young.

"Well, well, then, we will talk about the other matter. I will not pretend to disguise the fact that your mother is distressed at the idea of parting from you, and thinks it would be as sad for your brothers and sisters, whom she says you influence for their good. Do you think that you do?"

"Yes."

"How do you know this?"

"Do you know why you know everything?"

"No, my dear, and I have great respect for your instincts. But your sisters and brothers are now old enough to take care of themselves. They must be of poor stuff if they cannot live properly without the aid of a child. Moreover, they will be marrying soon. That will also mean that your mother will have many little grandchildren to console her for your loss. I will be the one bereft, if you leave me. I am the only one who really needs you. I don't say I will go to the bad, as you may have very foolishly persuaded yourself your family will do without you, but I trust to your instincts to make you realize how unhappy, how inconsolable I shall be. I shall be the loneliest man on earth!"

She rubbed her face deeper into his flannels, and tightened her embrace. "Can't you come, too?" she asked.

"No; you must live with me wholly or not at all. Your people are not my people, their ways are not my ways. We should not get along. And if you lived with me over there you might as well stay here, for your influence over them would be quite as removed. Moreover, if they are of the right stuff, the memory of you will be quite as potent for good as your actual presence."

"Not unless I died."

Again something within him trembled. "Do you believe you are going to die young?" he blurted out.

But she would not answer.

He entered the nursery abruptly the next day and found her packing her dolls. When she saw him, she sat down and began to weep hopelessly. He knew then that his fate was sealed. And when, a year later, he received her last little scrawl, he was almost glad that she went when she did.

E.T.A. Hoffman (1776–1822)

THE SAND-MAN

Ernst Theodor Wihelm Hoffman, who in 1808 changed one of his middle names from Wilhelm to Amadeus in honor of Mozart, is the only candidate to rival Poe (who was influenced by him) as the creator of the modern supernatural tale. His stories are a large part of the founding texts of the "fantastic" in European literature. His reputation rivalled those of Lord Byron and Sir Walter Scott in the Europe of his day. He is the greatest fantasy writer of the nineteenth century; his most famous stories include "The Golden Pot," which Everett Bleiler calls the greatest fantasy story of the nineteenth century, "Nutcracker and the King of the Mice," the source of Tchaikovsky's *The Nutcracker,* "Mademoiselle De Scudéry," arguably the first detective story. His great innovation was to bring the fantastic into the everyday present (fairy and folk tales had traditionally been set long ago and far away), a foundation of all horror literature since. His novella, "The Sand-man," a nightmarish piece that fascinated Sigmund Freud so much that he used it as the basic text of his essay, "The Uncanny," was written in 1816. As John Sladek pointed out in *Horror: The 100 Best Books*, "This dark tale was written two years before Mary Shelley's *Frankenstein*, in a similar spirit of horrified fascination with science and its application to artificial life. Hoffman is concerned with the horror of automata indistinguishable from real people." This theme has grown and reverberated through literature since, and is particulary common in science fiction. It is interesting to compare "The Sand-man" to George R.R.

Martin's "Sandkings," Philip K. Dick's "Faith of Our Fathers," and John W. Campbell's "Who Goes There?"

Nathanael to Lothair

I know you are all very uneasy because I have not written for such a long, long time. Mother, to be sure, is angry, and Clara, I dare say, believes I am living here in riot and revelry, and quite forgetting my sweet angel, whose image is so deeply engraved upon my heart and mind. But that is not so; daily and hourly do I think of you all, and my lovely Clara's form comes to gladden me in my dreams, and smiles upon me with her bright eyes, as graciously as she used to do in the days when I went in and out amongst you. Oh! how could I write to you in the distracted state of mind in which I have been, and which, until now, has quite bewildered me! A terrible thing has happened to me. Dark forebodings of some awful fate threatening me are spreading themselves out over my head like black clouds, impenetrable to every friendly ray of sunlight. I must now tell you what has taken place; I must, that I see well enough, but only to think upon it makes the wild laughter burst from my lips. Oh! my dear, dear Lothair, what shall I say to make you feel, if only in an inadequate way, that that which happened to me a few days ago could thus really exercise such a hostile and disturbing influence upon my life? Oh that you were here to see for yourself! but now you will, I suppose, take me for a superstitious ghost-seer. In a word, the terrible thing which I have experienced, the fatal effect of which I in vain exert every effort to shake off, is simply that some days ago, namely, on the 30th October, at twelve o'clock

at noon, a dealer in weather-glasses came into my room
and wanted to sell me one of his wares. I bought nothing,
and threatened to kick him downstairs, whereupon he
went away of his own accord.

You will conclude that it can only be very peculiar
relations—relations intimately intertwined with my life
—that can give significance to this event, and that it
must be the person of this unfortunate hawker which has
had such a very inimical effect upon me. And so it really
is. I will summon up all my faculties in order to narrate
to you calmly and patiently as much of the early days of
my youth as will suffice to put matters before you in such
a way that your keen sharp intellect may grasp everything clearly and distinctly, in bright and living pictures.
Just as I am beginning, I hear you laugh and Clara say,
"What's all this childish nonsense about!" Well, laugh at
me, laugh heartily at me, pray do. But, good God! my
hair is standing on end, and I seem to be entreating you
to laugh at me in the same sort of frantic despair in
which Franz Moor entreated Daniel to laugh him to
scorn. But to my story.

Except at dinner we, *i.e.,* I and my brothers and sisters,
saw but little of our father all day long. His business no
doubt took up most of his time. After our evening meal,
which, in accordance with an old custom, was served at
seven o'clock, we all went, mother with us, into father's
room, and took our places around a round table. My
father smoked his pipe, drinking a large glass of beer to
it. Often he told us many wonderful stories, and got so
excited over them that his pipe always went out; I
used then to light it for him with a spill, and this formed
my chief amusement. Often, again, he would give us
picture-books to look at, whilst he sat silent and motionless in his easy-chair, puffing out such dense
clouds of smoke that we were all as it were enveloped in
mist. On such evenings mother was very sad; and
directly it struck nine she said, "Come, children! off to

bed! Come! The 'Sand-man' is come I see." And I always
did seem to hear something trampling upstairs with slow
heavy steps; that must be the Sand-man. Once in particular I was very much frightened at this dull trampling and
knocking; as mother was leading us out of the room I
asked her, "O mamma! but who is this nasty Sand-man
who always sends us away from papa? What does he look
like?" "There is no Sand-man, my dear child," mother
answered; "when I say the Sand-man is come, I only
mean that you are sleepy and can't keep your eyes open,
as if somebody had put sand in them." This answer of
mother's did not satisfy me; nay, in my childish mind the
thought clearly unfolded itself that mother denied there
was a Sand-man only to prevent us being afraid,—why, I
always heard him come upstairs. Full of curiosity to
learn something more about this Sand-man and what he
had to do with us children, I at length asked the old
woman who acted as my youngest sister's attendant,
what sort of a man he was—the Sand-man? "Why,
'thanael, darling, don't you know?" she replied. "Oh!
he's a wicked man, who comes to little children when
they won't go to bed and throws handfuls of sand in their
eyes, so that they jump out of their heads all bloody; and
he puts them into a bag and takes them to the half-moon
as food for his little ones; and they sit there in the nest
and have hooked beaks like owls, and they pick naughty
little boys' and girls' eyes out with them." After this I
formed in my own mind a horrible picture of the cruel
Sand-man. When anything came blundering upstairs at
night I trembled with fear and dismay; and all that my
mother could get out of me were the stammered words
"The Sand-man! the Sand-man!" whilst the tears
coursed down my cheeks. Then I ran into my bedroom,
and the whole night through tormented myself with the
terrible apparition of the Sand-man. I was quite old
enough to perceive that the old woman's tale about the
Sand-man and his little ones' nest in the half-moon

couldn't be altogether true; nevertheless the Sand-man continued to be for me a fearful incubus, and I was always seized with terror—my blood always ran cold, not only when I heard anybody come up the stairs, but when I heard anybody noisily open my father's room door and go in. Often he stayed away for a long season altogether; then he would come several times in close succession.

This went on for years, without my being able to accustom myself to this fearful apparition, without the image of the horrible Sand-man growing any fainter in my imagination. His intercourse with my father began to occupy my fancy ever more and more; I was restrained from asking my father about him by an unconquerable shyness; but as the years went on the desire waxed stronger and stronger within me to fathom the mystery myself and to see the fabulous Sand-man. He had been the means of disclosing to me the path of the wonderful and the adventurous, which so easily find lodgment in the mind of the child. I liked nothing better than to hear or read horrible stories of goblins, witches, Tom Thumbs, and so on; but always at the head of them all stood the Sand-man, whose picture I scribbled in the most extraordinary and repulsive forms with both chalk and coal everywhere, on the tables, and cupboard doors, and walls. When I was ten years old my mother removed me from the nursery into a little chamber off the corridor not far from my father's room. We still had to withdraw hastily whenever, on the stroke of nine, the mysterious unknown was heard in the house. As I lay in my little chamber I could hear him go into father's room, and soon afterwards I fancied there was a fine and peculiar smelling steam spreading itself through the house. As my curiosity waxed stronger, my resolve to make somehow or other the Sand-man's acquaintance took deeper root. Often when my mother had gone past, I slipped quickly out of my room into the corridor, but I could never see anything, for always before I could reach the place where I could get sight of him, the Sand-man was well inside the door. At last, unable to resist the impulse any longer, I determined to conceal myself in father's room and there wait for the Sand-man.

One evening I perceived from my father's silence and mother's sadness that the Sand-man would come; accordingly, pleading that I was excessively tired, I left the room before nine o'clock and concealed myself in a hiding-place close beside the door. The street door creaked, and slow, heavy, echoing steps crossed the passage towards the stairs. Mother hurried past me with my brothers and sisters. Softly—softly—I opened father's room door. He sat as usual, silent and motionless, with his back towards it; he did not hear me; and in a moment I was in and behind a curtain drawn before my father's open wardrobe, which stood just inside the room. Nearer and nearer and nearer came the echoing footsteps. There was a strange coughing and shuffling and mumbling outside. My heart beat with expectation and fear. A quick step now close, close beside the door, a noisy rattle of the handle, and the door flies open with a bang. Recovering my courage with an effort, I take a cautious peep out. In the middle of the room in front of my father stands the Sand-man, the bright light of the lamp falling full upon his face. The Sand-man, the terrible Sand-man, is the old advocate *Coppelius* who often comes to dine with us.

But the most hideous figure could not have awakened greater trepidation in my heart than this Coppelius did. Picture to yourself a large broad-shouldered man, with an immensely big head, a face the colour of yellow-ochre, grey bushy eyebrows, from beneath which two piercing, greenish, cat-like eyes glittered, and a prominent Roman nose hanging over his upper lip. His distorted mouth was often screwed up into a malicious smile; then two dark-red spots appeared on his cheeks, and a strange hissing noise proceeded from between his tightly clenched teeth. He always wore an ash-grey coat of an old-fashioned cut, a waistcoat of the same, and nether extremeties to match, but black stockings and buckles set with stones on his shoes. His little wig scarcely extended beyond the crown of his head, his hair was curled round high up above his big red ears, and plastered to his temples with cosmetic, and a broad closed hair-bag stood out prominently from his neck, so that you could see the silver buckle that fastened his folded neck-cloth. Altogether he was a most disagreeable and horribly ugly figure; but what we children detested most of all was his big coarse hairy hands; we could never fancy anything that he had once touched. This he had noticed; and so, whenever our good mother quietly placed a piece of cake or sweet fruit on our plates, he delighted to touch it under some pretext or other, until the bright tears stood in our eyes, and from disgust and loathing we lost the enjoyment of the tit-bit that was intended to please us. And he did just the same thing when father gave us a glass of sweet wine on holidays. Then he would quickly pass his hand over it, or even sometimes raise the glass to his blue lips, and he laughed quite sardonically when all we dared do was to express our vexation in stifled sobs. He habitually called us the "little brutes"; and when he was present we might not utter a sound; and we cursed the ugly spiteful man who deliberately and intentionally spoilt all our little pleasures. Mother seemed to dislike this hateful Coppelius as much as we did; for as soon as he appeared her cheerfulness and bright and natural manner were transformed into sad, gloomy seriousness. Father treated him as if he were a being of some higher race, whose ill-manners were to be tolerated, whilst no efforts ought to be spared to keep him in good-humour. He had only to give a slight hint, and his favourite dishes were cooked for him and rare wine uncorked.

As soon as I saw this Coppelius, therefore, the fearful and hideous thought arose in my mind that he, and he alone, must be the Sand-man; but I no longer conceived of the Sand-man as the bugbear in the old nurse's fable, who fetched children's eyes and took them to the half-moon as food for his little ones—no! but as an ugly spectre-like fiend bringing trouble and misery and ruin, both temporal and everlasting, everywhere wherever he appeared.

I was spell-bound on the spot. At the risk of being discovered, and, as I well enough knew, of being severely punished, I remained as I was, with my head thrust through the curtains listening. My father received Coppelius in a ceremonious manner. "Come, to work!" cried the latter, in a hoarse snarling voice, throwing off his coat. Gloomily and silently my father took off his dressing-gown, and both put on long black smock-frocks. Where they took them from I forgot to notice. Father opened the folding-doors of a cupboard in the wall; but I saw that what I had so long taken to be a cupboard was really a dark recess, in which was a little hearth. Coppelius approached it, and a blue flame crackled upwards from it. Round about were all kinds of strange utensils. Good God! as my old father bent down over the fire how different he looked! His gentle and venerable features seemed to be drawn up by some dreadful convulsive pain into an ugly, repulsive Satanic mask. He looked like Coppelius. Coppelius plied the red-hot tongs and drew bright glowing masses out of the thick smoke and began assiduously to hammer them. I fancied that there were men's faces visible round about, but without eyes, having ghastly deep black holes where the eyes should have been. "Eyes here! Eyes here!" cried Coppelius, in a hollow sepulchral voice. My blood ran cold with horror; I screamed and tumbled out of my hiding-place onto the floor. Coppelius immediately seized upon me. "You little brute! You little brute!" he bleated, grinding his teeth. Then, snatching me up, he threw me on the hearth, so that the flames began to singe my hair. "Now we've got eyes—eyes—a beautiful pair of children's eyes," he whispered, and, thrusting his hands into the flames he took out some red-hot grains and was about to strew them into my eyes. Then my father clasped his hands and entreated him, saying, "Master, master, let my Nathanael keep his eyes—oh! do let him keep them." Coppelius laughed shrilly and replied, "Well then, the boy may keep his eyes and whine and pule his way through the world; but we will now at any rate observe the mechanism of the hand and the foot." And there with he roughly laid hold upon me, so that my joints cracked, and twisted my hands and my feet, pulling them now this way, and now that, "That's not quite right altogether! It's better as it was!—the old fellow knew what he was about." Thus lisped and hissed Coppelius; but all around me grew black and dark; a sudden convulsive pain shot through all my nerves and bones; I knew nothing more.

I felt a soft warm breath fanning my cheek; I awakened as if out of the sleep of death; my mother was bending over me. "Is the Sand-man still there?" I stammered. "No, my dear child; he's been gone a long, long time; he'll not hurt you." Thus spoke my mother, as she kissed her recovered darling and pressed him to her heart. But why should I tire you, my dear Lothair? why do I dwell at such length on these details, when there's so much remains to be said? Enough—I was detected in my eavesdropping, and roughly handled by Coppelius. Fear and terror had brought on a violent fever, of which I lay ill several weeks. "Is the Sand-man still there?" These were the first words I uttered on coming to myself again, the first sign of my recovery, of my safety. Thus, you see, I have only to relate to you the most terrible moment of my youth for you to thoroughly understand that it must not be ascribed to the weakness of my eyesight if all that I see is colourless, but to the fact that a mysterious destiny has hung a dark veil of clouds about my life, which I shall perhaps only break through when I die.

Coppelius did not show himself again; it was reported he had left the town.

It was about a year later when, in pursuance of the old unchanged custom, we sat around the round table in the evening. Father was in very good spirits, and was telling us amusing tales about his youthful travels. As it was striking nine we all at once heard the street door creak on its hinges, and slow ponderous steps echoed across the passage and up the stairs. "That is Coppelius," said my mother, turning pale. "Yes, it is Coppelius," replied my father in a faint broken voice. The tears started from my mother's eyes. "But, father, father," she cried, "must it be so?" "This is the last time," he replied; "this is the last time he will come to me, I promise you. Go now, go and take the children. Go, go to bed—good-night."

As for me, I felt as if I were converted into cold, heavy stone; I could not get my breath. As I stood there immovable my mother seized me by the arm. "Come, Nathanael! do come along!" I suffered myself to be led away; I went into my room. "Be a good boy and keep quiet," mother called after me; "get into bed and go to sleep." But, tortured by indescribable fear and uneasiness, I could not close my eyes. That hateful, hideous Coppelius stood before me with his glittering eyes, smiling maliciously down upon me; in vain did I strive to banish the image. Somewhere about midnight there was a terrific crack, as if a cannon were being fired off. The whole house shook; something went rustling and clattering past my door; the house-door was pulled to with a bang. "That is Coppelius," I cried, terror-stricken, and leaped out of bed. Then I heard a wild heart-rending scream; I rushed into my father's room; the door stood open, and clouds of suffocating smoke came rolling towards me. The servant maid shouted, "Oh! my master! my master!" On the floor in front of the smoking hearth lay my father, dead, his face burned black and fearfully distorted, my sisters weeping and moaning around him, and my mother lying near them in a swoon.

"Coppelius, you atrocious fiend, you've killed my father," I shouted. My senses left me. Two days later, when my father was placed in his coffin, his features were mild and gentle again as they had been when he was alive. I found great consolation in the thought that his association with the diabolical Coppelius could not have ended in his everlasting ruin.

Our neighbours had been awakened by the explosion; the affair got talked about, and came before the magisterial authorities, who wished to cite Coppelius to clear himself. But he had disappeared from the place, leaving no traces behind him.

Now when I tell you, my dear friend, that the peddler I spoke of was the villain Coppelius, you will not blame me for seeing impending mischief in his inauspicious reappearance. He was differently dressed; but Coppelius's figure and features are too deeply impressed upon my mind for me to be capable of making a mistake in the matter. Moreover, he has not even changed his name. He proclaims himself here, I learn, to be a Piedmontese mechanician, and styles himself Giuseppe Coppola.

I am resolved to enter the lists against him and avenge my father's death, let the consequences be what they may.

Don't say a word to mother about the reappearance of this odious monster. Give my love to my darling Clara; I will write to her when I am in a somewhat calmer frame of mind. Adieu, &c.

Clara to Nathanael

You are right, you have not written to me for a very long time, but nevertheless I believe that I still retain a place in your mind and thoughts. It is a proof that you were thinking a good deal about me when you were sending off your last letter to brother Lothair, for instead of directing it to him you directed it to me. With joy I tore open the envelope, and did not perceive the mistake until I read the words, "Oh! my dear, dear Lothair."

Now I know I ought not to have read any more of the letter, but ought to have given it to my brother. But as you have so often in innocent raillery made it a sort of reproach against me that I possessed such a calm and, for a woman, cool-headed temperament that I should be like the woman we read of—if the house was threatening to tumble down, I should stop before hastily fleeing, to smooth down a crumple in the window curtains—I need hardly tell you that the beginning of your letter quite upset me. I could scarcely breathe; there was a bright mist before my eyes.

Oh! my darling Nathanael! what could this terrible thing be that had happened? Separation from you— never to see you again, the thought was like a sharp knife in my heart. I read on and on. Your description of that horrid Coppelius made my flesh creep. I now learned for the first time what a terrible and violent death your good old father died. Brother Lothair, to whom I handed over his property, sought to comfort me, but with little success. That horrid peddler Giuseppe Coppola followed me everywhere; and I am almost ashamed to confess it, but he was able to disturb my sound and in general calm sleep with all sorts of wonderful dream-shapes. But soon—the next day—I saw everything in a different light. Oh! do not be angry with me, my best-beloved, if, despite your strange presentiment that Coppelius will do you some mischief, Lothair tells you I am in quite as good spirits, and just the same as ever.

I will frankly confess, it seems to me that all that was fearsome and terrible of which you speak, existed only in your own self, and that the real true outer world had but little to do with it. I can quite admit that old Coppelius may have been highly obnoxious to you children, but your real detestation of him arose from the fact that he hated children.

Naturally enough the gruesome Sand-man of the old nurse's story was associated in your childish mind with old Coppelius, who, even though you had not believed in the Sand-man, would have been to you a ghostly bug-bear, especially dangerous to children. His mysterious labours along with your father at night-time were, I daresay, nothing more than secret experiments in alche-my, with which your mother could not be over well pleased, owing to the large sums of money that most likely were thrown away upon them; and besides, your father, his mind full of the deceptive striving after higher knowledge, may probably have become rather indiffer-ent to his family, as so often happens in the case of such experimentalists. So also it is equally probable that your father brought about his death by his own imprudence, and that Coppelius is not to blame for it. I must tell you that yesterday I asked our experienced neighbour, the chemist, whether in experiments of this kind an explo-sion could take place which would have a momentarily fatal effect. He said, "Oh, certainly!" and described to me in his prolix and circumstantial way how it could be occasioned, mentioning at the same time so many strange and funny words that I could not remember them at all. Now I know you will be angry at your Clara, and will say, "Of the Mysterious which often clasps man in its invisible arms there's not a ray can find its way into this cold heart. She sees only the varied surface of the things of the world, and, like the little child, is pleased with the golden glittering fruit, at the kernel of which lies the fatal poison."

Oh! my beloved Nathanael, do you believe then that the intuitive prescience of a dark power working within us to our own ruin cannot exist also in minds which are cheerful, natural, free from care? But please forgive me that I, a simple girl, presume in any way to indicate to you what I really think of such an inward strife. After all, I should not find the proper words, and you would only laugh at me, not because my thoughts were stupid, but because I was so foolish as to attempt to tell them to you.

If there is a dark and hostile power which traitorously fixes a thread in our hearts in order that, laying hold of it and drawing us by means of it along a dangerous road to ruin, which otherwise we should not have trod—if, I say, there is such a power, it must assume within us a form like ourselves, nay, it must be ourselves; for only in that way can we believe in it, and only so understood do we yield to it so far that it is able to accomplish its secret purpose. So long as we have sufficient firmness, fortified by cheerfulness, to always acknowledge foreign hostile influences for what they really are, whilst we quietly pursue the path pointed out to us by both inclination and calling, then this mysterious power perishes in its futile struggles to attain the form which is to be the reflected image of ourselves. It is also certain, Lothair adds, that if we have once voluntarily given ourselves up to this dark physical power, it often reproduces within us the strange forms which the outer world throws in our way, so that thus it is we ourselves who engender within ourselves the spirit which by some remarkable delusion we imagine to speak in that outer form. It is the phantom of our own self whose intimate relationship with, and whose powerful influence upon our soul either plunges us into hell or elevates us to heaven. Thus you will see, my beloved Nathanael, that I and brother Lothair have well talked over the subject of dark powers and forces; and now, after I have with some difficulty written down the principal results of our discussion, they seem to me to contain many really profound thoughts. Lothair's last words, however, I don't quite understand altogether; I only dimly guess what he means; and yet I cannot help thinking it is all very true. I beg you, dear, strive to forget the ugly advocate Coppelius as well as the weather-glass hawker Giuseppe Coppola. Try and convince yourself that these foreign influences can have no power over you, that it is only the belief in their hostile power which can in reality make them dangerous to you. If every line of your letter did not betray the violent excitement of your mind, and if I did not sympathise with your condition from the bottom of my heart, I could in truth jest about the advocate Sand-man and weather-glass hawker Coppelius. Pluck up your spirits! Be cheerful! I have resolved to appear to you as your guardian-angel if that ugly man Coppola should dare take it into his head to bother you in your dreams, and drive him away with a good hearty laugh. I'm not afraid of him and his nasty hands, not the least little bit; I won't let him either as advocate spoil any dainty tit-bit I've taken, or as Sand-man rob me of my eyes.

> My darling, darling Nathanael,
> Eternally yours, &c. &c.

Nathanael to Lothair

I am very sorry that Clara opened and read my last letter to you; of course the mistake is to be attributed to my own absence of mind. She has written me a very deep philosophical letter, proving conclusively that Coppelius and Coppola only exist in my own mind and are phantoms of my own self, which will at once be dissipated, as soon as I look upon them in that light. In very truth one can hardly believe that the mind which so often sparkles in those bright, beautifully smiling, childlike eyes of hers like a sweet lovely dream could draw such subtle and scholastic distinctions. She also mentions your name. You have been talking about me. I suppose you have been giving her lectures, since she sifts and refines everything so acutely. But enough of this! I must now tell you it is most certain that the weather-glass hawker Giuseppe Coppola is not the advocate Coppelius. I am attending the lectures of our recently appointed Professor of Physics, who, like the distinguished naturalist, is called Spalanzani, and is of Italian origin. He has known Coppola for many years; and it is also easy to tell from his accent that he really is a Piedmontese. Coppelius was a German, though no honest German, I fancy. Nevertheless I am not quite satisfied. You and Clara will perhaps take me for a gloomy dreamer, but nohow can I get rid of the impression which Coppelius's cursed face made upon me. I am glad to learn from Spalanzani that he has left the town. This Professor Spalanzani is a very queer fish. He is a little fat man, with prominent cheek-bones, thin nose, projecting lips, and small piercing eyes. You cannot get a better picture of him than by turning over one of the Berlin pocket-almanacs and looking at Cagliostro's portrait engraved by Chodowiecki; Spalanzani looks just like him.

Once lately, as I went up the steps to his house, I perceived that beside the curtain which generally covered a glass door there was a small chink. What it was that excited my curiosity I cannot explain; but I looked through. In the room I saw a female, tall, very slender, but of perfect proportions, and splendidly dressed, sitting at a little table, on which she had placed both her arms, her hands being folded together. She sat opposite the door, so that I could easily see her angelically beautiful face. She did not appear to notice me, and there was moreover a strangely fixed look about her eyes, I might almost say they appeared as if they had no power of vision; I thought she was sleeping with her eyes open. I felt quite uncomfortable, and so I slipped away quietly into the Professor's lecture-room, which was close at hand. Afterwards I learnt that the figure which I had seen was Spalanzani's daughter, Olimpia, whom he keeps locked in a most wicked and unaccountable way, and no man is ever allowed to come near her. Perhaps, however, there is after all something peculiar about her; perhaps she's an idiot or something of that sort. But why am I telling you all this? I could have told you it all better and more in detail when I see you. For in a fortnight I shall be amongst you. I must see my dear sweet angel, my Clara, again. Then the little bit of ill-temper, which, I must confess, took possession of me after her fearfully sensible letter, will be blown away. And that is the reason why I am not writing to her as well today. With all best wishes, &c.

Nothing more strange and extraordinary can be imagined, gracious reader, than what happened to my poor friend, the young student Nathanael, and which I have undertaken to relate to you. Have you ever lived to experience anything that completely took possession of your heart and mind and thoughts to the utter exclusion of everything else? All was seething and boiling within you; your blood, heated to fever pitch, leapt through your veins and inflamed your cheeks. Your gaze was so peculiar, as if seeking to grasp in empty space forms not seen of any other eye, and all your words ended in sighs betokening some mystery. Then your friends asked you, "What is the matter with you, my dear friend? What do you see?" And, wishing to describe the inner pictures in all their vivid colours, with their lights and their shades, you in vain struggled to find words with which to express yourself. But you felt as if you must gather up all the events that had happened, wonderful, splendid, terrible, jocose, and awful, in the very first word, so that the whole might be revealed by a single electric discharge, so to speak. Yet every word and all that partook of the nature of communication by intelligible sounds seemed to be colourless, cold, and dead. Then you try and try again, and stutter and stammer, whilst your friends' prosy questions strike like icy winds upon your heart's hot fire until they extinguish it. But if, like a bold painter, you had first sketched in a few audacious strokes the outline of the picture you had in your soul, you would then easily have been able to deepen and intensify the colours one after the other, until the varied throng of living figures carried your friends away, and they, like you, saw themselves in the midst of the scene that had proceeded out of your own soul.

Strictly speaking, indulgent reader, I must indeed confess to you, nobody has asked me for the history of young Nathanael; but you are very well aware that I belong to that remarkable class of authors who, when they are bearing anything about in their minds in the manner I have just described, feel as if everybody who comes near them, and also the whole world to boot, were asking, "Oh! what is it? Oh! do tell us, my good sir?" Hence I was most powerfully impelled to narrate to you Nathanael's ominous life. My soul was full of the elements of wonder and extraordinary peculiarity in it; but, for this very reason, and because it was necessary in the very beginning to dispose you, indulgent reader, to bear with what is fantastic—and that is not a little thing—I racked my brain to find a way of commencing the story in a significant and original manner, calculated to arrest your attention. To begin with "Once upon a time," the best beginning for a story, seemed to me too tame; with "In the small country town S—— lived," rather better, at any rate allowing plenty of room to work up to the climax; or to plunge at one *in medias res,* "'Go to the devil!' cried the student Nathanael, his eyes blazing wildly with rage and fear, when the weather-glass hawker

Giuseppe Coppola"—well, that is what I really had written, when I thought I detected something of the ridiculous in Nathanael's wild glance; and the history is anything but laughable. I could not find any words which seemed fitted to reflect in even the feeblest degree the brightness of the colours of my mental vision. I determined not to begin at all. So I pray you, gracious reader, accept the three letters which my friend Lothair has been so kind as to communicate to me as the outline of the picture, into which I will endeavour to introduce more and more colour as I proceed with my narrative. Perhaps, like a good portrait-painter, I may succeed in depicting more than one figure in such wise that you will recognise it as a good likeness without being acquainted with the original, and feel as if you had very often seen the original with your own bodily eyes. Perhaps, too, you will then believe that nothing is more wonderful, nothing more fantastic than real life, and that all that a writer can do is to present it as a dark reflection from a dim cut mirror.

In order to make the very commencement more intelligible, it is necessary to add to the letters that, soon after the death of Nathanael's father, Clara and Lothair, the children of a distant relative, who had likewise died, leaving them orphans, were taken by Nathanael's mother into her own house. Clara and Nathanael conceived a warm affection for each other, against which not the slightest objection in the world could be urged. When therefore Nathanael left home to prosecute his studies in G———, they were betrothed. It is from G——— that his last letter is written, where he is attending the lectures of Spalanzani, the distinguished Professor of Physics.

I might now proceed comfortably with my narration, did not at this moment Clara's image rise up so vividly before my eyes that I cannot turn them away from it, just as I never could when she looked upon me and smiled so sweetly. Nowhere would she have passed for beautiful; that was the unanimous opinion of all who professed to have any technical knowledge of beauty. But whilst architects praised the pure proportions of her figure and form, painters averred that her neck, shoulders, and bosom were almost too chastely modelled, and yet, on the other hand, one and all were in love with her glorious Magdalene hair, and talked a good deal of nonsense about Battoni-like colouring. One of them, a veritable romanticist, strangely enough likened her eyes to a lake by Ruisdael, in which is reflected the pure azure of the cloudless sky, the beauty of woods and flowers, and all the bright and varied life of a living landscape. Poets and musicians went still further and said, "What's all this talk about seas and reflections? How can we look upon the girl without feeling that wonderful heavenly songs and melodies beam upon us from her eyes, penetrating deep down into our hearts, till all becomes awake and throbbing with emotion? And if we cannot sing anything at all passable then, why, we are not worth much; and this we can also plainly read in the rare smile which flits around her lips when we have the hardihood to squeak out something in her presence which we pretend to call singing, in spite of the fact that it is nothing more than a few single notes confusedly linked together." And it really was so. Clara had the powerful fancy of a bright, innocent, unaffected child, a woman's deep and sympathetic heart, and an understanding clear, sharp, and discriminating. Dreamers and visionaries had but a bad time of it with her; for without saying very much—she was not by nature of a talkative disposition—she plainly asked, by her calm steady look, and rare ironical smile, "How can you imagine, my dear friends, that I can take these fleeting shadowy images for true living and breathing forms?" For this reason many found fault with her as being cold, prosaic, and devoid of feeling; others, however, who had reached a clearer and deeper conception of life, were extremely fond of the intelligent, childlike, large-hearted girl. But none had such an affection for her as Nathanael, who was a zealous and cheerful cultivator of the fields of science and art. Clara clung to her lover with all her heart; the first clouds she encountered in life were when he had to separate from her. With what delight did she fly into his arms when, as he had promised in his last letter to Lothair, he really came back to his native town and entered his mother's room! And as Nathanael had foreseen, the moment he saw Clara again he no longer thought about either the advocate Coppelius or her sensible letter; his ill-humour had quite disappeared.

Nevertheless Nathanael was right when he told his friend Lothair that the repulsive vendor of weather-glasses, Coppola, had exercised a fatal and disturbing influence upon his life. It was quite patent to all; for even during the first few days he showed that he was completely and entirely changed. He gave himself up to gloomy reveries, and moreover acted so strangely; they had never observed anything at all like it in him before. Everything, even his own life, was to him but dreams and presentiments. His constant theme was that every man who delusively imagined himself to be free was merely the plaything of the cruel sport of mysterious powers, and it was vain for man to resist them; he must humbly submit to whatever destiny had decreed for him. He went so far as to maintain that it was foolish to believe that a man could do anything in art or science of his own accord; for the inspiration in which alone any true artistic work could be done did not proceed from the spirit within outwards, but was the result of the operation directed inwards of some Higher Principle existing without and beyond ourselves.

This mystic extravagance was in the highest degree repugnant to Clara's clear intelligent mind, but it seemed vain to enter upon any attempt at refutation. Yet when

Nathanael went on to prove that Coppelius was the Evil Principle which had entered into him and taken possession of him at the time he was listening behind the curtain, and that this hateful demon would in some terrible way ruin their happiness, then Clara grew grave and said, "Yes, Nathanael. You are right; Coppelius is an Evil Principle; he can do dreadful things, as bad as could a Satanic power which should assume a living physical form, but only—only if you do not banish him from your mind and thoughts. So long as you believe in him he exists and is at work; your belief in him is his only power." Whereupon Nathanael, quite angry because Clara would only grant the existence of the demon in his own mind, began to dilate at large upon the whole mystic doctrine of devils and awful powers, but Clara abruptly broke off the theme by making, to Nathanael's very great disgust, some quite commonplace remark. Such deep mysteries are sealed books to cold, unsusceptible characters, he thought, without being clearly conscious to himself that he counted Clara amongst these inferior natures, and accordingly he did not remit his efforts to initiate her into these mysteries. In the morning, when she was helping to prepare breakfast, he would take his stand beside her, and read all sorts of mystic books to her, until she begged him—"But, my dear Nathanael, I shall have to scold you as the Evil Principle which exercises a fatal influence upon my coffee. For if I do as you wish, and let things go their own way, and look into your eyes whilst you read, the coffee will all boil over into the fire, and you will none of you get any breakfast." Then Nathanael hastily banged the book to and ran away in great displeasure to his own room.

Formerly he had possessed a peculiar talent for writing pleasing, sparkling tales, which Clara took the greatest delight in listening to; but now his productions were gloomy, unintelligible, and wanting in form, so that, although Clara out of forbearance towards him did not say so, he nevertheless felt how very little interest she took in them. There was nothing that Clara disliked so much as what was tedious; at such times her intellectual sleepiness was not to be overcome; it was betrayed both in her glances and in her words. Nathanael's effusions were, in truth, exceedingly tedious. His ill-humour at Clara's cold prosaic temperament continued to increase; Clara could not conceal her distaste of his dark, gloomy, wearying mysticism; and thus both began to be more and more estranged from each other without exactly being aware of it themselves. The image of the ugly Coppelius had, as Nathanael was obliged to confess to himself, faded considerably in his fancy, and it often cost him great pains to present him in vivid colours in his literary efforts, in which he played the part of the ghoul of Destiny. At length it entered into his head to make his dismal presentiment that Coppelius would ruin his happiness the subject of a poem. He made himself and Clara, united by true love, the central figures, but represented a black hand as being from time to time thrust into their life and plucking out a joy that had blossomed for them. At length, as they were standing at the altar, the terrible Coppelius appeared and touched Clara's lovely eyes, which leapt into Nathanael's own bosom, burning and hissing like bloody sparks. Then Coppelius laid hold upon him, and hurled him into a blazing circle of fire, which spun round with the speed of a whirlwind, and, storming and blustering, dashed away with him. The fearful noise it made was like a furious hurricane lashing the foaming sea-waves until they rise up like black, white-headed giants in the midst of the raging struggle. But through the midst of the savage fury of the tempest he heard Clara's voice calling, "Can you not see me, dear? Coppelius has deceived you; they were not my eyes which burned so in your bosom; they were fiery drops of your own heart's blood. Look at me, I have got my own eyes still." Nathanael thought, "Yes, that is

Clara, and I am hers forever." Then this thought laid a powerful grasp upon the fiery circle so that it stood still, and the riotous turmoil died away rumbling down a dark abyss. Nathanael looked into Clara's eyes; but it was death whose gaze rested so kindly upon him.

Whilst Nathanael was writing this work he was very quiet and sober-minded; he filed and polished every line, and as he had chosen to submit himself to the limitations of metre, he did not rest until all was pure and musical. When, however, he had at length finished it and read it aloud to himself he was seized with horror and awful dread, and he screamed, "Whose hideous voice is this?" But he soon came to see in it again nothing beyond a very successful poem, and he confidently believed it would enkindle Clara's cold temperament, though to what end she should be thus aroused was not quite clear to his own mind, nor yet what would be the real purpose served by tormenting her with these dreadful pictures, which prophesied a terrible and ruinous end to her affection.

Nathanael and Clara sat in his mother's little garden. Clara was bright and cheerful, since for three entire days her lover, who had been busy writing his poem, had not teased her with his dreams or forebodings. Nathanael, too, spoke in a gay and vivacious way of things of merry import, as he formerly used to do, so that Clara said, "Ah! now I have you again. We have driven away that ugly Coppelius, you see." Then it suddenly occurred to him that he had got the poem in his pocket which he wished to read to her. He at once took out the manuscript and began to read. Clara, anticipating something tedious as usual, prepared to submit to the infliction, and calmly resumed her knitting. But as the sombre clouds rose up darker and darker she let her knitting fall on her lap and sat with her eyes fixed in a set stare upon Nathanael's face. He was quite carried away by his own work, the fire of enthusiasm coloured his cheeks a deep red, and tears started from his eyes. At length he concluded, groaning and showing great lassitude; grasping Clara's hand, he sighed as if he were being utterly melted in inconsolable grief, "Oh! Clara! Clara!" She drew him softly to her heart and said in a low but very grave and impressive tone, "Nathanael, my darling Nathanael, throw that foolish, senseless, stupid thing into the fire." Then Nathanael leapt indignantly to his feet, crying, as he pushed Clara from him, "You damned lifeless automaton!" and rushed away. Clara was cut to the heart, and wept bitterly. "Oh! he has never loved me, for he does not understand me," she sobbed.

Lothair entered the arbour. Clara was obliged to tell him all that had taken place. He was passionately fond of his sister; and every word of her complaint fell like a spark upon his heart, so that the displeasure which he had long entertained against his dreamy friend Nathanael was kindled into furious anger. He hastened to find Nathanael, and upbraided him in harsh words for his irrational behaviour towards his beloved sister. The fiery Nathanael answered him in the same style. "A fantastic, crack-brained fool," was retaliated with, "A miserable, common, everyday sort of fellow." A meeting was the inevitable consequence. They agreed to meet on the following morning behind the garden-wall, and fight, according to the custom of the students of the place, with sharp rapiers. They went about silent and gloomy; Clara had both heard and seen the violent quarrel, and also observed the fencing-master bring the rapiers in the dusk of the evening. She had a presentiment of what was to happen. They both appeared at the appointed place wrapped up in the same gloomy silence, and threw off their coats. Their eyes flaming with the bloodthirsty light of pugnacity, they were about to begin their contest when Clara burst through the garden door. Sobbing, she screamed, "You savage, terrible men! Cut me down before you attack each other; for how can I live when my lover has slain my brother, or my brother slain my lover?" Lothair let his weapon fall and gazed silently upon the ground, whilst Nathanael's heart was rent with sorrow, and all the affection which he had felt for his lovely Clara in the happiest days of her golden youth was awakened within him. His murderous weapon, too, fell from his hand; he threw himself at Clara's feet. "Oh! can you ever forgive me, my only, my dearly loved Clara? Can you, my dear brother Lothair, also forgive me?" Lothair was touched by his friend's great distress; the three young people embraced each other amidst endless tears, and swore never again to break their bond of love and fidelity.

Nathanael felt as if a heavy burden that had been weighing him down to the earth was now rolled from off him, nay, as if by offering resistance to the dark power which had possessed him, he had rescued his own self from the ruin which had threatened him. Three happy days he now spent amidst the loved ones, and then returned to G———, where he had still a year to stay before settling down in his native town for life.

Everything having reference to Coppelius had been concealed from the mother, for they knew she could not think of him without horror, since she as well as Nathanael believed him to be guilty of causing her husband's death.

When Nathanael came to the house where he lived he was greatly astonished to find it burnt down to the ground, so that nothing but the bare outer walls were left standing amidst a heap of ruins. Although the fire had broken out in the laboratory of the chemist who lived on the ground-floor, and had therefore spread upwards, some of Nathanael's bold, active friends had succeeded in time in forcing a way into his room in the upper storey and saving his books and manuscripts and instruments. They had carried them all uninjured into another house, where they engaged a room for him; this he now at once took possession of. That he lived opposite Professor Spalanzani did not strike him particularly, nor did it occur to him as anything more singular that he could, as he observed, by looking out of his window, see straight into the room where Olimpia often sat alone. Her figure he could plainly distinguish, although her features were uncertain and confused. It did at length occur to him, however, that she remained for hours together in the same position in which he had first discovered her through the glass door, sitting at a little table without any occupation whatever, and it was evident that she was constantly gazing across in his direction. He could not but confess to himself that he had never seen a finer figure. However, with Clara mistress of his heart, he remained perfectly unaffected by Olimpia's stiffness and apathy; and it was only occasionally that he sent a fugitive glance over his compendium across to her—that was all.

He was writing to Clara; a light tap came at the door. At his summons to "Come in," Coppola's repulsive face appeared peeping in. Nathanael felt his heart beat with trepidation; but, recollecting what Spalanzani had told him about his fellow-countryman Coppola, and what he had himself so faithfully promised his beloved in respect to the Sand-man Coppelius, he was ashamed at himself for this childish fear of spectres. Accordingly, he controlled himself with an effort, and said, as quietly and as calmly as he possibly could, "I don't want to buy any weather-glasses, my good friend; you had better go elsewhere." Then Coppola came right into the room, and said in a hoarse voice, screwing up his wide mouth into a hideous smile, whilst his little eyes flashed keenly from beneath his long grey eyelashes, "What! Nee weather-gless? Nee weather-gless? 've got foine oyes as well—foine oyes!" Affrighted, Nathanael cried, "You stupid man, how can you have eyes?—eyes—eyes?" But

Coppola, laying aside his weather-glasses, thrust his
hands into his big coat-pockets and brought out several
spy-glasses and spectacles, and put them on the table.
"Theer! Theer! Spect'cles! Spect'cles to put 'n nose!
Them's my oyes—foine oyes." And he continued to
produce more and more spectacles from his pockets until
the table began to gleam and flash all over. Thousands of
eyes were looking and blinking convulsively, and staring
up at Nathanael; he could not avert his gaze from the
table. Coppola went on heaping up his spectacles, whilst
wilder and ever wilder burning flashes crossed through
and through each other and darted their blood-red rays
into Nathanael's breast. Quite overcome, and frantic
with terror, he shouted, "Stop! stop! you terrible man!"
and he seized Coppola by the arm, which he had again
thrust into his pocket in order to bring out still more
spectacles, although the whole table was covered all over
with them. With a harsh disagreeable laugh Coppola
gently freed himself; and with the words "So! went none!
Well, here foine gless!" he swept all his spectacles
together, and put them back into his coat-pockets, whilst
from a breast-pocket he produced a great number of
larger and smaller perspectives. As soon as the spectacles
were gone Nathanael recovered his equanimity again;
and, bending his thoughts upon Clara, he clearly discerned that the gruesome incubus had proceeded only
from himself, as also that Coppola was a right honest
mechanician and optician, and far from being Coppelius's dreaded double and ghost. And then, besides, none
of the glasses which Coppola now placed on the table had
anything at all singular about them, at least nothing so
weird as the spectacles; so, in order to square accounts
with himself, Nathanael now really determined to buy
something of the man. He took up a small, very beautifully cut pocket perspective, and by way of proving it
looked through the window. Never before in his life had
he had a glass in his hands that brought out things so

clearly and sharply and distinctly. Involuntarily he directed the glass upon Spalanzani's room; Olimpia sat at the little table as usual, her arms laid upon it and her hands folded. Now he saw for the first time the regular and exquisite beauty of her features. The eyes, however, seemed to him to have a singular look of fixity and lifelessness. But as he continued to look closer and more carefully through the glass he fancied a light like humid moonbeams came into them. It seemed as if their power of vision was now being enkindled; their glances shone with ever-increasing vivacity. Nathanael remained standing at the window as if glued to the spot by a wizard's spell, his gaze rivetted unchangeably upon the divinely beautiful Olimpia. A coughing and shuffling of the feet awakened him out of his enchaining dream, as it were. Coppola stood behind him, "Tre zechini" (three ducats). Nathanael had completely forgotten the optician; he hastily paid the sum demanded. "Ain't 't? Foine gless? foine gless?" asked Coppola in his harsh, unpleasant voice, smiling sardonically. "Yes, yes, yes," rejoined Nathanael impatiently; "adieu, my good friend." But Coppola did not leave the room without casting many peculiar side-glances upon Nathanael; and the young student heard him laughing loudly on the stairs. "Ah well!" thought he, "he's laughing at me because I've paid him too much for this little perspective—because I've given him too much money—that's it." As he softly murmured these words he fancied he detected a gasping sigh as of a dying man stealing awfully through the room; his heart stopped beating with fear. But to be sure he had heaved a deep sigh himself; it was quite plain. "Clara is quite right," said he to himself, "in holding me to be an incurable ghost-seer; and yet it's very ridiculous—ay, more than ridiculous, that the stupid thought of having paid Coppola too much for his glass should cause me this strange anxiety; I can't see any reason for it."

Now he sat down to finish his letter to Clara; but a

glance through the window showed him Olimpia still in her former posture. Urged by an irresistible impulse he jumped up and seized Coppola's perspective; nor could he tear himself away from the fascinating Olimpia until his friend and brother Siegmund called for him to go to Professor Spalanzani's lecture. The curtains before the door of the all-important room were closely drawn, so that he could not see Olimpia. Nor could he even see her from his own room during the two following days, notwithstanding that he scarcely ever left his window, and maintained a scarce interrupted watch through Coppola's perspective upon her room. On the third day curtains even were drawn across the window. Plunged into the depths of despair,—goaded by longing and ardent desire, he hurried outside the walls of the town. Olimpia's image hovered about his path in the air and stepped forth out of the bushes, and peeped up at him with large and lustrous eyes from the bright surface of the brook. Clara's image was completely faded from his mind; he had no thoughts except for Olimpia. He uttered his love-plaints aloud and in a lachrymose tone, "Oh! my glorious, noble star of love, have you only risen to vanish again, and leave me in the darkness and hopelessness of night?"

Returning home, he became aware that there was a good deal of noisy bustle going on in Spalanzani's house. All the doors stood wide open; men were taking in all kinds of gear and furniture; the windows of the first floor were all lifted off their hinges; busy maid-servants with immense hair-brooms were driving backwards and forwards dusting and sweeping, whilst within could be heard the knocking and hammering of carpenters and upholsterers. Utterly astonished, Nathanael stood still in the street; then Siegmund joined him, laughing, and said, "Well, what do you say to our old Spalanzani?" Nathanael assured him that he could not say anything, since he knew not what it all meant; to his great astonishment, he could hear, however, that they were turning the quiet gloomy house almost inside out with their dusting and cleaning and making of alterations. Then he learned from Siegmund that Spalanzani intended giving a great concert and ball on the following day, and that half the university was invited. It was generally reported that Spalanzani was going to let his daughter Olimpia, whom he had so long so jealously guarded from every eye, make her first appearance.

Nathanael received an invitation. At the appointed hour, when the carriages were rolling up and the lights were gleaming brightly in the decorated halls, he went across to the Professor's, his heart beating high with expectation. The company was both numerous and brilliant. Olimpia was richly and tastefully dressed. One could not but admire her figure and the regular beauty of her features. The striking inward curve of her back, as well as the wasp-like smallness of her waist, appeared to be the result of too-tight lacing. There was something stiff and measured in her gait and bearing that made an unfavourable impression upon many; it was ascribed to the constraint imposed upon her by the company. The concert began. Olimpia played on the piano with great skill; and sang as skilfully an *aria di bravura,* in a voice which was, if anything, almost too sharp, but clear as glass bells. Nathanael was transported with delight; he stood in the background farthest from her, and owing to the blinding lights could not quite distinguish her features. So, without being observed, he took Coppola's glass out of his pocket, and directed it upon the beautiful Olimpia. Oh! then he perceived how her yearning eyes sought him, how every note only reached its full purity in the loving glance which penetrated to and inflamed his heart. Her artificial *roulades* seemed to him to be the exultant cry towards heaven of the soul refined by love; and when at last, after the *cadenza,* the long trill rang shrilly and loudly through the hall, he felt as if he were suddenly grasped by burning arms and could no longer control himself,—he could not help shouting aloud in his mingled pain and delight, "Olimpia!" All eyes were turned upon him; many people laughed. The face of the cathedral organist wore a still more gloomy look than it had done before, but all he said was, "Very well!"

The concert came to an end, and the ball began. Oh! to dance with her—with her—that was now the aim of all Nathanael's wishes, of all his desires. But how should he have courage to request her, the queen of the ball, to grant him the honour of a dance? And yet he couldn't tell how it came about, just as the dance began, he found himself standing close beside her, nobody having as yet asked her to be his partner; so, with some difficulty stammering out a few words, he grasped her hand. It was cold as ice; he shook with an awful, frosty shiver. But, fixing his eyes upon her face, he saw that her glance was beaming upon him with love and longing, and at the same moment he thought that the pulse began to beat in her cold hand, and the warm life-blood to course through her veins. And passion burned more intensely in his own heart also; he threw his arm round her beautiful waist and whirled her round the hall. He had always thought that he kept good and accurate time in dancing, but from the perfectly rhythmical evenness with which Olimpia danced, and which frequently put him quite out, he perceived how very faulty his own time really was. Notwithstanding, he would not dance with any other lady; and everybody else who approached Olimpia to call upon her for a dance, he would have liked to kill on the spot. This, however, only happened twice; to his astonishment Olimpia remained after this without a partner, and he failed not on each occasion to take her out again. If Nathanael had been able to see anything else except the beautiful Olimpia, there would inevitably have been a good deal of unpleasant quarrelling and strife; for it was evident that Olimpia was the object of the smothered laughter only with difficulty suppressed, which was heard in various corners amongst the young people; and they followed her with very curious looks, but nobody knew for what reason. Nathanael, excited by dancing and the plentiful supply of wine he had consumed, had laid aside the shyness which at other times characterised him. He sat beside Olimpia, her hand in his own, and declared his love enthusiastically and passionately in words which neither of them understood, neither he nor Olimpia. And yet she perhaps did, for she sat with her eyes fixed unchangeably upon his, sighing repeatedly, "Ach! Ach! Ach!" Upon this Nathanael would answer, "Oh, you glorious heavenly lady! You ray from the promised paradise of love! Oh! what a profound soul you have! my whole being is mirrored in it!" and a good deal more in the same strain. But Olimpia only continued to sigh "Ach! Ach!" again and again.

Professor Spalanzani passed by the two happy lovers once or twice, and smiled with a look of peculiar satisfaction. All at once it seemed to Nathanael, albeit he was far away in a different world, as if it were growing perceptibly darker down below at Professor Spalanzani's. He looked about him, and to his very great alarm became aware that there were only two lights left burning in the hall, and they were on the point of going out. The music and dancing had long ago ceased. "We must part—part!" he cried, wildly and despairingly; he kissed Olimpia's hand; he bent down to her mouth, but ice-cold lips met his burning ones. As he touched her cold hand, he felt his heart thrilled with awe; the legend of "The Dead Bride" shot suddenly through his mind. But Olimpia had drawn him closer to her, and the kiss appeared to warm her lips into vitality. Professor Spalanzani strode slowly through the empty apartment, his footsteps giving a hollow echo; and his figure had, as the flickering shadows played about him, a ghostly, awful appearance. "Do you love me? Do you love me,

Olimpia? Only one little word—Do you love me?"
whispered Nathanael, but she only sighed, "Ach! Ach!"
as she rose to her feet. "Yes, you are my lovely, glorious
star of love," said Nathanael, "and will shine forever,
purifying and ennobling my heart." "Ach! Ach!" replied
Olimpia, as she moved along. Nathanael followed her;
they stood before the Professor. "You have had an
extraordinarily animated conversation with my daughter," said he, smiling; "well, well, my dear Mr. Nathanael, if you find pleasure in talking to the stupid girl, I am
sure I shall be glad for you to come and do so."
Nathanael took his leave, his heart singing and leaping in
a perfect delirium of happiness.

During the next few days Spalanzani's ball was the
general topic of conversation. Although the Professor
had done everything to make the thing a splendid
success, yet certain gay spirits related more than one
thing that had occurred which was quite irregular and
out of order. They were especially keen in pulling
Olimpia to pieces for her taciturnity and rigid stiffness;
in spite of her beautiful form they alleged that she was
hopelessly stupid, and in this fact they discerned the
reason why Spalanzani had so long kept her concealed
from publicity. Nathanael heard all this with inward
wrath, but nevertheless he held his tongue; for, thought
he, would it indeed be worth while to prove to these
fellows that it is their own stupidity which prevents them
from appreciating Olimpia's profound and brilliant
parts? One day Siegmund said to him, "Pray, brother,
have the kindness to tell me how you, a sensible fellow,
came to lose your head over that Miss Wax-face—that
wooden doll across there?" Nathanael was about to fly
into a rage, but he recollected himself and replied, "Tell
me, Siegmund, how came it that Olimpia's divine
charms could escape your eye, so keenly alive as it always
is to beauty, and your acute perception as well? But
Heaven be thanked for it, otherwise I should have had

you for a rival, and then the blood of one of us would have had to be spilled." Siegmund, perceiving how matters stood with his friend, skilfully interposed and said, after remarking that all argument with one in love about the object of his affections was out of place, "Yet it's very strange that several of us have formed pretty much the same opinion about Olimpia. We think she is—you won't take it ill, brother?—that she is singularly statuesque and soulless. Her figure is regular, and so are her features, that can't be gainsaid; and if her eyes were not so utterly devoid of life, I may say, of the power of vision, she might pass for a beauty. She is strangely measured in her movements, they all seem as if they were dependent upon some wound-up clock-work. Her playing and singing has the disagreeably perfect, but insensitive time of a singing machine, and her dancing is the same. We felt quite afraid of this Olimpia, and did not like to have anything to do with her; she seemed to us to be only acting *like* a living creature, and as if there was some secret at the bottom of it all." Nathanael did not give way to the bitter feelings which threatened to master him at these words of Siegmund's; he fought down and got the better of his displeasure, and merely said, very earnestly, "You cold prosaic fellows may very well be afraid of her. It is only to its like that the poetically organised spirit unfolds itself. Upon me alone did her loving glances fall, and through my mind and thoughts alone did they radiate; and only in her love can I find my own self again. Perhaps, however, she doesn't do quite right not to jabber a lot of nonsense and stupid talk like other shallow people. It is true, she speaks but few words; but the few words she does speak are genuine hieroglyphs of the inner world of Love and of the higher cognition of the intellectual life revealed in the intuition of the Eternal beyond the grave. But you have no understanding for all these things, and I am only wasting words." "God be with you, brother," said Siegmund very gently, almost sadly, "but it seems to me that you are in a very bad way. You may rely upon me, if all—No, I can't say any more." It all at once dawned upon Nathanael that his cold prosaic friend Siegmund really and sincerely wished him well, and so he warmly shook his proffered hand.

Nathanael had completely forgotten that there was a Clara in the world, whom he had once loved—and his mother and Lothair. They had all vanished from his mind; he lived for Olimpia alone. He sat beside her every day for hours together, rhapsodising about his love and sympathy enkindled into life, and about psychic elective affinity—all of which Olimpia listened to with great reverence. He fished up from the very bottom of his desk all the things that he had ever written—poems, fancy sketches, visions, romances, tales, and the heap was increased daily with all kinds of aimless sonnets, stanzas, canzonets. All these he read to Olimpia hour after hour without growing tired; but then he had never had such an exemplary listener. She neither embroidered, nor knitted; she did not look out of the window, or feed a bird, or play with a little pet dog or a favourite cat, neither did she twist a piece of paper or anything of that kind round her finger; she did not forcibly convert a yawn into a low affected cough—in short, she sat hour after hour with her eyes bent unchangeably upon her lover's face, without moving or altering her position, and her gaze grew more ardent and more ardent still. And it was only when at last Nathanael rose and kissed her lips or her hand that she said, "Ach! Ach!" and then "Good-night, dear." Arrived in his own room, Nathanael would break out with, "Oh! what a brilliant—what a profound mind! Only you—you alone understand me." And his heart trembled with rapture when he reflected upon the wondrous harmony which daily revealed itself between his own and his Olimpia's character; for he fancied that she had expressed in respect to his works and his poetic genius the identical sentiments which he himself cherished deep down in his own heart in respect to the same, and even as if it was his own heart's voice speaking to him. And it must indeed have been so; for Olimpia never uttered any other words than those already mentioned. And when Nathanael himself in his clear and sober moments, as, for instance, directly after waking in a morning, thought about her utter passivity and taciturnity, he only said, "What are words—but words? The glance of her heavenly eyes says more than any tongue of earth. And how can, anyway, a child of heaven accustom herself to the narrow circle which the exigencies of a wretched mundane life demand?"

Professor Spalanzani appeared to be greatly pleased at the intimacy that had sprung up between his daughter Olimpia and Nathanael, and showed the young man many unmistakable proofs of his good feeling towards him; and when Nathanael ventured at length to hint very delicately at an alliance with Olimpia, the Professor smiled all over his face at once, and said he should allow his daughter to make a perfectly free choice. Encouraged by these words, and with the fire of desire burning in his heart, Nathanael resolved the very next day to implore Olimpia to tell him frankly, in plain words, what he had long read in her sweet loving glances,—that she would be his for ever. He looked for the ring which his mother had given him at parting; he would present it to Olimpia as a symbol of his devotion, and of the happy life he was to lead with her from that time onwards. Whilst looking for it he came across his letters from Clara and Lothair; he threw them carelessly aside, found the ring, put it in his pocket, and ran across to Olimpia. Whilst still on the stairs, in the entrance-passage, he heard an extraordinary hubbub; the noise seemed to proceed from Spalanzani's study. There was a stamping—a rattling—pushing—knocking against the door, with curses and oaths intermingled. "Leave hold—leave hold—you monster—you rascal—staked your life and honour upon it?—Ha! ha! ha! ha!—That was not our wager—I, I made the eyes—I the clock-work.—Go to the devil with your clock-work—you damned dog of a watch-maker—be off—Satan—stop—you paltry turner—you infernal beast!—stop—begone—let me go." The voices which were thus making all this racket and rumpus were those of Spalanzani and the fearsome Coppelius. Na-thanael rushed in, impelled by some nameless dread. The Professor was grasping a female figure by the shoulders, the Italian Coppola held her by the feet; and they were pulling and dragging each other backwards and forwards, fighting furiously to get possession of her. Nathanael recoiled with horror on recognising that the figure was Olimpia. Boiling with rage, he was about to tear his beloved from the grasp of the madmen, when Coppola by an extraordinary exertion of strength twisted the figure out of the Professor's hands and gave him such a terrible blow with her, that he reeled backwards and fell over the table all amongst the phials and retorts, the bottles and glass cylinders, which covered it: all these things were smashed into a thousand pieces. But Coppola threw the figure across his shoulder, and, laugh-ing shrilly and horribly, ran hastily down the stairs, the figure's ugly feet hanging down and banging and rattling like wood against the steps. Nathanael was stupefied;— he had seen only too distinctly that in Olimpia's pallid waxed face there were no eyes, merely black holes in their stead; she was an inanimate puppet. Spalanzani was rolling on the floor; the pieces of glass had cut his head and breast and arm; the blood was escaping from him in streams. But he gathered his strength together by an effort.

"After him—after him! What do you stand staring there for? Coppelius—Coppelius—he's stolen my best automaton—at which I've worked for twenty years— staked my life upon it—the clock-work—speech—

movement—mine—your eyes—stolen your eyes—
damn him—curse him—after him—fetch me back
Olimpia—there are the eyes." And now Nathanael saw a
pair of bloody eyes lying on the floor staring at him;
Spalanzani seized them with his uninjured hand and
threw them at him, so that they hit his breast. Then
madness dug her burning talons into him and swept
down into his heart, rending his mind and thoughts to
shreds. "Aha! aha! aha! Fire-wheel—fire-wheel! Spin
round, fire-wheel! merrily, merrily! Aha! wooden doll!
spin round, pretty wooden doll!" and he threw himself
upon the Professor, clutching him fast by the throat. He
would certainly have strangled him had not several
people, attracted by the noise, rushed in and torn away
the madman; and so they saved the Professor, whose
wounds were immediately dressed. Siegmund, with all
his strength, was not able to subdue the frantic lunatic,
who continued to scream in a dreadful way, "Spin
round, wooden doll!" and to strike out right and left with
his doubled fists. At length the united strength of several
succeeded in overpowering him by throwing him on the
floor and binding him. His cries passed into a brutish
bellow that was awful to hear; and thus raging with the
harrowing violence of madness, he was taken away to the
madhouse.

Before continuing my narration of what happened
further to the unfortunate Nathanael, I will tell you,
indulgent reader, in case you take any interest in that
skilful mechanician and fabricator of automata, Spalanzani, that he recovered completely from his wounds.
He had, however, to leave the university, for Nathanael's fate had created a great sensation; and the opinion
was pretty generally expressed that it was an imposture
altogether unpardonable to have smuggled a wooden
puppet instead of a living person into intelligent tea-
circles,—for Olimpia had been present at several with
success. Lawyers called it a cunning piece of knav-

ery, and all the harder to punish since it was directed against the public; and it had been so craftily contrived that it had escaped unobserved by all except a few preternaturally acute students, although everybody was very wise now and remembered to have thought of several facts which occurred to them as suspicious. But these latter could not succeed in making out any sort of a consistent tale. For was it, for instance, a thing likely to occur to any one as suspicious that, according to the declaration of an elegant beau of these tea-parties, Olimpia had, contrary to all good manners, sneezed oftener than she had yawned? The former must have been, in the opinion of this elegant gentleman, the winding up of the concealed clock-work; it had always been accompanied by an observable creaking, and so on. The Professor of Poetry and Eloquence took a pinch of snuff, and, slapping the lid to and clearing his throat, said solemnly, "My most honourable ladies and gentlemen, don't you see then where the rub is? The whole thing is an allegory, a continuous metaphor. You understand me? *Sapienti sat.*" But several most honourable gentlemen did not rest satisfied with this explanation; the history of this automaton had sunk deeply into their souls, and an absurd mistrust of human figures began to prevail. Several lovers, in order to be fully convinced that they were not paying court to a wooden puppet, required that their mistress should sing and dance a little out of time, should embroider or knit or play with her little pug, &c., when being read to, but above all things else that she should do something more than merely listen—that she should frequently speak in such a way as to really show that her words presupposed as a condition some thinking and feeling. The bonds of love were in many cases drawn closer in consequence, and so of course became more engaging; in other instances they gradually relaxed and fell away. "I cannot really be made responsible for it," was the remark of more than one young gallant. At the tea-gatherings everybody, in order to ward off suspicion, yawned to an incredible extent and never sneezed. Spalanzani was obliged, as has been said, to leave the place in order to escape a criminal charge of having fraudulently imposed an automaton upon human society. Coppola, too, had also disappeared.

When Nathanael awoke he felt as if he had been oppressed by a terrible nightmare; he opened his eyes and experienced an indescribable sensation of mental comfort, whilst a soft and most beautiful sensation of warmth pervaded his body. He lay on his own bed in his own room at home; Clara was bending over him, and at a little distance stood his mother and Lothair. "At last, at last, O my darling Nathanael; now we have you again; now you are cured of your grievous illness, now you are mine again." And Clara's words came from the depths of her heart; and she clasped him in her arms. The bright scalding tears streamed from his eyes, he was so overcome with mingled feelings of sorrow and delight; and he gasped forth, "My Clara, my Clara!" Siegmund, who had staunchly stood by his friend in his hour of need, now came into the room. Nathanael gave him his hand— "My faithful brother, you have not deserted me." Every trace of insanity had left him, and in the tender hands of his mother and his beloved, and his friends, he quickly recovered his strength again. Good fortune had in the meantime visited the house; a niggardly old uncle, from whom they had never expected to get anything, had died, and left Nathanael's mother not only a considerable fortune, but also a small estate, pleasantly situated not far from the town. There they resolved to go and live, Nathanael and his mother, and Clara, to whom he was now to be married, and Lothair. Nathanael was become gentler and more childlike than he had ever been before, and now began really to understand Clara's supremely pure and noble character. None of them ever reminded him, even in the remotest degree, of the past. But when

Siegmund took leave of him, he said, "By heaven, brother! I was in a bad way, but an angel came just at the right moment and led me back upon the path of light. Yes, it was Clara." Siegmund would not let him speak further, fearing lest the painful recollections of the past might arise too vividly and too intensely in his mind.

The time came for the four happy people to move to their little property. At noon they were going through the streets. After making several purchases they found that the lofty tower of the townhouse was throwing its giant shadows across the marketplace. "Come," said Clara, "let us go up to the top once more and have a look at the distant hills." No sooner said than done. Both of them, Nathanael and Clara, went up the tower; their mother, however, went on with the servant-girl to her new home, and Lothair, not feeling inclined to climb up all the many steps, waited below. There the two lovers stood arm-in-arm on the topmost gallery of the tower, and gazed out into the sweet-scented wooded landscape, beyond which the blue hills rose up like a giant's city.

"Oh! do look at that strange little grey bush, it looks as if it were actually walking towards us," said Clara. Mechanically he put his hand into his side-pocket; he found Coppola's perspective and looked for the bush; Clara stood in front of the glass. Then a convulsive thrill shot through his pulse and veins; pale as a corpse, he fixed his staring eyes upon her; but soon they began to roll, and a fiery current flashed and sparkled in them, and he yelled fearfully, like a hunted animal. Leaping up high in the air and laughing horribly at the same time, he began to shout, in a piercing voice, "Spin round, wooden doll! Spin round, wooden doll!" With the strength of a giant he laid hold upon Clara and tried to hurl her over, but in an agony of despair she clutched fast hold of the railing that went round the gallery. Lothair heard the madman raging and Clara's scream of terror: a fearful presentiment flashed across his mind. He ran up the

steps; the door of the second flight was locked. Clara's
scream for help rang out more loudly. Mad with rage and
fear, he threw himself against the door, which at length
gave way. Clara's cries were growing fainter and fainter,
—"Help! save me! save me!" and her voice died away in
the air. "She is killed—murdered by that madman,"
shouted Lothair. The door to the gallery was also locked.
Despair gave him the strength of a giant; he burst the
door off its hinges. Good God! there was Clara in
the grasp of the madman Nathanael, hanging over the
gallery in the air; she only held to the iron bar with one
hand. Quick as lightning, Lothair seized his sister and
pulled her back, at the same time dealing the madman a
blow in the face with his doubled fist, which sent him
reeling backwards, forcing him to let go his victim.

Lothair ran down with his insensible sister in his arms.
She was saved. But Nathanael ran round and round the
gallery, leaping up in the air and shouting, "Spin round,
fire-wheel! Spin round, fire-wheel!" The people heard the
wild shouting, and a crowd began to gather. In the midst
of them towered the advocate Coppelius, like a giant; he
had only just arrived in the town, and had gone straight
to the marketplace. Some were going up to overpower
and take charge of the madman, but Coppelius laughed
and said, "Ha! ha! wait a bit; he'll come down of his own
accord"; and he stood gazing upwards along with the
rest. All at once Nathanael stopped as if spell-bound; he
bent down over the railing, and perceived Coppelius.
With a piercing scream, "Ha! foine oyes! foine oyes!" he
leapt over.

When Nathanael lay on the stone pavement with a
broken head, Coppelius had disappeared in the crush
and confusion.

Several years afterwards it was reported that, outside
the door of a pretty country house in a remote district,
Clara had been seen sitting hand in hand with a pleasant
gentleman, whilst two bright boys were playing at her

feet. From this it may be concluded that she eventually found that quiet domestic happiness which her cheerful, blithesome character required, and which Nathanael, with his tempest-tossed soul, could never have been able to give her.

Octavia Butler (b. 1947)

BLOODCHILD

Octavia Butler is one of a small number of distinguished black writers writing science fiction today, and of them, the only woman. Her most famous novels are *Wild Seed* (1980) and *Kindred* (1979). Butler's stories are characterized by literal or metaphorical issues of class or race, by strong moral consciousness, and careful attention to detail. Science fiction, her chosen genre, is particularly rich in possibilities for constructing imagined societies that reflect metaphorically upon our own, and Butler has taken full advantage of them in her works. Sometimes the possibilities are horrifying, and she often uses horrific effects in her work, with grim realism. Her most significant story to date is "Bloodchild," which won the 1985 Hugo Award, and the Nebula Award of the Science Fiction Writers of America. An initiation story of considerable power, it plays with great virtuosity upon her usual themes and adds an extraordinary emotional warmth to a dark and horrifying depiction of brutal sexual and social enslavement. It is also a departure for her, in that she characteristically uses women as central characters. Perhaps the most important influence on Butler are the darkly ironic works of Harlan Ellison, her mentor.

M y last night of childhood began with a visit home. T'Gatoi's sisters had given us two sterile eggs.

T'Gatoi gave one to my mother, brother, and sisters. She insisted that I eat the other one alone. It didn't matter. There was still enough to leave everyone feeling good. Almost everyone. My mother wouldn't take any. She sat, watching everyone drifting and dreaming without her. Most of the time she watched me.

I lay against T'Gatoi's long, velvet underside, sipping from my egg now and then, wondering why my mother denied herself such a harmless pleasure. Less of her hair would be gray if she indulged now and then. The eggs prolonged life, prolonged vigor. My father, who had never refused one in his life, had lived more than twice as long as he should have. And toward the end of his life, when he should have been slowing down, he had married my mother and fathered four children.

But my mother seemed content to age before she had to. I saw her turn away as several of T'Gatoi's limbs secured me closer. T'Gatoi liked our body heat, and took advantage of it whenever she could. When I was little and at home more, my mother used to try to tell me how to behave with T'Gatoi—how to be respectful and always obedient because T'Gatoi was the Tlic government official in charge of the Preserve, and thus the most important of her kind to deal directly with Terrans. It was an honor, my mother said, that such a person had chosen to come into the family. My mother was at her most formal and severe when she was lying.

I had no idea why she was lying, or even what she was lying about. It *was* an honor to have T'Gatoi in the family, but it was hardly a novelty. T'Gatoi and my mother had been friends all my mother's life, and T'Gatoi was not interested in being honored in the house she considered her second home. She simply came in, climbed onto one of her special couches and called me over to keep her warm. It was impossible to be formal with her while lying against her and hearing her complain as usual that I was too skinny.

"You're better," she said this time, probing me with six or seven of her limbs. "You're gaining weight finally. Thinness is dangerous." The probing changed subtly, became a series of caresses.

"He's still too thin," my mother said sharply.

T'Gatoi lifted her head and perhaps a meter of her body off the couch as though she were sitting up. She looked at my mother and my mother, her face lined and old-looking, turned away.

"Lien, I would like you to have what's left of Gan's egg."

"The eggs are for the children," my mother said.

"They are for the family. Please take it."

Unwillingly obedient, my mother took it from me and put it to her mouth. There were only a few drops left in the now-shrunken, elastic shell, but she squeezed them out, swallowed them, and after a few moments some of the lines of tension began to smooth from her face.

"It's good," she whispered. "Sometimes I forget how good it is."

"You should take more," T'Gatoi said. "Why are you in such a hurry to be old?"

My mother said nothing.

"I like being able to come here," T'Gatoi said. "This place is a refuge because of you, yet you won't take care of yourself."

T'Gatoi was hounded on the outside. Her people wanted more of us made available. Only she and her political faction stood between us and the hordes who did not understand why there was a Preserve—why any Terran could not be courted, paid, drafted, in some way made available to them. Or they did understand, but in their desperation, they did not care. She parceled us out to the desperate and sold us to the rich and powerful for their political support. Thus, we were necessities, status symbols, and an independent people. She oversaw the joining of families, putting an end to the final remnants of the earlier system of breaking up Terran families to suit impatient Tlic. I had lived outside with her. I had seen the desperate eagerness in the way some people looked at me. It was a little frightening to know that only she stood between us and that desperation that could so easily swallow us. My mother would look at her sometimes and say to me, "Take care of her." And I would remember that she too had been outside, had seen.

Now T'Gatoi used four of her limbs to push me away from her onto the floor. "Go on, Gan," she said. "Sit down there with your sisters and enjoy not being sober. You had most of the egg. Lien, come warm me."

My mother hesitated for no reason that I could see. One of my earliest memories is of my mother stretched alongside T'Gatoi, talking about things I could not understand, picking me up from the floor and laughing as she sat me on one of T'Gatoi's segments. She ate her share of eggs then. I wondered when she had stopped, and why.

She lay down now against T'Gatoi, and the whole left row of T'Gatoi's limbs closed around her, holding her loosely, but securely. I had always found it comfortable to lie that way but, except for my older sister, no one else in the family liked it. They said it made them feel caged.

T'Gatoi meant to cage my mother. Once she had, she moved her tail slightly, then spoke. "Not enough egg, Lien. You should have taken it when it was passed to you. You need it badly now."

T'Gatoi's tail moved once more, its whip motion so swift I wouldn't have seen it if I hadn't been watching for it. Her sting drew only a single drop of blood from my mother's bare leg.

My mother cried out—probably in surprise. Being stung doesn't hurt. Then she sighed and I could see her body relax. She moved languidly into a more comfortable position within the cage of T'Gatoi's limbs. "Why did you do that?" she asked, sounding half asleep.

"I could not watch you sitting and suffering any longer."

My mother managed to move her shoulders in a small shrug. "Tomorrow," she said.

"Yes. Tomorrow you will resume your suffering—if you must. But for now, just for now, lie here and warm me and let me ease your way a little."

"He's still mine, you know," my mother said suddenly. "Nothing can buy him from me." Sober, she would not have permitted herself to refer to such things.

"Nothing," T'Gatoi agreed, humoring her.

"Did you think I would sell him for eggs? For long life? My son?"

"Not for anything," T'Gatoi said, stroking my mother's shoulders, toying with her long, graying hair.

I would like to have touched my mother, shared that moment with her. She would take my hand if I touched her now. Freed by the egg and the sting, she would smile and perhaps say things long held in. But tomorrow, she would remember all this as a humiliation. I did not want to be part of a remembered humiliation. Best just to be still and know she loved me under all the duty and pride and pain.

"Xuan Hoa, take off her shoes," T'Gatoi said. "In a little while I'll sting her again and she can sleep."

My older sister obeyed, swaying drunkenly as she stood up. When she had finished, she sat down beside me and took my hand. We had always been a unit, she and I.

My mother put the back of her head against T'Gatoi's underside and tried from that impossible angle to look up into the broad, round face. "You're going to sting me again?"

"Yes, Lien."

"I'll sleep until tomorrow noon."

"Good. You need it. When did you sleep last?"

My mother made a wordless sound of annoyance. "I should have stepped on you when you were small enough," she muttered.

It was an old joke between them. They had grown up together, sort of, though T'Gatoi had not, in my mother's lifetime, been small enough for any Terran to step on. She was nearly three times my mother's present age, yet would still be young when my mother died of age. But T'Gatoi and my mother had met as T'Gatoi was coming into a period of rapid development—a kind of Tlic adolescence. My mother was only a child, but for a while they developed at the same rate and had no better friends than each other.

T'Gatoi had even introduced my mother to the man who became my father. My parents, pleased with each other in spite of their very different ages, married as T'Gatoi was going into her family's business—politics. She and my mother saw each other less. But sometime before my older sister was born, my mother promised T'Gatoi one of her children. She would have to give one of us to someone, and she preferred T'Gatoi to some stranger.

Years passed. T'Gatoi traveled and increased her influence. The Preserve was hers by the time she came back to my mother to collect what she probably saw as her just reward for her hard work. My older sister took an instant liking to her and wanted to be chosen, but my mother was just coming to term with me and T'Gatoi liked the idea of choosing an infant and watching and taking part in all the phases of development. I'm told I was first caged within T'Gatoi's many limbs only three minutes after my birth. A few days later, I was given my first taste of egg. I tell Terrans that when they ask whether I was ever afraid of her. And I tell it to Tlic when T'Gatoi suggests a young Terran child for them and they, anxious and ignorant, demand an adolescent. Even my brother who had somehow grown up to fear and distrust the Tlic could probably have gone smoothly into one of their families if he had been adopted early enough. Sometimes, I think for his sake he should have been. I looked at him, stretched out on the floor across the room, his eyes open, but glazed as he dreamed his egg dream. No matter what he felt toward the Tlic, he always demanded his share of egg.

"Lien, can you stand up?" T'Gatoi asked suddenly.

"Stand?" my mother said. "I thought I was going to sleep."

"Later. Something sounds wrong outside." The cage was abruptly gone.

"What?"

"Up, Lien!"

My mother recognized her tone and got up just in time to avoid being dumped on the floor. T'Gatoi whipped her three meters of body off her couch, toward the door, and out at full speed. She had bones—ribs, a long spine, a skull, four sets of limbbones per segment. But when she moved that way, twisting, hurling herself into controlled falls, landing running, she seemed not only boneless, but aquatic—something swimming through the air as though it were water. I loved watching her move.

I left my sister and started to follow her out the door, though I wasn't very steady on my own feet. It would have been better to sit and dream, better yet to find a girl and share a waking dream with her. Back when the Tlic saw us as not much more than convenient big warm-blooded animals, they would pen several of us together, male and female, and feed us only eggs. That way they could be sure of getting another generation of us no matter how we tried to hold out. We were lucky that didn't go on long. A few generations of it and we would have *been* little more than convenient big animals.

"Hold the door open, Gan," T'Gatoi said. "And tell the family to stay back."

"What is it?" I asked.

"N'Tlic."

I shrank back against the door. "Here? Alone?"

"He was trying to reach a call box, I suppose." She

carried the man past me, unconscious, folded like a coat over some of her limbs. He looked young—my brother's age perhaps—and he was thinner than he should have been. What T'Gatoi would have called dangerously thin.

"Gan, go to the call box," she said. She put the man on the floor and began stripping off his clothing.

I did not move.

After a moment, she looked up at me, her sudden stillness a sign of deep impatience.

"Send Qui," I told her. "I'll stay here. Maybe I can help."

She let her limbs begin to move again, lifting the man and pulling his shirt over his head. "You don't want to see this," she said. "It will be hard. I can't help this man the way his Tlic could."

"I know. But send Qui. He won't want to be of any help here. I'm at least willing to try."

She looked at my brother—older, bigger, stronger, certainly more able to help her here. He was sitting up now, braced against the wall, staring at the man on the floor with undisguised fear and revulsion. Even she could see that he would be useless.

"Qui, go!" she said.

He didn't argue. He stood up, swayed briefly, then steadied, frightened sober.

"This man's name is Bram Lomas," she told him, reading from the man's arm band. I fingered my own arm band in sympathy. "He needs T'Khotgif Teh. Do you hear?"

"Bram Lomas, T'Khotgif Teh," my brother said. "I'm going." He edged around Lomas and ran out the door.

Lomas began to regain consciousness. He only moaned at first and clutched spasmodically at a pair of T'Gatoi's limbs. My younger sister, finally awake from her egg dream, came close to look at him, until my mother pulled her back.

T'Gatoi removed the man's shoes, then his pants, all

the while leaving him two of her limbs to grip. Except for the final few, all her limbs were equally dexterous. "I want no argument from you this time, Gan," she said.

I straightened. "What shall I do?"

"Go out and slaughter an animal that is at least half your size."

"Slaughter? But I've never—"

She knocked me across the room. Her tail was an efficient weapon whether she exposed the sting or not.

I got up, feeling stupid for having ignored her warning, and went into the kitchen. Maybe I could kill something with a knife or an ax. My mother raised a few Terran animals for the table and several thousand local ones for their fur. T'Gatoi would probably prefer something local. An achti, perhaps. Some of those were the right size, though they had about three times as many teeth as I did and a real love of using them. My mother, Hoa, and Qui could kill them with knives. I had never killed one at all, had never slaughtered any animal. I had spent most of my time with T'Gatoi while my brother and sisters were learning the family business. T'Gatoi had been right. I should have been the one to go to the call box. At least I could do that.

I went to the corner cabinet where my mother kept her larger house and garden tools. At the back of the cabinet there was a pipe that carried off waste water from the kitchen—except that it didn't anymore. My father had rerouted the waste water before I was born. Now the pipe could be turned so that one half slid around the other and a rifle could be stored inside. This wasn't our only gun, but it was our most easily accessible one. I would have to use it to shoot one of the biggest of the achti. Then T'Gatoi would probably confiscate it. Firearms were illegal in the Preserve. There had been incidents right after the Preserve was established—Terrans shooting Tlic, shooting N'Tlic. This was before the joining of families began, before everyone had a personal stake in keeping the peace. No one had shot a Tlic in my lifetime or my mother's, but the law still stood—for our protection, we were told. There were stories of whole Terran families wiped out in reprisal back during the assassinations.

I went out to the cages and shot the biggest achti I could find. It was a handsome breeding male and my mother would not be pleased to see me bring it in. But it was the right size, and I was in a hurry.

I put the achti's long, warm body over my shoulder—glad that some of the weight I'd gained was muscle—and took it to the kitchen. There, I put the gun back in its hiding place. If T'Gatoi noticed the achti's wounds and demanded the gun, I would give it to her. Otherwise, let it stay where my father wanted it.

I turned to take the achti to her, then hesitated. For several seconds, I stood in front of the closed door wondering why I was suddenly afraid. I knew what was going to happen. I hadn't seen it before but T'Gatoi had shown me diagrams, and drawings. She had made sure I knew the truth as soon as I was old enough to understand it.

Yet I did not want to go into that room. I wasted a little time choosing a knife from the carved, wooden box in which my mother kept them. T'Gatoi might want one, I told myself, for the tough, heavily furred hide of the achti.

"Gan!" T'Gatoi called, her voice harsh with urgency.

I swallowed. I had not imagined a simple moving of the feet could be so difficult. I realized I was trembling and that shamed me. Shame impelled me through the door.

I put the achti down near T'Gatoi and saw that Lomas was unconscious again. She, Lomas, and I were alone in the room, my mother and sisters probably sent out so they would not have to watch. I envied them.

But my mother came back into the room as T'Gatoi

seized the achti. Ignoring the knife I offered her, she extended claws from several of her limbs and slit the achti from throat to anus. She looked at me, her yellow eyes intent. "Hold this man's shoulders, Gan."

I stared at Lomas in panic, realizing that I did not want to touch him, let alone hold him. This would not be like shooting an animal. Not as quick, not as merciful, and, I hoped, not as final, but there was nothing I wanted less than to be part of it.

My mother came forward. "Gan, you hold his right side," she said. "I'll hold his left." And if he came to, he would throw her off without realizing he had done it. She was a tiny woman. She often wondered aloud how she had produced, as she said, such "huge" children.

"Never mind," I told her, taking the man's shoulders. "I'll do it."

She hovered nearby.

"Don't worry," I said. "I won't shame you. You don't have to stay and watch."

She looked at me uncertainly, then touched my face in a rare caress. Finally, she went back to her bedroom.

T'Gatoi lowered her head in relief. "Thank you, Gan," she said with courtesy more Terran than Tlic. "That one . . . she is always finding new ways for me to make her suffer."

Lomas began to groan and make choked sounds. I had hoped he would stay unconscious. T'Gatoi put her face near his so that he focused on her.

"I've stung you as much as I dare for now," she told him. "When this is over, I'll sting you to sleep and you won't hurt anymore."

"Please," the man begged. "Wait . . ."

"There's no more time, Bram. I'll sting you as soon as it's over. When T'Khotgif arrives she'll give you eggs to help you heal. It will be over soon."

"T'Khotgif!" the man shouted, straining against my hands.

"Soon, Bram." T'Gatoi glanced at me, then placed a claw against his abdomen slightly to the right of the middle, just below the last rib. There was movement on the right side—tiny, seemingly random pulsations moving his brown flesh, creating a concavity here, a convexity there, over and over until I could see the rhythm of it and knew where the next pulse would be.

Lomas's entire body stiffened under T'Gatoi's claw, though she merely rested it against him as she wound the rear section of her body around his legs. He might break my grip, but he would not break hers. He wept helplessly as she used his pants to tie his hands, then pushed his hands above his head so that I could kneel on the cloth between them and pin them in place. She rolled up his shirt and gave it to him to bite down on.

And she opened him.

His body convulsed with the first cut. He almost tore himself away from me. The sounds he made . . . I had never heard such sounds come from anything human. T'Gatoi seemed to pay no attention as she lengthened and deepened the cut, now and then pausing to lick away blood. His blood vessels contracted, reacting to the chemistry of her saliva, and the bleeding slowed.

I felt as though I were helping her torture him, helping her consume him. I knew I would vomit soon, didn't know why I hadn't already. I couldn't possibly last until she was finished.

She found the first grub. It was fat and deep red with his blood—both inside and out. It had already eaten its own egg case, but apparently had not yet begun to eat its host. At this stage, it would eat any flesh except its mother's. Let alone, it would have gone on excreting the poisons that had both sickened and alerted Lomas. Eventually it would have begun to eat. By the time it ate its way out of Lomas's flesh, Lomas would be dead or dying—and unable to take a revenge on the thing that was killing him. There was always a grace period between the time the host sickened and the time the grubs began to eat him.

T'Gatoi picked up the writhing grub carefully, and looked at it, somehow ignoring the terrible groans of the man.

Abruptly, the man lost consciousness.

"Good." T'Gatoi looked down at him. "I wish you Terrans could do that at will." She felt nothing. And the thing she held . . .

It was limbless and boneless at this stage, perhaps fifteen centimeters long and two thick, blind and slimy with blood. It was like a large worm. T'Gatoi put it into the belly of the achti, and it began at once to burrow. It would stay there and eat as long as there was anything to eat.

Probing through Lomas's flesh, she found two more, one of them smaller and more vigorous. "A male!" she said happily. He would be dead before I would. He would be through his metamorphosis and screwing everything that would hold still before his sisters even had limbs. He was the only one to make a serious effort to bite T'Gatoi as she placed him in the achti.

Paler worms oozed to visibility in Lomas's flesh. I closed my eyes. It was worse than finding something dead, rotting, and filled with tiny animal grubs. And it was far worse than any drawing or diagram.

"Ah, there are more," T'Gatoi said, plucking out two long, thick grubs. "You may have to kill another animal, Gan. Everything lives inside you Terrans."

I had been told all my life that this was a good and necessary thing Tlic and Terran did together—a kind of birth. I had believed it until now. I knew birth was painful and bloody, no matter what. But this was something else, something worse. And I wasn't ready to see it. Maybe I never would be. Yet I couldn't *not* see it. Closing my eyes didn't help.

T'Gatoi found a grub still eating its egg case. The

remains of the case were still wired into a blood vessel by their own little tube or hook or whatever. That was the way the grubs were anchored and the way they fed. They took only blood until they were ready to emerge. Then they ate their stretched, elastic egg cases. Then they ate their hosts.

T'Gatoi bit away the egg case, licked away the blood. Did she like the taste? Did childhood habits die hard—or not die at all?

The whole procedure was wrong, alien. I wouldn't have thought anything about her could seem alien to me.

"One more, I think," she said. "Perhaps two. A good family. In a host animal these days, we would be happy to find one or two alive." She glanced at me. "Go outside, Gan, and empty your stomach. Go now while the man is unconscious."

I staggered out, barely made it. Beneath the tree just beyond the front door, I vomited until there was nothing left to bring up. Finally, I stood shaking, tears streaming down my face. I did not know why I was crying but I could not stop. I went farther from the house to avoid being seen. Every time I closed my eyes I saw red worms crawling over redder human flesh.

There was a car coming toward the house. Since Terrans were forbidden motorized vehicles except for certain farm equipment, I knew this must be Lomas's Tlic with Qui and perhaps a Terran doctor. I wiped my face on my shirt, struggled for control.

"Gan," Qui called as the car stopped. "What happened?" He crawled out of the low, round, Tlic-convenient car door. Another Terran crawled out the other side and went into the house without speaking to me. The doctor. With his help and a few eggs, Lomas might make it.

"T'Khotgif Teh?" I said.

The Tlic driver surged out of her car, reared up half her length before me. She was paler and smaller than T'Gatoi—probably born from the body of an animal.

Tlic from Terran bodies were always larger as well as more numerous.

"Six young," I told her. "Maybe seven, all alive. At least one male."

"Lomas?" she said harshly. I liked her for the question and the concern in her voice when she asked it. The last coherent thing he had said was her name.

"He's alive," I said.

She surged away to the house without another word.

"She's been sick," my brother said, watching her go. "When I called, I could hear people telling her she wasn't well enough to go out even for this."

I said nothing. I had extended courtesy to the Tlic. Now I didn't want to talk to anyone. I hoped he would go in—out of curiosity if nothing else.

"Finally found out more than you wanted to know, eh?"

I looked at him.

"Don't give me one of *her* looks," he said. "You're not her. You're just her property."

One of her looks. Had I picked up even an ability to imitate her expressions?

"What'd you do, puke?" He sniffed the air. "So now you know what you're in for."

I walked away from him. He and I had been close when we were kids. He would let me follow him around when I was home and sometimes T'Gatoi would let me bring him along when she took me into the city. But something had happened when he reached adolescence. I never knew what. He began keeping out of T'Gatoi's way. Then he began running away—until he realized there was no "away." Not in the Preserve. Certainly not outside. After that he concentrated on getting his share of every egg that came into the house, and on looking out for me in a way that made me all but hate him—a way that clearly said, as long as I was all right, he was safe from the Tlic.

"How was it, really?" he demanded, following me.

"I killed an achti. The young ate it."

"You didn't run out of the house and puke because they ate an achti."

"I had . . . never seen a person cut open before." That was true, and enough for him to know. I couldn't talk about the other. Not with him.

"Oh," he said. He glanced at me as though he wanted to say more, but he kept quiet.

We walked, not really headed anywhere. Toward the back, toward the cages, toward the fields.

"Did he say anything?" Qui asked. "Lomas, I mean."

Who else would he mean? "He said 'T'Khotgif.'"

Qui shuddered. "If she had done that to me, she'd be the last person I'd call for."

"You'd call for her. Her sting would ease your pain without killing the grubs in you."

"You think I'd care if they died?"

No. Of course he wouldn't. Would I?

"Shit!" He drew a deep breath. "I've seen what they do. You think this thing with Lomas was bad? It was nothing."

I didn't argue. He didn't know what he was talking about.

"I saw them eat a man," he said.

I turned to face him. "You're lying!"

"I saw them eat a man." He paused. "It was when I was little. I had been to the Hartmund house and I was on my way home. Halfway here, I saw a man and a Tlic and the man was N'Tlic. The ground was hilly. I was able to hide from them and watch. The Tlic wouldn't open the man because she had nothing to feed the grubs. The man couldn't go any farther and there were no houses around. He was in so much pain he told her to kill him. He begged her to kill him. Finally, she did. She cut his throat. One swipe of one claw. I saw the grubs eat their way out, then burrow in again, still eating."

His words made me see Lomas's flesh again, parasitized, crawling. "Why didn't you tell me that?" I whispered.

He looked startled, as though he'd forgotten I was listening. "I don't know."

"You started to run away not long after that, didn't you?"

"Yeah. Stupid. Running inside the Preserve. Running in a cage."

I shook my head, said what I should have said to him long ago. "She wouldn't take you, Qui. You don't have to worry."

"She would . . . if anything happened to you."

"No. She'd take Xuan Hoa. Hoa . . . wants it." She wouldn't if she had stayed to watch Lomas.

"They don't take women," he said with contempt.

"They do sometimes." I glanced at him. "Actually, they prefer women. You should be around them when they talk among themselves. They say women have more body fat to protect the grubs. But they usually take men to leave the women free to bear their own young."

"To provide the next generation of host animals," he said, switching from contempt to bitterness.

"It's more than that!" I countered. Was it?

"If it were going to happen to me, I'd want to believe it was more, too."

"It *is* more!" I felt like a kid. Stupid argument.

"Did you think so while T'Gatoi was picking worms out of that guy's guts?"

"It's not supposed to happen that way."

"Sure it is. You weren't supposed to see it, that's all. And his Tlic was supposed to do it. She could sting him unconscious and the operation wouldn't have been as painful. But she'd still open him, pick out the grubs, and if she missed even one, it would poison him and eat him from the inside out."

There was actually a time when my mother told me to show respect for Qui because he was my older brother. I walked away, hating him. In his way, he was gloating. He was safe and I wasn't. I could have hit him, but I didn't think I would be able to stand it when he refused to hit back, when he looked at me with contempt and pity.

He wouldn't let me get away. Longer-legged, he swung ahead of me and made me feel as though I were following him.

"I'm sorry," he said.

I strode on, sick and furious.

"Look, it probably won't be that bad with you. T'Gatoi likes you. She'll be careful."

I turned back toward the house, almost running from him.

"Has she done it to you yet?" he asked, keeping up easily. "I mean, you're about the right age for implantation. Has she—"

I hit him. I didn't know I was going to do it, but I think I meant to kill him. If he hadn't been bigger and stronger, I think I would have.

He tried to hold me off, but in the end, had to defend himself. He only hit me a couple of times. That was plenty. I don't remember going down, but when I came to, he was gone. It was worth the pain to be rid of him.

I got up and walked slowly toward the house. The back was dark. No one was in the kitchen. My mother and sisters were sleeping in their bedrooms—or pretending to.

Once I was in the kitchen, I could hear voices—Tlic and Terran from the next room. I couldn't make out what they were saying—didn't want to make it out.

I sat down at my mother's table, waiting for quiet. The table was smooth and worn, heavy and well-crafted. My father had made it for her just before he died. I remembered hanging around underfoot when he built it. He didn't mind. Now I sat leaning on it, missing him. I could have talked to him. He had done it three times in his long life. Three clutches of eggs, three times being opened and sewed up. How had he done it? How did anyone do it?

I got up, took the rifle from its hiding place, and sat down again with it. It needed cleaning, oiling.

All I did was load it.

"Gan?"

She made a lot of little clicking sounds when she walked on bare floor, each limb clicking in succession as it touched down. Waves of little clicks.

She came to the table, raised the front half of her body above it, and surged onto it. Sometimes she moved so smoothly she seemed to flow like water itself. She coiled herself into a small hill in the middle of the table and looked at me.

"That was bad," she said softly. "You should not have seen it. It need not be that way."

"I know."

"T'Khotgif—Ch'Khotgif now—she will die of her disease. She will not live to raise her children. But her sister will provide for them, and for Bram Lomas." Sterile sister. One fertile female in every lot. One to keep the family going. That sister owed Lomas more than she could ever repay.

"He'll live then?"

"Yes."

"I wonder if he would do it again."

"No one would ask him to do that again."

I looked into the yellow eyes, wondering how much I saw and understood there, and how much I only imagined. "No one ever asks us," I said. "You never asked me."

She moved her head slightly. "What's the matter with your face?"

"Nothing. Nothing important." Human eyes probably wouldn't have noticed the swelling in the darkness. The only light was from one of the moons, shining through a window across the room.

"Did you use the rifle to shoot the achti?"

"Yes."

"And do you mean to use it to shoot me?"

I stared at her, outlined in moonlight—coiled, graceful body. "What does Terran blood taste like to you?"

She said nothing.

"What are you?" I whispered. "What are we to you?"

She lay still, rested her head on her topmost coil. "You know me as no other does," she said softly. "You must decide."

"That's what happened to my face," I told her.

"What?"

"Qui goaded me into deciding to do something. It didn't turn out very well." I moved the gun slightly, brought the barrel up diagonally under my own chin. "At least it was a decision I made."

"As this will be."

"Ask me, Gatoi."

"For my children's lives?"

She would say something like that. She knew how to manipulate people, Terran and Tlic. But not this time.

"I don't want to be a host animal," I said. "Not even yours."

It took her a long time to answer. "We use almost no host animals these days," she said. "You know that."

"You use us."

"We do. We wait long years for you and teach you and join our families to yours." She moved restlessly. "You know you aren't animals to us."

I stared at her, saying nothing.

"The animals we once used began killing most of our eggs after implantation long before your ancestors arrived," she said softly. "You know these things, Gan. Because your people arrived, we are relearning what it means to be a healthy, thriving people. And your ancestors, fleeing from their homeworld, from their own kind who would have killed or enslaved them—they survived because of us. We saw them as people and gave them the Preserve when they still tried to kill us as worms."

At the word "worms" I jumped. I couldn't help it, and she couldn't help noticing it.

"I see," she said quietly. "Would you really rather die than bear my young, Gan?"

I didn't answer.

"Shall I go to Xuan Hoa?"

"Yes!" Hoa wanted it. Let her have it. She hadn't had to watch Lomas. She'd be proud . . . Not terrified.

T'Gatoi flowed off the table onto the floor, startling me almost too much.

"I'll sleep in Hoa's room tonight," she said. "And sometime tonight or in the morning, I'll tell her."

This was going too fast. My sister. Hoa had had almost as much to do with raising me as my mother. I was still close to her—not like Qui. She could want T'Gatoi and still love me.

"Wait! Gatoi!"

She looked back, then raised nearly half her length off the floor and turned it to face me. "These are adult things, Gan. This is my life, my family!"

"But she's . . . my sister."

"I have done what you demanded. I have asked you!"

"But—"

"It will be easier for Hoa. She has always expected to carry other lives inside her."

Human lives. Human young who would someday drink at her breasts, not at her veins.

I shook my head. "Don't do it to her, Gatoi." I was not Qui. It seemed I could become him, though, with no effort at all. I could make Xuan Hoa my shield. Would it be easier to know that red worms were growing in her flesh instead of mine?

"Don't do it to Hoa," I repeated.

She stared at me, utterly still.

I looked away, then back at her. "Do it to me."

I lowered the gun from my throat and she leaned forward to take it.

"No," I told her.

"It's the law," she said.

"Leave it for the family. One of them might use it to save my life someday."

She grasped the rifle barrel, but I wouldn't let go. I was pulled into a standing position over her.

"Leave it here!" I repeated. "If we're not your animals, if these are adult things, accept the risk. There is risk, Gatoi, in dealing with a partner."

It was clearly hard for her to let go of the rifle. A shudder went through her and she made a hissing sound of distress. It occurred to me that she was afraid. She was old enough to have seen what guns could do to people. Now her young and this gun would be together in the same house. She did not know about our other guns. In this dispute, they did not matter.

"I will implant the first egg tonight," she said as I put the gun away. "Do you hear, Gan?"

Why else had I been given a whole egg to eat while the rest of the family was left to share one? Why else had my mother kept looking at me as though I were going away from her, going where she could not follow? Did T'Gatoi imagine I hadn't known?

"I hear."

"Now!" I let her push me out of the kitchen, then walked ahead of her toward my bedroom. The sudden urgency in her voice sounded real. "You would have done it to Hoa tonight!" I accused.

"I must do it to someone tonight."

I stopped in spite of her urgency and stood in her way. "Don't you care who?"

She flowed around me and into my bedroom. I found her waiting on the couch we shared. There was nothing in Hoa's room that she could have used. She would have done it to Hoa on the floor. The thought of her doing it to Hoa at all disturbed me in a different way now, and I was suddenly angry.

Yet I undressed and lay down beside her. I knew what to do, what to expect. I had been told all my life. I felt the familiar sting, narcotic, mildly pleasant. Then the blind probing of her ovipositor. The puncture was painless, easy. So easy going in. She undulated slowly against me, her muscles forcing the egg from her body into mine. I held on to a pair of her limbs until I remembered Lomas holding her that way. Then I let go, moved inadvertently, and hurt her. She gave a low cry of pain and I expected to be caged at once within her limbs. When I wasn't, I held on to her again, feeling oddly ashamed.

"I'm sorry," I whispered.

She rubbed my shoulders with four of her limbs.

"Do you care?" I asked. "Do you care that it's me?"

She did not answer for some time. Finally, "You were the one making choices tonight, Gan. I made mine long ago."

"Would you have gone to Hoa?"

"Yes. How could I put my children into the care of one who hates them?"

"It wasn't . . . hate."

"I know what it was."

"I was afraid."

Silence.

"I still am." I could admit it to her here, now.

"But you came to me . . . to save Hoa."

"Yes." I leaned my forehead against her. She was cool velvet, deceptively soft. "And to keep you for myself," I said. It was so. I didn't understand it, but it was so.

She made a soft hum of contentment. "I couldn't believe I had made such a mistake with you," she said. "I'll chose you. I believed you had grown to choose me."

"I had, but . . ."

"Lomas."

"Yes."

"I have never known a Terran to see a birth and take it well. Qui has seen one, hasn't he?"

"Yes."

"Terrans should be protected from seeing."

I didn't like the sound of that—and I doubted that it was possible. "Not protected," I said. "Shown. Shown when we're young kids, and shown more than once. Gatoi, no Terran ever sees a birth that goes right. All we see is N'Tlic—pain and terror and maybe death."

She looked down at me. "It is a private thing. It has always been a private thing."

Her tone kept me from insisting—that and the knowledge that if she changed her mind, I might be the first public example. But I had planted the thought in her mind. Chances were it would grow, and eventually she would experiment.

"You won't see it again," she said. "I don't want you thinking any more about shooting me."

The small amount of fluid that came into me with her egg relaxed me as completely as a sterile egg would have, so that I could remember the rifle in my hands and my feelings of fear and revulsion, anger and despair. I could remember the feelings without reviving them. I could talk about them.

"I wouldn't have shot you," I said. "Not you." She had been taken from my father's flesh when he was my age.

"You could have," she insisted.

"Not you." She stood between us and her own people, protecting, interweaving.

"Would you have destroyed yourself?"

I moved carefully, uncomfortably. "I could have done that. I nearly did. That's Qui's 'away.' I wonder if he knows."

"What?"

I did not answer.

"You will live now."

"Yes." *Take care of her,* my mother used to say. Yes.

"I'm healthy and young," she said. "I won't leave you as Lomas was left—alone, N'Tlic. I'll take care of you."

Richard Matheson (b. 1926)

DUEL

Richard Matheson won instant notoriety in 1950 with his first short story, "Born of Man and Woman," published in *The Magazine of Fantasy and Science Fiction*. There followed a number of clean, sharp stories of dark fantasy and horrific science fiction, enough to fill several collections in the fifties alone. His first novel, *I Am Legend* (1954), the classic science fiction vampire story, and his second, *The Shrinking Man* (1956), basis for the popular fifties' film, established him as the premier science fiction horror writer of the decade. He went on to a career in Hollywood and is recognized as scriptwriter of stories for "The Twilight Zone" and many television movies. His contemporary classic horror novel, *Hell House* (1971), was successfully filmed. *Bid Time Return* (1975) won the World Fantasy Award for best novel. "Duel" was the basis of a notable 1971 television movie directed by Steven Spielberg, for which Matheson wrote the teleplay. He is one of the finest living writers of horror. Without a hint of science fiction or an overt whiff of the supernatural, "Duel" manages to invoke both the science fiction tradition of the menace of the intelligent machine and the monster tradition of the horror genre. It is a psychological monster story, subtly shocking, compelling, fantastic.

At 11:32 AM, Mann passed the truck.

He was heading west, en route to San Francisco. It was Thursday and unseasonably hot for April. He had his suitcoat off, his tie removed and shirt collar opened, his sleeve cuffs folded back. There was sunlight on his left arm and on part of his lap. He could feel the heat of it through his dark trousers as he drove along the two-lane highway. For the past twenty minutes, he had not seen another vehicle going in either direction.

Then he saw the truck ahead, moving up a curving grade between two high green hills. He heard the grinding strain of its motor and saw a double shadow on the road. The truck was pulling a trailer.

He paid no attention to the details of the truck. As he drew behind it on the grade, he edged his car toward the opposite lane. The road ahead had blind curves and he didn't try to pass until the truck had crossed the ridge. He waited until it started around a left curve on the downgrade, then, seeing that the way was clear, pressed down on the accelerator pedal and steered his car into the eastbound lane. He waited until he could see the truck front in his rearview mirror before he turned back into the proper lane.

Mann looked across the countryside ahead. There were ranges of mountains as far as he could see and, all around him, rolling green hills. He whistled softly as the car sped down the winding grade, its tires making crisp sounds on the pavement.

At the bottom of the hill, he crossed a concrete bridge and, glancing to the right, saw a dry streambed strewn with rocks and gravel. As the car moved off the bridge, he saw a trailer park set back from the highway to his right. How can anyone live out here? he thought. His shifting gaze caught sight of a pet cemetery ahead and he smiled. Maybe those people in the trailers wanted to be close to the graves of their dogs and cats.

The highway ahead was straight now. Mann drifted into a reverie, the sunlight on his arm and lap. He wondered what Ruth was doing. The kids, of course, were in school and would be for hours yet. Maybe Ruth was shopping; Thursday was the day she usually went. Mann visualized her in the supermarket, putting various items into the basket cart. He wished he were with her instead of starting on another sales trip. Hours of driving yet before he'd reach San Francisco. Three days of hotel sleeping and restaurant eating, hoped-for contacts and likely disappointments. He sighed; then, reaching out impulsively, he switched on the radio. He revolved the tuning knob until he found a station playing soft, innocuous music. He hummed along with it, eyes almost out of focus on the road ahead.

He started as the truck roared past him on the left, causing his car to shudder slightly. He watched the truck and trailer cut in abruptly for the westbound lane and frowned as he had to brake to maintain a safe distance behind it. What's with you? he thought.

He eyed the truck with cursory disapproval. It was a huge gasoline tanker pulling a tank trailer, each of them having six pairs of wheels. He could see that it was not a new rig but was dented and in need of renovation, its tanks painted a cheap-looking silvery color. Mann wondered if the driver had done the painting himself. His gaze shifted from the word FLAMMABLE printed across the back of the trailer tank, red letters on a white background, to the parallel reflector lines painted in red across the bottom of the tank to the massive rubber flaps swaying behind the rear tires, then back up again. The reflector lines looked as though they'd been clumsily applied with a stencil. The driver must be an independent trucker, he decided, and not too affluent a one, from the looks of his outfit. He glanced at the trailer's license plate. It was a California issue.

Mann checked his speedometer. He was holding steady at 55 miles an hour, as he invariably did when he drove without thinking on the open highway. The truck driver must have done a good 70 to pass him so quickly. That seemed a little odd. Weren't truck drivers supposed to be a cautious lot?

He grimaced at the smell of the truck's exhaust and looked at the vertical pipe to the left of the cab. It was spewing smoke, which clouded darkly back across the trailer. Christ, he thought. With all the furor about air pollution, why do they keep allowing that sort of thing on the highways?

He scowled at the constant fumes. They'd make him nauseated in a little while, he knew. He couldn't lag back here like this. Either he slowed down or he passed the truck again. He didn't have the time to slow down. He'd gotten a late start. Keeping it at 55 all the way, he'd just about make his afternoon appointment. No, he'd have to pass.

Depressing the gas pedal, he eased his car toward the opposite lane. No sign of anything ahead. Traffic on this route seemed almost nonexistent today. He pushed down harder on the accelerator and steered all the way into the eastbound lane.

As he passed the truck, he glanced at it. The cab was too high for him to see into. All he caught sight of was the back of the truck driver's left hand on the steering wheel. It was darkly tanned and square-looking, with large veins knotted on its surface.

When Mann could see the truck reflected in the rearview mirror, he pulled back over to the proper lane and looked ahead again.

He glanced at the rearview mirror in surprise as the truck driver gave him an extended horn blast. What was that? he wondered; a greeting or a curse? He grunted with amusement, glancing at the mirror as he drove. The front fenders of the truck were a dingy purple color, the paint faded and chipped; another amateurish job. All he could see was the lower portion of the truck; the rest was cut off by the top of his rear window.

To Mann's right, now, was a slope of shalelike earth with patches of scrub grass growing on it. His gaze jumped to the clapboard house on top of the slope. The television aerial on its roof was sagging at an angle of less than 40 degrees. Must give great reception, he thought.

He looked to the front again, glancing aside abruptly at a sign printed in jagged block letters on a piece of plywood: NIGHT CRAWLERS—BAIT. What the hell is a night crawler? he wondered. It sounded like some monster in a low-grade Hollywood thriller.

The unexpected roar of the truck motor made his gaze jump to the rearview mirror. Instantly, his startled look jumped to the side mirror. By God, the guy was passing him *again*. Mann turned his head to scowl at the leviathan form as it drifted by. He tried to see into the cab but couldn't because of its height. What's with him, anyway? he wondered. What the hell are we having here, a contest? See which vehicle can stay ahead the longest?

He thought of speeding up to stay ahead but changed his mind. When the truck and trailer started back into the westbound lane, he let up on the pedal, voicing a newly incredulous sound as he saw that if he hadn't slowed down, he would have been prematurely cut off again. Jesus Christ, he thought. What's *with* this guy?

His scowl deepened as the odor of the truck's exhaust reached his nostrils again. Irritably, he cranked up the window on his left. Damn it, was he going to have to breathe that crap all the way to San Francisco? He couldn't afford to slow down. He had to meet Forbes at a quarter after three and that was that.

He looked ahead. At least there was no traffic complicating matters. Mann pressed down on the accelerator pedal, drawing close behind the truck. When the highway curved enough to the left to give him a completely open view of the route ahead, he jarred down on the pedal, steering out into the opposite lane.

The truck edged over, blocking his way.

For several moments, all Mann could do was stare at it in blank confusion. Then, with a startled noise, he braked, returning to the proper lane. The truck moved back in front of him.

Mann could not allow himself to accept what apparently had taken place. It had to be a coincidence. The truck driver couldn't have blocked his way on purpose. He waited for more than a minute, then flicked down the turn-indicator lever to make his intentions perfectly clear and, depressing the accelerator pedal, steered again into the eastbound lane.

Immediately, the truck shifted, barring his way.

"Jesus Christ!" Mann was astounded. This was unbelievable. He'd never seen such a thing in twenty-six years of driving. He returned to the westbound lane, shaking his head as the truck swung back in front of him.

He eased up on the gas pedal, falling back to avoid the truck's exhaust. Now what? he wondered. He still had to make San Francisco on schedule. Why in God's name hadn't he gone a little out of his way in the beginning, so he could have traveled by freeway? This damned highway was two lanes all the way.

Impulsively, he sped into the eastbound lane again. To his surprise, the truck driver did not pull over. Instead, the driver stuck his left arm out and waved him on. Mann started pushing down on the accelerator. Suddenly, he let up on the pedal with a gasp and jerked the steering wheel around, raking back behind the truck so quickly that his car began to fishtail. He was fighting to control its zigzag whipping when a blue convertible shot by him in the opposite lane. Mann caught a momentary vision of the man inside it glaring at him.

The car came under his control again. Mann was sucking breath in through his mouth. His heart was pounding almost painfully. My God! he thought. *He wanted me to hit that car head-on.* The realization stunned him. True, he should have seen to it himself that the road ahead was clear; that was his failure. But to wave him on . . . Mann felt appalled and sickened. Boy, oh, boy, oh, boy, he thought. This was really one for the books. That son of a bitch had meant for not only him to be killed but a totally uninvolved passerby as well. The idea seemed beyond his comprehension. On a California highway on a Thursday morning? *Why?*

Mann tried to calm himself and rationalize the incident. Maybe it's the heat, he thought. Maybe the truck driver had a tension headache or an upset stomach; maybe both. Maybe he'd had a fight with his wife. Maybe she'd failed to put out last night. Mann tried in vain to smile. There could be any number of reasons. Reaching out, he twisted off the radio. The cheerful music irritated him.

He drove behind the truck for several minutes, his face a mask of animosity. As the exhaust fumes started putting his stomach on edge, he suddenly forced down the heel of his right hand on the horn bar and held it there. Seeing that the route ahead was clear, he pushed in the accelerator pedal all the way and steered into the opposite lane.

The movement of his car was paralleled immediately by the truck. Mann stayed in place, right hand jammed down on the horn bar. Get out of the way, you son of a bitch! he thought. He felt the muscles of his jaw hardening until they ached. There was a twisting in his stomach.

"Damn!" He pulled back quickly to the proper lane, shuddering with fury. "You miserable son of a bitch," he muttered, glaring at the truck as it was shifted back in front of him. What the hell is wrong with you? I pass your goddamn rig a couple of times and you go flying off the deep end? Are you nuts or something? Mann nodded tensely. Yes, he thought; he *is.* No other explanation.

He wondered what Ruth would think of all this, how

she'd react. Probably, she'd start to honk the horn and would keep on honking it, assuming that, eventually, it would attract the attention of a policeman. He looked around with a scowl. Just where in hell *were* the policemen out here, anyway? He made a scoffing noise. What policemen? Here in the boondocks? They probably had a sheriff on horseback, for Christ's sake.

He wondered suddenly if he could fool the truck driver by passing on the right. Edging his car toward the shoulder, he peered ahead. No chance. There wasn't room enough. The truck driver could shove him through that wire fence if he wanted to. Mann shivered. And he'd want to, sure as hell, he thought.

Driving where he was, he grew conscious of the debris lying beside the highway: beer cans, candy wrappers, ice-cream containers, newspaper sections browned and rotted by the weather, a FOR SALE sign torn in half. Keep America beautiful, he thought sardonically. He passed a boulder with the name WILL JASPER painted on it in white. Who the hell is Will Jasper? he wondered. What would he think of this situation?

Unexpectedly, the car began to bounce. For several anxious moments, Mann thought that one of his tires had gone flat. Then he noticed that the paving along this section of highway consisted of pitted slabs with gaps between them. He saw the truck and trailer jolting up and down and thought: I hope it shakes your brains loose. As the truck veered into a sharp left curve, he caught a fleeting glimpse of the driver's face in the cab's side mirror. There was not enough time to establish his appearance.

"Ah," he said. A long, steep hill was looming up ahead. The truck would have to climb it slowly. There would doubtless be an opportunity to pass somewhere on the grade. Mann pressed down on the accelerator pedal, drawing as close behind the truck as safety would allow.

Halfway up the slope, Mann saw a turnout for the

eastbound lane with no oncoming traffic anywhere in sight. Flooring the accelerator pedal, he shot into the opposite lane. The slow-moving truck began to angle out in front of him. Face stiffening, Mann steered his speeding car across the highway edge and curved it sharply on the turnout. Clouds of dust went billowing up behind his car, making him lose sight of the truck. His tires buzzed and crackled on the dirt, then, suddenly, were humming on the pavement once again.

He glanced at the rearview mirror and a barking laugh erupted from his throat. He'd only meant to pass. The dust had been an unexpected bonus. Let the bastard get a sniff of something rotten-smelling in *his* nose for a change! he thought. He honked the horn elatedly, a mocking rhythm of bleats. Screw you, Jack!

He swept across the summit of the hill. A striking vista lay ahead: sunlit hills and flatland, a corridor of dark trees, quadrangles of cleared-off acreage and bright-green vegetable patches; far off, in the distance, a mammoth water tower. Mann felt stirred by the panoramic sight. Lovely, he thought. Reaching out, he turned the radio back on and started humming cheerfully with the music.

Seven minutes later, he passed a billboard advertising CHUCK'S CAFE. No thanks, Chuck, he thought. He glanced at a gray house nestled in a hollow. Was that a cemetery in its front yard or a group of plaster statuary for sale?

Hearing the noise behind him, Mann looked at the rearview mirror and felt himself go cold with fear. The truck was hurtling down the hill, pursuing him.

His mouth fell open and he threw a glance at the speedometer. He was doing more than 60! On a curving downgrade, that was not at all a safe speed to be driving. Yet the truck must be exceeding that by a considerable margin, it was closing the distance between them so rapidly. Mann swallowed, leaning to the right as he steered his car around a sharp curve. Is the man *insane?* he thought.

His gaze jumped forward searchingly. He saw a turnoff

half a mile ahead and decided that he'd use it. In the rearview mirror, the huge square radiator grille was all he could see now. He stamped down on the gas pedal and his tires screeched unnervingly as he wheeled around another curve, thinking that, surely, the truck would have to slow down here.

He groaned as it rounded the curve with ease, only the sway of its tanks revealing the outward pressure of the turn. Mann bit trembling lips together as he whipped his car around another curve. A straight descent now. He depressed the pedal farther, glanced at the speedometer. Almost 70 miles an hour! He wasn't used to driving this fast!

In agony, he saw the turnoff shoot by on his right. He couldn't have left the highway at this speed, anyway; he'd have overturned. Goddamn it, what was wrong with that son of a bitch? Mann honked his horn in frightened rage. Cranking down the window suddenly, he shoved his left arm out to wave the truck back. *"Back!"* he yelled. He honked the horn again. "Get back, you crazy bastard!"

The truck was almost on him now. He's going to kill me! Mann thought, horrified. He honked the horn repeatedly, then had to use both hands to grip the steering wheel as he swept around another curve. He flashed a look at the rearview mirror. He could see only the bottom portion of the truck's radiator grille. He was going to lose control! He felt the rear wheels start to drift and let up on the pedal quickly. The tire treads bit in, the car leaped on, regaining its momentum.

Mann saw the bottom of the grade ahead, and in the distance there was a building with a sign that read CHUCK'S CAFE. The truck was gaining ground again. This is insane! he thought, enraged and terrified at once. The highway straightened out. He floored the pedal: 74 now—75. Mann braced himself, trying to ease the car as far to the right as possible.

Abruptly, he began to brake, then swerved to the right, raking his car into the open area in front of the cafe. He

cried out as the car began to fishtail, then careened into a
skid. *Steer with it!* screamed a voice in his mind. The rear
of the car was lashing from side to side, tires spewing dirt
and raising clouds of dust. Mann pressed harder on the
brake pedal, turning further into the skid. The car began
to straighten out and he braked harder yet, conscious, on
the sides of his vision, of the truck and trailer roaring by
on the highway. He nearly sideswiped one of the cars
parked in front of the cafe, bounced and skidded by it,
going almost straight now. He jammed in the brake pedal
as hard as he could. The rear end broke to the right and
the car spun half around, sheering sideways to a neck-
wrenching halt thirty yards beyond the cafe.

Mann sat in pulsing silence, eyes closed. His heart-
beats felt like club blows in his chest. He couldn't seem
to catch his breath. If he were ever going to have a heart
attack, it would be now. After a while, he opened his eyes
and pressed his right palm against his chest. His heart
was still throbbing laboredly. No wonder, he thought. It
isn't every day I'm almost murdered by a truck.

He raised the handle and pushed out the door, then
started forward, grunting in surprise as the safety belt
held him in place. Reaching down with shaking fingers,
he depressed the release button and pulled the ends of
the belt apart. He glanced at the cafe. What had its
patrons thought of his breakneck appearance? he wondered.

He stumbled as he walked to the front door of the cafe.
TRUCKERS WELCOME, read a sign in the window. It gave
Mann a queasy feeling to see it. Shivering, he pulled
open the door and went inside, avoiding the sight of its
customers. He felt certain they were watching him, but
he didn't have the strength to face their looks. Keeping
his gaze fixed straight ahead, he moved to the rear of the
cafe and opened the door marked GENTS.

Moving to the sink, he twisted the right-hand faucet
and leaned over to cup cold water in his palms and

splash it on his face. There was a fluttering of his stomach muscles he could not control.

Straightening up, he tugged down several towels from their dispenser and patted them against his face, grimacing at the smell of the paper. Dropping the soggy towels into a wastebasket beside the sink, he regarded himself in the wall mirror. Still with us, Mann, he thought. He nodded, swallowing. Drawing out his metal comb, he neatened his hair. You never know, he thought. You just never know. You drift along, year after year, presuming certain values to be fixed; like being able to drive on a public thoroughfare without somebody trying to murder you. You come to depend on that sort of thing. Then something occurs and all bets are off. One shocking incident and all the years of logic and acceptance are displaced and, suddenly, the jungle is in front of you again. *Man, part animal, part angel.* Where had he come across that phrase? He shivered.

It was entirely an animal in that truck out there.

His breath was almost back to normal now. Mann forced a smile at his reflection. All right, boy, he told himself. It's over now. It was a goddamned nightmare, but it's over. You are on your way to San Francisco. You'll get yourself a nice hotel room, order a bottle of expensive Scotch, soak your body in a hot bath and forget. Damn right, he thought. He turned and walked out of the washroom.

He jolted to a halt, his breath cut off. Standing rooted, heartbeat hammering at his chest, he gaped through the front window of the cafe.

The truck and trailer were parked outside.

Mann stared at them in unbelieving shock. It wasn't possible. He'd seen them roaring by at top speed. The driver had won; he'd *won!* He'd had the whole damn highway to himself! *Why had he turned back?*

Mann looked around with sudden dread. There were five men eating, three along the counter, two in booths.

He cursed himself for having failed to look at faces when he'd entered. Now there was no way of knowing who it was. Mann felt his legs begin to shake.

Abruptly, he walked to the nearest booth and slid in clumsily behind the table. Now wait, he told himself; just wait. Surely, he could tell which one it was. Masking his face with the menu, he glanced across its top. Was it that one in the khaki work shirt? Mann tried to see the man's hands but couldn't. His gaze flicked nervously across the room. Not that one in the suit, of course. Three remaining. That one in the front booth, square-faced, black-haired? If only he could see the man's hands, it might help. One of the two others at the counter? Mann studied them uneasily. Why hadn't he looked at faces when he'd come in?

Now *wait,* he thought. Goddamn it, *wait!* All right, the truck driver was in here. That didn't automatically signify that he meant to continue the insane duel. Chuck's Cafe might be the only place to eat for miles around. It *was* lunchtime, wasn't it? The truck driver had probably intended to eat here all the time. He'd just been moving too fast to pull into the parking lot before. So he'd slowed down, turned around and driven back, that was all. Mann forced himself to read the menu. Right, he thought. No point in getting so rattled. Perhaps a beer would help relax him.

The woman behind the counter came over and Mann ordered a ham sandwich on rye toast and a bottle of Coors. As the woman turned away, he wondered, with a sudden twinge of self-reproach, why he hadn't simply left the cafe, jumped into his car and sped away. He would have known immediately, then, if the truck driver was still out to get him. As it was, he'd have to suffer through an entire meal to find out. He almost groaned at his stupidity.

Still, what if the truck driver *had* followed him out and started after him again? He'd have been right back where he'd started. Even if he'd managed to get a good lead, the truck driver would have overtaken him eventually. It just wasn't in him to drive at 80 and 90 miles an hour in order to stay ahead. True, he might have been intercepted by a California Highway Patrol car. What if he weren't though?

Mann repressed the plaguing thoughts. He tried to calm himself. He looked deliberately at the four men. Either of two seemed a likely possibility as the driver of the truck: the square-faced one in the front booth and the chunky one in the jumpsuit sitting at the counter. Mann had an impulse to walk over to them and ask which one it was, tell the man he was sorry he'd irritated him, tell him anything to calm him, since, obviously, he wasn't rational, was a manic-depressive, probably. Maybe buy the man a beer and sit with him awhile to try to settle things.

He couldn't move. What if the truck driver were letting the whole thing drop? Mightn't his approach rile the man all over again? Mann felt drained by indecision. He nodded weakly as the waitress set the sandwich and the bottle in front of him. He took a swallow of the beer, which made him cough. Was the truck driver amused by the sound? Mann felt a stirring of resentment deep inside himself. What right did that bastard have to impose this torment on another human being? It was a free country, wasn't it? Damn it, he had every right to pass the son of a bitch on a highway if he wanted to!

"Oh, hell," he mumbled. He tried to feel amused. He was making entirely too much of this. Wasn't he? He glanced at the pay telephone on the front wall. What was to prevent him from calling the local police and telling them the situation? But, then, he'd have to stay here, lose time, make Forbes angry, probably lose the sale. And what if the truck driver stayed to face them? Naturally, he'd deny the whole thing. What if the police believed him and didn't do anything about it? After they'd gone, the truck driver would undoubtedly take it out on him again, only worse. *God!* Mann thought in agony.

The sandwich tasted flat, the beer unpleasantly sour. Mann stared at the table as he ate. For God's sake, why was he just *sitting* here like this? He was a grown man, wasn't he? Why didn't he settle this damn thing once and for all?

His left hand twitched so unexpectedly, he spilled beer on his trousers. The man in the jumpsuit had risen from the counter and was strolling toward the front of the cafe. Mann felt his heartbeat thumping as the man gave money to the waitress, took his change and a toothpick from the dispenser and went outside. Mann watched in anxious silence.

The man did not get into the cab of the tanker truck.

It had to be the one in the front booth, then. His face took form in Mann's remembrance: square, with dark eyes, dark hair; the man who'd tried to kill him.

Mann stood abruptly, letting impulse conquer fear. Eyes fixed ahead, he started toward the entrance. Anything was preferable to sitting in that booth. He stopped by the cash register, conscious of the hitching of his chest as he gulped in air. Was the man observing him? he wondered. He swallowed, pulling out the clip of dollar bills in his right-hand trouser pocket. He glanced toward the waitress. Come *on,* he thought. He looked at his check and, seeing the amount, reached shakily into his trouser pocket for change. He heard a coin fall onto the floor and roll away. Ignoring it, he dropped a dollar and a quarter onto the counter and thrust the clip of bills into his trouser pocket.

As he did, he heard the man in the front booth get up. An icy shudder spasmed up his back. Turning quickly to the door, he shoved it open, seeing, on the edges of his vision, the square-faced man approach the cash register. Lurching from the cafe, he started toward his car with long strides. His mouth was dry again. The pounding of his heart was painful in his chest.

Suddenly, he started running. He heard the cafe door bang shut and fought away the urge to look across his shoulder. Was that a sound of other running footsteps now? Reaching his car, Mann yanked open the door and jarred in awkwardly behind the steering wheel. He reached into his trouser pocket for the keys and snatched them out, almost dropping them. His hand was shaking so badly he couldn't get the ignition key into its slot. He whined with mounting dread. Come on! he thought.

The key slid in, he twisted it convulsively. The motor started and he raced it momentarily before jerking the transmission shift to drive. Depressing the accelerator pedal quickly, he raked the car around and steered it toward the highway. From the corners of his eyes, he saw the truck and trailer being backed away from the cafe.

Reaction burst inside him. "No!" he raged and slammed his foot down on the brake pedal. This was idiotic! Why the hell should he run away? His car slid sideways to a rocking halt and, shouldering out the door, he lurched to his feet and started toward the truck with angry strides. *All right, Jack,* he thought. He glared at the man inside the truck. You want to punch my nose, okay, but no more goddamn tournament on the highway.

The truck began to pick up speed. Mann raised his right arm. "Hey!" he yelled. He knew the driver saw him. *"Hey!"* He started running as the truck kept moving, engine grinding loudly. It was on the highway now. He sprinted toward it with a sense of martyred outrage. The driver shifted gears, the truck moved faster. "Stop!" Mann shouted. "Damn it, *stop!"*

He thudded to a panting halt, staring at the truck as it receded down the highway, moved around a hill and disappeared. "You son of a bitch," he muttered. "You goddamn, miserable son of a bitch."

He trudged back slowly to his car, trying to believe that the truck driver had fled the hazard of a fistfight. It was possible, of course, but, somehow, he could not believe it.

He got into his car and was about to drive onto the highway when he changed his mind and switched the motor off. That crazy bastard might just be tooling along at 15 miles an hour, waiting for him to catch up. Nuts to that, he thought. So he blew his schedule; screw it. Forbes would have to wait, that was all. And if Forbes didn't care to wait, that was all right, too. He'd sit here for a while and let the nut get out of range, let him think he'd won the day. He grinned. You're the bloody Red Baron, Jack; you've shot me down. Now go to hell with my sincerest compliments. He shook his head. Beyond belief, he thought.

He really should have done this earlier, pulled over, waited. Then the truck driver would have had to let it pass. *Or picked on someone else,* the startling thought occurred to him. Jesus, maybe that was how the crazy bastard whiled away his work hours! Jesus Christ Almighty! was it possible?

He looked at the dashboard clock. It was just past 12:30. Wow, he thought. All that in less than an hour. He shifted on the seat and stretched his legs out. Leaning back against the door, he closed his eyes and mentally perused the things he had to do tomorrow and the following day. Today was shot to hell, as far as he could see.

When he opened his eyes, afraid of drifting into sleep and losing too much time, almost eleven minutes had passed. The nut must be an ample distance off by now, he thought; at least 11 miles and likely more, the way he drove. Good enough. He wasn't going to try to make San Francisco on schedule now, anyway. He'd take it real easy.

Mann adjusted his safety belt, switched on the motor, tapped the transmission pointer into drive position and pulled onto the highway, glancing back across his shoulder. Not a car in sight. Great day for driving. Everybody was staying at home. That nut must have a reputation around here. When Crazy Jack is on the highway, lock your car in the garage. Mann chuckled at the notion as his car began to turn the curve ahead.

Mindless reflex drove his right foot down against the brake pedal. Suddenly, his car had skidded to a halt and he was staring down the highway. The truck and trailer were parked on the shoulder less than 90 yards away.

Mann couldn't seem to function. He knew his car was blocking the westbound lane, knew that he should either make a U-turn or pull off the highway, but all he could do was gape at the truck.

He cried out, legs retracting, as a horn blast sounded behind him. Snapping up his head, he looked at the rearview mirror, gasping as he saw a yellow station wagon bearing down on him at high speed. Suddenly, it veered off toward the eastbound lane, disappearing from the mirror. Mann jerked around and saw it hurtling past his car, its rear end snapping back and forth, its back tires screeching. He saw the twisted features of the man inside, saw his lips move rapidly with cursing.

Then the station wagon had swerved back into the westbound lane and was speeding off. It gave Mann an odd sensation to see it pass the truck. The man in that station wagon could drive on, unthreatened. Only he'd been singled out. What happened was demented. Yet it was happening.

He drove his car onto the highway shoulder and braked. Putting the transmission into neutral, he leaned back, staring at the truck. His head was aching again. There was a pulsing at his temples like the ticking of a muffled clock.

What was he to do? He knew very well that if he left his car to walk to the truck, the driver would pull away and repark farther down the highway. He may as well face the fact that he was dealing with a madman. He felt the tremor in his stomach muscles starting up again. His heartbeat thudded slowly, striking at his chest wall. Now what?

With a sudden, angry impulse, Mann snapped the transmission into gear and stepped down hard on the accelerator pedal. The tires of the car spun sizzlingly before they gripped; the car shot out onto the highway. Instantly, the truck began to move. He even had the motor on! Mann thought in raging fear. He floored the pedal, then, abruptly, realized he couldn't make it, that the truck would block his way and he'd collide with its trailer. A vision flashed across his mind, a fiery explosion and a sheet of flame incinerating him. He started braking fast, trying to decelerate evenly, so he wouldn't lose control.

When he'd slowed down enough to feel that it was safe, he steered the car onto the shoulder and stopped it again, throwing the transmission into neutral.

Approximately eighty yards ahead, the truck pulled off the highway and stopped.

Mann tapped his fingers on the steering wheel. *Now* what? he thought. Turn around and head east until he reached a cutoff that would take him to San Francisco by another route? How did he know the truck driver wouldn't follow him even then? His cheeks twisted as he bit his lips together angrily. No! He wasn't going to turn around!

His expression hardened suddenly. Well, he wasn't going to *sit* here all day, that was certain. Reaching out, he tapped the gearshift into drive and steered his car onto the highway once again. He saw the massive truck and trailer start to move but made no effort to speed up. He tapped at the brakes, taking a position about 30 yards behind the trailer. He glanced at his speedometer. Forty miles an hour. The truck driver had his left arm out of the cab window and was waving him on. What did that mean? Had he changed his mind? Decided, finally, that this thing had gone too far? Mann couldn't let himself believe it.

He looked ahead. Despite the mountain ranges all around, the highway was flat as far as he could see. He tapped a fingernail against the horn bar, trying to make up his mind. Presumably, he could continue all the way to San Francisco at this speed, hanging back just far enough to avoid the worst of the exhaust fumes. It didn't seem likely that the truck driver would stop directly on the highway to block his way. And if the truck driver pulled onto the shoulder to let him pass, he could pull off the highway, too. It would be a draining afternoon but a safe one.

On the other hand, outracing the truck might be worth just one more try. This was obviously what that son of a bitch wanted. Yet, surely, a vehicle of such size couldn't be driven with the same daring as, potentially, his own. The laws of mechanics were against it, if nothing else. Whatever advantage the truck had in mass, it had to lose in stability, particularly that of its trailer. If Mann were to drive at, say, 80 miles an hour and there were a few steep grades—as he felt sure there were—the truck would have to fall behind.

The question was, of course, whether he had the nerve to maintain such a speed over a long distance. He'd never done it before. Still, the more he thought about it, the more it appealed to him; far more than the alternative did.

Abruptly, he decided. *Right,* he thought. He checked ahead, then pressed down hard on the accelerator pedal and pulled into the eastbound lane. As he neared the truck, he tensed, anticipating that the driver might block his way. But the truck did not shift from the westbound lane. Mann's car moved along its mammoth side. He glanced at the cab and saw the name KELLER printed on its door. For a shocking instant, he thought it read KILLER and started to slow down. Then, glancing at the name again, he saw what it really was and depressed the pedal sharply. When he saw the truck reflected in the rearview mirror, he steered his car into the westbound lane.

He shuddered, dread and satisfaction mixed together, as he saw that the truck driver was speeding up. It was strangely comforting to know the man's intentions definitely again. That plus the knowledge of his face and name seemed, somehow, to reduce his stature. Before, he had been faceless, nameless, an embodiment of unknown terror. Now, at least, he was an individual. All right, Keller, said his mind, let's see you beat me with that purple-silver relic now. He pressed down harder on the pedal. *Here we go,* he thought.

He looked at the speedometer, scowling as he saw that he was doing only 74 miles an hour. Deliberately, he pressed down on the pedal, alternating his gaze between the highway ahead and the speedometer until the needle turned past 80. He felt a flickering of satisfaction with himself. All right, Keller, you son of a bitch, top that, he thought.

After several moments, he glanced into the rearview mirror again. Was the truck getting closer? Stunned, he checked the speedometer. Damn it! He was down to 76! He forced in the accelerator pedal angrily. *He mustn't go less than 80!* Mann's chest shuddered with convulsive breath.

He glanced aside as he hurtled past a beige sedan parked on the shoulder underneath a tree. A young couple sat inside it, talking. Already they were far behind, their world removed from his. Had they even glanced aside when he'd passed? He doubted it.

He started as the shadow of an overhead bridge whipped across the hood and windshield. Inhaling raggedly, he glanced at the speedometer again. He was holding at 81. He checked the rearview mirror. Was it his imagination that the truck was gaining ground? He looked forward with anxious eyes. There had to be some kind of town ahead. To hell with time; he'd stop at the police station and tell them what had happened. They'd have to believe him. Why would he stop to tell them such a story if it weren't true? For all he knew, Keller had a police record in these parts. *Oh, sure, we're on to him,* he heard a faceless officer remark. *That crazy bastard's asked for it before and now he's going to get it.*

Mann shook himself and looked at the mirror. The truck *was* getting closer. Wincing, he glanced at the speedometer. Goddamn it, pay attention! raged his mind. He was down to 74 again! Whining with frustration, he depressed the pedal. Eighty!—80! he demanded of himself. There was a murderer behind him!

His car began to pass a field of flowers; lilacs, Mann saw, white and purple stretching out in endless rows. There was a small shack near the highway, the words FIELD FRESH FLOWER painted on it. A brown-cardboard square was propped against the shack, the word FUNERALS printed crudely on it. Mann saw himself, abruptly, lying in a casket, painted like some grotesque mannequin. The overpowering smell of flowers seemed to fill his nostrils. Ruth and the children sitting in the first row, heads bowed. All his relatives—

Suddenly, the pavement roughened and the car began to bounce and shudder, driving bolts of pain into his head. He felt the steering wheel resisting him and clamped his hands around it tightly, harsh vibrations running up his arms. He didn't dare look at the mirror now. He had to force himself to keep the speed unchanged. Keller wasn't going to slow down; he was sure of that. *What if he got a flat tire, though?* All control would vanish in an instant. He visualized the somersaulting of his car, its grinding, shrieking tumble, the explosion of its gas tank, his body crushed and burned and—

The broken span of pavement ended and his gaze jumped quickly to the rearview mirror. The truck was no closer, but it hadn't lost ground, either. Mann's eyes shifted. Up ahead were hills and mountains. He tried to reassure himself that upgrades were on his side, that he could climb them at the same speed he was going now. Yet all he could imagine were the downgrades, the immense truck close behind him, slamming violently into his car and knocking it across some cliff edge. He had a horrifying vision of dozens of broken, rusted cars lying unseen in the canyons ahead, corpses in every one of them, all flung to shattering deaths by Keller.

Mann's car went rocketing into a corridor of trees. On each side of the highway was a eucalyptus windbreak, each trunk three feet from the next. It was like speeding through a high-walled canyon. Mann gasped, twitching, as a large twig bearing dusty leaves dropped down across the windshield, then slid out of sight. Dear God! he thought. He was getting near the edge himself. If he should lose his nerve at this speed, it was over. Jesus! That would be ideal for Keller! he realized suddenly. He visualized the square-faced driver laughing as he passed the burning wreckage, knowing that he'd killed his prey without so much as touching him.

Mann started as his car shot out into the open. The route ahead was not straight now but winding up into the foothills. Mann willed himself to press down on the pedal even more. Eighty-three now, almost 84.

To his left was a broad terrain of green hills blending into mountains. He saw a black car on a dirt road, moving toward the highway. *Was its side painted white?* Mann's heartbeat lurched. Impulsively, he jammed the heel of his right hand down against the horn bar and held it there. The blast of the horn was shrill and racking to his ears. His heart began to pound. Was it a police car? *Was it?*

He let the horn bar up abruptly. *No, it wasn't.* Damn! his mind raged. Keller must have been amused by his pathetic efforts. Doubtless, he was chuckling to himself right now. He heard the truck driver's voice in his mind, coarse and sly. *You think you gonna get a cop to save you, boy? Shee-it. You gonna die.* Mann's heart contorted with savage hatred. *You son of a bitch!* he thought. Jerking his right hand into a fist, he drove it down against the seat. Goddamn you, Keller! I'm going to kill you, if it's the last thing I do!

The hills were closer now. There would be slopes directly, long steep grades. Mann felt a burst of hope within himself. He was sure to gain a lot of distance on the truck. No matter how he tried, that bastard Keller couldn't manage 80 miles an hour on a hill. But *I* can! cried his mind with fierce elation. He worked up saliva in his mouth and swallowed it. The back of his shirt was drenched. He could feel sweat trickling down his sides. A bath and a drink, first order of the day on reaching San Francisco. A long, hot bath, a long, cold drink. Cutty Sark. He'd splurge, by Christ. He rated it.

The car swept up a shallow rise. Not steep enough, goddamn it! The truck's momentum would prevent its losing speed. Mann felt mindless hatred for the landscape. Already, he had topped the rise and tilted over to a shallow downgrade. He looked at the rearview mirror. *Square,* he thought, everything about the truck was square: the radiator grille, the fender shapes, the bumper ends, the outline of the cab, even the shape of Keller's hands and face. He visualized the truck as some great entity pursuing him, insentient, brutish, chasing him with instinct only.

Mann cried out, horror-stricken, as he saw the ROAD REPAIRS sign up ahead. His frantic gaze leaped down the highway. Both lanes blocked, a huge black arrow pointing toward the alternate route! He groaned in anguish, seeing it was dirt. His foot jumped automatically to the brake pedal and started pumping it. He threw a dazed look at the rearview mirror. The truck was moving as fast as ever! It *couldn't,* though! Mann's expression froze in terror as he started turning to the right.

He stiffened as the front wheels hit the dirt road. For an instant, he was certain that the back part of the car was going to spin; he felt it breaking to the left. "No, don't!" he cried. Abruptly, he was jarring down the dirt road, elbows braced against his sides, trying to keep from losing control. His tires battered at the ruts, almost tearing the wheel from his grip. The windows rattled noisily. His neck snapped back and forth with painful jerks. His jolting body surged against the binding of the safety belt and slammed down violently on the seat. He felt the bouncing of the car drive up his spine. His clenching teeth slipped and he cried out hoarsely as his upper teeth gouged deep into his lip.

He gasped as the rear end of the car began surging to the right. He started to jerk the steering wheel to the left, then, hissing, wrenched it in the opposite direction, crying out as the right rear fender cracked into a fence pole, knocking it down. He started pumping at the brakes, struggling to regain control. The car rear yawed sharply to the left, tires shooting out a spray of dirt. Mann felt a scream tear upward in his throat. He twisted wildly at the steering wheel. The car began careening to the right. He hitched the wheel around until the car was on course again. His head was pounding like his heart now, with gigantic, throbbing spasms. He started coughing as he gagged on dripping blood.

The dirt road ended suddenly, the car regained momentum on the pavement and he dared to look at the rearview mirror. The truck was slowed down but was still behind him, rocking like a freighter on a storm-tossed sea, its huge tires scouring up a pall of dust. Mann shoved in the accelerator pedal and his car surged forward. A good, steep grade lay just ahead; he'd gain that distance now. He swallowed blood, grimacing at the taste, then fumbled in his trouser pocket and tugged out his handkerchief. He pressed it to his bleeding lip, eyes fixed on the slope ahead. Another fifty yards or so. He writhed his back. His undershirt was soaking wet, adhering to his skin. He glanced at the rearview mirror. The truck had just regained the highway. *Tough!* he thought with venom. Didn't get me, did you, Keller?

His car was on the first yards of the upgrade when steam began to issue from beneath its hood. Mann stiffened suddenly, eyes widening with shock. The steam increased, became a smoking mist. Mann's gaze jumped down. The red light hadn't flashed on yet but had to in a moment. How could this be happening? Just as he was set to get away! The slope ahead was long and gradual, with many curves. He knew he couldn't stop. Could he

U-turn unexpectedly and go back down? the sudden thought occurred. He looked ahead. The highway was too narrow, bound by hills on both sides. There wasn't room enough to make an uninterrupted turn and there wasn't time enough to ease around. If he tried that, Keller would shift direction and hit him head-on. "Oh, my God!" Mann murmured suddenly.

He was going to die.

He stared ahead with stricken eyes, his view increasingly obscured by steam. Abruptly, he recalled the afternoon he'd had the engine steam-cleaned at the local car wash. The man who'd done it had suggested he replace the water hoses, because steam-cleaning had a tendency to make them crack. He'd nodded, thinking that he'd do it when he had more time. *More time!* The phrase was like a dagger in his mind. He'd failed to change the hoses and, for that failure, he was now about to die.

He sobbed in terror as the dashboard light flashed on. He glanced at it involuntarily and read the word HOT, black on red. With a breathless gasp, he jerked the transmission into low. Why hadn't he done that right away! He looked ahead. The slope seemed endless. Already, he could hear a boiling throb inside the radiator. How much coolant was there left? Steam was clouding faster, hazing up the windshield. Reaching out, he twisted at a dashboard knob. The wipers started flicking back and forth in fan-shaped sweeps. There had to be enough coolant in the radiator to get him to the top. *Then* what? cried his mind. He couldn't drive without coolant, even downhill. He glanced at the rearview mirror. The truck was falling behind. Mann snarled with maddened fury. *If it weren't for that goddamned hose, he'd be escaping now!*

The sudden lurching of the car snatched him back to terror. If he braked now, he could jump out, run and scrabble up that slope. Later, he might not have the time. He couldn't make himself stop the car, though. As long as it kept on running, he felt bound to it, less vulnerable. God knows what would happen if he left it.

Mann started up the slope with haunted eyes, trying not to see the red light on the edges of his vision. Yard by yard, his car was slowing down. Make it, make it, pleaded his mind, even though he thought that it was futile. The car was running more and more unevenly. The thumping percolation of its radiator filled his ears. Any moment now, the motor would be choked off and the car would shudder to a stop, leaving him a sitting target. *No,* he thought. He tried to blank his mind.

He was almost to the top, but in the mirror he could see the truck drawing up on him. He jammed down on the pedal and the motor made a grinding noise. He groaned. It had to make the top! Please, God, help me! screamed his mind. The ridge was just ahead. Closer. Closer. Make it. "Make it." The car was shuddering and clanking, slowing down—oil, smoke and steam gushing from beneath the hood. The windshield wipers swept from side to side. Mann's head throbbed. Both his hands felt numb. His heartbeat pounded as he stared ahead. Make it, please, God, make it. Make it. *Make* it!

Over! Mann's lips opened in a cry of triumph as the car began descending. Hand shaking uncontrollably, he shoved the transmission into neutral and let the car go into a glide. The triumph strangled in his throat as he saw that there was nothing in sight but hills and more hills. Never mind! He was on a downgrade now, a long one. He passed a sign that read, TRUCKS USE LOW GEARS NEXT 12 MILES. Twelve miles! Something would come up. It had to.

The car began to pick up speed. Mann glanced at the speedometer. Forty-seven miles an hour. The red light still burned. He'd save the motor for a long time, too, though; let it cool for twelve miles, if the truck was far enough behind.

His speed increased. Fifty . . . 51. Mann watched the needle turning slowly toward the right. He glanced at the rearview mirror. The truck had not appeared yet. With a little luck, he might still get a good lead. Not as good as he might have if the motor hadn't overheated but enough to work with. There had to be some place along the way to stop. The needle edged past 55 and started toward the 60 mark.

Again, he looked at the rearview mirror, jolting as he saw that the truck had topped the ridge and was on its way down. He felt his lips begin to shake and crimped them together. His gaze jumped fitfully between the steam-obscured highway and the mirror. The truck was accelerating rapidly. Keller doubtless had the gas pedal floored. It wouldn't be long before the truck caught up to him. Mann's right hand twitched unconsciously toward the gearshift. Noticing, he jerked it back, grimacing, glanced at the speedometer. The car's velocity had just passed 60. Not enough! He had to use the motor now! He reached out desperately.

His right hand froze in midair as the motor stalled; then, shooting out the hand, he twisted the ignition key. The motor made a grinding noise but wouldn't start. Mann glanced up, saw that he was almost on the shoulder, jerked the steering wheel around. Again, he turned the key, but there was no response. He looked up at the rearview mirror. The truck was gaining on him swiftly. He glanced at the speedometer. The car's speed was fixed at 62. Mann felt himself crushed in a vise of panic. He stared ahead with haunted eyes.

Then he saw it, several hundred yards ahead: an escape route for trucks with burned-out brakes. There was no alternative now. Either he took the turnout or his car would be rammed from behind. The truck was frighteningly close. He heard the high-pitched wailing of its motor. Unconsciously, he started easing to the right, then jerked the wheel back suddenly. He mustn't give the move away! He had to wait until the last possible moment. Otherwise, Keller would follow him in.

Just before he reached the escape route, Mann

wrenched the steering wheel around. The car rear started breaking to the left, tires shrieking on the pavement. Mann steered with the skid, braking just enough to keep from losing all control. The rear tires grabbed and, at 60 miles an hour, the car shot up the dirt trail, tires slinging up a cloud of dust. Mann began to hit the brakes. The rear wheels sideslipped and the car slammed hard against the dirt bank to the right. Mann gasped as the car bounced off and started to fishtail with violent whipping motions, angling toward the trail edge. He drove his foot down on the brake pedal with all his might. The car rear skidded to the right and slammed against the bank again. Mann heard a grinding rend of metal and felt himself heaved downward suddenly, his neck snapped, as the car plowed to a violent halt.

As in a dream, Mann turned to see the truck and trailer swerving off the highway. Paralyzed, he watched the massive vehicle hurtle toward him, staring at it with a blank detachment, knowing he was going to die but so stupefied by the sight of the looming truck that he couldn't react. The gargantuan shape roared closer, blotting out the sky. Mann felt a strange sensation in his throat, unaware that he was screaming.

Suddenly, the truck began to tilt. Mann stared at it in choked-off silence as it started tipping over like some ponderous beast toppling in slow motion. Before it reached his car, it vanished from his rear window.

Hands palsied, Mann undid the safety belt and opened the door. Struggling from the car, he stumbled to the trail edge, staring downward. He was just in time to see the truck capsize like a foundering ship. The tanker followed, huge wheels spinning as it overturned.

The storage tank on the truck exploded first, the violence of its detonation causing Mann to stagger back and sit down clumsily on the dirt. A second explosion roared below, its shock wave buffeting across him hotly, making his ears hurt. His glazed eyes saw a fiery column shoot up toward the sky in front of him, then another.

Mann crawled slowly to the trail edge and peered down at the canyon. Enormous gouts of flame were towering upward, topped by thick, black, oily smoke. He couldn't see the truck or trailer, only flames. He gaped at them in shock, all feeling drained from him.

Then, unexpectedly, emotion came. Not dread, at first, and not regret; not the nausea that followed soon. It was a primeval tumult in his mind: the cry of some ancestral beast above the body of its vanquished foe.

Edgar Pangborn (1909–1976)

LONGTOOTH

Edgar Pangborn was one of the most admired fantasy and science fiction writers of the 1950s-70s. He wrote two classic novels of the genre, *A Mirror for Observers*, winner of the International Fantasy Award (1954) and *Davy* (1954), and a number of highly regarded short stories, many of them set in the same future world as the latter novel. He also wrote historical fiction. His work is notable for its precise and polished prose style and for his ability to round characters, in a field where either talent is comparatively rare. His few horror stories were mostly cast in the science fiction mode, with the exception of ''Longtooth,'' his masterpiece. A monster story set in the Maine woods, it is an unusual piece of pastoral horror in the tradition of Algernon Blackwood, with perhaps an admixture of Theodore Sturgeon, a writer who admired Pangborn and to whom Pangborn was often compared. The mixture of horror of, and compassion for, the monster together with the suggestion of a scientific rationale places ''Longtooth'' firmly in the twentieth century horror tradition.

M y word is good. How can I prove it? Born in Darkfield, wasn't I? Stayed away thirty more years after college, but when I returned I was still Ben Dane, one of the Darkfield Danes, Judge Marcus Dane's eldest.

And they knew my word was good. My wife died and I sickened of all cities; then my bachelor brother Sam died, too, who'd lived all his life here in Darkfield, running his one-man law office over in Lohman—our nearest metropolis, pop. 6437. A fast coronary at fifty; I had loved him. Helen gone, then Sam—I wound up my unimportances and came home, inheriting Sam's house-keeper Adelaide Simmons, her grim stability and celestial cooking. Nostalgia for Maine is a serious matter, late in life: I had to yield. I expected a gradual drift into my childless old age playing correspondence chess, translating a few of the classics. I thought I could take for granted the continued respect of my neighbors. I say my word is good.

I will remember again that middle of March a few years ago, the snow skimming out of an afternoon sky as dirty as the bottom of an old aluminum pot. Harp Ryder's back road had been plowed since the last snowfall; I supposed Bolt-Bucket could make the mile and a half in to his farm and out again before we got caught. Harp had asked me to get him a book if I was making a trip to Boston, any goddamn book that told about Eskimos, and I had one for him, De Poncins's *Kabloona*. I saw the midget devils of white running crazy down a huge slope of wind, and recalled hearing at the Darkfield News Bureau, otherwise Cleve's General Store, somebody mentioning a forecast of the worst blizzard in forty years. Joe Cleve, who won't permit a radio in the store because it pesters his ulcers, inquired of his Grand Inquisitor who dwells ten yards behind your right shoulder: "Why's it always got to be the worst in so-and-so many years, that going to help anybody?" The bureau was still analyzing this difficult inquiry when I left, with my cigarettes and as much as I could remember of Adelaide's grocery list after leaving it on the dining table. It wasn't yet three when I turned in on Harp's back road, and a gust slammed at Bolt-Bucket like death with a shovel.

I tried to win momentum for the rise to the high ground, swerved to avoid an idiot rabbit and hit instead a patch of snow-hidden melt-and-freeze, skidding to a full stop from which nothing would extract me but a tow.

I was fifty-seven that year, my wind bad from too much smoking and my heart (I now know) no stronger than Sam's. I quit cursing—gradually, to avoid sudden actions—and tucked *Kabloona* under my parka. I would walk the remaining mile to Ryder's, stay just to leave the book, say hello, and phone for a tow; then, since Harp never owned a car and never would, I could walk back and meet the truck.

If Leda Ryder knew how to drive, it didn't matter much after she married Harp. They farmed it, back in there, in almost the manner of Harp's ancestors of Jefferson's time. Harp did keep his two hundred laying hens by methods that were considered modern before the poor wretches got condemned to batteries, but his other enterprises came closer to antiquity. In his big kitchen garden he let one small patch of weeds fool themselves for an inch or two, so he'd have it to work at; they survived nowhere else. A few cows, a team, four acres for market crops, and a small dog Droopy, whose grandmother had made it somehow with a dachshund. Droopy's only menace in obese old age was a wheezing bark. The Ryders must have grown nearly all vital necessities except chewing tobacco and once in a while a new dress for Leda. Harp could snub the twentieth century, and I doubt if Leda was consulted about it in spite of his obsessive devotion for her. She was almost thirty years younger, and yes, he should not have married her. Other side up just as scratchy; she should not have married him, but she did.

Harp was a dinosaur perhaps, but I grew up with him, he a year the younger. We swam, fished, helled around together. And when I returned to Darkfield growing old, he was one of the few who acted glad to see me, so far as you can trust what you read in a face like a granite promontory. Maybe twice a week Harp Ryder smiled.

I pushed on up the ridge, and noticed a going-and-coming set of wide tire tracks already blurred with snow. That would be the egg truck I had passed a quarter hour since on the main road. Whenever the west wind at my back lulled, I could swing around and enjoy one of my favorite prospects of birch and hemlock lowland. From Ryder's Ridge there's no sign of Darkfield two miles southwest except one church spire. On clear days you glimpse Bald Mountain and his two big brothers, more than twenty miles west of us.

The snow was thickening. It brought relief and pleasure to see the black shingles of Harp's barn and the roof of his Cape Codder. Foreshortened, so that it looked snug against the barn; actually house and barn were connected by a two-story shed fifteen feet wide and forty feet long—woodshed below, hen loft above. The Ryders' sunrise-facing bedroom window was set only three feet above the eaves of that shed roof. They truly went to bed with the chickens. I shouted, for Harp was about to close the big shed door. He held it for me. I ran, and the storm ran after me. The west wind was bouncing off the barn; eddies howled at us. The temperature had tumbled ten degrees since I left Darkfield. The thermometer by the shed door read fifteen degrees, and I knew I'd been a damn fool. As I helped Harp fight the shed door closed, I thought I heard Leda, crying.

A swift confused impression. The wind was exploring new ranges of passion, the big door squawked, and Harp was asking: "Ca' break down?" I do still think I heard Leda wail. If so, it ended as we got the door latched and Harp drew a newly fitted two-by-four bar across it. I couldn't understand that: the old latch was surely proof against any wind short of a hurricane.

"Bolt-Bucket never breaks down. Ought to get one, Harp—lots of company. All she did was go in the ditch."

"You might see her again come spring." His hens were scratching overhead, not yet scared by the storm. Harp's eyes were small gray glitters of trouble. "Ben, you figure a man's getting old at fifty-six?"

"No." My bones (getting old) ached for the warmth of his kitchen-dining-living-everything room, not for sad philosophy. "Use your phone, okay?"

"If the wires ain't down," he said, not moving, a man beaten on by other storms. "Them loafers didn't cut none of the overhang branches all summer. I told 'em of course, I told 'em how it would be . . . I meant, Ben, old enough to get dumb fancies?" My face may have told him I thought he was brooding about himself with a young wife. He frowned, annoyed that I hadn't taken his meaning. "I meant, *seeing* things. Things that can't be so, but—"

"We can all do some of that at any age, Harp."

That remark was a stupid brushoff, a stone for bread, because I was cold, impatient, wanted in. Harp had always a tense one-way sensitivity. His face chilled. "Well, come in, warm up. Leda ain't feeling too good. Getting a cold or something."

When she came downstairs and made me welcome, her eyes were reddened. I don't think the wind made that noise. Droopy waddled from her basket behind the stove to snuff my feet and give me my usual low passing mark.

Leda never had it easy there, young and passionate with scant mental resources. She was twenty-eight that year, looking tall because she carried her firm body handsomely. Some of the sullenness in her big mouth and lucid gray eyes was sexual challenge, some pure discontent. I liked Leda; her nature was not one for animosity or meanness. Before her marriage the Dark-field News Bureau used to declare with its customary scrupulous fairness that Leda had been covered by every goddamn thing in pants within thirty miles. For once the bureau may have spoken a grain of truth in the malice, for Leda did have the smoldering power that draws men

without word or gesture. After her abrupt marriage to
Harp—Sam told me all this; I wasn't living in Darkfield
then and hadn't met her—the garbage-gossip went hastily underground: enraging Harp Ryder was never healthy.

The phone wires weren't down, yet. While I waited for
the garage to answer, Harp said, "Ben, I can't let you
walk back in that. Stay over, huh?"

I didn't want to. It meant extra work and inconven-
ience for Leda, and I was ancient enough to crave my
known safe burrow. But I felt Harp wanted me to stay for
his own sake. I asked Jim Short at the garage to go ahead
with Bolt-Bucket if I wasn't there to meet him. Jim
roared: "Know what it's doing right now?"

"Little spit of snow, looks like."

"Jesus!" He covered the mouthpiece imperfectly. I
heard his enthusiastic voice ring through cold-iron ech-
oes: "Hey, old Ben's got that thing into the ditch again!
Ain't that something . . . ? Listen, Ben, I can't make no
promises. Got both tow trucks out already. You better
stop over and praise the Lord you got that far."

"Okay," I said. "It wasn't much of a ditch."

Leda fed us coffee. She kept glancing toward the
landing at the foot of the stairs where a night-darkness
already prevailed. A closed-in stairway slanted down at a
never-used front door; beyond that landing was the other
ground floor room-parlor, spare, guestroom—where I
would sleep. I don't know what Leda expected to encounter in that shadow. Once when a chunk of firewood
made an odd noise in the range, her lips clamped shut on
a scream.

The coffee warmed me. By that time the weather left
no loophole for argument. Not yet 3:30, but west and
north were lost in furious black. Through the hissing
white flood I could just see the front of the barn forty feet
away. "Nobody's going no place into that," Harp said.
His little house shuddered, enforcing the words. "Leda,
you don't look too brisk. Get you some rest."

"I better see to the spare room for Ben."

Neither spoke with much tenderness, but it glowed openly in him when she turned her back. Then some other need bent his granite face out of its normal seams. His whole gaunt body leaning forward tried to help him talk. "You wouldn't figure me for a man'd go off his rocker?" he asked.

"Of course not. What's biting, Harp?"

"There's something in the woods, got no right to be there." To me that came as a letdown of relief: I would not have to listen to another's marriage problems. "I wish, b'Jesus Christ, it would hit somebody else once, so I could say what I know and not be laughed at all to hell. I *ain't* one for dumb fancies."

You walked on eggs, with Harp. He might decide any minute that *I* was laughing. "Tell me," I said. "If anything's out there now, it must feel a mite chilly."

"Ayah." He went to the north window, looking out where we knew the road lay under white confusion. Harp's land sloped down the other side of the road to the edge of mighty evergreen forest. Katahdin stands more than fifty miles north and a little east of us. We live in a withering shrink-world, but you could still set out from Harp's farm and, except for the occasional country road and the rivers—not many large ones—you could stay in deep forest all the way to the tundra, or Alaska. Harp said, "This kind of weather is when it comes."

He sank into his beat-up kitchen armchair and reached for *Kabloona*. He had barely glanced at the book while Leda was with us. "Funny name."

"Kabloona's an Eskimo word for white man."

"He done these pictures . . . ? Be they good, Ben?"

"I like 'em. Photographs in the back."

"Oh." He turned the pages hastily for those, but studied only the ones that showed the strong Eskimo faces, and his interest faded. Whatever he wanted was not here. "These people, be they—civilized?"

"In their own way, sure."

"Ayah, this guy looks like he could find his way in the woods."

"Likely the one thing he couldn't do, Harp. They never see a tree unless they come south, and they hate to do that. Anything below the Arctic is too warm."

"That a fact . . . ? Well, it's a nice book. How much was it?" I'd found it secondhand; he paid me to the exact penny. "I'll be glad to read it." He never would. It would end up on the shelf in the parlor with the Bible, an old almanac, a Longfellow, until someday this place went up for auction and nobody remembered Harp's way of living.

"What's this all about, Harp?"

"Oh . . . I was hearing things in the woods, back last summer. I'd think, fox, then I'd know it wasn't. Make your hair stand right on end. Lost a cow, last August, from the north pasture acrosst the rud. Section of board fence tore out. I mean, Ben, the two top boards was *pulled out from the nail holes.* No hammer marks."

"Bear?"

"Only track I found looked like bear except too small. You know a bear wouldn't *pull* it out, Ben."

"Cow slamming into it, panicked by something?"

He remained patient with me. "Ben, would I build a cow-pasture fence nailing the crosspieces from the outside? Cow hit it with all her weight she might bust it, sure. And kill herself doing it, be blood and hair all over the split boards, and she'd be there, not a mile and a half away into the woods. Happened during a big thunderstorm. I figured it had to be somebody with a spite ag'inst me, maybe some son of a bitch wanting the prop'ty, trying to scare me off that's lived here all my life and my family before me. But that don't make sense. I found the cow a week later, what was left. Way into the woods. The head and the bones. Hide tore up and flang around. Any *person* dressing off a beef, he'll cut whatever he wants and take off with it. He don't sit down and chaw the meat off the *bones,* b'Jesus Christ. He don't tear the thighbone out of the joint. . . . All right, maybe bear. But no bear did that job on that fence and then driv old Nell a mile and a half into the woods to kill her. Nice little Jersey, clever's a kitten. Leda used to make over her, like she don't usually do with the stock. . . . I've looked plenty in the woods since then, never turned up anything. Once and again I did smell something. Fishy, like bear-smell but—*different.*"

"But Harp, with snow on the ground—"

"Now you'll really call me crazy. When the weather is clear, I ain't once found his prints. I hear him then, at night, but I go out by daylight where I think the sound was, there's no trail. Just the usual snow tracks. I know. He lives in the trees and don't come down except when it's storming, I got to believe that? Because then he does come, Ben, when the weather's like now, like right now. And old Ned and Jerry out in the stable go wild, and sometimes we hear his noise under the window. I shine my flashlight through the glass—never catch sight of him. I go out with the ten gauge if there's any light to see by, and there's prints around the house—holes filling up with snow. By morning there'll be maybe some marks left, and they'll lead off to the north woods, but under the trees you won't find it. So he gets up in the branches and travels thataway? . . . Just once I have seen him, Ben. Last October. I better tell you one other thing first. A day or so after I found what was left of old Nell, I lost six roaster chickens. I made over a couple box stalls, maybe you remember, so the birds could be out on range and roost in the barn at night. Good doors, and I always locked 'em. Two in the morning, Ned and Jerry go crazy. I got out through the barn into the stable, and they was spooked, Ned trying to kick his way out. I got 'em quiet, looked all over the stable—loft, harness room, every-where. Not a thing. Dead quiet night, no moon. It had to be something the horses smelled. I come back into the barn, and found one of the chicken-pen doors open—

tore out from the lock. Chicken thief would bring along something to pry with—wouldn't he be a Christly idjut if he didn't . . . ? Took six birds, six nice eight-pound roasters, and left the heads on the floor—bitten off."

"Harp—some lunatic. People *can* go insane that way. There are old stories—"

"Been trying to believe that. Would a man live the winter out there? Twenty below zero?"

"Maybe a cave—animal skins."

"I've boarded up the whole back of the barn. Done the same with the hen-loft windows—two-by-fours with four-inch spikes driv slantwise. They be twelve feet off the ground, and he ain't come for 'em, not yet. . . . So after that happened I sent for Sheriff Robart. Son of a bitch happens to live in Darkfield, you'd think he might've took an interest."

"Do any good?"

Harp laughed. He did that by holding my stare, making no sound, moving no muscle except a disturbance at the eye corners. A New England art; maybe it came over on the *Mayflower*. "Robart he come by, after a while. I showed him that door. I showed him them chicken heads. Told him how I'd been spending my nights out there on my ass, with the ten gauge." Harp rose to unload tobacco juice into the range fire; he has a theory it purifies the air. "Ben, I might've showed him them chicken heads a shade close to his nose. By the time he got here, see, they wasn't all that fresh. He made out he'd look around and let me know. Mid-September. Ain't seen him since."

"Might've figured he wouldn't be welcome?"

"Why, he'd be welcome as shit on a tablecloth."

"You spoke of—seeing it, Harp?"

"Could call it seeing . . . all right. It was during them Indian summer days—remember? Like June except them pretty colors, smell of windfalls—God, I like that, I like October. I'd gone down to the slope acrosst the rud where I mended my fence after losing old Nell. Just leaning there, guess I was tired. Late afternoon, sky pinking up. You know how the fence cuts acrosst the slope to my east wood lot. I've let the bushes grow free—lot of elder, other stuff the birds come for. I was looking down toward that little break between the north woods and my wood lot, where a bit of old growed-up pasture shows through. Pretty spot. Painter fella come by a few years ago and done a picture of it, said the place looked like a coro, dunno what the hell that is, he didn't say."

I pushed at his brown study. "You saw it there?"

"No. Off to my right in them elder bushes. Fifty feet from me, I guess. By God, I didn't turn my head. I got it with the tail of my eye and turned the other way as if I meant to walk back to the rud. Made like busy with something in the grass, come wandering back to the fence some nearer. He stayed for me, a brownish patch in them bushes by the big yellow birch. Near the height of a man. No gun with me, not even a stick . . . Big shoulders, couldn't see his goddamn feet. He don't stand more'n five feet tall. His hands, if he's got real ones, hung out of my sight in a tangle of elder bushes. He's got brown fur, Ben, reddy-brown fur all over him. His face, too, his head, his big thick neck. There's a shine to fur in sunlight, you can't be mistook. So—I did look at him direct. Tried to act like I still didn't see him, but he knowed. He melted back and got the birch between him and me. Not a sound." And then Harp was listening for Leda upstairs. He went on softly: "Ayah, I ran back for a gun, and searched the woods, for all the good it did me. You'll want to know about his face. I ain't told Leda all this part. See, she's scared, I don't want to make it no worse, I just said it was some animal that snuck off before I could see it good. A big face, Ben. Head real human except it sticks out too much around the jaw. Not much nose—open spots in the fur. Ben, the—the *teeth!* I seen his mouth drop open and he pulled up one side of his lip to show me them stabbing things. I've seen as big as that on a full-growed bear. That's what I'll hear, I ever try to tell this. They'll say I seen a bear. Now, I shot my first bear when I was sixteen and Pa took me over toward Jackman. I've got me one maybe every other year since then. I know 'em, all their ways. But that's what I'll hear if I tell the story.''

I am a frustrated naturalist, loaded with assorted facts. I know there aren't any monkeys or apes that could stand our winters except maybe the harmless Himalayan langur. No such beast as Harp described lived anywhere on the planet. It didn't help. Harp was honest; he was rational; he wanted a reasonable explanation as much as I did. Harp wasn't the village atheist for nothing. I said, "I guess you will, Harp. People mostly won't take the—unusual.''

"Maybe you'll hear him tonight, Ben.''

Leda came downstairs, and heard part of that. "He's been telling you, Ben. What do you think?''

"I don't know what to think.''

"Led', I thought, if I imitate that noise for him—''

"No!'' She had brought some mending and was about to sit down with it, but froze as if threatened by attack. "I couldn't stand it, Harp. And—it might bring them.''

"Them?'' Harp chuckled uneasily. "I don't guess I could do it that good he'd come for it.''

"Don't *do* it, Harp!''

"All right, hon.'' Her eyes were closed, her head drooping back. "Don't git nerved up so.''

I started wondering whether a man still seeming sane could dream up such a horror for the unconscious purpose of tormenting a woman too young for him, a woman he could never imagine he owned. If he told her a fox bark wasn't right for a fox, she'd believe him. I said, "We shouldn't talk about it if it upsets her.''

He glanced at me like a man floating up from underwater. Leda said in a small, aching voice: "I wish to *God* we could move to Boston.''

The granite face closed in defensiveness. "Led', we

been over all that. Nothing is going to drive me off of my
land. I got no time for the city at my age. What the Jesus
would I do? Night watchman? Sweep out somebody's
back room, b'Jesus Christ? Savings'd be gone in no time.
We been all over it. We ain't moving nowhere."

"I could find work." For Harp, of course, that was the
worst thing she could have said. She probably knew it
from his stricken silence. She said clumsily, "I forgot
something upstairs." She snatched up her mending and
she was gone.

We talked no more of it the rest of the day. I followed
through the milking and other chores, lending a hand
where I could, and we made everything as secure as we
could against storm and other enemies. The long-
toothed furry thing was the spectral guest at dinner, but
we cut him, on Leda's account, or so we pretended.
Supper would have been awkward anyway. They weren't
in the habit of putting up guests, and Leda was a rather
deadly cook because she cared nothing about it. A
Darkfield girl, I suppose she had the usual twentieth-
century mishmash of television dreams until some impulse or maybe false signs of pregnancy tricked her into
marrying a man out of the nineteenth. We had venison
treated like beef and overdone vegetables. I don't like
venison even when it's treated right.

At six Harp turned on his battery radio and sat
stone-faced through the day's bad news and the weather
forecast—"a blizzard which may prove the worst in
forty-two years. Since three PM, eighteen inches have
fallen at Bangor, twenty-one at Boston. Precipitation is
not expected to end until tomorrow. Winds will increase
during the night with gusts up to seventy miles per
hour." Harp shut it off, with finality. On other evenings I
had spent there he let Leda play it after supper only kind
of soft, so there had been a continuous muted bleat and
blatter all evening. Tonight Harp meant to listen for
other sounds. Leda washed the dishes, said an early good
night, and fled upstairs.

Harp didn't talk, except as politeness obliged him to answer some blah of mine. We sat and listened to the snow and the lunatic wind. An hour of it was enough for me; I said I was beat and wanted to turn in early. Harp saw me to my bed in the parlor and placed a new chunk of rock maple in the pot-bellied stove. He produced a difficult granite smile, maybe using up his allowance for the week, and pulled out a bottle from a cabinet that had stood for many years below a parlor print—George Washington, I think, concluding a treaty with some offbeat sufferer from hepatitis who may have been General Cornwallis if the latter had two left feet. The bottle contained a brand of rye that Harp sincerely believed to be drinkable, having charred his gullet forty-odd years trying to prove it. While my throat healed, Harp said, "Shouldn't've bothered you with all this crap, Ben. Hope it ain't going to spoil your sleep." He got me his spare flashlight, then let me be, and closed the door.

I heard him drop back into his kitchen armchair. Under too many covers, lamp out, I heard the cruel whisper of the snow. The stove muttered, a friend, making me a cocoon of living heat in a waste of outer cold. Later I heard Leda at the head of the stairs, her voice timid, tired, and sweet with invitation: "You comin' up to bed, Harp?" The stairs creaked under him. Their door closed; presently she cried out in that desired pain that is brief release from trouble.

I remembered something Adelaide Simmons had told me about this house, where I had not gone upstairs since Harp and I were boys. Adelaide, one of the very few women in Darkfield who never spoke unkindly of Leda, said that the tiny west room across from Harp and Leda's bedroom was fixed up for a nursery, and Harp wouldn't allow anything in there but baby furniture. Had been so since they were married seven years before.

Another hour dragged on, in my exasperations of sleeplessness.

Then I heard Longtooth.

The noise came from the west side, beyond the snow-hidden vegetable garden. When it snatched me from the edge of sleep, I tried to think it was a fox barking, the ringing, metallic shriek the little red beast can belch dragonlike from his throat. But wide awake, I knew it had been much deeper, chestier. Horned owl?—no. A sound that belonged to ancient times when men relied on chipped stone weapons and had full reason to fear the dark.

The cracks in the stove gave me firelight for groping back into my clothes. The wind had not calmed at all. I stumbled to the west window, buttoning up, and found it a white blank. Snow had drifted above the lower sash. On tiptoe I could just see over it. A light appeared, dimly illuminating the snowfield beyond. That would be coming from a lamp in the Ryders' bedroom, shining through the nursery room and so out, weak and diffused, into the blizzard chaos.

Yaaarrhh!

Now it had drawn horribly near. From the north windows of the parlor I saw black nothing. Harp squeaked down to my door.

"'Wake, Ben?"

"Yes. Come look at the west window."

He had left no night-light burning in the kitchen, and only a scant glow came down to the landing from the bedroom. He murmured behind me, "Ayah, snow's up some. Must be over three foot on the level by now."

Yaaarrhh!

The voice had shouted on the south side, the blinder side of the house, overlooked only by one kitchen window and a small one in the pantry where the hand pump stood. The view from the pantry window was mostly blocked by a great maple that overtopped the house. I heard the wind shrilling across the tree's winter bones.

"Ben, you want to git your boots on? Up to you—can't ask it. I might have to go out." Harp spoke in an undertone as if the beast might understand him through the tight walls.

"Of course." I got into my knee boots and caught up my parka as I followed him into the kitchen. A .30-caliber rifle and his heavy shotgun hung on deerhorn over the door to the woodshed. He found them in the dark.

What courage I possessed that night came from being shamed into action, from fearing to show a poor face to an old friend in trouble. I went through the Normandy invasion. I have camped out alone, when I was younger and healthier, and slept nicely. But that noise of Longtooth stole courage. It ached along the channel of the spine.

I had the spare flashlight, but knew Harp didn't want me to use it here. I could make out the furniture, and Harp reaching for the gun rack. He already had on his boots, fur cap, and mackinaw. "You take this'n," he said, and put the ten gauge in my hands. "Both barrels loaded. Ain't my way to do that, ain't right, but since this thing started—"

Yaaarrhh!

"Where's he got to now?" Harp was by the south window. "Round this side?"

"I thought so. . . . Where's Droopy?"

Harp chuckled thinly. "Poor little shit! She come upstairs at the first sound of him and went under the bed. I told Led' to stay upstairs. She'd want a light down here. Wouldn't make sense."

Then, apparently from the east side of the hen loft and high, booming off some resonating surface: *Yaaarrhh!*

"He can't! Jesus, that's twelve foot off the ground!" But Harp plunged out into the shed, and I followed. "Keep your light on the floor, Ben." He ran up the narrow stairway. "Don't shine it on the birds, they'll act up."

So far the chickens, stupid and virtually blind in the dark, were making only a peevish tut-tutting of alarm.

But something was clinging to the outside of the barricaded east window, snarling, chattering teeth, pounding on the two-by-fours. With a fist?—it sounded like nothing else. Harp snapped, "Get your light on the window!" And he fired through the glass.

We heard no outcry. Any noise outside was covered by the storm and the squawks of the hens scandalized by the shot. The glass was dirty from their continual disturbance of the litter; I couldn't see through it. The bullet had drilled the pane without shattering it, and passed between the two-by-fours, but the beast could have dropped before he fired. "I got to go out there. You stay, Ben." Back in the kitchen he exchanged rifle for shotgun. "Might not have no chance to aim. You remember this piece, don't y'?—eight in the clip."

"I remember it."

"Good. Keep your ears open." Harp ran out through the door that gave on a small paved area by the woodshed. To get around under the east loft window he would have to push through the snow behind the barn, since he had blocked all the rear openings. He could have circled the house instead, but only by bucking the west wind and fighting deeper drifts. I saw his big shadow melt out of sight.

Leda's voice quavered down to me: "He—get it?"

"Don't know. He's gone to see. Sit tight. . . ."

I heard that infernal bark once again before Harp returned, and again it sounded high off the ground; it must have come from the big maple. And then moments later—I was still trying to pierce the dark, watching for Harp—a vast smash of broken glass and wood, and the violent bang of the door upstairs. One small wheezing shriek cut short, and one scream such as no human being should ever hear. I can still hear it.

I think I lost some seconds in shock. Then I was groping up the narrow stairway, clumsy with the rifle and flashlight. Wind roared at the opening of the kitchen door, and Harp was crowding past me, thrusting me aside. But I was close behind him when he flung the bedroom door open. The blast from the broken window that had slammed the door had also blown out the lamp. But our flashlights said at once that Leda was not there. Nothing was, nothing living.

Droopy lay in a mess of glass splinters and broken window sash, dead from a crushed neck—something had stamped on her. The bedspread had been pulled almost to the window—maybe Leda's hand had clenched on it. I saw blood on some of the glass fragments, and on the splintered sash, a patch of reddish fur.

Harp ran back downstairs. I lingered a few seconds. The arrow of fear was deep in me, but at the moment it made me numb. My light touched up an ugly photograph on the wall, Harp's mother at fifty or so, petrified and acid-faced before the camera, a puritan deity with shallow, haunted eyes. I remembered her.

Harp had kicked over the traces when his father died, and quit going to church. Mrs. Ryder "disowned" him. The farm was his; she left him with it and went to live with a widowed sister in Lohman, and died soon, unreconciled. Harp lived on as a bachelor, crank, recluse, until his strange marriage in his fifties. Now here was Ma still watchful, pucker-faced, unforgiving. In my dullness of shock I thought: Oh, they probably always made love with the lights out.

But now Leda wasn't there.

I hurried after Harp, who had left the kitchen door to bang in the wind. I got out there with rifle and flashlight, and over across the road I saw his torch. No other light, just his small gleam and mine.

I knew as soon as I had forced myself beyond the corner of the house and into the fantastic embrace of the storm that I could never make it. The west wind ground needles into my face. The snow was up beyond the middle of my thighs. With weak lungs and maybe an imperfect heart I could do nothing out here except die

quickly to no purpose. In a moment Harp would be
starting down the slope of the woods. His trail was
already disappearing under my beam. I drove myself a
little farther, and an instant's lull in the storm allowed
me to shout: "Harp! I can't follow!"

He heard. He cupped his mouth and yelled back:
"Don't try! Git back to the house! Telephone!" I waved
to acknowledge the message and struggled back.

I only just made it. Inside the kitchen doorway I fell
flat, gun and flashlight clattering off somewhere, and
there I stayed until I won back enough breath to keep
myself living. My face and hands were ice blocks, then
fires. While I worked at the task of getting air into my
body, one thought continued, an inner necessity: *There
must be a rational cause. I do not abandon the rational
cause.* At length I hauled myself up and stumbled to the
telephone. The line was dead.

I found the flashlight and reeled upstairs with it. I
stepped past poor Droopy's body and over the broken
glass to look through the window space. I could see that
snow had been pushed off the shed roof near the bedroom window; the house sheltered that area from the full
drive of the west wind, so some evidence remained. I
guessed that whatever came must have jumped to the
house roof from the maple, then down to the shed roof
and then hurled itself through the closed window without regard for it as an obstacle. Losing a little blood and a
little fur.

I glanced around and could not find that fur now.
Wind must have pushed it out of sight. I forced the door
shut. Downstairs, I lit the table lamps in kitchen and
parlor. Harp might need those beacons—if he came
back. I refreshed the fires, and gave myself a dose of
Harp's horrible whiskey. It was nearly one in the morning. If he never came back?

It might be days before they could plow out the road.
When the storm let up I could use Harp's snowshoes,
maybe . . .

Harp came back at 1:20, bent and staggering. He let me support him to the armchair. When he could speak he said, "No trail. No trail." He took the bottle from my hands and pulled on it. "Christ Jesus! What can I do? Ben . . . ? I got to go to the village, get help. If they got any help to give."

"Do you have an extra pair of snowshoes?"

He stared toward me, battling confusion. "Hah? No, I ain't. Better you stay anyhow. I'll bring yours from your house if you want, if I can git there." He drank again and slammed in the cork with the heel of his hand. "I'll leave you the ten gauge."

He got his snowshoes from a closet. I persuaded him to wait for coffee. Haste could accomplish nothing now; we could not say to each other that we knew Leda was dead. When he was ready to go, I stepped outside with him into the mad wind. "Anything you want me to do before you get back?" He tried to think about it.

"I guess not, Ben . . . God, ain't I *lived* right? No, that don't make sense? God? That's a laugh." He swung away. Two or three great strides and the storm took him.

That was about two o'clock. For four hours I was alone in the house. Warmth returned, with the bedroom door closed and fires working hard. I carried the kitchen lamp into the parlor, and then huddled in the nearly total dark of the kitchen with my back to the wall, watching all the windows, the ten gauge near my hand, but I did not expect a return of the beast, and there was none.

The night grew quieter, perhaps because the house was so drifted in that snow muted the sounds. I was cut off from the battle, buried alive.

Harp would get back. The seasons would follow their natural way, and somehow we would learn what had happened to Leda. I supposed the beast would have to be something in the human pattern—mad, deformed, gone wild, but still human.

After a time I wondered why we had heard no excitement in the stable. I forced myself to take up gun and flashlight and go look. I groped through the woodshed, big with the jumping shadows of Harp's cordwood, and into the barn. The cows were peacefully drowsing. In the center alley I dared to send my weak beam swooping and glimmering through the ghastly distances of the hayloft. Quiet, just quiet; natural rustling of mice. Then to the stable, where Ned whickered and let me rub his brown cheek, and Jerry rolled a humorous eye. I suppose no smell had reached them to touch off panic, and perhaps they had heard the barking often enough so that it no longer disturbed them. I went back to my post, and the hours crawled along a ridge between the pits of terror and exhaustion. Maybe I slept.

No color of sunrise that day, but I felt paleness and change; even a blizzard will not hide the fact of dayshine somewhere. I breakfasted on bacon and eggs, fed the hens, forked down hay, and carried water for the cows and horses. The one cow in milk, a jumpy Ayrshire, refused to concede that I meant to be useful. I'd done no milking since I was a boy, the knack was gone from my hands, and relief seemed less important to her than kicking over the pail; she was getting more amusement than discomfort out of it, so for the moment I let it go. I made myself busy work shoveling a clear space by the kitchen door. The wind was down, the snowfall persistent but almost peaceful. I pushed out beyond the house and learned that the stuff was up over my hips.

Out of that, as I turned back, came Harp in his long, snowshoe stride, and down the road three others. I recognized Sheriff Robart, overfed but powerful; and Bill Hastings, wry and ageless, a cousin of Harp's and one of his few friends; and last, Curt Davidson, perhaps a friend to Sheriff Robart but certainly not to Harp.

I'd known Curt as a thickwitted loudmouth when he was a kid; growing to man's years hadn't done much for him. And when I saw him I thought, irrationally perhaps: Not good for our side. A kind of absurdity, and yet Harp and I were joined against the world simply because we had experienced together what others were going to call impossible, were going to interpret in harsh, even damnable ways; and no help for it.

I saw the white thin blur of the sun, the strength of it growing. Nowhere in all the white expanse had the wind and the new snow allowed us any mark of the visitation of the night.

The men reached my cleared space and shook off snow. I opened the woodshed. Harp gave me one hopeless glance of inquiry and I shook my head.

"Having a little trouble?" That was Robart, taking off his snowshoes.

Harp ignored him. "I got to look after my chores." I told him I'd done it except for that damn cow. "Oh, Bess, ayah, she's nervy. I'll see to her." He gave me my snowshoes that he had strapped to his back. "Adelaide, she wanted to know about your groceries. Said I figured they was in the ca'."

"Good as an icebox," says Robart, real friendly.

Curt had to have his pleasures too. "Ben, you sure you got hold of old Bess by the right end, where the tits was?" Curt giggles at his own jokes, so nobody else is obliged to. Bill Hastings spat in the snow.

"Okay if I go in?" Robart asked. It wasn't a simple inquiry: He was present officially and meant to have it known. Harp looked him up and down.

"Nobody stopping you. Didn't bring you here to stand around, I suppose."

"Harp," said Robart pleasantly enough, "don't give me a hard time. You come tell me certain things has happened, I got to look into it is all." But Harp was already striding down the woodshed to the barn entrance. The others came into the house with me, and I put on water for fresh coffee. "Must be your ca' down the rud a piece, Ben? Heard you kind of went into a ditch. All's you can see now is a hump in the snow. Deep freeze might be good for her, likely you've tried everything else." But I wasn't feeling comic, and never had been on those terms with Robart. I grunted, and his face shed mirth as one slips off a sweater. "Okay, what's the score? Harp's gone and told me a story I couldn't feed to the dogs, so what about it? Where's Mrs. Ryder?"

Davidson giggled again. It's a nasty little sound to come out of all that beef. I don't think Robart had much enthusiasm for him either, but it seems he had sworn in the fellow as a deputy before they set out. "Yes, sir," said Curt, "that was *really* a story, that was."

"Where's Mrs. Ryder?"

"Not here," I told him. "We think she's dead."

He glowered, rubbing cold out of his hands. "Seen that window. Looks like the frame is smashed."

"Yes, from the outside. When Harp gets back you'd better look. I closed the door on that room and haven't opened it. There'll be more snow, but you'll see about what we saw when we got up there."

"Let's look right now," said Curt.

Bill Hastings said, "Curt, ain't you a mite busy for a dep'ty? Mr. Dane said when Harp gets back." Bill and I are friends; normally he wouldn't mister me. I think he was trying to give me some flavor of authority.

I acknowledged the alliance by asking: "You a deputy too, Bill?" Giving him an opportunity to spit in the stove, replace the lid gently, and reply: "Shit no."

Harp returned and carried the milk pail to the pantry. Then he was looking us over. "Bill, I got to try the woods again. You want to come along?"

"Sure, Harp. I didn't bring no gun."

"Take my ten gauge."

"Curt here'll go along," said Robart. "Real good man on snowshoes. Interested in wild life."

Harp said, "That's funny, Robart. I guess that's the funniest thing I heard since Cutler's little girl fell under the tractor. You joining us too?"

"Fact is, Harp, I kind of pulled a muscle in my back coming up here. Not getting no younger neither. I believe

I'll just look around here a little. Trust you got no objection? To me looking around a little?"

"Coffee's dripped," I said.

"Thing of it is, if I'd've thought you had any objection, I'd've been obliged to get me a warrant."

"Thanks, Ben." Harp gulped the coffee scalding. "Why, if looking around the house is the best you can do, Sher'f, I got no objection. Ben, I shouldn't be keeping you away from your affairs, but would you stay? Kind of keep him company? Not that I got much in the house, but still—you know—"

"I'll stay." I wished I could tell him to drop that manner; it only got him deeper in the mud.

Robart handed Davidson his gun belt and holster. "Better have it, Curt, so to be in style."

Harp and Bill were outside getting on their snowshoes; I half heard some remark of Harp's about the sheriff's aching back. They took off. The snow had almost ceased. They passed out of sight down the slope to the north, and Curt went plowing after them. Behind me Robart said, "You'd think Harp believed it himself."

"That's how it's to be? You make us both liars before you've even done any looking?"

"I got to try to make sense of it is all." I followed him up to the bedroom. It was cruelly cold. He touched Droopy's stiff corpse with his foot. "Hard to figure a man killing his own dog."

"We get nowhere with that kind of idea."

"Ben, you got to see this thing like it looks to other people. And keep out of my hair."

"That's what scares me, Jack. Something unreasonable did happen, and Harp and I were the only ones to experience it—except Mrs. Ryder."

"You claim you saw this—animal?"

"I didn't say that. I heard her scream. When we got upstairs this room was the way you see it." I looked around, and again couldn't find that scrap of fur, but I spoke of it, and I give Robart credit for searching. He shook out the bedspread and blankets, examined the floor and the closet. He studied the window space, leaned out for a look at the house wall and the shed roof. His big feet avoided the broken glass, and he squatted for a long gaze at the pieces of window sash. Then he bore down on me, all policeman personified, a massive, rather intelligent, conventionally honest man with no patience for imagination, no time for any fact not already in the books. "Piece of fur, huh?" He made it sound as if I'd described a Jabberwock with eyes of flame. "Okay, we're done up here." He motioned me downstairs—all policemen who'd ever faced a crowd's dangerous stupidity with their own.

As I retreated I said, "Hope you won't be too busy to have a chemist test the blood on that sash."

"We'll do that." He made move-along motions with his slab hands. "Going to be a pleasure to do that little thing for you and your friend."

Then he searched the entire house, shed, barn, and stable. I had never before watched anyone on police business; I had to admire his zeal. I got involved in the farce of holding the flashlight for him while he rooted in the cellar. In the shed I suggested that if he wanted to restack twenty-odd cords of wood he'd better wait till Harp could help him; he wasn't amused. He wasn't happy in the barn loft either. Shifting tons of hay to find a hypothetical corpse was not a one-man job. I knew he was capable of returning with a crew and machinery to do exactly that. And by his lights it was what he ought to do. Then we were back in the kitchen, Robart giving himself a manicure with his jackknife, and I down to my last cigarette, almost the last of my endurance.

Robart was not unsubtle. I answered his questions as temperately as I could—even, for instance: "Wasn't you a mite sweet on Leda yourself?" I didn't answer any of them with flat silence; to do that right you need an accompanying act like spitting in the stove, and I'm not a chewer. From the north window he said: "Comin' back. It figures." They had been out a little over an hour.

Harp stood by the stove with me to warm his hands. He spoke as if alone with me: "No trail, Ben." What followed came in an undertone: "Ben, you told me about a friend of yours, scientist or professor—"

"Professor Malcolm?" I remembered mentioning him to Harp a long while before; I was astonished at his recalling it. Johnny Malcolm is a professor of biology who has avoided too much specialization. Not a really close friend. Harp was watching me out of a granite despair as if he had asked me to appeal to some higher court. I thought of another acquaintance in Boston, too, whom I might consult—Dr. Kahn, a psychiatrist who had once seen my wife, Helen, through a difficult time. . . .

"Harp," said Robart, "I got to ask you a couple, three things. I sent word to Dick Hammond to get that goddamned plow of his into this road as quick as he can. Believe he'll try. Whiles we wait on him, we might's well talk. You know I don't like to get tough."

"Talk away," said Harp, "only Ben here he's got to get home without waiting on no Dick Hammond."

"That a fact, Ben?"

"Yes. I'll keep in touch."

"Do that," said Robart, dismissing me. As I left he was beginning a fresh manicure, and Harp waited rigidly for the ordeal to continue. I felt morbidly that I was abandoning him.

Still—corpus delicti—nothing much more would happen until Leda Ryder was found. Then if her body were found dead by violence, with no acceptable evidence of Longtooth's existence—well, what then?

I don't think Robart would have let me go if he'd known my first act would be to call Short's brother Mike and ask him to drive me into Lohman, where I could get a bus for Boston.

* * *

Johnny Malcolm said, "I can see this is distressing you, and you wouldn't lie to me. But, Ben, as biology it won't do. Ain't no such animile. You know that."

He wasn't being stuffy. We were having dinner at a quiet restaurant, and I had, of course, enjoyed the roast duckling too much. Johnny is a rock-ribbed beanpole who can eat like a walking famine with no regrets. "Suppose," I said, "just for argument and because it's not biologically inconceivable, that there's a basis for the yeti legend."

"Not inconceivable. I'll give you that. So long as any poorly known corners of the world are left—the Himalayan uplands, jungles, tropic swamps, the tundra—legends will persist and some of them will have little gleams of truth. You know what I think about moon flights and all that?" He smiled; privately I was hearing Leda scream. "One of our strongest reasons for them, and for the biggest flights we'll make if we don't kill civilization first, is a hunt for new legends. We've used up our best ones, and that's dangerous."

"Why don't we look at the countries inside us?" But Johnny wasn't listening much.

"Men can't stand it not to have closed doors and a chance to push at them. Oh, about your yeti—he might exist. Shaggy anthropoid able to endure severe cold, so rare and clever the explorers haven't tripped over him yet. Wouldn't have to be a carnivore to have big ugly canines—look at the baboons. But if he was active in a Himalayan winter, he'd have to be able to use meat, I think. Mind you, I don't believe any of this, but you can have it as a biological not-impossible. How'd he get to Maine?"

"Strayed? Tibet—Mongolia—Arctic ice."

"Maybe." Johnny had begun to enjoy the hypothesis as something to play with during dinner. Soon he was helping along the brute's passage across the continents, and having fun till I grumbled something about alternatives, extraterrestrials. He wouldn't buy that, and got cross. Still hearing Leda scream, I assured him I wasn't watching for little green men.

"Ben, how much do you know about this—Harp?"

"We grew up along different lines, but he's a friend. Dinosaur, if you like, but a friend."

"Hardshell Maine bachelor picks up dizzy young wife—"

"She's not dizzy. Wasn't. Sexy, but not dizzy."

"All right. Bachelor stewing in his own juices for years. Sure he didn't get up on that roof himself?"

"Nuts. Unless all my senses were more paralyzed than I think, there wasn't time."

"Unless they were more paralyzed than you think."

"Come off it! I'm not senile yet. . . . What's he supposed to have done with her? Tossed her into the snow?"

"Mph," said Johnny, and finished his coffee. "All right. Some human freak with abnormal strength and the endurance to fossick around in a Maine blizzard stealing women. I liked the yeti better. You say you suggested a madman to Ryder yourself. Pity if you had to come all the way here just so I could repeat your own guesswork. To make amends, want to take in a bawdy movie?"

"Love it."

The following day Dr. Kahn made time to see me at the end of the afternoon, so polite and patient that I felt certain I was keeping him from his dinner. He seemed undecided whether to be concerned with the traumas of Harp Ryder's history or those of mine. Mine were already somewhat known to him. "I wish you had time to talk all this out to me. You've given me a nice summary of what the physical events appear to have been, but—"

"Doctor," I said, "it *happened*. I heard the animal. The window *was* smashed—ask the sheriff. Leda Ryder did scream, and when Harp and I got up there together, the dog had been killed and Leda was gone."

"And yet, if it was all as clear as that, I wonder why you thought of consulting me at all, Ben. I wasn't there. I'm just a headshrinker."

"I wanted . . . Is there any way a delusion could take hold of Harp *and* me, disturb our senses in the same way? Oh, just saying it makes it ridiculous."

Dr. Kahn smiled. "Let's say, difficult."

"Is it possible Harp could have killed her, thrown her out through the window of the *west* bedroom—the snow must have drifted six feet or higher on that side—and then my mind distorted my time sense? So I might've stood there in the dark kitchen all the time it went on, a matter of minutes instead of seconds? Then he jumped down by the shed roof, came back into the house the normal way while I was stumbling upstairs? Oh, hell."

Dr. Kahn had drawn a diagram of the house from my description, and peered at it with placid interest. "Benign" was a word Helen had used for him. He said, "Such a distortion of the time sense would be —unusual. . . . Are you feeling guilty about anything?"

"About standing there and doing nothing? I can't seriously believe it was more than a few seconds. Anyway, that would make Harp a monster out of a detective story. He's not that. How could he count on me to freeze in panic? Absurd. I'd've heard the struggle, steps, the window of the west room going up. Could he have killed her and I known all about it at the time, even witnessed it, and then suffered amnesia for that one event?"

He still looked so patient, I wished I hadn't come. "I won't say any trick of the mind is impossible, but I might call that one highly improbable. Academically, however, considering your emotional involvement—"

"I'm not emotionally involved!" I yelled that. He smiled, looking much more interested. I laughed at myself. That was better than poking him in the eye. "I'm upset, Doctor, because the whole thing goes against reason. If you start out knowing nobody's going to believe you, it's all messed up before you open your mouth."

He nodded kindly. He's a good joe. I think he'd stopped listening for what I didn't say long enough to hear a little of what I did say. "You're not unstable, Ben. Don't worry about amnesia. The explanation, perhaps some human intruder, will turn out to be within the human norm. The norm of possibility does include such things as lycanthropic delusions, maniacal behavior, and so on. Your police up there will carry on a good search for the poor woman. They won't overlook that snowdrift. Don't underestimate them, and don't worry about your own mind, Ben."

"Ever seen our Maine woods?"

"No, I go away to the Cape."

"Try it sometime. Take a patch of it, say about fifty miles by fifty, that's twenty-five hundred square miles. Drop some eager policemen into it, tell 'em to hunt for something they never saw before and don't want to see, that doesn't want to be found."

"But if your beast is human, human beings leave traces. Bodies aren't easy to hide, Ben."

"In those woods? A body taken by a carnivorous animal? Why not?" Well, our minds didn't touch. I thanked him for his patience and got up. "The maniac responsible," I said. "But whatever we call him, Doctor, he was *there*."

Mike Short picked me up at the Lohman bus station and told me something of a ferment in Darkfield. I shouldn't have been surprised. "They're all scared, Mr. Dane. They want to hurt somebody." Mike is Jim Short's younger brother. He scrapes up a living with his taxi service and occasional odd jobs at the garage. There's a droop in his shaggy ringlets, and I believe thirty is staring him in the face. "Like old Harp, he wants to tell it like it happened and nobody buys. That's sad, man. You been away what, three days? The fuzz was pissed off. You better connect with Mr. Sheriff Robart like soon. He climbed all over my ass just for driving you to the bus that day, like I should've known you shouldn't."

"I'll pacify him. They haven't found Mrs. Ryder?"

Mike spat out the car window, which was rolled down for the mild air. "Old Harp he never got such a job of snow-shoveling done in all his days. By the c'munity, for free. No, they won't find her." In that there was plenty of I-want-to-be-asked, and something more, a hint of the mythology of Mike's generation.

"So what's your opinion, Mike?"

He maneuvered a fresh cigarette against the stub of the last and drove on through tiresome silence. The road was winding between ridged mountains of plowed, rotting snow. I had the window down on my side, too, for the genial afternoon sun, and imagined a tang of spring. At last Mike said, "You prob'ly don't go along . . . Jim got your ca' out, by the way. It's at your place. . . . Well, you'll hear 'em talking it all to pieces. Some claim Harp's telling the truth. Some say he killed her himself. They don't say how he made her disappear. Ain't heard any talk against you, Mr. Dane, nothing that counts. The sheriff's peeved, but that's just on account you took off without asking." His vague, large eyes watched the melting landscape, the ambiguous messages of spring. "Well, I think, like, a demon took her, Mr. Dane. She was one of his own, see? You got to remember, I knew that chick. Okay, you can say it ain't scientific, only there is a science to these things, I read a book about it. You can laugh if you want."

I wasn't laughing. It wasn't my first glimpse of the contemporary medievalism and won't be my last if I survive another year or two. I wasn't laughing, and I said nothing. Mike sat smoking, expertly driving his twentieth-century artifact while I suppose his thoughts were in the seventeenth, sniffing after the wonders of the invisible world, and I recalled what Johnny Malcolm had said about the need for legends. Mike and I had no more talk.

Adelaide Simmons was dourly glad to see me. From her I learned that the sheriff and state police had swarmed all over Harp's place and the surrounding countryside, and were still at it. Result, zero. Harp had repeatedly told our story and was refusing to tell it anymore. "Does the chores and sets there drinking," she said, "or staring off. Was up to see him yesterday, Mr. Dane—felt I should. Couple days they didn't let him alone a minute, maybe now they've eased off some. He asked me real sharp, was you back yet. Well, I redd up his place, made some bread, least I could do."

When I told her I was going there, she prepared a basket while I sat in the kitchen and listened. "Some say she busted that window herself, jumped down, and run off in the snow, out of her mind. Any sense in that?"

"Nope."

"And some claim she deserted him. Earlier. Which'd make you a liar. And they say whichever way it was, Harp's made up this crazy story because he can't stand the truth." Her clever hands slapped sandwiches into shape. "They claim Harp got you to go along with it, they don't say how."

"Hypnotized me, likely. Adelaide, it all happened the way Harp told it. I heard the thing too. If Harp is ready for the squirrels, so am I."

She stared hard, and sighed. She likes to talk, but her mill often shuts off suddenly, because of a quality of hers which I find good as well as rare: I mean that when she has no more to say she doesn't go on talking.

I got up to Ryder's Ridge about suppertime. Bill Hastings was there. The road was plowed slick between the snow ridges, and I wondered how much of the litter of tracks and crumpled paper and spent cigarette packages had been left by sight-seers. Ground frost had not yet yielded to the mud season, which would soon make normal driving impossible for a few weeks. Bill let me in, with the look people wear for serious illness. But Harp heaved himself out of that armchair, not sick in body at least. "Ben, I heard him last night. Late."

"What direction?"

"North."

"You hear it, Bill?" I set down the basket.

My pint-size friend shook his head. "Wasn't here." I couldn't guess how much Bill accepted of the tale.

Harp said, "What's the basket?—oh. Obliged. Adelaide's a nice woman." But his mind was remote. "It was north, Ben, a long way, but I think I know about where it would be. I wouldn't've heard it except the night was so still, like everything had quieted for me. You know, they been adeviling me night and day. Robart, state cops, mess of smart little buggers from the papers. I couldn't sleep, I stepped outside like I was called. Why, he might've been the other side of the stars, the sky so full of 'em and nothing stirring. Cold . . . You went to Boston, Ben?"

"Yes. Waste of time. They want it to be something human—anyhow, something that fits the books."

Whittling, Bill said neutrally, "Always a man for the books yourself, wasn't you, Ben?"

I had to agree. Harp asked, "Hadn't no ideas?"

"Just gave me back my own thoughts in their language. We have to find it, Harp. Of course some wouldn't take it for true even if you had photographs."

Harp said, "Photographs be goddamned."

"I guess you got to go," said Bill Hastings. "We been talking about it, Ben. Maybe I'd feel the same if it was me. . . . I better be on my way or supper'll be cold and the old woman raising hellfire." He tossed his stick back in the woodbox.

"Bill," said Harp, "you won't mind feeding the stock couple, three days?"

"I don't mind. Be up tomorrow."

"Do the same for you sometime. I wouldn't want it mentioned anyplace."

"Harp, you know me better'n that. See you, Ben."

"Snow's going fast," said Harp when Bill had driven off. "Be in the woods a long time yet, though."

"You wouldn't start this late."

He was at the window, his lean bulk shutting off much light from the time-seasoned kitchen where most of his indoor life had been passed. "Morning, early. Tonight I got to listen."

"Be needing sleep, I'd think."

"I don't always get what I need," said Harp.

"I'll bring my snowshoes. About six? And my carbine—I'm best with a gun I know."

He stared at me awhile. "All right, Ben. You understand, though, you might have to come back alone. I ain't coming back till I get him, Ben. Not this time."

At sunup I found him with Ned and Jerry in the stable. He had lived eight or ten years with that team. He gave Ned's neck a final pat as he turned to me and took up our conversation as if night had not intervened. "Not till I get him. Ben, I don't want you drug into this ag'inst your inclination."

"Did you hear it again last night?"

"I heard it. North."

The sun was at the point of rising when we left on our snowshoes, like morning ghosts ourselves. Harp strode ahead down the slope to the woods without haste, perhaps with some reluctance. Near the trees he halted, gazing to his right, where a red blaze was burning the edge of the sky curtain; I scolded myself for thinking that he was saying good-bye to the sun.

The snow was crusted, sometimes slippery even for our web feet. We entered the woods along a tangle of tracks, including the fat tire marks of a snow scooter. "Guy from Lohman," said Harp. "Hired the goddamn thing out to the state cops and hisself with it. Goes pootin' around all over hell, fit to scare everything inside eight, ten miles." He cut himself a fresh plug to last the morning. "I b'lieve the thing is a mite farther off than that. They'll be messing around again today." His fingers dug into my arm. "See how it is, don't y'? They ain't looking for what we are. Looking for a dead body to hang on to my neck. And if they was to find her the way I found—the way I found—"

"Harp, you needn't borrow trouble."

"I know how they think," he said. "Was I to walk down the road beyond Darkfield, they'd pick me up. They ain't got me in shackles because they got no—no body, Ben. Nobody needs to tell me about the law. They got to have a body. Only reason they didn't leave a man here overnight, they figure I can't go nowhere. They think a man couldn't travel in three, four foot of snow. . . . Ben, I mean to find that thing and shoot it down. . . . We better slant off thisaway."

He set out at a wide angle from those tracks, and we soon had them out of sight. On the firm crust our snowshoes left no mark. After a while we heard a grumble of motors far back, on the road. Harp chuckled viciously. "Bright and early like yesterday." He stared back the way we had come. "They'll never pick that up without dogs. That son of a bitch Robart did talk about borrying a hound somewhere, to sniff Leda's clothes. More likely give 'em a sniff of mine, now."

We had already come so far that I didn't know the way back. Harp would know it. He could never be lost in any woods, but I have no mental compass such as his. So I followed him blindly, not trying to memorize our trail. It was a region of uniform old growth, mostly hemlock, no recent lumbering, few landmarks. The monotony wore down native patience to a numbness, and our snowshoes left no more impression than our thoughts.

An hour passed, or more; after that sound of motors faded. Now and then I heard the wind move peacefully overhead. Few bird calls, for most of our singers had not yet returned. "Been in this part before, Harp?"

"Not with snow on the ground, not lately." His voice was hushed and careful. "Summers. About a mile now, and the trees thin out some. Stretch of slash where they were taking out pine four, five years back and left everything a christly pile of shit like they always do."

No, Harp wouldn't get lost here, but I was well lost, tired, sorry I had come. Would he turn back if I collapsed? I didn't think he could, now, for any reason. My pack with blanket roll and provisions had become infernal. He had said we ought to have enough for three or four days. Only a few years earlier I had carried heavier camping loads than this without trouble, but now I was blown, a stitch beginning in my side. My wristwatch said only nine o'clock.

The trees thinned out as he had promised, and here the land rose in a long slope to the north. I looked up across a tract of eight or ten acres, where the devastation of stupid lumbering might be healed if the hurt region could be let alone for sixty years. The deep snow, blinding out here where only scrub growth interfered with the sunlight, covered the worst of the wreckage. "Good place for wild ras'berries," Harp said quietly. "Been time for 'em to grow back. Guess it was nearer seven years ago when they cut here and left this mess. Last summer I couldn't hardly find their logging road. Off to the left—"

He stopped, pointing with a slow arm to a blurred gray line that wandered up from the left to disappear over the rise of ground. The nearest part of that gray curve must have been four hundred feet away, and to my eyes it might have been a shadow cast by an irregularity of the snow surface; Harp knew better. Something had passed there, heavy enough to break the crust. "You want to rest a mite, Ben? Once over that rise I might not want to stop again."

I let myself down on the butt of an old log that lay

tilted toward us, cut because it had happened to be in the way, left to rot because they happened to be taking pine. "Can you really make anything out of that?"

"Not enough," said Harp. "But it could be him." He did not sit by me but stood relaxed with his load, snowshoes spaced so he could spit between them. "About half a mile over that rise," he said, "there's a kind of gorge. Must've been a good brook, former times, still a stream along the bottom in summer. Tangle of elders and stuff. Couple, three caves in the bank at one spot. I guess it's three summers since I been there. Gloomy goddamn place. There was foxes into one of them caves. Natural caves, I b'lieve. I didn't go too near, not then."

I sat in the warming light, wondering whether there was any way I could talk to Harp about the beast—if it existed, if we weren't merely a pair of aging men with disordered minds. Any way to tell him the creature was important to the world outside our dim little village? That it ought somehow to be kept alive, not just shot down and shoveled aside? How could I say this to a man without science, who had lost his wife and also the trust of his fellow men?

Take away that trust and you take away the world.

Could I ask him to shoot it in the legs, get it back alive? Why, to my own self, irrationally, that appeared wrong, horrible, as well as beyond our powers. Better if he shot to kill. Or if I did. So in the end I said nothing, but shrugged my pack into place and told him I was ready to go on.

With the crust uncertain under that stronger sunshine, we picked our way slowly up the rise, and when we came at length to that line of tracks, Harp said matter-of-factly, "Now you've seen his mark. It's him."

Sun and overnight freezing had worked on the trail. Harp estimated it had been made early the day before. But wherever the weight of Longtooth had broken through, the shape of his foot showed clearly down there in its pocket of snow, a foot the size of a man's but broader, shorter. The prints were spaced for the stride of a short-legged person. The arch of the foot was low, but the beast was not actually flat-footed. Beast or man. I said, "This is a man's print, Harp. Isn't it?"

He spoke without heat. "No. You're forgetting, Ben. I seen him."

"Anyhow, there's only one."

He said slowly, "Only one set of tracks."

"What d'you mean?"

Harp shrugged. "It's heavy. He could've been carrying something. Keep your voice down. That crust yesterday, it would've held me without no web feet, but he went through, and he ain't as big as me." Harp checked his rifle and released the safety. "Half a mile to them caves. B'lieve that's where he is, Ben. Don't talk unless you got to, and take it slow."

I followed him. We topped the rise, encountering more of that lumberman's desolation on the other side. The trail crossed it, directly approaching a wall of undamaged trees that marked the limit of the cutting. Here forest took over once more, and where it began, Longtooth's trail ended. "Now you seen how it goes," Harp said. "Anyplace where he can travel above ground he does. He don't scramble up the trunks, seems like. Look here—he must've got aholt of that branch and swung hisself up. Knocked off some snow, but the wind knocks off so much, too, you can't tell nothing. See, Ben, he—he figures it out. He knows about trails. He'll have come down out of these trees far enough from where we are now so there ain't no chance of us seeing the place from here. Could be anywhere in a half circle, and draw it as big as you please."

"Thinking like a man."

"But he ain't a man," said Harp. "There's things he don't know. How a man feels, acts. I'm going on to them caves." From necessity, I followed him. . . .

I ought to end this quickly. Prematurely I am an old

man, incapacitated by the effects of a stroke and a
damaged heart. I keep improving a little—sensible diet,
no smoking, Adelaide's care. I expect several years of
tolerable health on the way downhill. But I find, as Harp
did, that it is even more crippling to lose the trust of
others. I will write here once more, and not again, that
my word is good.

It was noon when we reached the gorge. In that place
some melancholy part of night must always remain.
Down the center of the ravine between tangles of alder,
water murmured under ice and rotting snow, which here
and there had fallen in to reveal the dark brilliance. Harp
did not enter the gorge itself but moved slowly through
tree cover along the left edge, eyes flickering for danger. I
tried to imitate his caution. We went a hundred yards or
more in that inching advance, maybe two hundred. I
heard only the occasional wind of spring.

He turned to look at me with a sickly triumph, a
grimace of disgust and of justification too. He touched
his nose and then I got it also, a rankness from down
ahead of us, a musky foulness with an ammoniacal tang
and some smell of decay. Then on the other side of the
gorge, off in the woods but not far, I heard Longtooth.

A bark, not loud. Throaty, like talk.

Harp suppressed an answering growl. He moved on
until he could point down to a black cave mouth on the
opposite side. The breeze blew the stench across to us.
Harp whispered, "See, he's got like a path. Jumps down
to that flat rock, then to the cave. We'll see him in a
minute." Yes, there were sounds in the brush. "You keep
back." His left palm lightly stroked the underside of his
rifle barrel.

So intent was he on the opening where Longtooth
would appear, I may have been first to see the other who
came then to the cave mouth and stared up at us with
animal eyes. Longtooth had called again, a rather gentle
sound. The woman wrapped in filthy hides may have
been drawn by that call or by the noise of our approach.

Then Harp saw her.

He knew her. In spite of the tangled hair, scratched face, dirt, and the shapeless deer pelt she clutched around herself against the cold, I am sure he knew her. I don't think she knew him, or me. An inner blindness, a look of a beast wholly centered on its own needs. I think human memories had drained away. She knew Longtooth was coming. I think she wanted his warmth and protection, but there were no words in the whimper she made before Harp's bullet took her between the eyes.

Longtooth shoved through the bushes. He dropped the rabbit he was carrying and jumped down to that flat rock snarling, glancing sidelong at the dead woman who was still twitching. If he understood the fact of death, he had no time for it. I saw the massive overdevelopment of thigh and leg muscles, their springy motions of preparation. The distance from the flat rock to the place where Harp stood must have been fifteen feet. One spear of sunlight touched him in that blue-green shade, touched his thick red fur and his fearful face.

Harp could have shot him. Twenty seconds for it, maybe more. But he flung his rifle aside and drew out his hunting knife, his own long tooth, and had it waiting when the enemy jumped.

So could I have shot him. No one needs to tell me I ought to have done so.

Longtooth launched himself, clawed fingers out, fangs exposed. I felt the meeting as if the impact had struck my own flesh. They tumbled roaring into the gorge, and I was cold, detached, an instrument for watching.

It ended soon. The heavy brownish teeth clenched in at the base of Harp's neck. He made no more motion except the thrust that sent his blade into Longtooth's left side. Then they were quiet in that embrace, quiet all three. I heard the water flowing under the ice.

I remember a roaring in my ears, and I was moving with slow care, one difficult step after another, along the lip of the gorge and through mighty corridors of white and green. With my hard-won detached amusement I supposed this might be the region where I had recently followed poor Harp Ryder to some destination or other, but not (I thought) one of those we talked about when we were boys. A band of iron had closed around my forehead, and breathing was an enterprise needing great effort and caution, in order not to worsen the indecent pain that clung as another band around my diaphragm. I leaned against a tree for thirty seconds or thirty minutes, I don't know where. I knew I mustn't take off my pack in spite of the pain, because it carried provisions for three days. I said once: "Ben, you are lost."

I had my carbine, a golden bough, staff of life, and I recall the shrewd management and planning that enabled me to send three shots into the air. Twice.

It seems I did not want to die, and so hung on the cliff edge of death with a mad stubborness. They tell me it could not have been the second day that I fired the second burst, the one that was heard and answered—because they say a man can't suffer the kind of attack I was having and then survive a whole night of exposure. They say that when a search party reached me from Wyndham Village (eighteen miles from Darkfield), I made some garbled speech and fell flat on my face.

I woke immoblized, without power of speech or any motion except for a little life in my left hand, and for a long time memory was only a jarring of irrelevancies. When that cleared, I still couldn't talk for another long deadly while. I recall someone saying with exasperated admiration that with cerebral hemorrhage on top of coronary infarction, I had no damn right to be alive; this was the first sound that gave me any pleasure. I remember recognizing Adelaide and being unable to thank her for her presence. None of this matters to the story, except the fact that for months I had no bridge of communication with the world; and yet I loved the world and did not want to leave it.

One can always ask: What will happen next?

Sometime in what they said was June my memory was (I think) clear. I scrawled a little, with the nurse supporting the deadened part of my arm. But in response to what I wrote, the doctor, the nurses, Sheriff Robart, even Adelaide Simmons and Bill Hastings, looked— sympathetic. I was not believed. I am not believed now, in the most important part of what I wish I might say: that there are things in our world that we do not understand, and that this ignorance ought to generate humility. People find this obvious, bromidic—oh, they always have!—and therefore they do not listen, retaining the pride of their ignorance intact.

Remnants of the three bodies were found in late August, small thanks to my efforts, for I had no notion what compass direction we took after the cut-over area, and there are so many such areas of desolation I couldn't tell them where to look. Forest scavengers, including a pack of dogs, had found the bodies first. Water had moved them, too, for the last of the big snow melted suddenly, and for a couple of days at least there must have been a small river raging through that gorge. The head of what they are calling the "lunatic" got rolled downstream, bashed against rocks, partly buried in silt. Dogs had chewed and scattered what they speak of as "the man's fur coat."

It will remain a lunatic in a fur coat, for they won't have it any other way. So far as I know, no scientist ever got a look at the wreckage, unless you glorify the coroner by that title. I believe he was a good vet before he got the job. When my speech was more or less regained, I was already through trying to talk about it. A statement of mine was read at the inquest—that was before I could talk or leave the hospital. At this ceremony society officially decided that Harper Harrison Ryder, of this township, shot to death his wife, Leda, and an individual, male, of unknown identity, while himself temporarily of unsound mind, and died of knife injuries received in a struggle with the said individual of unknown, and so forth.

I don't talk about it because that only makes people more sorry for me, to think a man's mind should fail so, and he not yet sixty.

I cannot even ask them: "What is truth?" They would only look more saddened, and I suppose shocked, and perhaps find reasons for not coming to see me again.

They are kind. They will do anything for me, except think about it.

Mary Wilkins Freeman (1852–1930)

LUELLA MILLER

Mary E. Wilkins Freeman was in her day one of the best-known American writers. She was championed by William Dean Howells for her literary value and awarded the Howells Medal for fiction of the American Academy in 1926. Her reputation however, and her work, declined after entering an oppressive marriage in 1902. Like Kate Chopin, Sarah Orne Jewett, and others, she has been consigned to the ghetto of "local colorists" by critics for most of this century. Primarily a short story writer, Freeman was popular and prolific, but produced only eleven supernatural stories, six of which were collected in her volume, *The Wind in the Rose-Bush and Other Stories of the Supernatural* (1903), which is, according to Everett Bleiler, "of greater critical and historical importance than its uniqueness might suggest. It is one of the very few bodies of work that combine domestic realism with supernaturalism, and it has been the founding document of a minor school within supernatural fiction (notably August Derleth and his followers)." Derleth ranked her as one of the four "absolute formative masters" of the horror genre following the Gothic vogue. His press, Arkham House, released the definitive *Collected Ghost Stories* (1974), with a useful introduction by Edward Wagenknecht. "Luella Miller" is her most horrific tale. Told by an unreliable narrator, it is at the same time an attack on the helpless child-woman and paradoxically on the independent single woman, the outsider. It is a ghost story and a vampire story at once. One must gauge the narrator's prejudices. It is an interesting contrast to

Violet Hunt, Madeline Yale Wynne, and at an opposite pole from Le Fanu, M.R. James, and the Lovecraftians. It is perhaps one of the ancestors of Ray Bradbury.

C lose to the village street stood the one-story house in which Luella Miller, who had an evil name in the village, had dwelt. She had been dead for years, yet there were those in the village who, in spite of the clearer light which comes on a vantage-point from a long-past danger, half believed in the tale which they had heard from their childhood. In their hearts, although they scarcely would have owned it, was a survival of the wild horror and frenzied fear of their ancestors who had dwelt in the same age with Luella Miller. Young people even would stare with a shudder at the old house as they passed, and children never played around it as was their wont around an untenanted building. Not a window in the old Miller house was broken: the panes reflected the morning sunlight in patches of emerald and blue, and the latch of the sagging front door was never lifted, although no bolt secured it. Since Luella Miller had been carried out of it, the house had had no tenant except one friendless old soul who had no choice between that and the far-off shelter of the open sky. This old woman, who had survived her kindred and friends, lived in the house one week, then one morning no smoke came out of the chimney, and a body of neighbours, a score strong, entered and found her dead in her bed. There were dark whispers as to the cause of her death, and there were those who testified to an expression of fear so exalted that it showed forth the state of the departing soul upon the dead face. The old woman had been hale and hearty when she entered the house, and in seven days she was dead; it seemed that she had fallen a victim to some uncanny power. The minister talked in the pulpit with covert severity against the sin of superstition; still the belief prevailed. Not a soul in the village but would have chosen the almshouse rather than that dwelling. No vagrant, if he heard the tale, would seek shelter beneath that old roof, unhallowed by nearly half a century of superstitious fear.

There was only one person in the village who had actually known Luella Miller. That person was a woman well over eighty, but a marvel of vitality and unextinct youth. Straight as an arrow, with the spring of one recently let loose from the bow of life, she moved about the streets, and she always went to church, rain or shine. She had never married, and had lived alone for years in a house across the road from Luella Miller's.

This woman had none of the garrulousness of age, but never in all her life had she ever held her tongue for any will save her own, and she never spared the truth when she essayed to present it. She it was who bore testimony to the life, evil, though possibly wittingly or designedly so, of Luella Miller, and to her personal appearance. When this old woman spoke—and she had the gift of description, although her thoughts were clothed in the rude vernacular of her native village—one could seem to see Luella Miller as she had really looked. According to this woman, Lydia Anderson by name, Luella Miller had been a beauty of a type rather unusual in New England. She had been a slight, pliant sort of creature, as ready with a strong yielding to fate and as unbreakable as a willow. She had glimmering lengths of straight, fair hair, which she wore softly looped round a long, lovely face. She had blue eyes full of soft pleading, little slender, clinging hands, and a wonderful grace of motion and attitude.

"Luella Miller used to sit in a way nobody else could if they sat up and studied a week of Sundays," said Lydia Anderson, "and it was a sight to see her walk. If one of them willows over there on the edge of the brook could start up and get its roots free of the ground, and move off, it would go just the way Luella Miller used to. She had a green shot silk she used to wear, too, and a hat with green ribbon streamers, and a lace veil blowing across her face and out sideways, and a green ribbon flyin' from her waist. That was what she came out bride in when she married Erastus Miller. Her name before she was married was Hill. There was always a sight of 'ls' in her name, married or single. Erastus Miller was good lookin', too, better lookin' than Luella. Sometimes I used to think that Luella wa'n't so handsome after all. Erastus just about worshiped her. I used to know him pretty well. He lived next door to me, and we went to school together. Folks used to say he was waitin' on me, but he wa'n't. I never thought he was except once or twice when he said things that some girls might have suspected meant somethin'. That was before Luella came here to teach the district school. It was funny how she came to get it, for folks said she hadn't any education, and that one of the big girls, Lottie Henderson, used to do all the teachin' for her, while she sat back and did embroidery work on a cambric pocket-handkerchief. Lottie Henderson was a real smart girl, a splendid scholar, and she just set her eyes by Luella, as all the girls did. Lottie would have made a real smart woman, but she died when Luella had been here about a year—just faded away and died: nobody knew what ailed her. She dragged herself to that schoolhouse and helped Luella teach till the very last minute. The committee all knew how Luella didn't do much of the work herself, but they winked at it. It wa'n't long after Lottie died that Erastus married her. I always thought he hurried it up because she wa'n't fit to teach. One of the big boys used to help her after Lottie died, but he hadn't much government, and the school didn't do very well, and Luella might have had to give it up, for the committee couldn't have shut their eyes to things much longer. The boy that helped her was a real honest, innocent sort of fellow, and he was a good scholar, too. Folks said he overstudied, and that was the reason he was took crazy the year after Luella married, but I don't know. And I don't know what made Erastus Miller go into consumption of the blood the year after he was married: consumption wa'n't in his family. He just grew weaker and weaker, and went almost bent double when he tried to wait on Luella, and he spoke feeble, like an old man. He worked terrible hard till the last trying to save up a little to leave Luella. I've seen him out in the worst storms on a wood-sled—he used to cut and sell wood—and he was hunched up on top lookin' more dead than alive. Once I couldn't stand it: I went over and helped him pitch some wood on the cart—I was always strong in my arms. I wouldn't stop for all he told me to, and I guess he was glad enough for the help. That was only a week before he died. He fell on the kitchen floor while he was gettin' breakfast. He always got the breakfast and let Luella lay abed. He did all the sweepin' and the washin' and the ironin' and most of the cookin'. He couldn't bear to have Luella lift her finger, and she let him do for her. She lived like a queen for all the work she did. She didn't even do her sewin'. She said it made her shoulder ache to sew, and poor Erastus's sister Lily used to do all her sewin'. She wa'n't able to, either; she was never strong in her back, but she did it beautifully. She had to, to suit Luella, she was so dreadful particular. I never saw anythin' like the fagottin' and hemstitchin' that Lily Miller did for Luella. She made all Luella's weddin' outfit, and that green silk dress, after Maria Babbit cut it. Maria she cut it for nothin', and she did a lot more cuttin' and fittin' for nothin' for Luella, too. Lily Miller went to live with Luella after Erastus died. She gave up her home, though she was real attached to it and wa'n't a mite afraid to stay alone. She rented it and she went to live with Luella right away after the funeral."

Then this old woman, Lydia Anderson, who remembered Luella Miller, would go on to relate the story of

Lily Miller. It seemed that on the removal of Lily Miller to the house of her dead brother, to live with his widow, the village people first began to talk. This Lily Miller had been hardly past her first youth, and a most robust and blooming woman, rosy-cheeked, with curls of strong, black hair overshadowing round, candid temples and bright dark eyes. It was not six months after she had taken up her residence with her sister-in-law that her rosy colour faded and her pretty curves became wan hollows. White shadows began to show in the black rings of her hair, and the light died out of her eyes, her features sharpened, and there were pathetic lines at her mouth, which yet wore always an expression of utter sweetness and even happiness. She was devoted to her sister; there was no doubt that she loved her with her whole heart, and was perfectly content in her service. It was her sole anxiety lest she should die and leave her alone.

"The way Lily Miller used to talk about Luella was enough to make you mad and enough to make you cry," said Lydia Anderson. "I've been in there sometimes toward the last when she was too feeble to cook and carried her some blanc-mange or custard—somethin' I thought she might relish, and she'd thank me, and when I asked her how she was, say she felt better than she did yesterday, and asked me if I didn't think she looked better, dreadful pitiful, and say poor Luella had an awful time takin' care of her and doin' the work—she wa'n't strong enough to do anythin'—when all the time Luella wa'n't liftin' her finger and poor Lily didn't get any care except what the neighbours gave her, and Luella eat up everythin' that was carried in for Lily. I had it real straight that she did. Luella used to just sit and cry and do nothin'. She did act real fond of Lily, and she pined away considerable, too. There was those that thought she'd go into a decline herself. But after Lily died, her Aunt Abby Mixter came, and then Luella picked up and grew as fat and rosy as ever. But poor Aunt Abby begun to droop just the way Lily had, and I guess somebody wrote to her married daughter, Mrs. Sam Abbot, who lived in Barre, for she wrote her mother that she must leave right away and come and make her a visit, but Aunt Abby wouldn't go. I can see her now. She was a real good-lookin' woman, tall and large, with a big, square face and a high forehead that looked of itself kind of benevolent and good. She just tended out on Luella as if she had been a baby, and when her married daughter sent for her she wouldn't stir one inch. She'd always thought a lot of her daughter, too, but she said Luella needed her and her married daughter didn't. Her daughter kept writin' and writin', but it didn't do any good. Finally she came, and when she saw how bad her mother looked, she broke down and cried and all but went on her knees to have her come away. She spoke her mind out to Luella, too. She told her that she'd killed her husband and everybody that had anythin' to do with her, and she'd thank her to leave her mother alone. Luella went into hysterics, and Aunt Abby was so frightened that she called me after her daughter went. Mrs. Sam Abbot she went away fairly cryin' out loud in the buggy, the neighbours heard her, and well she might, for she never saw her mother again alive. I went in that night when Aunt Abby called for me, standin' in the door with her little green-checked shawl over her head. I can see her now. 'Do come over here, Miss Anderson,' she sung out, kind of gasping for breath. I didn't stop for anythin'. I put over as fast as I could, and when I got there, there was Luella laughin' and cryin' all together, and Aunt Abby trying to hush her, and all the time she herself was white as a sheet and shakin' so she could hardly stand. 'For the land sakes, Mrs. Mixter,' says I, 'you look worse than she does. You ain't fit to be up out of your bed.'

"'Oh, there ain't anythin' the matter with me,' says she. Then she went on talkin' to Luella. 'There, there, don't, don't, poor little lamb,' says she. 'Aunt Abby is here. She ain't goin' away and leave you. Don't, poor little lamb.'

"'Do leave her with me, Mrs. Mixter, and you get back to bed,' says I, for Aunt Abby had been layin' down considerable lately, though somehow she contrived to do the work.

"'I'm well enough,' says she. 'Don't you think she had better have the doctor, Miss Anderson?'

"'The doctor,' says I, 'I think *you* had better have the doctor. I think you need him much worse than some folks I could mention.' And I looked right straight at Luella Miller laughin' and cryin' and goin' on as if she was the centre of all creation. All the time she was actin' so—seemed as if she was too sick to sense anythin'—she was keepin' a sharp lookout as to how we took it out of the corner of one eye. I see her. You could never cheat me about Luella Miller. Finally I got real mad and I run home and I got a bottle of valerian I had, and I poured some boilin' hot water on a handful of catnip, and I mixed up that catnip tea with most half a wineglass of valerian, and I went with it over to Luella's. I marched right up to Luella, a-holdin' out of that cup, all smokin'. 'Now,' says I, 'Luella Miller, *you swaller this!*'

"'What is—what is it, oh, what is it?' she sort of screeches out. Then she goes off a-laughin' enough to kill.

"'Poor lamb, poor little lamb,' says Aunt Abby, standin' over her, all kind of tottery, and tryin' to bathe her head with camphor.

"'*You swaller this right down,*' says I. And I didn't waste any ceremony. I just took hold of Luella Miller's chin and I tipped her head back, and I caught her mouth open with laughin' and I clapped that cup to her lips, and I fairly hollered at her: 'Swaller, swaller, swaller!' and she gulped it right down. She had to, and I guess it did her good. Anyhow, she stopped cryin' and laughin' and let me put her to bed, and she went to sleep like a baby inside of half an hour. That was more than poor Aunt Abby did. She lay awake all that night and I stayed with her, though she tried not to have me; said she wa'n't sick enough for watchers. But I stayed, and I made some good cornmeal gruel and I fed her a teaspoon every little while all night long. It seemed to me as if she was jest dyin' from bein' all wore out. In the mornin' as soon as it was light I run over to the Bisbees and sent Johnny Bisbee for the doctor. I told him to tell the doctor to hurry, and he come pretty quick. Poor Aunt Abby didn't seem to know much of anythin' when he got there. You couldn't hardly tell she breathed, she was so used up. When the doctor had gone, Luella came into the room lookin' like a baby in her ruffled nightgown. I can see her now. Her eyes were as blue and her face all pink and white like a blossom, and she looked at Aunt Abby in the bed sort of innocent and surprised. 'Why,' says she, 'Aunt Abby ain't got up yet?'

"'No, she ain't,' says I, pretty short.

"'I thought I didn't smell the coffee,' says Luella.

"'Coffee,' says I. 'I guess if you have coffee this mornin' you'll make it yourself.'

"'I never made the coffee in all my life,' says she, dreadful astonished. 'Erastus always made the coffee as long as he lived, and then Lily she made it, and then Aunt Abby made it. I don't believe I *can* make the coffee, Miss Anderson.'

"'You can make it or go without, jest as you please,' says I.

"'Ain't Aunt Abby goin' to get up?' says she.

"'I guess she won't get up,' says I, 'sick as she is.' I was gettin' madder and madder. There was somethin' about that little pink-and-white thing standin' there and talkin' about coffee, when she had killed so many better folks than she was, and had jest killed another, that made me feel 'most as if I wished somebody would up and kill her before she had a chance to do any more harm.

"'Is Aunt Abby sick?' says Luella, as if she was sort of aggrieved and injured.

"'Yes,' says I, 'she's sick, and she's goin' to die, and then you'll be left alone, and you'll have to do for yourself and wait on yourself, or do without things.' I don't know but I was sort of hard, but it was the truth, and if I was any harder than Luella Miller had been I'll give up. I ain't never been sorry that I said it. Well, Luella, she up and had hysterics again at that, and I jest let her have 'em. All I did was to bundle her into the room on the other side of the entry where Aunt Abby couldn't hear her, if she wa'n't past it—I don't know but she was—and set her down hard in a chair and told her not to come back into the other room, and she minded. She had her hysterics in there till she got tired. When she found out that nobody was comin' to coddle her and do for her she stopped. At least I supposed she did. I had all I could do with poor Aunt Abby tryin' to keep the breath of life in her. The doctor had told me that she was dreadful low, and give me some very strong medicine to give to her in drops real often, and told me real particular about the nourishment. Well, I did as he told me real faithful till she wa'n't able to swaller any longer. Then I had her daughter sent for. I had begun to realize that she wouldn't last any time at all. I hadn't realized it before, though I spoke to Luella the way I did. The doctor he came, and Mrs. Sam Abbot, but when she got there it was too late; her mother was dead. Aunt Abby's daughter just give one look at her mother layin' there, then she turned sort of sharp and sudden and looked at me.

"'Where is she?' says she, and I knew she meant Luella.

"'She's out in the kitchen,' says I. 'She's too nervous to see folks die. She's afraid it will make her sick.'

"The Doctor he speaks up then. He was a young man. Old Doctor Park had died the year before, and this was a young fellow just out of college. 'Mrs. Miller is not strong,' says he, kind of severe, 'and she is quite right in not agitating herself.'

"'You are another, young man; she's got her pretty claw on you,' think I, but I didn't say anythin' to him. I just said over to Mrs. Sam Abbot that Luella was in the kitchen, and Mrs. Sam Abbot she went out there, and I went, too, and I never heard anythin' like the way she talked to Luella Miller. I felt pretty hard to Luella myself, but this was more than I ever would have dared to say. Luella she was too scared to go into hysterics. She jest flopped. She seemed to jest shrink away to nothin' in that kitchen chair, with Mrs. Sam Abbot standin' over her and talkin' and tellin' her the truth. I guess the truth was most too much for her and no mistake, because Luella presently actually did faint away, and there wa'n't any sham about it, the way I always suspected there was about them hysterics. She fainted dead away and we had to lay her flat on the floor, and the Doctor he came runnin' out and he said somethin' about a weak heart dreadful fierce to Mrs. Sam Abbot, but she wa'n't a mite scared. She faced him jest as white as even Luella was layin' there lookin' like death and the Doctor feelin' of her pulse.

"'Weak heart,' says she, 'weak heart; weak fiddlesticks! There ain't nothin' weak about that woman. She's got strength enough to hang onto other folks till she kills 'em. Weak? It was my poor mother that was weak: this woman killed her as sure as if she had taken a knife to her.'

"But the Doctor he didn't pay much attention. He was bendin' over Luella layin' there with her yellow hair all streamin' and her pretty pink-and-white face all pale, and her blue eyes like stars gone out, and he was holdin' onto her hand and smoothin' her forehead, and tellin' me to get the brandy in Aunt Abby's room, and I was sure as I wanted to be that Luella had got somebody else to hang onto, now Aunt Abby was gone, and I thought of poor Erastus Miller, and I sort of pitied the poor young Doctor, led away by a pretty face, and I made up my mind I'd see what I could do.

"I waited till Aunt Abby had been dead and buried about a month, and the Doctor was goin' to see Luella steady and folks were beginnin' to talk; then one evenin', when I knew the Doctor had been called out of town and wouldn't be round, I went over to Luella's. I found her all dressed up in a blue muslin with white polka dots on it, and her hair curled jest as pretty, and there wa'n't a young girl in the place could compare with her. There was somethin' about Luella Miller seemed to draw the heart right out of you, but she didn't draw it out of *me*. She was settin' rocking in the chair by her sittin'-room window, and Maria Brown had gone home. Maria Brown had been in to help her, or rather to do the work, for Luella wa'n't helped when she didn't do anythin'. Maria Brown was real capable and she didn't have any ties; she wa'n't married, and lived alone, so she'd offered. I couldn't see why she should do the work any more than Luella; she wa'n't any too strong; but she seemed to think she could and Luella seemed to think so, too, so she went over and did all the work—washed, and ironed, and baked, while Luella sat and rocked. Maria didn't live long afterward. She began to fade away just the same fashion the others had. Well, she was warned, but she acted real mad when folks said anythin': said Luella was a poor, abused woman, too delicate to help herself, and they'd ought to be ashamed, and if she died helpin' them that couldn't help themselves she would—and she did.

"'I s'pose Maria has gone home,' says I to Luella, when I had gone in and sat down opposite her.

"'Yes, Maria went half an hour ago, after she had got supper and washed the dishes,' says Luella, in her pretty way.

"'I suppose she has got a lot of work to do in her own house tonight,' says I, kind of bitter, but that was all thrown away on Luella Miller. It seemed to her right that other folks that wa'n't any better able than she was herself should wait on her, and she couldn't get it through her head that anybody should think it *wa'n't* right.

"'Yes,' says Luella, real sweet and pretty, 'yes, she said she had to do her washin' tonight. She has let it go for a fortnight along of comin' over here.'

"'Why don't she stay home and do her washin' instead of comin' over here and doin' *your* work, when you are just as well able, and enough sight more so, than she is to do it?' says I.

"Then Luella she looked at me like a baby who has a rattle shook at it. She sort of laughed as innocent as you please. 'Oh, I can't do the work myself, Miss Anderson,' says she. 'I never did. Maria *has* to do it.'

"Then I spoke out: 'Has to do it!' says I. 'Has to do it! She don't have to do it, either. Maria Brown has her own house and enough to live on. She ain't beholden to you to come over here and slave for you and kill herself.'

"Luella she jest set and stared at me for all the world like a doll-baby that was so abused that it was comin' to life.

"'Yes,' says I, 'she's killin' herself. She's goin' to die just the way Erastus did, and Lily, and your Aunt Abby. You're killin' her jest as you did them. I don't know what there is about you, but you seem to bring a curse,' says I. 'You kill everybody that is fool enough to care anythin' about you and do for you.'

"She stared at me and she was pretty pale.

"'And Maria ain't the only one you're goin' to kill,' says I. 'You're goin' to kill Doctor Malcom before you're done with him.'

"Then a red colour came flamin' all over her face. 'I ain't goin' to kill him, either,' says she, and she begun to cry.

"'Yes, you *be*!' says I. Then I spoke as I had never spoke before. You see, I felt it on account of Erastus. I told her that she hadn't any business to think of another man after she'd been married to one that had died for her: that she was a dreadful woman; and she was, that's true enough, but sometimes I have wondered lately if she knew it—if she wa'n't like a baby with scissors in its hand cuttin' everybody without knowin' what it was doin'.

"Luella she kept gettin' paler and paler, and she never

took her eyes off my face. There was somethin' awful about the way she looked at me and never spoke one word. After awhile I quit talkin' and I went home. I watched that night, but her lamp went out before nine o'clock, and when Doctor Malcom came drivin' past and sort of slowed up he see there wa'n't any light and he drove along. I saw her sort of shy out of meetin' the next Sunday, too, so he shouldn't go home with her, and I begun to think mebbe she did have some conscience after all. It was only a week after that that Maria Brown died—sort of sudden at the last, though everybody had seen it was comin'. Well, then there was a good deal of feelin' and pretty dark whispers. Folks said the days of witchcraft had come again, and they were pretty shy of Luella. She acted sort of offish to the Doctor and he didn't go there, and there wa'n't anybody to do anythin' for her. I don't know how she *did* get along. I wouldn't go in there and offer to help her—not because I was afraid of dyin' like the rest, but I thought she was just as well able to do her own work as I was to do it for her, and I thought it was about time that she did it and stopped killin' other folks. But it wa'n't very long before folks began to say that Luella herself was goin' into a decline jest the way her husband, and Lily, and Aunt Abby and the others had, and I saw myself that she looked pretty bad. I used to see her goin' past from the store with a bundle as if she could hardly crawl, but I remembered how Erastus used to wait and 'tend when he couldn't hardly put one foot before the other, and I didn't go out to help her.

"But at last one afternoon I saw the Doctor come drivin' up like mad with his medicine chest, and Mrs. Babbit came in after supper and said that Luella was real sick.

"'I'd offer to go in and nurse her,' says she, 'but I've got my children to consider, and mebbe it ain't true what they say, but it's queer how many folks that have done for her have died.'

"I didn't say anythin', but I considered how she had been Erastus's wife and how he had set his eyes by her, and I made up my mind to go in the next mornin', unless she was better, and see what I could do; but the next mornin' I see her at the window, and pretty soon she came steppin' out as spry as you please, and a little while afterward Mrs. Babbit came in and told me that the Doctor had got a girl from out of town, a Sarah Jones, to come there, and she said she was pretty sure that the Doctor was goin' to marry Luella.

"I saw him kiss her in the door that night myself, and I knew it was true. The woman came that afternoon, and the way she flew around was a caution. I don't believe Luella had swept since Maria died. She swept and dusted, and washed and ironed; wet clothes and dusters and carpets were flyin' over there all day, and every time Luella set her foot out when the Doctor wa'n't there there was that Sarah Jones helpin' of her up and down the steps, as if she hadn't learned to walk.

"Well, everybody knew that Luella and the Doctor were goin' to be married, but it wa'n't long before they began to talk about his lookin' so poorly, jest as they had about the others; and they talked about Sarah Jones, too.

"Well, the Doctor did die, and he wanted to be married first, so as to leave what little he had to Luella, but he died before the minister could get there, and Sarah Jones died a week afterward.

"Well, that wound up everything for Luella Miller. Not another soul in the whole town would lift a finger for her. There got to be a sort of panic. Then she began to droop in good earnest. She used to have to go to the store herself, for Mrs. Babbit was afraid to let Tommy go for her, and I've seen her goin' past and stoppin' every two or three steps to rest. Well, I stood it as long as I could, but one day I see her comin' with her arms full and stoppin' to lean against the Babbit fence, and I run out and took her bundles and carried them to her house. Then I went home and never spoke one word to her though she called after me dreadful kind of pitiful. Well, that night I was taken sick with a chill, and I was sick as I wanted to be for two weeks. Mrs. Babbit had seen me run out to help Luella and she come in and told me I was goin' to die on account of it. I didn't know whether I was or not, but I considered I had done right by Erastus's wife.

"That last two weeks Luella she had a dreadful hard time, I guess. She was pretty sick, and as near as I could make out nobody dared go near her. I don't know as she was really needin' anythin' very much, for there was enough to eat in her house and it was warm weather, and she made out to cook a little flour gruel every day, I know, but I guess she had a hard time, she that had been so petted and done for all her life.

"When I got so I could go out, I went over there one morning. Mrs. Babbit had just come in to say she hadn't seen any smoke and she didn't know but it was somebody's duty to go in, but she couldn't help thinkin' of her children, and I got right up, though I hadn't been out of the house for two weeks, and I went in there, and Luella she was layin' on the bed, and she was dyin'.

"She lasted all that day and into the night. But I sat there after the new doctor had gone away. Nobody else dared to go there. It was about midnight that I left her for a minute to run home and get some medicine I had been takin', for I begun to feel rather bad.

"It was a full moon that night, and just as I started out of my door to cross the street back to Luella's, I stopped short, for I saw something."

Lydia Anderson at this juncture always said with a certain defiance that she did not expect to be believed, and then proceeded in a hushed voice:

"I saw what I saw, and I know I saw it, and I will swear on my death bed that I saw it. I saw Luella Miller and Erastus Miller, and Lily, and Aunt Abby, and Maria, and the Doctor, and Sarah, all goin' out of her door, and all but Luella shone white in the moonlight, and they were all helpin' her along till she seemed to fairly fly in the midst of them. Then it all disappeared. I stood a minute with my heart poundin', then I went over there. I thought of goin' for Mrs. Babbit, but I thought she'd be afraid. So I went alone, though I knew what had happened. Luella was layin' real peaceful, dead on her bed."

This was the story that the old woman, Lydia Anderson, told, but the sequel was told by the people who survived her, and this is the tale which has become folklore in the village.

Lydia Anderson died when she was eighty-seven. She had continued wonderfully hale and hearty for one of her years until about two weeks before her death.

One bright moonlight evening she was sitting beside a window in her parlour when she made a sudden exclamation, and was out of the house and across the street before the neighbour who was taking care of her could stop her. She followed as fast as possible and found Lydia Anderson stretched on the ground before the door of Luella Miller's deserted house, and she was quite dead.

The next night there was a red gleam of fire athwart the moonlight and the old house of Luella Miller was burned to the ground. Nothing is now left of it except a few old cellar stones and a lilac bush, and in summer a helpless trail of morning glories among the weeds, which might be considered emblematic of Luella herself.

Gerald Durrell (b. 1925)

THE ENTRANCE

Gerald Durrell is the brother of Lawrence Durrell, who exceeded his sibling's literary success and reputation in the 1950s with *The Alexandria Quartet*. Yet Gerald, the world-famous naturalist, always made more money, principally on nonfiction. Gerald's short fiction is not well known and "The Entrance" seems to spring from nowhere in the body of his work. It was a serious project for him, and he was reportedly pleased that Lawrence praised the piece that moved in a new direction, over which he had taken some time. One suspects that, like Fuentes' "Aura," the story was generated not by genre reading but by rich reading experiences and, perhaps, images of mirrors. The device of a tale told by a manuscript is common in horror, from Le Fanu and M.R. James through, for instance, Jean Ray's "The Shadowy Street" (which makes an interesting comparison). Another literary antecedent might well be Oscar Wilde's classic novella, "The Portrait of Dorian Gray." Another, *Through The Looking Glass*. In any case, "The Entrance" is a polished and effective tale of horror that deserves wide recognition and repays careful reading. It is a monster story about the nature of identity.

M y friends Paul and Marjorie Glenham are both failed artists or, perhaps, to put it more charitably, they are both unsuccessful. But they enjoy their failure more than most successful artists enjoy their success, and this is what makes them such good company and is one of the reasons why I always go and stay with them when I am in France. Their rambling farmhouse in Provence was always in a state of chaos, with sacks of potatoes, piles of dried herbs, plates of garlic and forests of dried maize jostling with piles of half-finished water-colors and oil paintings of the most hideous sort, perpetrated by Marjorie, and strange Neanderthal sculpture, which was Paul's handiwork. Throughout this market-like mess prowled cats of every shade and marking and a river of dogs, from an Irish wolfhound the size of a pony to an old English bulldog that made noises like Stevenson's Rocket. Around the walls in ornate cages were housed Marjorie's collection of roller canaries, who sang with undiminished vigor regardless of the hour, thus making speech difficult. It was a warm, friendly cacophonous atmosphere and I loved it.

When I arrived in the early evening I had had a long drive and was tired, a condition that Paul set about remedying with a hot brandy and lemon of Herculean proportions. I was glad to have got there, for during the last half hour a summer storm had moved ponderously over the landscape like a great black cloak, and thunder reverberated among the crags like a million rocks cascading down a wooden staircase. I had only just reached the safety of the warm, noisy kitchen, redolent with the mouth-watering smells of Marjorie's cooking, when the rain started in torrents. The noise of it on the tile roof, combined with the massive thunder claps that made even the solid stone farmhouse shudder, aroused the competitive spirit in the canaries and they all burst into song simultaneously. It was the noisiest storm I had ever encountered.

"Another noggin, dear boy?" enquired Paul hopefully.

"No, no!" shouted Marjorie above the bubbling songs of the birds and the roar of the rain. "The food's ready and it will spoil if you keep it waiting. Have some wine. Come and sit down, Gerry dear."

"Wine, wine, that's the thing: I've got something special for you, dear boy," said Paul, and he went off into the cellar to reappear a moment later with his arms full of bottles, which he placed reverently on the table near me. "A special Gigondas I have discovered," he said. "Brontosaurus blood, I do assure you my dear fellow, pure prehistoric monster juice. It will go well with the truffles and the guinea fowl Marjorie's run up."

He uncorked a bottle and splashed the deep red wine into a generously large goblet. He was right. The wine slid into your mouth like red velvet and then, when it reached the back of your tongue, it exploded like a fireworks display into your brain cells.

"Good, eh?" said Paul, watching my expression. "I found it in a small *cave* near Avignon. It was a blistering hot day and the *cave* was so nice and cool that I sat and drank two bottles of it before I realized what I was doing. It's a seducing wine, alright. Of course, when I got out in the sun again the damn stuff hit me like a sledgehammer. Marjorie had to drive."

"I was so ashamed," said Marjorie, placing in front of me a black truffle the size of a peach, encased in a fragile, feather-light overcoat of crisp brown pastry. "He paid for the wine and then bowed to the *Patron* and fell flat on his face. The *Patron* and his sons had to lift him into the car. It was disgusting."

"Nonsense," said Paul. "The *Patron* was enchanted. It gave his wine the accolade it needed."

"That's what you think," said Marjorie. "Now start, Gerry, before it gets cold."

I cut into the globe of golden pastry in front of me and released the scent of the truffle, like the delicious aroma of a damp autumn wood, a million leafy, earthy smells rolled up into one. With the Gigondas as an accompaniment, this promised to be a meal for the Gods. We fell silent as we attacked our truffles and listened to the rain on the roof, the roar of thunder and the almost apoplectic singing of the canaries. The bulldog, who had for no apparent reason fallen suddenly and deeply in love with me, sat by my chair watching me fixedly with his protuberant brown eyes, panting gently and wheezing.

"Magnificent, Marjorie," I said as the last fragment of pastry dissolved like a snowflake on my tongue. "I don't know why you and Paul don't set up a restaurant: with your cooking and Paul's choice of wines you'd be one of the three-star *Michelin* jobs in next to no time."

"Thank you, dear," said Marjorie, sipping her wine, "but I prefer to cook for a small audience of gourmets rather than a large audience of gourmands."

"She's right; there's no gainsaying it," agreed Paul, splashing wine into our glasses with gay abandon.

A sudden prolonged roar of thunder directly overhead precluded speech for a long minute and was so fierce and sustained that even the canaries fell silent, intimidated by the sound. When it had finished, Marjorie waved her fork at her spouse.

"You mustn't forget to give Gerry your thingummy," she said.

"Thingummy?" asked Paul blankly. "What thingummy?"

"You *know*," said Marjorie impatiently, "your thingummy . . . your manuscript . . . It's just the right sort of night for him to read it."

"Oh, the manuscript . . . *yes*," said Paul enthusiastically. "The *very* night for him to read it."

"I refuse," I protested. "Your paintings and sculptures are bad enough. I'm damned if I'll read your literary efforts as well."

"Heathen," said Marjorie good-naturedly. "Anyway, it's not Paul's, it's someone else's."

"I don't think he *deserves* to read it after those disparaging remarks about my art," said Paul. "It's too good for him."

"What is it?" I asked.

"It's a very curious manuscript I picked up," Paul began when Marjorie interrupted.

"Don't tell him about it; let him read it," she said. "I might say it gave *me* nightmares."

While Marjorie was serving helpings of guinea fowl wrapped in an almost tangible aroma of herbs and garlic, Paul went over to the corner of the kitchen, where a tottering mound of books, like some ruined castle, lay between two sacks of potatoes and a large barrel of wine. He rummaged around for a bit and then emerged triumphantly with a fat red notebook, very much the worse for wear, and came and put it on the table.

"There!" he said with satisfaction. "The moment I'd read it I thought of you. I got it among a load of books I bought from the library of old Doctor Lepitre, who used to be prison doctor down in Marseilles. I don't know whether it's a hoax or what."

I opened the book, and on the inside of the cover I found a bookplate in black, three cyprus trees and a sundial under which was written, in Gothic script, *Ex Libras Lepitre*. I flipped over the pages and saw that the manuscript was in longhand, some of the most beautiful and elegant copperplate handwriting I had seen, the ink now faded to a rusty brown.

"I wish I had waited until daylight to read it," said Marjorie with a shudder.

"What is it? A ghost story?" I asked curiously.

"No," said Paul uncertainly, "at least, not exactly. Old Lepitre is dead, unfortunately, so I couldn't find out about it. It's a very curious story. But the moment I read it I thought of you, knowing your interest in the occult and things that go bump in the night. Read it and tell me what you think. You can have the manuscript if you want it. It might amuse you, anyway."

"I would hardly call it amusing," said Marjorie, "anything but amusing. I think it's horrid."

Some hours later, full of good food and wine, I took the giant golden oil lamp, carefully trimmed, and in its gentle daffodil-yellow light I made my way upstairs to the guest room and a feather bed the size of a barn door. The bulldog had followed me upstairs and had sat wheezing, watching me undress and climb into bed. He sat by the bed looking at me soulfully. The storm continued unabated, and the rumble of thunder was almost continuous while the dazzling flashes of lightning lit up the whole room at intervals. I adjusted the wick of the lamp, moved it closer to me, picked up the red notebook and settled myself back against the pillows to read. The manuscript began without preamble:

March 16th, 1901, Marseilles.

I have all night lying ahead of me, and as I know I cannot sleep—in spite of my resolve—I thought I would try and write down in detail the thing that has just happened to me. I am afraid that even setting it down like this will not make it any the more believable, but it will pass the time until dawn comes and with it my release.

Firstly, I must explain a little about myself and my relationship with Gideon de Teildras Villeray so that the reader (if there ever is one) will understand how I came to be in the depths of France in midwinter. I am an antiquarian bookseller and I can say, in all modesty, I am at the top of my profession. Or perhaps it would be more accurate to say that I *was* at the top of my profession. I was even once described by one of my fellow booksellers—I hope more in a spirit of levity than one of jealousy—as a "literary truffle hound," a description that I suppose, in its amusing way, does describe me. A hundred or more libraries have passed through my hands, and I have been responsible for a number of important finds, the original Gottenstein manuscript, for example, the rare "Conrad" illustrated *Bible,* said by some to be as beautiful as the *Book of Kells,* the five new poems by Blake that I unearthed at an unpromising country house sale in the Midlands, and many lesser but nonetheless satisfying discoveries, such as the signed first edition of *Alice in Wonderland* that I found in a trunk full of rag books and toys in the nursery of a vicarage in Shropshire and a presentation copy of *Sonnets from the Portuguese,* signed and with a six-line verse written on the flyleaf by both Robert and Elizabeth Browning. I think to be able to unearth such things in unlikely places is a gift that you are born with. It is really rather like water divining; either you are born with the gift or not, but it is not a gift you can acquire, though most certainly, with practice, you are able to sharpen your perceptions and make your eye keener. In my spare time I also catalogue some of the smaller and more important libraries, as I get enormous pleasure out of simply *being* with books. To me the quietness of a library, the smell and the feel of the books is like the smell and texture of food to a gourmet. It may sound fanciful, but I can stand in the middle of a library and hear the myriad voices around me as though I were standing in the middle of a vast choir, a choir of knowledge and beauty.

Naturally, because of my work, it was at Sotheby's that I first met Gideon. I had unearthed in a house in Sussex a small but quite interesting collection of first editions, and being interested to see what they would fetch, I had attended the sale myself. As the bidding was in progress I got the rather uncomfortable feeling that I was being watched. I glanced around but could see no one whose attention was not upon the auctioneer. Yet, as the sale proceeded I got more and more uncomfortable. Perhaps this is too strong a word, but I became convinced that I was the object of an intense scrutiny. At last the crowd in the salesroom moved slightly and I saw who it was. He was a man of medium height with a handsome but somewhat plump face, piercing and very large dark eyes and smoky black curly hair, worn rather long. He was dressed in a very well cut dark overcoat with an astrakhan collar, and in his elegantly gloved hands he carried the sales catalogue and a wide-brimmed dark velour hat.

His glittering, gypsylike eyes were fixed on me intently but then, when he saw me looking at him, the fierceness of his gaze faded, and he gave me a faint smile and a tiny nod of his head, as if to acknowledge that he had been caught out in staring at me in such a vulgar fashion. He turned then and shouldered his way through the people who surrounded him and was soon lost to my sight. I don't know why but the intense scrutiny of this stranger somewhat disconcerted me, to such an extent that I did not follow the rest of the sale with any degree of attention, except to note that the items I had put up fetched more than I had anticipated they would. The bidding over, I made my way through the crush and out into the street. It was a dank, raw day in February, with that unpleasant smoky smell in the air that augers fog and makes the back of your throat raw. As it looked unpleasantly as though it might drizzle, I hailed a cab. I have one of those tall, narrow houses in Smith Street, just off the Kings Road. It was bequeathed to me by my mother and does me very well. It is not in a fashionable part of town, but the house is quite big enough for a bachelor like myself and his books, for I have, over the years, collected a small but extremely nice library on the various subjects that interest me: Indian art, particularly miniatures; some of the early natural histories; a small but rather rare collection of books on the occult; a number of volumes on plants and great gardens; and a very nice collection of first editions of contemporary novelists. My home is simply furnished but comfortable, and although I am not rich, I have suffucient for my needs and I keep a good table and very reasonable wine cellar.

As I paid off the cab and mounted the steps to my front door, I saw that, as I had predicted, the fog was starting to descend upon the city and already it was difficult to see the end of the street. It was obviously going to turn out to be a real pea-souper and I was glad to be home. My housekeeper, Mrs. Manning, had a bright and cheerful fire burning in my small drawing room, and next to my favorite chair she had, as usual, laid out my slippers (for who can relax without slippers?) and on a small table all the accoutrements for a warming punch. I took off my coat and hat, slipped off my shoes and put on my slippers.

Presently Mrs. Manning appeared from the kitchen below and asked me, in view of the weather, if I would mind if she went home since it seemed as if the fog was getting thicker. She had left me some soup, a steak-and-kidney pie and an apple tart, all of which only needed heating. I said that this would do splendidly, since on many occasions I had looked after myself in this way when the weather had forced Mrs. Manning to leave early.

"There was a gentleman come to see you a bit earlier," said Mrs. Manning.

"A gentleman? What was his name?" I asked, astonished that anyone should call on an evening like this.

"He wouldn't give no name, sir," she replied, "but said he'd call again."

I thought that, in all probability, it had something to do with a library I was cataloguing then, and thought no more about it. Presently Mrs. Manning reappeared, dressed for the street, and I let her out of the front door and bolted it securely behind her, before returning to my drink and the warm fire. My cat Neptune appeared from my study upstairs, where his comfortable basket was, gave a faint meow of greeting and jumped gracefully onto my lap where, after paddling with his forepaws for a short while, he settled down to dream and doze, purring like a great tortoiseshell hive of bees. Lulled by the fire, the punch and the loud purrs of Neptune, I dropped off to sleep.

I must have slept heavily for I awoke with a start and was unable to recall what it was that had awakened me. On my lap Neptune rose and stretched and yawned as if he knew he was going to be disturbed. I listened but the house was silent. I had just decided that it must have been the rustling scrunch of coals shifting in the grate when there came an imperious knocking at the front door. I made my way to the front door, repairing, as I went, the damage that sleep had perpetrated on my neat appearance, straightening my collar and tie and smoothing down my hair, which is unruly at the best of times. I lit the light in the hall, unbolted the front door and threw it open. Shreds of mist swirled in, and there, standing on the top step, was the curious, gypsylike man that I had seen watching me so intently at Sotheby's. Now he was dressed in a well-cut evening suit and was wearing an opera cloak lined with red silk. On his head was a top hat whose shining appearance was blurred by the tiny drops of moisture deposited on it by the fog, which moved, like an unhealthy yellow backdrop, behind him. In one gloved hand he held a slender ebony cane with a beautifully worked gold top and he swung this gently between his fingers like a pendulum. When he saw that it was I who had opened the door and not a butler or some skivvy, he straightened up and removed his hat.

"Good evening," he said, giving me a most charming smile that showed very fine, white, even teeth. His voice had a peculiar husky, lilting musical quality about it that was most attractive and enhanced by his slight but noticeable French intonation.

"Good evening," I said, puzzled as to what this stranger could possibly want of me.

"Am I addressing Mr. Letting . . . Mr. Peter Letting?" he asked.

"Yes," I said, "I am Peter Letting."

He smiled again, removed his glove and held out a well-manicured hand on which a large blood opal gleamed in a gold ring.

"I am more delighted than I can say at this opportunity of meeting you, sir," he said, as he shook my hand, "and I must first of all apologize for disturbing you at such a time, on such a night."

He drew his cloak around him slightly and glanced at the damp, yellow fog that swirled behind him. Noting this, I felt it incumbent on me to ask him to step inside and state his business, for I felt it would hardly be good manners to keep him standing on the step in such unpleasant weather. He entered the hall, and when I had turned from closing and bolting the front door, I found that he had divested himself of his hat, stick and cloak, and was standing there, rubbing his hands together, looking at me expectantly.

"Come into the drawing room Mr. . . ." I paused on a note of interrogation.

A curious, childlike look of chagrin passed across his face, and he looked at me contritely. "My dear sir," he said, "my dear Mr. Letting. How excessively remiss of me. You will be thinking me totally lacking in social graces, forcing my way into your home on such a night and then not even bothering to introduce myself. I do apologize. I am Gideon de Teildras Villeray."

"I am pleased to meet you," I said politely, though in truth I must confess that, in spite of his obvious charm, I was slightly uneasy for I could not see what a Frenchman of his undoubted aristocratic lineage would want of an antiquarian bookseller such as myself. "Perhaps," I continued, "you would care to come in and partake of a little refreshment—some wine perhaps, or maybe, since the night is so chilly, a little brandy?"

"You are very kind and very forgiving," he said with a slight bow, still smiling his beguiling smile. "A glass of wine would be most welcome, I do assure you."

I showed him into my drawing room and he walked to the fire and held his hands out to the blaze, clenching and unclenching his white fingers so that the opal in his ring fluttered like a spot of blood against his white skin. I selected an excellent bottle of Margaux and transported it carefully up to the drawing room with two of my best crystal glasses. My visitor had left the fire and was standing by my bookshelves, a volume in his hands. He glanced up as I entered and held up the book.

"What a superb copy of Eliphas Levi," he said enthusiastically, "and what a lovely collection of *grimoires* you have got. I did not know you were interested in the occult."

"Not really," I said, uncorking the wine. "After all, no sane man would believe in witches and warlocks and sabbaths and spells and all that tarradiddle. No, I merely collect them as interesting books which are of value and, in many cases, because of their contents, exceedingly amusing."

"Amusing?" he said, coming forward to accept the glass of wine I held out to him. "How do you mean, amusing?"

"Well, don't you find it amusing, the thought of all those grown men mumbling all those silly spells and standing about for hours in the middle of the night expecting Satan to appear? I confess I find it very amusing indeed."

"I do not," he said, and then, as if he feared that he had been too abrupt and perhaps rude, he smiled and raised his glass. "Your very good health, Mr. Letting."

He drank, and he rolled the wine round his mouth and then raised his eyebrows. "May I compliment you on your cellar," he said. "This is an excellent bottle of Margaux."

"Thank you," I said, flattered, I must confess, that this aristocratic Frenchman should approve my choice in wine. "Won't you have a chair and perhaps explain to me how I may be of service to you."

He seated himself elegantly in a chair by the fire, sipped his wine and stared at me thoughtfully for a moment. When his face was in repose like that, one noticed the size and blackness and luster of his eyes. They seemed to probe you; they seemed almost as if they could read one's very thoughts. The impression they gave made one uncomfortable, to say the least. But then he smiled and immediately the eyes flashed with mischief, good humor and an overwhelming charm.

"I'm afraid that my unexpected arrival so late at night—and on such a night—must lend an air of mystery to what is, I'm afraid, a very ordinary request that I have to make of you. Simply, it is that I should like you to catalogue a library for me, a comparatively small collection of books, not above twelve hundred, I surmise, which was left to me by my aunt when she died last year. As I say, it is only a small collection of books and I have done no more than give it a cursory glance. However, I believe it to contain some quite rare and valuable things, and I feel it necessary to have it properly catalogued, a precaution my aunt never took, poor dear. She was a woman with a mind of cotton wool and never, I dare swear, opened a book from the start of her life until the end of it. She led an existence untrammelled and unruffled by the slightest breeze of culture. She had inherited the books from her father, and from the day they came into her possession she never paid them the slightest regard. They are a muddled and confused mess, and I would be grateful if you would lend me your expertise in sorting them out. The reason I have invaded your house at such an hour is force of circumstances, for I must go back to France tomorrow morning very early, and this was my only chance of seeing you. I do hope you can spare the time to do this for me?"

"I shall be happy to be of what assistance I can," I said, for I must admit that the idea of a trip to France was a pleasant thought, "but I am curious to know why you have picked on me when there are so many people who could do the job just as well, if not better."

"I think you do yourself an injustice," said my visitor.

"You must be aware of the excellent reputation you enjoy. I asked a number of people for their advice and when I found that they all, of their own free will, advised me to ask you, then I was sure that, if you agreed to do the work, I would be getting the very best, my dear Mr. Letting."

I confess I flushed with pleasure, since there was no way of doubting the man's sincerity, and it was pleasant to know that my colleagues thought so highly of me. "When would you wish me to commence?" I asked.

He spread his hands and gave an expressive shrug. "I'm in no hurry," he said. "Naturally I would have to fall in with your plans. But I was wondering if, say, sometime in the spring? The Loire valley is particularly beautiful then and there is no reason why you should not enjoy the countryside as well as catalogue books."

"The spring would suit me admirably," I said, pouring out some more wine. "Would April be alright?"

"Excellent," he said. "I would think that the job should take you a month or so, but from my point of view, please stay as long as is necessary. I have a good cellar and a good chef, so I can minister to the wants of the flesh, at any rate."

I fetched my diary and we settled on April the fourteenth as being a suitable date for both of us, and my visitor rose to go.

"Just one other thing," he said as he swirled his cloak around his shoulders. "I would be the first to admit that I have a difficult name to remember and pronounce. Therefore, if you would not consider it presumptuous of me, I would like you to call me Gideon, and may I call you Peter?"

"Of course," I said immediately and with some relief, for the name de Teildras Villeray was not one that slid easily off the tongue.

He shook my hand warmly, once again apologized for disturbing me, promised he would write with full details of how to reach him in France and then strode off confidently into the swirling yellow fog and was soon lost to view.

I returned to my warm and comfortable drawing room and finished the bottle of wine while musing on my strange visitor. The more I thought about it the more curious the whole incident became. For example, why had Gideon not approached me when he first saw me at Sotheby's? He said that he was in no hurry to have his library catalogued and yet felt it imperative that he should see me, late at night, as if the matter were of great urgency. Surely he could have written to me? Or did he perhaps think the force of his personality would make me accept a commission that I might otherwise refuse? I was in two minds about the man himself. As I said, when his face was in repose, his eyes were so fiercely brooding and penetrating that they made one uneasy and one was filled almost with a sense of repugnance. But then when he smiled and his eyes filled with laughter and he spoke with that husky, musical voice, one was charmed in spite of oneself. He was, I decided, a very curious character, and I determined that I would try and find out more about him before I went over to France. Having made this resolution, I made my way down to the kitchen, preceded by a now hungry Neptune, and fixed myself my late supper.

A few days later I ran into my old friend Edward Wallenger at a sale, and during the course of it I asked him casually if he knew of Gideon. He gave me a very penetrating look from over the top of his glasses.

"Gideon de Teildras Villeray?" he asked. "D'you mean the Count . . . the nephew of the old Marquis de Teildras Villeray?"

"He didn't tell me he was a Count, but I suppose it must be the same one," I said. "Do you know anything about him?"

"When the sale is over we'll go and have a drink and

I'll tell you," said Edward. "They are a very odd family . . . at least, the old Marquis is distinctly odd."

The sale over, we repaired to the local pub and over a drink Edward told me what he knew of Gideon. It appeared that, many years previously, the Marquis de Teildras Villeray had asked my friend to go to France (just as Gideon had done with me) to catalogue and value his extensive library. Edward had accepted the commission and had set off for the Marquis' place in the Gorge du Tarn.

"Do you know that area of France?" Edward asked.

"I have never been to France at all," I confessed.

"Well, it's a desolate area. The house is in a wild and remote district right in the Gorge itself. It's a rugged country, with huge cliffs and deep gloomy gorges, waterfalls and rushing torrents, not unlike the Gustave Doré drawings for Dante's *Inferno,* you know." Edward paused to sip his drink thoughtfully and then occupied himself with lighting a cigar. When it was drawing to his satisfaction, he went on. "In the house, apart from the family retainers of which there seemed to be only three (a small number for such a large establishment), was the uncle and his nephew, who, I take it, was your visitor of the other night. The uncle was—well, not to put too fine a point on it—a most unpleasant old man. He must have been about eighty-five, I suppose, with a really evil, leering face, and an oily manner that he obviously thought was charm. The boy was about fourteen, I suppose, with huge dark eyes in a pale face. He seemed an intelligent lad, old for his age, but the thing that worried me was that he seemed to be suffering from intense fear, a fear, it seemed to me, of his uncle. The first night I arrived, after we had had dinner which was, to my mind, meager and badly cooked fare for France, I went to bed early, for I was fatigued after my journey. The old man and the boy stayed up. As luck would have it, the dining room was directly below my bedroom, and so although I could not hear clearly all that passed between them, I could hear enough to discern that the old man was doing his best to persuade his nephew into some course of action that the boy found repugnant, for he was vehement in his refusal. The argument went on for some time, the uncle's voice getting louder and louder and more angry. Suddenly, I heard the scrape of a chair as the boy stood and shouted—positively shouted, my dear Peter—in French at his uncle, 'No, no, I will not be devoured so that you may live . . . I hate you.' I heard it quite clearly and I thought it an astonishing statement for a young boy to make. Then I heard the door of the dining salon open and bang shut, and I heard the boy's footsteps running up the stairs and, eventually, the banging of what I assumed was his bedroom door. After a short while I heard the uncle get up from the table and come upstairs. There was no mistaking his footfall, for one of his feet was twisted and misshapen, and so he walked slowly with a pronounced limp, dragging his left foot. He came slowly up the stairs, and I do assure you, my dear Peter, there was positive evil in this slow, shuffling approach that really made my hair stand on end. I heard him go to the boy's bedroom door, open it and enter. He called the boy's name two or three times, softly and cajolingly, but with indescribable menace. Then he said one sentence that I could not catch. After this he closed the boy's door and for some moments I could hear him dragging and shuffling down the long corridor to his own quarters. I opened my door and from the boy's room I could hear muffled weeping, as though the poor child had his head under the bedclothes. It went on for a long time, and I was very worried. I wanted to go and comfort the lad, but I felt it might embarrass him, and in any case it was really none of my business. But I did not like the situation at all. The whole atmosphere, my dear Peter, was charged with something unpleasant. I am not a superstitious man, as you well know, but I lay awake for a long time and wondered if I could stay in the atmosphere of that house for the two or three weeks it would take me to finish the job I had agreed to do. Fortunately, fate gave me the chance I needed: the very next day I received a telegram saying that my sister had fallen gravely ill and so, quite legitimately, I could ask de Teildras Villeray to release me from my contract. He was, of course, most reluctant to do so, but he eventually agreed with ill grace. While I was waiting for the dogcart to arrive to take me to the station, I had a quick look round some of his library which, since it was really extensive, spread all over the house. But the bulk of it was housed in what he referred to as the Long Gallery, a very handsome long room that would not have disgraced one of our aristocratic country houses. It was all hung with giant mirrors between the bookcases. In fact, the whole house was full of mirrors. I can never remember being in a house with so many before. Well, he certainly had a rare and valuable collection, particularly on one of your pet subjects, Peter: the occult. I noticed, in my hurried browse, among other things some most interesting Hebrew manuscripts on witchcraft, as well as an original copy of Mathew Hopkin's *Discovery of Witches* and a truly beautiful copy of Dee's *De Mirabilius Naturae*. But then the dogcart arrived and, making my farewells, I left. I can tell you, my dear boy, I was never so glad in my life to be quit of a house. I truly believe the old man to have been evil and would not be surprised to learn that he practiced witchcraft and was trying to involve that nice young lad in his foul affairs. However, I have no proof of this, you understand, so that is why I would not wish you to repeat it. I should imagine that the uncle is now dead, or if not, he must be in his nineties. As to the boy, I later heard from friends in Paris that there were rumors that his private life was not all it should be, some talk of his attachment to certain women, you know, but this was all circumstantial, and in any case, as you know, dear boy, foreigners have a totally different set of morals to an Englishman. It is one of the many things that sets us apart from the rest of the world, thank God."

I had listened with great interest to Edward's account, and I resolved to ask Gideon about his uncle if I got the chance.

So I prepared myself for my trip to France with, I must admit, pleasurable anticipation, and on April the fourteenth I embarked on the train to Dover, thence uneventfully (even to *mal de mer*) to Calais. I spent the night in Paris, sampling the delights of French food and wine, and the following day I embarked once more on the train. Eventually, I arrived at the bustling station at Tours, and Gideon was there to meet me, as he had promised he would. He seemed in great spirits and greeted me as if I were an old and valued friend, which, I confess, flattered me. I thanked him for coming to meet me, but he waved my thanks away.

"It's nothing, my dear Peter," he said. "I have nothing to do except eat, drink and grow fat. A visit from someone like you is a rare pleasure."

Outside the station we entered a handsome brougham drawn by two beautiful bay horses, and we set off at a spanking pace through the most delicious countryside, all green and gold and shimmering in the sunlight. We drove for an hour along roads that got progressively narrower and narrower, until we were travelling along between high banks emblazoned with flowers of every sort, while overhead, the branches of the trees on each side of the road entwined branches covered with the delicate green leaves of spring. Occasionally, there would be a gap in the trees and high banks, and I could see the silver gleam of the Loire between the trees and realized that we were driving parallel to the great river. Once, we passed the massive stone gateposts and huge wrought iron gates that guarded the wide paths up to an immense and very beautiful *château* in gleaming pinky-yellow stone. Gideon saw me looking at it, perhaps with an expression of wonder, for it did look like something out of a fairy tale, and he smiled.

"I hope, my dear Peter, that you do not expect to find me living in a monster like that? If so, you will be doomed to disappointment. I am afraid that my *château* is a miniature one, but big enough for my needs."

I protested that I did not care if he lived in a cow shed: for me the experience of being in France for the first time and seeing all these new sights, and with the prospect of a fascinating job at the end of it, was more than sufficient.

It was not until evening, when the mauve tree shadows were stretched long across the green meadows that we came to Gideon's establishment, the Château St. Claire. The gateposts were surmounted by two large, delicately carved owls in a pale honey-colored stone, and I saw that the same motif had been carried out most skillfully in the wrought iron gates that hung from the pillars. As soon as we entered the grounds, I was struck by the contrast to the countryside we had been passing through, which had been exuberant and unkempt, alive with wild flowers and meadows, shaggy with long rich grass. Here the drive was lined with giant oak and chestnut trees, each the circumference of a small room, gnarled and ancient, with bark as thick as an elephant's hide. How many hundred years these trees had guarded the entrance to the Château St. Claire, I could not imagine, but many of them must have been well-grown trees when Shakespeare was a young man. The greensward under them was as smooth as baize on a billiard table, and responsible for this were several herds of spotted fallow deer, grazing peacefully in the setting sun's rays. The bucks, with their fine twisted antlers, threw up their heads and gazed at us without fear as we clopped past them and down the avenue. Beyond the greensward I could see a line of gigantic poplars and, gleaming between them, the Loire. Then the drive turned away from the river and the *château* came into sight. It was, as Gideon had said, small but perfect, as a miniature is perfect. In the evening sun its pale straw-colored walls glowed and the light gave a soft and delicate patina to the bluish slate of the roofs of the main house and its two turrets. It was surrounded by a wide verandah of great flagstone, hemmed in by a wide balustrade on which were perched above thirty peacocks, their magnificent tails trailing down towards the well-kept lawn. Around the balustrade, the flower beds, beautifully kept, were ablaze with flowers in a hundred different colors that seemed to merge with the peacocks' tails which trailed amongst them. It was a magnificent and breathtaking sight. The carriage pulled up by the wide steps, the butler threw open the door of the brougham, and Gideon dismounted, took off his hat and swept me a low bow, grinning mischievously.

"Welcome to the Château St. Claire," he said.

Thus for me began an enchanted three weeks, for it was more of a holiday than work. The miniature but impeccably kept and furnished *château* was a joy to live in. The tiny park that meandered along the riverbank was also beautifully kept, for every tree looked as if it were freshly groomed; the emerald lawns looked as if they were combed each morning; and the peacocks, trailing their glittering tails amongst the massive trees, looked as if they had just left the careful hands of Fabergé. Combined with a fine cellar and a kitchen ruled over by a red balloon of a chef whose deft hands could conjour up the most delicate and aromatic of meals, you had a close approach to an earthly paradise. The mornings would be spent sorting and cataloguing the books (and a most interesting collection it was), and then in the afternoon Gideon would insist that we go swimming or for a ride round the park, for he possessed a small stable of very nice horses. In the evenings, after dinner, we would sit out on the still sun-warmed terrace and talk, our conversation made warm and friendly with the wine we had consumed and the excellent meal we had eaten. Gideon was an excellent host, a brilliant raconteur and this, together with his extraordinary gift for mimicry, made him a most entertaining companion. I shall never know now, of course, whether he deliberately exerted all his charm in order to ensnare my liking and friendship. I like to think not; I like to think that he quite genuinely liked me and my company. Not that I suppose it matters now. But certainly, as day followed day, I grew fonder and fonder of Gideon. I am a solitary creature by nature, and I have only a very small circle of friends—close friends—whom I see perhaps once or twice a year, preferring, for my part, my own company. However, my time spent at the *château* with Gideon had an extraordinary effect upon me. It began to dawn upon me that I had perhaps made myself into too much of a recluse. It was also borne upon me most forceably that all my friends were of a different age group; they were all much older than I was. Gideon, if I could count him as a friend (and by this time, I certainly did), was the only friend I had who was, roughly speaking, my own age. Under his influence I began to expand. As he said to me one night, a slim cigar crushed between his strong white teeth, squinting at me past the blue smoke, "The trouble with you, Peter, is that you are in danger of becoming a young fogey." I had laughed, of course, but on reflection I knew he was right. I also knew that when the time came for me to leave the *château,* I would miss his volatile company a great deal, probably more than I cared to admit, even to myself.

In all our talks Gideon discussed his extensive family with me with a sort of ironic affection, telling me anecdotes to illustrate their stupidity or their eccentricity, never maliciously but rather with a sort of detached good humor. However, the curious thing was that he never once mentioned his uncle, the Marquis, until one evening. We were sitting out on the terrace, watching the white owls that lived in the hollow oaks along the drive doing their first hunting swoops across the greensward in front of us. I had been telling him of a book which I knew was to be put up for sale in the autumn and which I thought could be purchased for some two thousand pounds, a large price, but it was an important work and I felt he should have it in his library, as it complemented the other works he had on the subject. Did he want me to bid for him? He had flipped his cigar butt over the balustrade into the flower bed, where it lay gleaming like a monstrous red glowworm, and he chuckled softly.

"Two thousand pounds?" he said. "My dear Peter, I am not rich enough to indulge my hobby to that extent unfortunately. If my uncle were to die now it would be a different story."

"Your uncle?" I queried cautiously. "I did not know you had any uncles."

"Only one, thank God," said Gideon, "but unfortunately he holds the purse strings of the family fortunes and the old swine appears to be indestructible. He is ninety-one and when I last saw him, a year or two back, he did not look a day over fifty. However, in spite of all his efforts I do not believe him to be immortal, and so one day the devil will gather him to his bosom, and on that happy day I will inherit a very large sum of money and a library that will make even you, my dear Peter, envious. But until that day comes I cannot go around spending two thousand pounds on a book. But waiting for dead men's shoes is a tedious occupation, and my uncle is an unsavory topic of conversation, so let's have some more wine and talk of something pleasant."

"If he is unsavory, then he is in contrast to the rest of your relatives you have told me about," I said lightly, hoping he would give me further information about his infamous uncle.

Gideon was silent for a moment.

"Yes, a great contrast," he said, "but as every village must have its idiot, so every family must have its black sheep or its madman."

"Oh, come now, Gideon," I protested, "surely that's a bit too harsh a criticism?"

"You think so?" he asked and in the half light I could see that his face was shining with sweat. "You think I am being harsh to my dear relative? But then you have not had the pleasure of meeting him, have you?"

"No," I said, worried by the savage bitterness in his voice and wishing I had let the subject drop since it seemed to disturb him so much.

"When my mother died, I had to go and live with my 'dear' uncle for several years until I inherited the modest amount of money my father left me in trust and then I could be free of him. But for ten years I lived in purgatory with that corrupt old swine. For ten years not a day or night passed without my being terrified out of my soul. There are no words to describe how evil he is, and there are no lengths to which he will not go to achieve his ends. If Satan prowls the earth in the guise of a man, then he surely inhabits the filthy skin of my uncle."

He got up abruptly and went into the house, leaving me puzzled and alarmed at the vehemence with which he had spoken. I did not know whether to follow him or not. But presently he returned carrying the brandy decanter and two glasses. He sat down and poured us both a generous amount of the spirit.

"I must apologize, my dear Peter, for all my histrionics, for inflicting on you melodrama that would be more in keeping in the *Grande Guignol* than on this terrace," he said, handing me my drink. "Talking of my old swine of an uncle always has that effect on me, I'm afraid. At one time I lived in fear because I thought he had captured my soul . . . you know the stupid ideas children get? It was many years before I grew out of that. But it still, as you can see, upsets me to talk of him, so let's drink and talk of other things, eh?"

I agreed wholeheartedly, and we talked pleasantly for a couple of hours or so. But that night was the only time I saw Gideon go to bed the worse for liquor, and I felt most guilty since I felt it was due to my insistence that he talked to me about his uncle who had obviously made such a deep, lasting and unpleasant impression on his mind.

Over the next four years I grew to know Gideon well. He came to stay with me whenever he was in England and I paid several delightful visits to the Château St. Claire. Then for a period of six months I heard nothing from him, and I could only presume that he had been overcome by what he called his "travel disease" and had gone off to Egypt or the Far East or even America on one of his periodic jaunts. However, this coincided with a time when I was, myself, extremely busy and so I had little time to ponder on the whereabouts of Gideon. Then one evening, I returned home to Smith Street dead tired after a long journey from Aberdeen and I found awaiting me a telegram from Gideon:

ARRIVING LONDON MONDAY THIRTY CAN I STAY STOP UNCLE PUT TO DEATH I INHERIT LIBRARY WOULD YOU CATALOGUE VALUE MOVE STOP EXPLAIN ALL WHEN WE MEET REGARDS GIDEON.

I was amused that Gideon, who prided himself on his impeccable English, should have written "put to death" instead of "died" until he arrived and I discovered that this is exactly what had happened to his uncle, or at least, what appeared to have happened. Gideon arrived quite late on the Monday evening, and as soon as I looked at him I could see that he had been undergoing some harrowing experience. But surely, I thought, it could not be the death of his uncle that was affecting him so. If anything, I would have thought he would be glad. But my friend had lost weight, his handsome face was gaunt and white and he had dark circles under his eyes, which themselves seemed to have suddenly lost all their sparkle and luster. When I poured him a glass of his favorite wine he took it with a hand that trembled slightly and tossed it back in one gulp as if it had been mere water.

"You look tired Gideon," I said. "You must have a few glasses of wine and then I suggest an early dinner and bed. We can discuss all there is to be discussed in the morning."

"Dear old Peter," he said, giving me a shadow of his normally effervescent smile, "please don't act like an English nanny, and take that worried look off your face. I am not sickening for anything. It's just that I have had rather a hard time these last few weeks and I'm suffering from reaction. However, it's all over now, thank God. I'll tell you all about it over dinner, but before then I would be grateful if I could have a bath, my dear chap."

"Of course," I said immediately, and went to ask Mrs. Manning to draw a bath for my friend and to take his baggage up to the guest room.

He went upstairs to bathe and change, and very shortly I followed him. Both my bedroom and the guest room each had its own bathroom, for there was sufficient room on that floor to allow this little luxury. I was just about to start undressing in order to start my own ablutions when I was startled by a loud moaning cry, almost a strangled scream, followed by a crash of breaking glass which appeared to emanate from Gideon's bathroom. I hastened across the narrow landing and tapped on his door.

"Gideon?" I called, "Gideon, are you alright . . . can I come in?"

There was no reply and so, greatly agitated, I entered the room. I found my friend in his bathroom, bent over the basin and holding on to it for support, his face the ghastly white of cheese, sweat streaming down it. The big mirror over the basin had been shattered and the fragments, together with a broken bottle of what looked like shampoo, littered the basin and the floor around.

"He did it . . . he did it . . . he did it . . ." muttered Gideon to himself, swaying, clutching hold of the basin. He seemed oblivious of my presence. I seized him by the arm and helped him into the bedroom, where I made him lie down on the bed and called down the stairs for Mrs. Manning to bring up some brandy and look sharp about it.

When I went back into the room, Gideon was looking a little better, but he was lying there with his eyes closed, taking deep shuddering breaths like a man who has just run a gruelling race. When he heard me approach the bed, he opened his eyes and gave me a ghastly smile.

"My dear Peter," he said, "I do apologize . . . so stupid of me . . . I suddenly felt faint . . . I think it must be the journey and lack of food, plus your excellent wine . . . I fear I fell forward with that bottle in my hand and shattered your beautiful mirror. . . . I'm so sorry . . . of course, I will replace it."

I told him, quite brusquely, not to be so silly, and when Mrs. Manning came panting up the stairs with the brandy, I forced him to take some in spite of his protests. While he was drinking it, Mrs. Manning cleaned up the mess in the bathroom.

"Ah. That's better," said Gideon at last. "I feel quite revived now. All I want is a nice relaxing bath and I shall be a new man."

I felt that he ought to have his food in bed, but he would not hear of it, and when he descended to the dining room half an hour later I must say he did look better and much more relaxed. He laughed and joked with Mrs. Manning as she served us and complimented her lavishly on her cooking, swearing that he would get rid of his own chef and kidnap Mrs. Manning and take her to his *château* in France to cook for him. Mrs.

Manning was enchanted by him, as indeed she always was, but I could see that it cost him some effort to be so charming and jovial. When at last we had finished the sweet and cheese and Mrs. Manning had put the decanter of port on the table and, saying goodnight, had left us, Gideon accepted a cigar, lighted it, and leant back in his chair and smiled at me through the smoke.

"Now, Peter," he said, "I can tell you something of what's been happening."

"I am most anxious to know what it is that has brought you to this low ebb, my friend," I said seriously.

He felt in his pocket and produced from it a large iron key with heavy teeth and an ornate butt. He threw it on the table, where it fell with a heavy thud. "This was one of the causes of the trouble," he said, staring at it moodily, "the key to life and death, as you might say."

"I don't understand you," I said, puzzled.

"Because of this key I was nearly arrested for murder," said Gideon with a smile.

"Murder? You?" I said, aghast. "But how can that possibly be?"

Gideon took a sip of port and settled himself back in his chair. "About two months ago," he said, "I got a letter from my uncle asking me to go and see him. This I did, with considerable reluctance as you may imagine for you know what my opinion of him was. Well, to cut a long story short, there were certain things he wanted me to do . . . er . . . family matters . . . which I refused to do. He flew into a rage and we quarrelled furiously. I am afraid that I left him in no doubt as to what I thought of him, and the servants heard us quarrel. I left his house and continued on my way to Marseilles to catch a boat for Morocco where I was going for a tour. Two days later my uncle was murdered."

"So that's why you put 'uncle put to death' in your telegram," I said. "I wondered."

"He *had* been put to death, and in the most mysterious

circumstances," said Gideon. "He was found in an empty attic at the top of the house which contained nothing but a large broken mirror. He was a hideous mess, his clothes torn off, his throat and body savaged as if by a mad dog. There was blood everywhere. I had to identify the body. It was not a pleasant task, for his face had been so badly mauled that it was almost unrecognizable." He paused and took another sip of port. Presently he went on. "But the curious thing about all this was that the attic was locked, *locked on the inside* with that key."

"But how could that be?" I asked, bewildered. "How did his assailant leave the room?"

"That's exactly what the police wanted to know," said Gideon dryly. "As you know, the French police are very efficient but lacking in imagination. Their logic worked something like this: I was the one who stood to gain by my uncle's death because I inherit the family fortune and his library and several extensive farms dotted about all over France. So as I was the one who stood to gain, *enfin*, I must be the one who committed murder."

"But that's ridiculous," I broke in indignantly.

"Not to a policeman," said Gideon, "especially when they heard that at my last meeting with my uncle we had quarrelled bitterly, and one of the things the servants heard me saying to him was that I wished he would drop dead and thus leave the world a cleaner place."

"But in the heat of a quarrel one is liable to say anything," I protested. "Everyone knows that . . . And how did they suggest you killed your uncle and then left the room locked on the inside?"

"Oh, it was possible, quite possible," said Gideon. "With a pair of long-nosed, very slender pliers, it could be done, but it would undoubtedly have left marks on the end of the key, and as you can see it's unmarked. The real problem was that at first I had no alibi. I had gone down to Marseilles, and as I had cut my visit to my uncle short, I was too early for my ship. I booked into a small hotel and enjoyed myself for those few days in exploring the port. I knew no one there so, naturally, there was no one to vouch for my movements. As you can imagine, it took time to assemble all the porters, maids, *maîtres d'hotels,* restaurant owners, hotel managers and so on and, through their testimony, prove to the police that I was, in fact, in Marseilles and minding my own business when my uncle was killed. It has taken me the last six weeks to do it, and it has been extremely exhausting.

"Why didn't you telegraph me?" I asked. "I could have come and at least have kept you company."

"You are very kind, Peter, but I did not want to embroil my friends in such a sordid mess. Besides, I knew that if all went well and the police released me (which they eventually did after much protest), I should want your help on something appertaining to this."

"Anything I can do," I said. "You know you have only to ask, my dear fellow."

"Well, as I told you, I spent my youth under my uncle's care, and after that experience I grew to loathe his house and everything about it. Now, with this latest thing, I really feel I cannot set foot in that place again. I am not exaggerating but I seriously think that if I were to go there and stay I should become seriously ill."

"I agree," I said firmly. "On no account must you even contemplate such a step."

"Well, the furniture and the house I can, of course, get valued and sold by a Paris firm; that is simple. But the most valuable thing in the house is, of course, the library. And this is where you come in, Peter. Would you be willing to go down and catalogue and value the books for me, and then I can arrange for them to be stored until I can build an extension to my library to house them?"

"Of course I will," I said, "with the greatest of pleasure. You just tell me when you want me to come."

"I shall not be with you; you'll be quite alone," Gideon warned.

"I am a solitary creature, as I have told you." I laughed. "And as long as I have a supply of books to amuse me I shall get along splendidly; don't worry."

"I would like it done as soon as possible," said Gideon, "so that I may get rid of the house. How soon could you come down?"

I consulted my diary and found that, fortunately, I was coming up to a rather slack period. "How about the end of next week?" I asked.

Gideon's face lit up. "So soon?" he said delightedly. "That would be splendid. I could meet you at the station at Fontaine next Friday. Would that be alright?"

"Perfectly alright," I said, "and I will soon have the books sorted out for you. Now, another glass of port and then you must away to bed."

"My dear Peter, what a loss you are to Harley Street," joked Gideon, but he took my advice.

Twice during the night I awakened, thinking that I heard him cry out, but after listening for a while and finding all was quiet, I concluded that it was just my imagination. The following morning he left for France and I started making my preparations to follow him, packing sufficient things for a prolonged stay at his late uncle's house.

The whole of Europe was in the grip of an icy winter and it was certainly not the weather to travel in. Indeed, no one but Gideon could have got me to leave home in such weather. Crossing the Channel was a nightmare, and I felt so sick on arrival in Paris that I could not do more than swallow a little broth and go straight to bed. On the following day it was icy cold, with a bitter wind, grey skies and driving veils of rain that stung one's face. Eventually, I reached the station and boarded the train for what seemed an interminable journey, during which I had to change and wait at more and more inhospitable stations, until I was so numbed with cold I could hardly think straight. All the rivers wore a rim of lacy ice along their shores, and the ponds and lakes turned blank frozen eyes to the steel grey sky.

At length, the local train I had changed to dragged itself, grimy and puffing, into the station of Fontaine and I disembarked and made my way with my luggage to the tiny booking office and minute waiting room. Here, to my relief, I found that there was an old-fashioned, pot-bellied stove stuffed with chestnut roots and glowing almost red hot. I piled my luggage in the corner and spent some time thawing myself out, for the heating on the train had been minimal. There was no sign of Gideon.

Presently, warmed by the fire and a nip of brandy I had taken from my travelling flask, I began to feel better. But half an hour later I began to worry about Gideon's absence. I went out onto the platform and discovered that the grey sky seemed to have moved closer to the earth and a few snowflakes were starting to fall, huge lacy ones the size of a half-crown, that augured a snowstorm of considerable dimensions in the not-too-distant future. I was just wondering if I should try walking to the village when I heard the clop of hooves and made out a dogcart coming along the road, driven by Gideon muffled up in a glossy fur coat and wearing an astrakhan hat.

"I'm so very sorry, Peter, for keeping you waiting like this," he said, wringing my hand, "but we seem to have one catastrophe after another. Come, let me help you with your bags and I will tell you all about it as we drive."

We collected my baggage, bundled it into the dogcart, and then I climbed up onto the box alongside Gideon and covered myself thankfully with the thick fur rug he had brought. He turned the horse, cracked his whip and we went bowling down the snowflakes which were now falling quite fast. The wind whipped our faces and made our eyes water, but still Gideon kept the horse at a fast trot.

"I am anxious to get there before the snowstorm really starts," he said. "That is why I am going at this uncivilized pace. Once these snowstorms start up here they can be very severe. One can even get snowed in for days at a time."

"It is certainly becoming a grim winter," I said.

"The worst we've had here for fifty years," said Gideon.

He came to the village and Gideon was silent as he guided his horse through the narrow, deserted streets, already white with settling snow. Occasionally a dog would run out of an alley and run barking alongside us for a way, but otherwise there was no sign of life and the village could have been deserted for all evidence to the contrary.

"I am afraid that once again, my dear Peter, I shall have to trespass upon your good nature," said Gideon, smiling at me, his hat and his eyebrows white with snow. "Sooner or later my demands on our friendship will exhaust your patience."

"Nonsense," I said. "Just tell me what the problem is."

"Well," said Gideon, "I was to leave you in charge of François and his wife, who were my uncle's servants. Unfortunately, when I went to the house this morning I found that François's wife, Marie, had slipped on the icy front steps and had fallen some thirty feet onto the rocks and broken her legs. They are, I'm afraid, splintered very badly, and I really don't hold out much hope for their being saved."

"Poor woman, how dreadful," I exclaimed.

"Yes," Gideon continued. "Of course, François was nearly frantic when I got there, and so there was nothing for it but to drive them both to the hospital in Milau, which took me over two hours, hence the reason I was late meeting you."

"That doesn't matter at all," I said. "Of course you had to drive them to the hospital."

"Yes, but it creates another problem as well," said Gideon. "You see, none of the villagers liked my uncle, and François and Marie were the only couple who would work for him. So with both of them in Milau, there is no one to look after you, at least for two or three days until François comes back."

"My dear chap, don't let that worry you." I laughed. "I am quite used to fending for myself, I do assure you. If I have food and wine and a fire I will be very well found I promise you."

"Oh, you'll have all that," said Gideon. "The larder is well stocked, and down in the game room there is a haunch of venison, half a wild boar, some pheasants and partridge, and a few brace of wild duck. There is wine aplenty, since my uncle kept quite a good cellar, and the cellar is full of chestnut roots and pine logs, so you will be warm. You will also have for company the animals."

"Animals, what animals?" I asked, curious.

"A small dog called Agrippa," said Gideon, laughing, "a very large and idiotic cat called Clair de Lune, or Clair for short, a whole cage full of canaries and various finches, and an extremely old parrot called Octavius."

"A positive menagerie," I exclaimed. "It's a good thing that I like animals."

"Seriously, Peter," said Gideon, giving me one of his very penetrating looks, "are you sure you will be alright? It seems a terrible imposition to me."

"Nonsense," I said heartily. "What are friends for?"

The snow was now coming down with a vengeance and we could see only a yard or two beyond the horse's ears, so dense were the whirling clouds of huge flakes. We had now entered one of the many tributary gorges that led into the Gorge du Tarn proper. On our left the brown and black cliffs, dappled with patches of snow on sundry crevices and ledges, loomed over us, in places actually overhanging the narrow road. On our right the ground dropped away, almost sheer, five or six hundred feet into the gorge below where, through the windblown curtains of snow, one could catch occasional glimpses of the green river, its tumbled rocks snow-wigged, their edges crusted with ice. The road was rough, snow and water worn, and in places covered with a sheet of ice that made the horse slip and stumble and slowed our progress. Once a small avalanche of snow slid down the cliff face with a hissing sound and thumped onto the road in front of us, making the horse shy so badly that Gideon had to fight to keep control, and for several hair-raising minutes I feared that we, the dogcart and the terrified horse might slide over the edge of the gorge and plunge down into the river below. But eventually Gideon got it under control and we crawled along our way.

At length the gorge widened a little, and presently we rounded a corner and there before us was the strange bulk of Gideon's uncle's house. It was a very extraordinary edifice and I feel I should describe it in some detail. To begin with, the whole thing was perched up on top of a massive rock that protruded from the river far below so that it formed what could only be described as an island, shaped not unlike an isosceles triangle, with the house on top. It was connected to the road by a massive and very old stone bridge. The tall outside walls of the house fell straight down to the rocks and river below, but as we crossed the bridge and drove under the huge arch, guarded by thick oak doors, we found that the house was built round a large center courtyard, cobblestoned and with a pond with a fountain in the middle. This last depicted a dolphin held up by cherubs, the whole thing polished with ice and with icicles hanging from it. All the many windows that looked down into the court were shuttered with a fringe of huge icicles hanging from every cornice. Between the windows were monstrous gargoyles depicting various forms of animal life, both known and unknown to science, each one seeming more malign than the last and their appearance not improved by the ice and snow that blurred their outlines so that they seemed to be peering at you from some snowy ambush. As Gideon drew the horse to a standstill by the steps that led to the front door, we could hear the barking of the dog inside. My friend opened the front door with a large rusty key and immediately the dog tumbled out, barking vociferously and wagging its tail with pleasure. The large black-and-white cat was more circumspect and did not deign to come out into the snow but merely stood, arching its back and mewing, in the doorway. Gideon helped me carry my bags into the large marble hall, where a handsome staircase led to the upper floors of the house. All the pictures, mirrors and furniture were covered with dust sheets.

"I am sorry about the covers," said Gideon, and it seemed to me that as soon as he entered the house he became increasingly nervous and ill at ease. "I meant to remove them all this morning and make it more habitable for you, but what with one thing and another I did not manage it."

"Don't worry," I said, making a fuss over the dog and cat, who were both vying for my attention. "I shan't be inhabiting all of the house, so I will just remove the sheets in those parts that I shall use."

"Yes, yes," said Gideon, running his hands through his hair in a nervous fashion. "Your bed is made up . . . the bedroom is the second door on the left as you reach the top of the stairs. Now, come with me and I'll show you the kitchen and cellar."

He led me across the hall to a door that was hidden under the main staircase. Opening this he made his way down broad stone steps that spiralled their way down into gloom. Presently we reached a passageway that led to a gigantic stone-flagged kitchen and, adjoining it, cavernous cellars and a capacious larder, cold as a glacier, with the carcasses of game, chicken and duck, and legs of lamb and saddles of beef hanging from hooks or lying on the marble shelves that ran around the walls. In the kitchen was a great range, each fire carefully laid, and on the great table in the center had been arranged various commodities that Gideon thought I may need: rice, lentils as black as soot, potatoes, carrots and other vegetables in large baskets, pottery jars of butter and preserves, and a pile of freshly baked loaves. On the other side of the kitchen, opposite to the cellars and larder, lay the wine store, approached through a heavy door, bolted and padlocked. Obviously Gideon's uncle had not trusted his staff when it came to alcoholic beverages. The cellar was small, but I saw at a glance that it contained some excellent vintages.

"Do not stint yourself, Peter," said Gideon. "There are some really quite nice wines in there and they will be some small compensation for staying in the gloomy place alone."

"You want me to spend my time in an inebriated state?" I laughed. "I would never get the books valued. But don't worry, Gideon; I shall be quite alright. As I told you before, I like being on my own, and here I have food and wine enough for an army, plenty of fuel for the fire, a dog and a cat and birds to keep me company and a large and interesting library. What more could any man want?"

"The books, by the way, are mainly in the Long Gallery, on the south side of the house. I won't show it to you—it's easy enough to find—but I really must be on my way," said Gideon, leading the way up into the hall once more. He delved into his pocket and produced a huge bunch of ancient keys. "The 'keys of the Kingdom,'" he said with a faint smile. "I don't think anything is locked, but if it is, please open it. I will tell François that he is to come back here and look after you as soon as his wife is out of danger, and I myself will return in about four weeks' time. By then you should have finished your task."

"Easily," I said. "In fact, if I get it done before then I will send you a telegram."

"Seriously, Peter," he said, taking my hand, "I am

really most deeply in your debt for what you are doing. I shall not forget it."

"Rubbish, my friend," I said. "It gives me great pleasure to be of service to you."

I stood in the doorway of the house, the dog panting by my side, the cat arching itself round my legs and purring loudly, and watched Gideon get back into the dogcart, wrap the rug around himself and then flick the horses with the reins. As they broke into a trot and he steered them towards the entrance to the courtyard, he raised his whip in salute. He disappeared through the archway and very soon the sound of the hoof beats were muffled by the snow and soon faded altogether. Picking up the warm silky body of the cat and whistling to the dog who had chased the dogcart to the archway, barking exuberantly, I went back into the house and bolted the front door behind me.

I decided that the first thing to do was to explore the house and ascertain where the various books were that I had come to work with, and thus to make up my mind which rooms I needed to open up. On a table in the hall I had spotted a large six-branched silver candelabra loaded with candles and a box of matches lying beside it. I decided to use this in my exploration since it would relieve me of the tedium of having to open and close innumerable shutters. So, lighting the candles and accompanied by the eager, bustling dog whose nails rattled on the bare floors like castanets, I started off. The whole of the ground floor consisted of three very large rooms and one smaller one, which comprised the drawing room, the dining room, a study and then this smaller salon. Strangely enough, this room—which I called the blue salon as it was decorated in various shades of blue and gold—was the only one that was locked, and it took me some time to find the right key for it. This salon formed one end of the house and so it was a long, narrow shoebox shape, with large windows at each end. The door by which you entered was midway down one of the longer walls and hanging on the wall opposite was one of the biggest mirrors I have ever seen. It must have been fully nine feet high, stretching from floor level to almost the ceiling, and some thirty-five feet in length. The mirror itself was slightly tarnished, which gave it a pleasant bluish tinge, like the waters of a shallow lake, but it still reflected clearly and accurately. The whole was encompassed in a wide and very ornate gold frame, carved to depict various nymphs and satyrs, unicorns, griffons and other fabulous beasts. The frame in itself was a work of art. By seating oneself in one of the comfortable chairs that stood one on each side of the fireplace, one could see the whole room reflected in this remarkable mirror, and although the room was somewhat narrow, this gave one a great sense of space. Owing to the size, the convenience and—I must admit—the novelty of the room, I decided to make it my living room, and so in a very short space of time I had the dust covers off the furniture and a roaring blaze of chestnut roots in the hearth. Then I moved in the cage of finches and canaries and placed them at one end of the room together with Octavius, the parrot, who seemed pleased by the change, for he shuffled his feathers, cocked his head to one side and whistled a few bars of the "Marseillaise." The dog and cat immediately stretched out in front of the blaze and fell into a contented sleep. Thus, deserted by my companions, I took my candelabra and continued my investigation of the house alone.

The next floor was comprised mainly of bed and bathrooms, but I found that one whole wing of the house (which formed the hollow square in which the courtyard lay) was one enormous room, the Long Gallery, as Gideon had called it. Down one side of this long, wide room—which would have done credit to any great country house in England—there were very tall windows, and opposite each window was a tall mirror, similar to the one downstairs but long and narrow.

Between these mirrors stood the bookcases of polished oak, and piled on the shelves haphazardly were a myriad of books, some on their sides, some upside down in total confusion. Even a cursory glance was enough to tell me that the library was so muddled it would take me some considerable time to sort the books into subjects before I could even start to catalogue and value them. Leaving the Long Gallery shrouded in dust sheets and with the shutters still closed, I went one floor higher. Here there were only attics, and in one of them I came upon the gilt frame of a mirror and I shivered, for I presumed that this was the attic in which Gideon's uncle had been found dead. The mirror frame was identical to the one in the blue salon but on a much smaller scale, of course. Here again were the satyrs, the unicorns, the griffons and hippographs, but in addition there was a small area at the top of the frame, carved like a medallion, in which were inscribed in French the words: *"I am your servant. Feed and liberate me. I am you."* It did not seem to make sense. I closed the attic door and, chiding myself for being a coward, I locked it securely and in consequence felt much better.

When I made my way downstairs to the blue salon, I was greeted with rapture by both dog and cat, as if I had been away on a journey of many days, and I realized that they were hungry. Simultaneously I realized that I was hungry too, for the excitement of arriving at the house and exploring it had quite made me forget to prepare myself any luncheon and it was now past six o'clock in the evening. So, accompanied by the eager animals, I made my way down to the kitchen to cook some food for us all. For the dog, I stewed some scraps of mutton, and a little chicken for the cat, both combined with some boiled rice and potatoes; they were delighted with this menu. For myself, I grilled a large steak with an assortment of vegetables and chose from the cellar an excellent bottle of red wine. When this was ready I carried it up to the blue salon and, pulling my chair up to the fire, made myself comfortable and fell on the food hungrily. Presently the dog and the cat, replete with food, joined me and spread out in front of the fire. I got up and closed the door once they were settled, for there was quite a cold draught from the big hall which, with its marble floor, was now as cold as an ice-chest. Finishing my food, I lay back contentedly in my chair, sipping my wine and watching the blue flames run to and fro over the chestnut roots in the fire. I was very relaxed and happy and the wine, rich and heavy, was having a soporific effect on me. I slept for perhaps an hour. Then, suddenly, I was fully awake with every nerve tingling, as if someone had shouted my name. I listened, but the only sounds were the soft breathing of the sleeping dog and the contented purr of the cat curled up on the chair opposite me. It was so silent that I could hear the faint bubble and crackle of the chestnut roots in the fire. Feeling sure I must have imagined a sound, and yet feeling unaccountably uneasy for no discernible reason, I threw another log on the fire and settled back in the chair to doze.

It was then I glanced across at the mirror opposite me and noticed that in the reflection the door to the salon which I had carefully closed was now ajar. Surprised, I twisted round in my chair and looked at the real door, only to find it was securely closed as I had left it. I looked again into the mirror and made sure my eyes—aided by the wine—were not playing tricks, but sure enough, in the reflection the door appeared to be slightly ajar. I was sitting there looking at it and wondering what trick of light and reflection could produce the effect of an open door when the door responsible for the reflection was securely closed, when I noticed something that made me sit up, astonished and uneasy. *The door in the reflection was being pushed open still further.* I looked at the real door again and saw that it was still firmly shut. Yet its reflection in the mirror was opening, very slowly, millimeter by millimeter. I sat watching it, the hair on the nape of my neck stirring, and suddenly round the edge of the door, on the carpet, there appeared something that at first glance I thought was some sort of caterpillar. It was long, wrinkled and yellowish-white in color, and at one end it had a long blackened horn. It humped itself up and scrabbled at the surface of the carpet with its horn in a way that I had seen no caterpillar behave. Then, slowly, it retreated behind the door. I found that I was sweating. I glanced once more at the real door to assure myself that it was closed because, for some reason or other, I did not fancy having that caterpillar or whatever it was crawling about the room with me. The door was still shut. I took a draught of wine to steady my nerves and was annoyed to see that my hand was shaking. I, who had never believed in ghosts, or hauntings, or magic spells or any of that claptrap, was imagining things in a mirror and convincing myself to such an extent they were real that I was actually afraid. It was ridiculous, I told myself as I drank the wine. There was some perfectly rational explanation for the whole thing. I sat forward in my chair and gazed at the reflection in the mirror with great intentness. For a long time nothing happened, and then the door in the mirror swung open a fraction and the caterpillar appeared again, but this time it was joined by another and then, after a pause, yet another and suddenly my blood ran cold for I realized what it was. They were not caterpillars but attenuated yellow fingers with long black nails twisted like gigantic misshapen rose thorns. The moment I realized this the whole hand came into view, feeling its way feebly along the carpet. The hand was a mere skeleton covered with the pale yellow, parchment-like skin through which the knuckles and joints showed like walnuts. It felt around on the carpet in a blind, groping sort of way, the hand moving from a bony wrist, like the tentacles of some strange sea anemone from the deep, one that has become pallid through living in perpetual dark. Then slowly it withdrew behind the door. I shuddered for I wondered what sort of body was attached to that horrible hand. I waited for perhaps quarter of an hour, dreading what might suddenly appear from behind the mirror door, but nothing happened.

After a while I became restive. I was still attempting to convince myself that the whole thing was an hallucination brought on by the wine and the heat of the fire, but without success. For there was the door of the blue salon carefully closed against the draught and the door in the mirror still ajar with apparently something lurking behind it. I wanted to walk over to the mirror and examine it, but I did not have the courage, I regret to say. Instead, I thought of a plan which, I felt, would show me whether I was imagining things or not. I woke Agrippa the dog and, crumpling up a sheet of the newspaper I had been reading into a ball, I threw it down the room so that it landed just by the closed door. In the mirror it lay just near the door that was ajar. Agrippa, more to please me than anything else for he was very sleepy, bounded after it. Gripping the arms of my chair, I watched his reflection in the mirror as he ran towards the door. He reached the ball of newspaper and paused to pick it up. And then something so hideous happened that I could scarcely believe my eyes. The mirror door was pushed open still further and the hand and a long white bony arm shot out. It grabbed the dog in the mirror by the scruff of its neck and pulled it speedily, kicking and struggling, behind the door. Agrippa had now come back to me, having retrieved the newspaper, but I took no notice of him, for my gaze was fixed on the reflection in the mirror. After a few minutes the hand suddenly reappeared. Was it my imagination or did it now seem stronger? At any event, it curved itself round the woodwork of the door and drew it completely shut, leaving on the white paint a series of bloody fingerprints that made me feel sick. The real Agrippa was nosing my leg, the newspaper in his mouth, seeking my approval, while behind the mirror door, God knows what fate had overtaken his reflection.

To say that I was shaken means nothing. I could scarcely believe the evidence of my senses. I sat staring at the mirror for a long time, but nothing further happened. Eventually, and with my skin prickling with fear, I got up and examined both the mirror and the door into the salon, but both bore a perfectly ordinary appearance. I wanted very much to open the door to the salon and see if the reflection in the mirror opened as well, but to tell the truth, I was too frightened of disturbing whatever it was that lurked behind the mirror door. I glanced up at the top of the mirror and saw for the first time that it bore the same inscription as the one I had found in the attic: *I am your servant. Feed and liberate me. I am you.* Did this mean the creature behind the door, I wondered? Feed and liberate me—was that what I had done by letting the dog go near the door? Was the creature now feasting upon the dog it had caught in the mirror? I shuddered at the thought. I determined that the only thing to do was to get a good night's rest, for I was tired and overwrought. In the morning, I assured myself, I would hit upon a ready explanation for all this mumbo-jumbo. So, picking up the cat and calling for the dog (for, if the truth be known, I needed the company of the animals), I left the blue salon. As I was closing the door I was frozen into immobility and the hair on my head prickled as I heard a cracked, harsh voice bid me *"Bon nuit"* in wheedling tones. It was a moment or two before I realized it was Octavius the parrot and went limp with relief.

Clair the cat drowsed peacefully in my arms, but Agrippa needed some encouragement to accompany me upstairs, for it was obvious that he had never been allowed above the ground floor before. At length, with reluctance that soon turned to excitement at the novelty, he followed me upstairs. The fire in the bedroom had died down, but the atmosphere was still warm. I made my toilet and, without further ado, climbed into bed with Agrippa lying on one side of me and Clair on the other. I received much comfort from the feel of their warm bodies but, in addition, I am not ashamed to say I left the candles burning and the door to the room securely locked.

The following morning when I awoke I was immediately conscious of the silence. Throwing open the shutters, I gazed out at a world muffled in snow. It must have been snowing steadily all night, and great drifts had piled up on the rock faces, on the bare trees, along the river bank and piled in a great cushion some seven feet deep along the crest of the bridge that joined the house to the mainland. Every windowsill and every projection of the eaves were a fearsome armory of icicles, and the sills themselves were varnished with a thin layer of ice. The sky was dark grey and lowering so that I could see we were in for yet more snow. Even if I had wanted to leave the house, the roads were already impassable, and with another snowfall, I would be completely cut off from the outside world. I must say that, thinking back on my experiences of the previous night, this fact made me feel somewhat uneasy. But I chided myself and by the time I had finished dressing, I had managed to convince myself that my experience in the blue salon was due entirely to a surfeit of good wine and an overexcited imagination.

Thus comforting myself, I went downstairs, picked up Clair in my arms, called Agrippa to heel and, steeling myself, threw open the door of the blue salon and entered. It was as I had left it, the dirty plates and wine bottle near my chair, the chestnut roots in the fire burnt to a delicate grey ash that stirred slightly at the sudden draught from the open door. But it was the only thing in the room that stirred. Everything was in order. Everything was normal and I heaved a sigh of relief. It was not until I was halfway down the room that I glanced at the mirror, and I stopped as suddenly as if I had walked into a brick wall and my blood froze, for I could not believe what I was seeing.

Reflected in the mirror was myself with the cat in my arms, but *there was no dog at my heels, although Agrippa was nosing at my ankles.*

For several seconds I stood there thunderstruck, unable to believe the evidence of my own senses, gazing first at the dog at my feet and then at the mirror with no reflection of the animal. I, the cat and the rest of the room were reflected with perfect clarity, but there was no reflection of Agrippa. I dropped the cat on the floor (and she remained reflected by the mirror) and picked Agrippa up in my arms. In the mirror I appeared to be carrying an imaginary object in my arms. Hastily I picked up the cat and so, with Clair under one arm and an invisible dog under the other, I left the blue salon and securely locked the door behind me.

Down in the kitchen I was ashamed to find that my hands were shaking. I gave the animals some milk (and the way Agrippa dealt with his, there was no doubt he was a flesh-and-blood animal) and made myself some breakfast. As I automatically fried eggs and some heavily smoked ham, my mind was busy with what I had seen in the blue salon. Unless I was mad—and I had never felt saner in my life—I was forced to admit that I had really experienced what I had seen, incredible though it seemed and indeed still seems to me. Although I was terrified at whatever it was that lurked behind the door in the mirror, yet I was filled with an overwhelming curiosity, a desire to see whatever creature it was that possessed that gaunt and tallow hand, yellow and emaciated arm. I determined that that very evening I would attempt to lure the creature out so that I could examine it. I was filled with horror at what I intended to do, but my curiosity was stronger than my fear. So I spent the day cataloguing the books in the study and, when darkness fell, I again lit the fire in the salon and cooked myself some supper and carried it and a bottle of wine upstairs and settled myself by the hearth. This time, however, I had taken the precaution of arming myself with a stout ebony cane and this gave me a certain confidence, though if I had thought about it, what use a cane was going to be to me against a looking-glass adversary, Heaven only knew. As it turned out eventually, arming myself with the stick was the worst thing I could have done and nearly cost me my life.

I ate my food, my eyes fixed on the mirror, the two animals lying asleep at my feet as they had done the night before. I finished my meal and still there was no change in the mirror image of the door. I sat back sipping my wine and watching. After an hour or so the fire was burning low and so I got up to put some logs on it; I had just settled back in my chair when I saw the handle of the mirror door start to turn very slowly. Then, millimeter by millimeter, the door was pushed open a foot or so. It was incredible that the opening of a door should be charged with such menace, but the slow furtive way it swung across the carpet was indescribably evil. Then the hand appeared, again moving very slowly, humping its way across the carpet until the wrist and part of the yellowish forearm was in view. It paused for a moment, lying flaccid on the carpet. Then, in a sickening sort of way, it started to grope around, as if the creature in control of the hand was blind. Now, it seemed to me, was the moment to put my carefully thought out plan into operation. I had deliberately starved Clair so that she would be hungry and so now I woke her up and waved under her nose a piece of meat which I had brought up from the kitchen for this purpose. Her eyes widened and she let out a loud mew of excitement. I waved the meat under her nose until she was frantic to get the morsel and then I threw it down the room so that it landed on the carpet near the firmly closed door of the salon. In the mirror I could see that it had landed near, but not too near the reflection of the hand which was still groping about blindly. Uttering a loud wail of hunger, Clair sped down the room after it. I had hoped that the cat would be so far away from the door that it would tempt the creature out into the open. But I realized that I had thrown the meat too close to the door for, as Clair's reflection stopped and the cat bent down to take the meat in her mouth, the hand ceased its blind groping, and shooting out with incredible speed, it seized Clair by the tail and dragged her, struggling and twisting, behind the door. As before, after a moment, the hand reappeared, curved round the door and slowly drew it shut, leaving bloody fingerprints on the woodwork. I think what made the whole thing doubly horrible was the contrast between the speed and ferocity with which the hand grabbed its prey, and the slow, furtive way it opened and closed the door. Clair now returned with the meat in her mouth to eat it in comfort by the fire, and like Agrippa, she seemed none the worse for now having no reflection. Although I waited up until after midnight the hand did not appear again, and so I took the animals and went to bed, determined that on the morrow I would work out a plan that would force the thing behind the door to show itself.

By evening on the following day I had finished my preliminary sorting and listing of the books on the ground floor of the house, and so the next step was to move upstairs to where the bulk of the library was housed in the Long Gallery. I felt somewhat tired that day and so, towards five o'clock, I decided to take a turn outside to get some fresh air in my lungs. Alas for my hopes! It had been snowing steadily since my arrival and now the glistening drifts were so high I could not walk through them. The only way to have got out of the central courtyard and across the bridge would have been to dig a path, and this would have been through snow lying in a great crusty blanket some six feet deep. Some of the icicles hanging from the guttering, the window ledges and the gargoyles were four and five feet long and as thick as my arm. The animals would not accompany me, but I tried walking a few steps into this spacious white world, as silent and as cold as the bottom of a well. The snow squeaked protestingly, like mice, beneath my shoes, and I sank in over my knees and soon had to struggle back to the house. The snow was still falling in flakes as big as dandelion blooms, thickening the white pie crusts on the roof ridges and gables. There was that complete silence that snow brings, no sound, no bird song, no whine of wind, just an almost tangible silence, as though the living world had been gagged with a crisp white scarf. Rubbing my frozen hands, I hastened inside, closed the front door and hastened down to the kitchen to prepare my evening meal. While this was cooking, I lit the fire in the blue salon once more and when the food was ready carried it up there as had become my habit, the animals accompanying me. Once again I armed myself with my stout stick and this gave me a small measure of comfort. I ate my food and drank my wine, watching the mirror but the hand did not put in an appearance. Where was it, I wondered. Did it stalk about and explore a reflection of the house that lay behind the door, a reflection I could not see? Or did it exist only when it became a reflection in the mirror that I looked at? Musing on this, I dozed, warmed by the fire, and presently slept deeply, which I had not meant to do. I must have slept for about an hour when I was suddenly shocked awake by the sound of a voice, a thin cracked voice, singing shrilly:

> *Auprès de ma blonde, auprès de ma blonde,*
> *qu'il fait bon dormir . . .*

This was followed by a grating peal of hysterical laughter. Half asleep as I was, it was a moment before I realized that the singing and laughter came from Octavius. But the shock of suddenly hearing a human voice like that was considerable, and my heart was racing. I glanced down the room and saw that the cages containing the canaries and Octavius were still as I had placed them. Then I glanced in the mirror and sat transfixed in my chair at the sight I saw. I suffered a revulsion and terror that surpassed anything I had felt before, for my wish had been granted and the thing from behind the door had appeared. As I watched it, how fervently I wished to God that I had left well alone, that I had locked the blue salon after the first night and never revisited it.

The creature—I must call it that for it seemed scarcely human—was small and humpbacked and clad in what I could only believe was a shroud, a yellowish linen garment spotted with gobbets of dirt and mould, torn in places where the fabric had worn thin, pulled over the thing's head and twisted round, like a scarf. At that moment, all that was visible of its face was a tattered fringe of faded orange hair on a heavily lined forehead and two large pale yellow eyes that glared with the fierce, impersonal arrogance of a goat, while below them the shroud was twisted round and held in place by one of the thing's pale, black-nailed hands.

It was standing behind the big cage that had contained the canaries. The cage was now twisted and wrenched and disembowelled, like a horse in a bull ring, and covered with a cloud of yellow feathers that stuck to the bloodstains on the bars. I noticed that there were a few yellow feathers between the fingers of the creature's hand. As I watched, it moved from the remains of the canary cage to the next table where the parrot cage had been placed. It moved slowly and limped heavily, appearing more to drag one foot after the other than anything else. It reached the cage in which the reflection of Octavius was weaving from side to side on his perch. The real bird in the room with me was still singing and cackling with laughter periodically. In the mirror the creature studied the parrot in its cage with its ferocious yellow eyes. Then suddenly, two things happened. The thing's hand shot out and the fingers entwined round the bars of the cage and wrenched and twisted them apart. While both hands were thus occupied, the piece of shroud that had been covering the face fell away and revealed the most disgusting face I have ever seen. Most of the features below the eyes appeared to have been eaten away, either by decay or some disease akin to leprosy. Where the nose should have been, there were just two black holes with tattered rims. The whole of one cheek was missing and so the upper and lower jaw, with mildewed gums and decaying teeth, were displayed, and trickles of saliva flooded out from the mouth and dripped down into the folds of the shroud. What was left of the lips were serrated with fine wrinkles so that they looked as though they had been stitched together and the cotton pulled tight. What made the whole thing even worse, as a macabre spectacle, was that on one of the creature's disgusting fingers it wore a large gold ring in which an opal flashed like flame as its hands moved, twisting the metal of the cage. This refinement on such a corpselike apparition only served to enhance its repulsive appearance. Presently it had twisted the wires enough so that there was room for it to put its hands inside the cage. The parrot was still bobbing and weaving on his perch, and the real Octavius was still singing and laughing. The creature grabbed the parrot in the reflection and it flapped and struggled in its hands, while Octavius continued to sing. The creature dragged the bird from the broken cage and lifted it to its obscene mouth and cracked the parrot's skull as it would a nut, and then with enjoyment started to suck out the brains, feathers and fragments of brain and skull mixing with the saliva that fell from the thing's mouth onto the shroud. I was filled with such revulsion and yet such rage at the creature's actions that I grasped my stick and leapt to my feet, trembling with anger. I approached the mirror and as I did so and my reflection appeared, I realized that (in the mirror) I was approaching the thing from behind. I moved forward until, in the reflection, I was close to the thing and then I raised my stick. But suddenly the creature's eyes appeared to blaze in its disintegrating face, and it stopped its revolting feast and dropped the corpse of the parrot to the ground at the same time whirling round to face my reflection with such speed that I was taken aback and stood there, staring at it, my stick raised. The creature did not hesitate for a second but dived forward and fastened its lean and powerful hands round my throat in the reflection. This sudden attack made my reflection stagger backwards and it dropped the stick. The creature and my reflection fell to the floor behind the table and I could see them both thrashing about together. Horrified, I dropped my stick and running to the mirror beat futilely against the glass. Presently all movement ceased behind the table. I could not see what was happening but, convinced the creature was dealing with my reflection as it had done with the dog and the cat, I continued to beat upon the mirror's surface. Presently, from behind the table, the creature rose up unsteadily, panting. It had its back to me. It remained like that for a moment or two and then it bent down and seizing my reflection body it dragged it slowly through the door. As it did so, I could see that the body had had its throat torn out. The creature then reappeared licking its lips in an anticipatory sort of way. It picked up the ebony stick and once more disappeared. It was gone some ten minutes and when it came back it was—to my horror and anger—feasting upon a severed hand, as a man might eat the wing of a chicken. Forgetting all fear, I beat on the mirror again. Slowly, as if trying to decide where the noise was coming from, the beast turned round, its eyes flashing terribly, its face covered with blood that could only be mine. Then it saw me and its eyes widened with a ferocious, knowing expression that turned me cold. Slowly it started to approach the mirror, and as it did so I stopped my futile hammering on the glass and backed away, appalled by the menace in the thing's goatlike eyes. Slowly it moved forward, its fierce eyes fixed on me as if stalking me. When it was close to the mirror, it put out its hands and touched the glass, *leaving bloody fingerprints and yellow and grey feathers stuck to the glass.* It felt the surface of the mirror delicately, as one would test the fragility of ice on a pond, and then it bunched its appalling hands into knobbly fists and beat a sudden furious tattoo on the glass, emitting a sudden, startling rattle of drums in the silent room. Then it unbunched its hands and felt the glass again. It stood for a moment watching me, as if it were musing. It was quite obvious that it could see me and I could only conclude that, although I possessed no reflection in my mirror, I must be visible as a reflection in the mirror that formed part of the looking-glass world which this creature inhabited. Suddenly, as if coming to a decision, it turned and limped off across the room and then, to my alarm, it disappeared through the door only to reappear a moment later carrying in its hands the ebony stick that my reflection had been carrying. Terrified, I realized that if I could hear the creature beating on the glass with its hands it must be in some way *solid,* and this meant that if it attacked the mirror with the stick the chances were the glass would shatter and that the creature could then, in some way, get through to me. As it limped down the room I made up my mind. I was determined that neither I nor the animals would stay in the blue salon any longer. I ran to where the cat and the dog lay asleep in front of the fire and gathered them up in my arms. I ran down the room and threw them unceremoniously into the hall. As I turned and hurried towards the bird cages, the creature reached the mirror, whirled the stick around its head and brought it crashing down. I saw that part of the mirror whiten and star in the way that ice on a pond does when struck with a stone. I did not wait. I seized the two cages and fled down the room with them and threw them into the hall and followed. As I grabbed the door to pull it shut, there was another crash and I saw a large portion of the mirror shower onto the floor and, sticking through the void, protruding into the blue salon, the emaciated, twisted arm of the creature brandishing the ebony cane. I did not wait to see more, but slammed the door and turned the key in the lock and leaned against the solid wood, the sweat running down my face, my heart hammering.

I collected my wits after a moment and made my way down to the kitchen where I poured myself a stiff brandy. My hand was trembling so much that I could hardly hold the glass. Desperately, I marshalled my wits and tried to think. It seemed to me that the mirror, when broken, acted as an *entrance* for the creature into my world. I did not know whether it was just this particular mirror or all mirrors. Furthermore, I did not know—if I broke any mirror that might act as an entrance for the thing— whether I would be preventing it or aiding it. I was shaking with fear but I knew that I would have to do something, for it was obvious that the creature would hunt me through the house. I went into the cellar and found myself a short, broad-bladed axe and then, picking up the candelabra, I made my way upstairs. The door to the blue salon was securely locked. I steeled myself and went into the study next door where there was, I knew, a medium-sized mirror hanging on the wall. I approached it, the candelabra held high, my axe ready. It was a curious sensation to stand in front of a mirror and not see yourself. I stood thus for a moment and then started with fright, for there appeared in the mirror suddenly, where my reflection should have been, the ghastly face of the creature glaring at me with a mad, lustful look in its eyes. I knew this was the moment that I would have to test my theory, but even so, I hesitated for a second before I smashed the axe head against the glass and saw it splinter and heard the pieces crash to the floor.

I stepped back after I had dealt the blow and stood with my weapon raised, ready to do battle should the creature try to get at me through the mirror, but with the disappearance of the glass, it was as if the creature had disappeared as well. Then I knew my idea was correct: if the mirror was broken from my side it ceased to be an entrance. I now knew that, to save myself, I had to destroy every mirror in the house and do it quickly, before the creature got to them and broke through. Picking up the candelabra, I moved swiftly to the dining salon where there was a large mirror and reached it just as the creature did. Luckily, I dealt the glass a shivering blow before the thing could break it with the cane that it still carried.

Moving as quickly as I could without quenching the candles, I made my way up to the first floor. Here I moved swiftly from bedroom to bedroom, bathroom to bathroom, wreaking havoc. Fear must have lent my feet wings because I arrived at all these mirrors before the creature did and managed to break them without seeing a sign of my adversary. Then all that was left was the Long Gallery with its ten or so huge mirrors hanging between the tall bookcases. I made my way there as rapidly as I could, walking for some stupid reason on tiptoe. When I reached the door, I was overcome with terror that the creature would have reached there before me and broken through and was, even now, waiting for me in the darkness. I put my ear to the door but could hear nothing. Taking a deep breath I threw open the door, holding the candelabra high.

Ahead of me lay the Long Gallery in soft velvety darkness, as anonymous as a mole's burrow. I stepped inside the door and the candle flames rocked and twisted on the ends of the candles, flapping the shadows like black funeral pennants on the floor and walls. I walked a little way into the room peering at the far end of the gallery, which was too far away to be illuminated by my candles, but it seemed to me that all the mirrors were intact. Hastily I placed the candelabra on a table and turned to the long row of mirrors. At that moment a sudden loud crash and tinkle sent my heart into my mouth, and it was a moment or so before I realized, with sick relief, that it was not the sound of a breaking mirror I heard but the noise of a great icicle that had broken loose from one of the windows and had fallen, with a sound like breaking glass, into the courtyard below.

I knew I had to act swiftly before that shuffling, limping monstrosity reached the Long Gallery and broke through. Taking a grip on the axe, I hurried from mirror to mirror, creating wreckage that no delinquent schoolboy could have rivalled. Again and again I smashed the head of the axe into the smooth surface like a man clearing ice from a lake, and the surface would star and whiten and then slip, the pieces chiming musically as they fell, to crash on the ground. The noise, in that silence, was extraordinarily loud. I reached the last mirror but one, and as my axe head splintered it, the one next door cracked and broke and the ebony stick, held in the awful hand, came through. Dropping the axe in my fright, I turned and fled, pausing only to snatch up the candelabra. As I slammed the door shut and locked it, I caught a glimpse of something white struggling to disentangle itself from the furthest mirror in the Gallery. I leaned against the door, shaking with fright, my heart hammering, listening. Dimly, through the locked door, I could hear faint sounds of tinkling glass and then there was silence. I strained my ears but could hear no more. Then, against my back, I could feel the handle of the door being slowly turned. Cold with fear, I leapt away and, fascinated, watched the handle move round until the creature realized that the door was locked. Then there came such an appalling scream of frustrated rage, shrill, raw and indescribably evil and menacing, that I almost dropped the candelabra in my fright. I leaned against the wall, shaking, wiping the sweat from my face but limp with relief. Now all the mirrors in the house were broken and the only two rooms that thing had access to were securely locked. For the first time in twenty-four hours, I felt safe. Inside the Long Gallery the creature was snuffling round the door like a pig in a trough. Then it gave another blood-curdling scream of frustrated rage and then there was silence. I listened for a few minutes but I could hear nothing so, taking up my candelabra, I started to make my way downstairs.

I paused frequently to listen. I moved slowly so that the tiny scraping noises of my sleeve against my coat would not distract my hearing. I held my breath. All I could hear was my heart, hammering against my ribs like a desperate hand, and the very faint rustle and flap of the candle flames as they danced to my movement. Thus, slowly, every sense alert, I made my way down to the lower floor of that gaunt, cold, empty house. It was not until I reached the bend in the staircase that led down into the hall that I realized I had made a grave mistake.

I paused at the bend to listen and I stood so still that even the candle flames stood upright, like a little grove of orange cypress trees. I could hear nothing. I let my breath out slowly in a sigh of relief and then I rounded the corner and saw the one thing I had forgotten, the tall pier glass that hung at the foot of the stairs.

In my horror I nearly dropped the candelabra. I gripped it more firmly in my sweating hands. The mirror hung there, innocently on the wall, reflecting nothing more alarming than the flight of steps I was about to descend. All was quiet. I prayed the thing was still upstairs snuffling around in the wreckage of a dozen broken mirrors. Slowly I started to descend the stairs.

Then halfway down, I stopped suddenly, paralyzed

with fear, for reflected in the top of the mirror, descending as I was towards the hall, appeared the bare, misshapen feet of the creature.

I was panic-stricken, did not know what to do. I knew that I should break the mirror before the creature descended to the level where it could see me. But to do this I would have to throw the candelabra at the mirror to shatter it and this would then leave me in the dark. And supposing I missed? To be trapped on the stairs, in the dark, by that monstrous thing was more than I could bear. I hesitated, and hesitated too long. For with surprising speed the limping creature descended the stairs, using the stick in one hand to support it while the other ghastly hand clasped the bannister rail, the opal ring glinting as it moved. Its head and decaying face came into view and it glared through the mirror at me and snarled. Still I could do nothing. I stood rooted to the spot, holding the candles high, unable to move.

It seemed to me more important that I should have light so that I could see what the thing was doing than that I should use the candelabra to break the mirror. But I hesitated too long. The creature drew back its emaciated arm, lifted the stick high and brought it down. There was a splintering crash; the mirror splinters became opaque, and through the falling glass the creature's arm appeared. More glass fell until it was all on the floor and the frame was clear. The creature, snuffling and whining eagerly, like a dog that has been shown a plate of food, stepped through the mirror and, its feet scrunching and squeaking, trod on the broken glass. Its blazing eyes fixed upon me, it opened its mouth and uttered a shrill, gurgling cry of triumph; the saliva flowed out of its decomposing ruins of cheeks, and I could hear its teeth squeak together as it ground them. It was such a fearful sight I was panicked into making a move. Praying that my aim would be sure, I raised the heavy candelabra and hurled it down at the creature. For a moment it seemed as though the candelabra hung in midair, the flames still on the candles, the creature standing in the wreckage of the mirror, glaring up at me, and then the heavy ornate weapon struck it. As the candles went out I heard the soggy thud and the grunt the creature gave, followed by the sound of the candelabra hitting the marble floor and the sound of a body falling. Then there was complete darkness and complete silence. I could not move. I was shaking with fear and at any minute I expected to feel those hideous white hands fasten around my throat or round my ankles, but nothing happened. How many minutes I stood there I do not know. At length I heard a faint, gurgling sigh and then there was silence again. I waited, immobile in the darkness, and still nothing happened. Taking courage I felt in my pocket for the matches. My hands were shaking so much that I could hardly strike one, but at length I succeeded. The feeble light it threw was not enough for me to discern anything except that the creature lay huddled below the mirror, a hunched heap that looked very dark in the flickering light. It was either unconscious or dead, I thought, and then cursed as the match burnt my hand and I dropped it. I lit another and made my way cautiously down the stairs. Again the match went out before I reached the bottom and I was forced to pause and light another. I bent over the thing, holding out the match and then recoiled at what I saw:

Lying with his head in a pool of blood was Gideon.

I stared down at his face in the flickering light of the match, my senses reeling. He was dressed as I had last seen him. His astrakhan hat had fallen from his head and the blood had gushed from his temple where the candelabra had hit him. I felt for his heartbeat and his pulse, but he was quite dead. His eyes, now lacking the fire of his personality, gazed blankly up at me. I relit the candles and then sat on the stairs and tried to work it out. I am still trying to work it out today.

I will spare the reader the details of my subsequent arrest and trial. All those who read newspapers will remember my humiliation, how they would not believe me (particularly as they found the strangled and half-eaten corpses of the dog, the cat and the birds) that after the creature appeared we had merely become the reflections in its mirror. If I was baffled to find an explanation, you may imagine how the police treated the whole affair. The newspapers called me the "Monster of the Gorge" and were shrill in calling for my blood. The police, dismissing my story of the creature, felt they had enough evidence in the fact that Gideon had left me a large sum of money in his will. In vain I protested that it was I, at God knows what cost to myself, who had fought my way through the snow to summon help. For the police, disbelievers in witchcraft (as indeed I had been before this), the answer was simple: I had killed my friend for money and then made up this tarradiddle of the creature in the mirror. The evidence was too strongly against me and the uproar of the Press, fanning the flames of public opinion, sealed my fate. I was a monster and must be punished. So I was sentenced to death, sentenced to die beneath the blade of the guillotine. Dawn is not far away, and it is then that I am to die. So I have whiled away the time writing down this story in the hopes that anyone who reads it might believe me. I have never fancied death by the guillotine; it has always seemed to me to be a most barbarous means of putting a man to death. I am watched, of course, so I cannot cheat what the French call "the widow," with macabre sense of humor. But I have been asked if I have a last request, and they have agreed to let me have a full-length mirror to dress myself for the occasion. I shall be interested to see what will happen.

Here the manuscript ended. Written underneath, in a different hand, was the simple statement: the prisoner was found dead in front of the mirror. Death was due to heart failure. Dr. Lepitre.

The thunder outside was still tumultuous and the lightning still lit up the room at intervals. I am not ashamed to say I went and hung a towel over the mirror on the dressing table and then, picking up the bulldog, I got back into bed and snuggled down with him.

Scott Baker (b. 1947)

THE LURKING DUCK

Scott Baker, originally from the American midwest, is the author of the subtle and startling horror novels *Webs* and *Dhampire* and a number of disturbing and original horror stories, of which "Nesting Instinct" won the World Fantasy Award for 1988. He is also the winner of the Prix Apollo, the distinguished French Award for science fiction. Characteristically, Baker works with the subtle accumulation of detail and atmosphere to create progressively more disturbing revelations. He has lived for many years in Paris with his wife, Suzy, who is a translator. This story first appeared in France, in a French collection of Baker's stories never published in English. A substantially shorter form appeared in *Omni* in 1987, and was a World Fantasy Award nominee, but the unabridged version, too short to be published as a full-length book, and too long for most magazines and anthologies, remained unpublished in English until now. When I asked Baker why he had chosen this particular title, he replied that he wanted that old Lovecraftian feel. Beware of Baker's deadpan humor, which underpins some of the finest moments of this piece. Here, for the first time, in the unabridged version is "The Lurking Duck."

Julie: 1981

It was Tuesday evening, just before dark, a few weeks
after my birthday. I was four years old. Mother and
Daddy had just had another fight. Daddy used to be a
policeman before he got paralyzed all below the neck but
Mother was still a policewoman and she was very strong
and every now and then she lost control and knocked
him around a little. That's what she called it and that's
what happened this time, but even after she got him to
shut up they were still both really mad at each other, so
she took me down to El Estero Lake to watch the ducks
and the swans while she ran around the lake to make
herself calm down. The swans were mean but I liked the
ducks a lot.

  She put me on one of the concrete benches and got out
the piece of string she always kept in her pocket when she
was with me, then made a circle around the bench with
it. The piece of string was about ten feet long but the
circle it made was a lot smaller and I had to stay inside it.
Then she went off to do her jogging.

  After a while I noticed that there was an old green car
with no one in it, one of those big bump-shaped cars like
the ones you see in the black-and-white movies on TV,
parked a little ways away from me on the gravel, up
under a tree where it was pretty close to the water. The
sun was already gone and it was almost dark but I could
still see that every now and then one of the ducks would
get curious about the car and waddle up to it and stick its
head underneath to look at something, then sort of
squeeze down and push itself the rest of the way under
the car. I couldn't see what happened to the ducks under
the car but none of them ever came out again. I saw two
of the ducks with the bright green heads—mallards—
and one brown duck go under the car before Mother
came back to do her jump-roping.

  When I told her about the ducks she got real mad

again. At first I thought she was mad at me but then she went and found a man hiding in the car under an old blanket and she arrested him. He was all dirty and ragged and skinny and he smelled bad. His hands were all big and red. Mother said that he was a drunk and that he was sick in the head but he wasn't very old. He'd made a hole in the bottom of his car and put a lot of duck food on the ground beneath it so the ducks would come underneath where he could grab them by the neck and kill them without anybody being able to see what he was doing. Mother said that Daddy'd arrested him for doing the same thing once back before the accident. She found five dead mallards and seven of the brown ducks and two white ducks under the blanket with him but they were all already dead.

JAMES PATRICK DUBIC

I. From the *SAND CITY SHORELINE RAG AND TATTLESHEET,* May 22, 1981:

DUCKNAPPER NABBED YET AGAIN!
by *RAG* Staff Writer Thom Homart

The *RAG* learned yesterday that twenty-nine-year-old aerospace heir James Patrick Dubic, a former part-time instructor in the department of computer sciences at Monterey Peninsula and Chapman Colleges, was arrested Monday evening by Police Officer Mrs. Virginia Matson on multiple charges stemming from the alleged theft and slaughter of fourteen ducks from El Estero Park in downtown Monterey.

Officer Matson, who was recently promoted to the head of the Monterey Municipal Police Tac Squad (where she replaces her husband, Thomas Philip Matson, paralyzed in a tragic skateboard accident during the Parent-Teacher Day celebrations at Monterey High School last fall), was off duty at the time of the arrest. She had taken her daughter Julie, four, to the lake to "get her out of the house for a while" when Julie noticed that there were a lot of ducks going under an old car parked near them but that none of the ducks that went under the car ever came out again! She told her mother and Officer Matson investigated, only to find James Patrick Dubic hidden under a blanket in the backseat. With him under the blanket she found a cloth sack labeled *Dewer's Duckfood* containing fourteen recently killed ducks. The floorboards of the car had been removed and duck pellets scattered on the ground beneath it to attract the birds.

Dubic is currently out on bail on previous charges stemming from the alleged sale of a large number of sea gulls and a smaller number of cats to five ethnic restaurants here on the Peninsula and in Salinas. The restaurants in question—Casa Miguel, La Poubelle de Luxe, The Ivory Pagoda, Shanghai Express and Ho's Terrace Cafe—have been charged with serving the sea gulls, which are protected by state, federal, county and city law, as duck and chicken in a variety of dishes such as *Cantonese duck, Pollo Mole,* and *Duck à l'orange.* The cats are alleged to have served as the basis for a number of beef and rabbit dishes.

Dubic, furthermore, has not only been convicted on three previous misdemeanor charges involving what might be termed violence against domestic birds and wildfowl but is also the man whom Monterey County Prosecutor Florio Volpone attempted last year to prove was the actual head of the dognapping ring that in the last five years has been responsible for the deaths of thousands of Central California Irish Setters and Afghans sold to the Mexican fur industry for their beautiful "pelts." Though we here at the *RAG* cannot disagree with Judge Hapgood's ruling to the effect that the evidence Prosecutor Volpone produced was insufficient to prove Dubic guilty before the law of the dognapping and related conspiracy charges—which is to say, guilty of them beyond the shadow of a reasonable doubt—yet we cannot help but feel that there is something at the very least quite *suggestive* about the fact that Dubic has been arrested and charged with similar crimes on at least *forty* other occasions in the recent past. Though it is not perhaps completely fair for those of us here at the *RAG*, in our capacity of armchair quarterbacks, to suggest that, as the saying goes, there's no smoke without fire and that there must have been some compelling reason for not just one but all of our local police forces to keep on arresting Dubic again and again for the same kind of alleged crime. . . .

II. The Trial

"Objection sustained," Hapgood said but it was already too late. Volpone'd been able to get the jury thinking about the dognapping charges again, with that bit about Mexico thrown in to appeal to their racism. The bastard. He knew as well as I did that that was all bullshit, that I'd never had anything against dogs. Or cats either, and he was trying to get them to believe I'd been killing cats too, and that wasn't true. I'd always loved cats, I'd even had one of my own for a while and he knew it, but it didn't make any difference to Volpone, he was going to try to get me for the cats anyway.

". . . a rubber duck," Wibsome was saying the next time I bothered to tune in to him. I hadn't been missing anything. I'd heard it all before time after time and anyway he was even clumsier than usual today. Probably because he knew there was no way his particular brand of rhetoric was going to get me out of anything this time, no matter how hard he tried, so he wasn't even trying.

"A rubber duck," he continued, "which the late Robert Tyrone Dubic had the habit of filling with bird shot and ball bearings before he used it to beat his defenseless five-year-old brother into unconsciousness. The same rubber duck with which he often threatened to kill that younger brother, James Patrick Dubic, here before you on charges from what the prosecution claims is a pathological hatred of birds in general and ducks in particular.

"But I ask you—is there anything really all *that* sick or irrational in the defendent's feelings about birds? Would *you,* any of you, have had a great fondness for the creatures if you had been repeatedly beaten by a sadistic older brother with a lead-filled rubber duck during your formative years? If you had been so badly mauled by your aunt's flock of geese that you were hospitalized for three days? Would you have had any overwhelming love for our feathered friends if your grandfather had disinherited you in favor of a bird sanctuary in Guatemala, a country which neither you nor he had ever visited? Is there anything odd about the fact that James Patrick Dubic is, as you yourselves have heard him testify, disgusted with the evident hypocrisy of people who publically demand increased protection for the California environment while at the same time spending a fortune in certain local restaurants for meat from wild boar they know perfectly well have been killed illegally inside the Los Padres Forest preserve?

"I'm not going to try to pretend to you that James Patrick Dubic is immensely likeable, or that he's just like everybody else. He isn't. But what he *is* is a man of intelligence and principle, a former teacher who was always respected by his students, and he is neither irrational nor insane. His dislike of birds, regrettable though it may be, is a perfectly normal reaction to the rather unique and unfortunate circumstances of his childhood. . . ."

It wasn't going to work. Not this time. Wibsome

wasn't even trying. They were going to lock me up again, and not just for a little while this time. Maybe even get me committed to Atascadero, put me away for the rest of my life by claiming I was criminally insane. That sounded like what Wibsome was really after this time. Get me out of Father's hair for good. And even if they let me out later he could always have me put back in if I made any more trouble for him. If they ever let me out. He'd like that now, with Mother remarried so she couldn't make him do anything for me anymore.

"We're going to appeal," Wibsome told me when he came back and sat down again. Meaning that there was no way they weren't going to find me guilty. "Those articles in the *RAG*—I'm pretty sure we can prove they prejudiced the jury and kept you from getting a fair trial. And there may be other things I can turn up when I've had the time to study the court recorder's transcripts of the trial for a while."

"Wibsome," I said, "you know I didn't have anything to do with the dogs, or with those cats either. You know how I've always liked dogs and cats—"

"Of course, Jimmy." He didn't believe me even though he was supposed to be on my side. "Not the dogs and cats. Just those nasty, nasty birds."

"Yes!" He was laughing at me again. Just like Bobby used to, before they shipped him off to Vietnam and killed him. But if I ever got out of here I was going to get him just like I was going to get all the rest of them. That oh-so-sweet little girl and her bull-dyke mother and her paralyzed father who was the one who'd lied about me at that other trial, the time that he'd been the one who'd arrested me. That bastard who'd written all those articles for the *RAG* and all those restaurant owners who'd tried to put each other out of business by accusing each other of having hired me to get their sea gulls and cats for them, when all the time they'd hired me to get sea gulls for them themselves and they knew I wouldn't have anything to do with killing cats. And Judge Hapgood and Florio Volpone and the jury and Wibsome and my father and the ducks.

All of them. But especially the ducks.

III. From the *SAND CITY SHORELINE RAG AND TATTLESHEET,* August 8, 1983:

. . . remember that the judge and jury agreed with our editorial staff and that Dubic was sentenced to three concurrent terms of ten to twenty years in the state penitentiary. Since then his lawyers have made repeated attempts to have his convictions overturned, most recently by charging that the *RAG*'s crusading editorials and reportage unfairly prejudiced the jury against him and so precluded the possibility of a fair trial. Dubic's lawyers accompanied this latest appeal with a simultaneous multimillion dollar suit against the *RAG* and its editorial staff for libel and defamation of character.

We are very happy indeed to report that Dubic's appeal has been denied and that all charges against us for libel and defamation of character have been unconditionally dismissed.

IV. From THE BUZZBOMB, House Organ of the Dubic Aerospace and Munitions Industrial Group, January, 1984:

Aerospace Guidance System Division Chief Damien Holmes announced today the purchase of THE OTHER CHESSPLAYER, INC., designers and manufacturers of the popular PROGRAMMED PRO line of computerized tennis opponents, as well as of the increasingly popular computer games SHARK ALERT, ROBOBRAWL, and GET THE PROWLER BEFORE HE GETS YOU. "With their genius for innovative software and our technical expertise," Vice President

Holmes told the *Buzzbomb*, "it shouldn't be more than a matter of months before we're not only light-years ahead of our competitors here in the United States but even further ahead of everybody else in the rest of the world, and most especially our counterparts in Soviet Russia."

V. From "Philanthropy for the Year 2000," a speech delivered by James Damien Dubic to the Orange County League of Republican Women, March 19, 1984

". . . not just new ways of doing things that have never really done anybody much real good. To put it another way, we don't want to compete with any of the other charitable and philanthropic organizations now operating, we want to put them out of business altogether by making the very need for charity and philanthropy obsolete.

"Furthermore, there's no question in any of our minds that our society's future lies with increased computerization. Now, there are some disadvantages to this, as I'm sure some of you may have noticed every now and then when you've caught a computer error on your bank statement or your Mastercharge, but that kind of problem doesn't come from using computers, it just comes from the fact that we haven't been using computers long enough to have learned everything there is to know about using them. A good comparison would be to think of yourselves in the same position as the first railway passengers, who inevitably got covered with soot and smoke from the locomotive's engines because nobody'd yet found out how to make them burn cleaner and how to keep the smoke away from the passengers. But after trains had been around for a while they found all sorts of solutions to the problems, so they weren't really problems at all anymore.

"But let me get back to what we at the Dubic Foundation are trying to do right now, which is to find new ways to use the future's increased computerization for the social good. Not just new ways of doing old things—like a robot soup-line to compete with the Salvation Army's human volunteers—but ways to do new things altogether, things that nobody's ever been able to do before. And we're pretty sure we've found some new ways of doing things, all of them so far based on the concepts of shared computer time and decentralization.

"Let me make that a little clearer for you. Take a look at oh, any of the big banks here in California. Bank of America, UCB, even the Japanese Maritime Bank, any bank with a lot of branches scattered all over the state. All their records are computerized, but there's no way that any of these banks could have ever afforded a separate computer system for every one of their branches, even if they'd wanted to have them for some reason. No, what they've got is a single master computer connected by telephone linkages to separate data terminals in every branch, so that each branch is sharing the master computer's capabilities with all the other branches. There are even a number of companies that rent their spare computer time to companies too small to have a cost-effective computer capacity of their own. Dubic Aerospace is one such company, which is one of the reasons I know what I do about the subject.

"Anyway, ladies, think about what would happen if you took the whole process one step further, and took at least some of the data terminals out of the branch offices or whatever and put them into the employees' homes, so that you had a double telephone linkage working for you, not only between the master computer and the branch offices, but also between the branch offices and the employees' home terminals. There are an awful lot of peripheral benefits we haven't yet had a chance to examine to be gained from having people work at home like that—no commuting time wasted and less traffic jams, for one thing, possible savings on expensive office space for another, to pick just two examples—but that sort of thing's not really what we, as philanthropists, are interested in right now. What we want to know is, how can we find new ways to use this development to make things better for people?

"Well, one of the first things we thought of was the way this could help shut-ins, perfectly competent and intelligent people who because of some accident or chronic illness are unable to leave their homes or, even worse, have been condemned to live the rest of their lives confined to their beds. Just think what it would do for these people's sense of self-esteem if they had a way of holding a real job and of becoming more or less self-supporting. Not to mention the savings to society involved in getting them off welfare. This wouldn't really affect all that many people, probably, but it could make an enormous difference in the lives of the people it did affect, and save the taxpayer some money in the process.

"But there's another kind of shut-in this kind of set-up could help, and help in a way that could quite possibly do all of us an enormous amount of incidental good. I'm talking about convicts, convicted criminals, all those men and women that society has been forced for its own protection, and in the hope of reforming them, to put behind bars. And there are a lot of them, make no mistake of that, all our jails, prisons, penitentiaries and work farms are not only full but dangerously overcrowded with men, women and adolescents whose care and keeping is paid for by the rest of us, all of us who pay taxes.

"And what we're paying for, really, is a kind of school system or fraternity where all the petty criminals—the kids who hot-wired cars to go joyriding or the clerk who for the first and only time in his life needed money so badly that he took a hundred dollars out of his employer's cash register and got caught at it—where all these people who have nothing better to do with their time than break rocks or stamp out license plates learn from the other prisoners, the real hardened criminals, how to become hardened criminals themselves. And when they finally do get out the only people they know are criminals, they can't get a job because of their records and because, especially if they were pretty young when they went in, all they know how to do is break rocks or make license plates or hang around with criminals. And so what their stay in prison has really done for them is just to put them on the road to becoming far more dangerous and expensive to society than they might ever have become on their own.

"But think about a convict who gets the training he needs to be a computer programmer of some sort in prison. He's already learned a skill that will be useful to society and that has a good chance of taking him away from the poverty and bad influences that may well have been what turned him to crime in the first place.

"So far, so good. But now let's assume that some company or group of companies has arranged to have some of its data terminals installed within the prison walls, in much the same way as the terminals for the shut-in patients I mentioned earlier would have been installed in their homes, and that this company agrees to accept qualifying prisoners for some sort of apprentice program, so that they can not only be gaining useful skills and on-the-job training while still in prison, but they can already have a job waiting for them when they get out AND have a bank account they've built up from what they were being paid during their apprenticeship waiting for them outside. That way, they'll be able to sidestep the whole grinding cycle of poverty and humiliation and living on welfare that right now drives so many ex-convicts straight back to a life of crime.

"Of course, there are still a few safeguards we're going to have to work out before we can put our pilot program in practice because these are, after all, convicted criminals we're talking about. To give you just one example of the kinds of things we're going to have to guard against, you wouldn't want to put a genius embezzler or even safecracker in total control of Bank of America's computer system. . . ."

Julie: 1988

It was a really hot night even though it was still only April and the air conditioner was broken again. Mother was yelling at Father and he was whining back at her again. Pretty soon he'd start yelling and then she'd start hitting him again. They'd been drinking a lot too, both of them, like they always did. I was eleven and they'd been doing the same thing ever since I could remember. I couldn't stand them, either of them.

I put my slingshot—the hunting kind you get at sporting goods stores that shoots steel balls, not one of those homemade rubber band things for little kids—into my bag and went down to the lake to sit around for a while. We lived about four blocks away, up by the Naval Postgraduate School. Sometimes when there wasn't anyone else at the lake I'd try to get one of the swans or even one of the ducks with my slingshot—I'd killed a swan once, one of the black ones with the red beaks, and hit one or two others and a couple of ducks—but there were a lot of people out on the lake on those stupid little two-person aquacycles, those boat-things you pedal like bicycles. Couples mainly, some high school kids but mainly old people, tourists and golfers. Some fathers with their kids. They all looked stupid.

I didn't like the park all that much but I didn't have any friends that lived close and I didn't feel like walking or even riding my bike very far, especially not all the way up Carmel Hill to where Beth lived. But I couldn't stand staying home any longer either, not while they were still fighting. It would be OK later on, when something they both wanted to watch came on TV or when Father had a little more to drink. After a while he just got quieter and

quieter until he went to sleep. Which was why I was glad
he drank all the time, even though he got pretty nasty in
the evening and when he first woke up in the morning.
And that was OK anyway, because he had a right to get
angry even if not at me, the way Mother treated him. She
treated him like shit and he never did anything wrong, all
he did was sit around all day watching television and
reading magazines and detective stories and drinking a
little beer through his tube. He didn't hurt anybody and
it wasn't his fault if he couldn't wash himself and if
sometimes he smelled bad and that he'd gotten all sort of
fat and droopy-faced and pasty-looking, not at all like he
looked in those pictures Mother still had of him from
before the accident, when he still looked a lot like that
mess sergeant Mother sometimes brought home with her
from Fort Ord, the one who kept telling me he was going
to fix the air conditioner but never did. Only Father'd
been a lot cleaner and handsomer and younger than the
mess sergent was, then.

The sun was going away even though it wasn't quite
dark yet and it looked like it was going to rain pretty
soon. A lot of people were coming back in to shore and
turning in their aquacycles to the man that rented them
out, though there were still a couple of chicano-looking
kids in an aluminum canoe who didn't look like they
were going to quit before dark. And I had to be careful, I
could still remember sitting there on that bench watching Mother arrest that man who'd been killing the ducks
under his car. I still had all the clippings that Mother'd
saved for me from that, including the ones with my
picture in them from the *Post-Sentinel* and the *RAG*, and
the other one where they'd had me talk a bit for the *Pine
Cone*.

The highschool kids in the canoe were down at the
other end of lake. I was watching the ducks and the
swans out on the lake feeding—I didn't want to try
anything with any of the ones up on shore, where

somebody could see what happened to it and where there wouldn't be that much skill involved anyway—because I had to know where they all were so I could find them again if I had to wait until it was almost all the way dark before everybody else went away. The swans were mean but I didn't dislike the ducks or anything—though I didn't much like them either, with their mean little suspicious eyes and the way they walked around when they were on land like they thought they were the most important things in the world—but there wasn't anything else I could do to go get back at something when I felt like this. Just like Father yelling at Mother whenever he got to thinking about how really bad it was to be paralyzed and that we had to feed him and help him go to the bathroom, or Mother hitting him whenever she couldn't stand to look at how horrible it was for him anymore.

A lot of the ducks and swans were up on the shore near me looking for food somebody might have left and quacking and honking at each other or lying down on their stomachs with their heads tucked in and sleeping. The swans that were in the water were down at the other end of the lake but the ducks in the water were all paddling around in groups and quacking at each other. A lot of the male mallards were doing that thing they do together when they all swim after one of the brown females without ever catching her and then they all take off together and they chase her through the air but they still don't catch her, and a few of them every now and then were doing that thing where they beat their wings and sort of get up out of the water like they were standing on their tiptoes and beating their chests like Tarzan. But most of them were just swimming around and sticking their heads down underwater the way they do when they're looking for something to eat down there but don't feel like diving for it, or doing that thing where they turn all the way upside down like they're standing on their heads with their tails sticking straight up out of the water.

There was an old lady down at the other end of the lake, near the kids in the canoe. She was throwing bread crumbs or something to the swans but she looked pretty busy and I didn't think she'd notice what I was doing if I waited until it got just a little darker.

One of the ducks, a mallard, a really pretty male with a bright green head and a big patch of shiny blue on his side, was off alone out in the middle, not doing much with the other ducks, just sort of floating there like he was half-asleep though he didn't have his head tucked back or anything. He was pretty far away but close enough so I thought I could hit him with a good enough shot.

Suddenly he started doing that thing that ducks do when they're real mad at each other or fighting over a female or that the females sort of do when they're telling all the males to go away and they stick their necks forward with their mouths wide open and charge at each other using their wings to go fast enough so they're almost running at each other on top of the water. But the weird thing was that the duck wasn't charging another male, he was charging a whole little group of four or five females—I could tell they were females because they were all brown and speckled and one of them even had some of her black and yellow baby ducklings swimming around her—and he wasn't making that sort of hissing warning noise that all the other ducks I'd ever seen make when they're charging like that.

He didn't stop when he was close enough to warn them off either, like they usually do. All at once he was in with the other ducks and they were all squacking and beating their wings and trying to fly away. I thought I saw something real bright flash, like a knife blade, only it was too dark for a piece of metal to flash like that, and then all but one of the females that had been trying to get away were up out of the water and flying off and the baby ducklings were running across the water peeping and trying to get away.

But one of the females—maybe the mother, I couldn't tell—was floating there with its belly up and its orange legs twitching. Then its legs quit twitching and I could tell it was dead. And the male was gone. It hadn't flown away with the others and it hadn't swum away and it wasn't anywhere I could see in the water. So it must have dived down to the bottom and stayed there or at least not come up until it was a long ways away. Maybe it was lurking down there like a snapping turtle.

The chicano high school kids were landing their canoe and I tried to get them to take me out in it again so I could get the dead duck and take a look at it and see what the male had done to it but they were already starting to put their canoe back in their pickup and they weren't interested.

It was getting too dark to see anything so I walked around for a while. I went down to the wharf to see if the organ-grinder was there with his monkey but he wasn't —it wasn't quite the beginning of the tourist season yet and anyway it was the middle of the week, so there weren't that many people around—so I walked back to McDonald's and bought a Big Mac with some money I took from Mother's purse when she left it lying around a few days before, then went the rest of the way home. Father was asleep but Mother was still up watching a movie on TV. I didn't have any homework so after I fed my turtles and guppies I sat down and watched the movie with her until she told me it was too late and I had to go to bed.

When I went down to the lake the next morning before school with a pair of binoculars the dead duck was gone. I looked for the other duck for a while, but I couldn't find it or if I did find it it looked just like all the other mallards and wasn't doing anything special.

But I spotted it for sure when I came back again after school. It was just floating around the same way it had the night before and it always stayed out near the middle, away from shore and the shallow water where all the other ducks liked to feed, and it wouldn't move at all except to keep away from the people on their aquacycles. That was how I noticed it, because when an aquacycle came within maybe fifteen feet of where it was resting it would move away so it stayed just fifteen feet away from the aquacycle, then move back to where it'd been as soon as the people on the cycle were far enough away. And it did the same thing once with some people in a boat.

And besides it never dived or quacked or preened itself or seemed to be looking for anything to eat and all the other ducks ignored it. They didn't seem scared of it, they just didn't pay any attention to it, and all it did was float there and keep away from people.

But that was only when the sun was shining on it. As soon as things clouded over it would start swimming towards the other ducks, but it always stopped and went back to floating on its own away from everything else when the sun came out from behind the clouds again.

All except one time, after I'd been there a couple of hours, when a lot of really dark clouds covered the sun and kept it covered for about fifteen minutes. The duck started swimming towards another duck the way it always did when the sun got covered over—the other duck was a male mallard just like it was this time—but it didn't stop like it had before, the times when the sun came out from behind the clouds again. I was watching it through the binoculars to try to see what it did if it attacked the other male the same way it'd attacked the females the night before.

Only it didn't attack the other duck. It just swam closer and closer to it until the two ducks were maybe three feet away from each other, then it put its head down and went forward a little like it was looking for food on the bottom and then it dived.

A second or two late the other mallard gave a sort of

shocked SQUAWK! and got pulled under, just like a giant snapping turtle had reached up from underneath and grabbed it in its jaws and pulled it down. Only I knew it wasn't a snapping turtle, it was the other duck.

I watched where it had gone under with the binoculars for a while but there wasn't any blood or feathers I could see, nothing to make it look like the duck was getting killed or eaten there under the water, except that it never came up again.

But about five minutes later the duck that had killed it came bobbing up again. It was all muddy and I thought that maybe it had been lying down there on the bottom in the mud eating the other duck and then had buried what was left of its body like a dog with a bone it's finished with. It preened itself for a while, looking pretty and silly and self-important like any other mallard, then paddled back to the middle and went back to its sunbathing.

It was getting near dinner time so I went home to take care of Father. Mother was still at the police station and he was in a pretty good mood and watching something he liked on TV so it wasn't so bad. I changed his urine bottle and washed him up a bit, then fed him a TV dinner and connected his drinking tube to a big bottle of one of those pre-mixed drinks—a whisky sour or a gin martini, I forget which—then left him there and went back down to the lake to watch the ducks for a while. I took some bread down with me to feed to the other ducks and swans in case somebody wanted to know what I was doing there. The day was still pretty bright out and the duck that was killing the other ducks was still floating out alone in the middle, though not quite in the same place, so I didn't have any trouble finding it again.

It pulled another duck down the same way before the sun went down, a different kind this time, one of those grey and white ones with the chocolate brown heads and necks with a white stripe running up each side. And then, just as the last light was going away, it did the same thing it'd done the night before, when it'd attacked the group of females. Only this time I had the binoculars ready and I knew what I was looking for, so I got to see what it did when it killed the other duck.

It charged just the way any other duck would've again, only it didn't stop when the other duck tried to get away. The duck it was after was another male mallard again—there were a whole lot of them out on the lake, like there always were—and the duck that was attacking it kept right on going faster and faster with its bill wide open until just before it was going to ram into the other duck something like a pair of shiny steel garden shears came out of its open mouth like a gigantic metal snake's tongue and cut the other duck's head off.

The scissors went back into the killer duck's mouth and it grabbed the dead duck's head in its bill then dived like it had the other times, when it had pulled the ducks down. Only this time it left the headless duck's body floating on the water and it didn't come up again.

I waited until it was too dark to see, then made sure I knew how to find the spot where the duck had disappeared and went home. Father was asleep in his wheelchair in front of the TV. Mother wasn't home yet. I changed Father's urine bag again then wheeled him into his bedroom and got him into bed, then fed the turtles and guppies and went to bed with a book I'd gotten out of the school library about ducks.

But I was out of bed the next morning before it got light out and by the time the sun came up I was already down at the lake with the binoculars, watching the spot where the duck had disappeared the night before. There was a whole cluster of five or six big water lilies there I hadn't noticed before but I was still pretty sure I had the right spot.

About an hour after the sun came up the water lillies disappeared like fishing-line bobbers being yanked down by a big fish and a moment later the duck bobbed to the surface. It was all muddy again but it preened itself for a while until it was all clean, then swam back to the middle of the lake, but not quite the same spot it had been in the day before.

I went back to the house. Mother hadn't come home at all last night but Father was already awake. I helped him get dressed and go to the bathroom, then cleaned him up and made us both some scrambled eggs and toast. After I fed him I wheeled him into the living room and put his book in the thing to turn the pages for him, then made myself two liver sausage sandwiches for lunch. Mother came home just as I was leaving and gave me a ride to school.

It rained all afternoon and I didn't get to see the duck with the scissors in its mouth, though most of the other ducks were still out in the rain and I looked for it for a long time. But I was down by the lake when it started to get light out again the next morning and I found its group of lily pads—they were cleaner-looking than the other water lilies, not as scummy and ragged, and they were farther out into deep water than they should have been and bigger than most of the others—and was there watching it through the binoculars when it came up. This time I noticed that it seemed to be preening itself real slowly, like it was very tired or something, and that when it swam out to the middle again it was swimming a lot slower than usual.

Father yelled at me at breakfast when I spilled some cereal and milk on his shirt so I just left him there in his wheelchair and went to school early, without any sandwiches. I had enough money so I could've bought myself lunch at school if I'd wanted to but I wanted to save it, so I told Beth I'd forgotten it and she gave me half of one of her sandwiches and bought me a carton of milk with her own money.

After school I went around to all the sporting goods

stores and checked out the prices they wanted for fishing nets. They were all too expensive and anyway the duck could've cut its way out of all of them with the scissors in its mouth. Besides, I didn't know what it did when it pulled the ducks under in the daytime. The scissors in its mouth meant it had to be some kind of machine or maybe it was a real duck that had been changed around so it was part duck and part machine like the bionic man and woman, so it could've had all sorts of other ways to break out of the net anyway. Maybe it had some kind of extra claws or a hooked sword or something like that hidden under its feathers that it used to drag the ducks under that it got in the daytime.

I went home and checked Mother's purse for some money I could take but all she had was an awful lot of ten- and twenty-dollar bills and even though she had so many I was sure she'd notice if any of them were missing. But she had five or six quarters and a fifty cent piece, so I took three of the quarters and put two nickels back in their place so it would feel like she still had the same amount of money. And that night one of her friends called to ask if I could baby-sit his two kids Saturday afternoon. All Mother's friends knew how good I was at taking care of Father, even the ones that didn't really know how bad *she* was at taking care of him—he never talked about it to anybody when she wasn't there, though he always made a lot of nasty remarks about the way she treated him when she was in the room with him and his friends and I were there—so I got a lot of offers to do baby-sitting. But Mother liked to keep me home to watch Father when she was working or had something else she wanted to do and she was always working or doing something and she didn't like to come home very much if she could get out of it, so I didn't get to do much baby-sitting. But this time she'd already decided to stay home all day Saturday, so she said go ahead and I ended up making seven and a half dollars.

The next morning I was up early again. I blew up a big white balloon and put it on the end of a long bamboo fishing pole made out of five sticks that screwed together we had out in the garage, but when I found the duck's lily pads they were too far away from shore for me to put the balloon by where the duck was going to come up and hold it there so I could see what he was going to do with it. They didn't rent out aquacycles until way too late and anyway the pole was long but it wasn't quite fifteen feet long so an aquacycle wouldn't have done me any good and there wasn't anything I could do.

It was the same way Monday and Tuesday and then it rained Wednesday and Thursday, so I didn't get to see the duck at all. But Friday even though it was too far out from shore for me to put the balloon next to its lily pads I saw it get a white duck and a black swan, which made me very happy.

Beth came over Saturday and we rented one of the aquacycles and I went pedaling after the duck but it just kept itself away from me. I didn't want to tell Beth what I was doing and she got really bored and angry with me after a while but I made her keep on pedaling until our time was up.

And then Saturday the robot duck finally killed another duck close to shore with the scissors in its mouth so that Sunday I had my balloon right by its lily pad when it came up in the morning. But the day was all sunny and starting to get hot and the duck just ignored the balloon and went off to float in the middle of the lake. And by that time I'd realized that even when it got cloudy out the duck never attacked another duck if the other duck was near an aquacycle or one of the aluminum canoes. So there wasn't any real way I could find out what it would and wouldn't attack, and anyway I was getting scared that people might be beginning to notice me, out there with my balloon on a pole every morning. So I stayed away from the lake for a week and I was glad I did, because there was a movie on TV that Saturday afternoon that I watched over at Beth's house, *The Invisible Boy* with Robbie the Robot, where this evil computer takes control over Robbie and makes him do things he doesn't want to do. And that made me think about those kids with their radio-controlled toy sailboats and I started wondering if there was someone who came down to watch the duck after it came up and who kept the controls he used to make the duck kill the other ducks hidden in his pocket or something. So after I'd stayed away from the lake for a week I came back and didn't do anything, just watched, but though there were some people who came down almost every day to watch the ducks and feed them, there wasn't anybody I could see who was there every day when the duck killed something by pulling it under and I watched for more than two weeks to make sure. Besides, the little old man who was there the most often even came when it was raining out and the duck stayed underwater.

By this time I had enough money from Mother's purse and my baby-sitting and even one time five dollars from the mess sergeant's wallet to buy a net if I wanted one but not one with a long handle. The only way I'd figured out to catch the duck was to wade or swim out to where its lily pads were some night when it was resting or turned off at the bottom and then scoop it up in the net and hope it would stay turned off or asleep or whatever until I got it into something dark and strong, like the ten-gallon grease can I'd already gotten from the gas station down on Del Monte by the Navy School. But I was scared to try it because for all I knew the duck never really turned itself off, it just went down to hide in the mud on the bottom of the lake where it could cut the ducks it had killed into little pieces with the scissors in its mouth so that nobody would ever find their bodies, and I couldn't think of any reason it couldn't kill me the same way it killed the ducks and swans, either with its scissors or with whatever it used when it got them from underwater. Besides which, I was afraid somebody'd come driving by and catch me. Or that a car would come by and the light from its headlights would turn the duck back on even if it had been turned off and *then* it would get me.

But I didn't want to give up, I wanted that duck a lot, especially after I found the headless body of one of the white ducks washed up early in the morning. I took it away and put it in somebody's garbage can a ways away from the lake, under the garbage so nobody else'd see it and figure out what was going on, and from then on I tried to check the shore as much as I could to make sure that none of the other bodies washed up but either the rest of them must have just sunk or dogs or cats came by in the nighttime and ate them as soon as they washed up.

I spent a few more days down by the lake feeding the ducks and pigeons and even the swans a lot of stale bread and other garbage to give myself an excuse for being there before I got the idea of putting some sort of noose at the end of the bamboo pole and using it to snag the whole group of lily pads. They had to be connected to the duck and made out of plastic or metal or something like that and be pretty strong, so I could use them to drag the duck up out of the water. The thing is, I didn't know if that would wake the duck up or not, or if the stems were really strong enough to pull the duck out of the water without breaking it somehow. If it was all made of metal except for its feathers it had to be very heavy. And if I woke the duck up dragging it out like that, I didn't know if it would just try to get away from me or if it would try to kill me to make me stop and keep anyone else from learning about it. I'd never seen it up on shore like the other ducks so for all I knew it couldn't even walk and I'd be safe as long as I didn't go in the water with it.

But then again I'd already seen it do that half-flying thing where it came partway up out of the water when it attacked the other ducks so for all I knew it could fly all the way. And I didn't really know how it dragged the ducks and swans under or what it did to them there. Perhaps it had big knives hidden in its wings or hooks, or maybe even it had some sort of built-in spear gun it used to harpoon them from the bottom so it could reel them down and then cut them up into little pieces there in the mud.

But the real thing that was wrong with trying to catch it at night in the dark was that I wouldn't be able to see it unless I used a light, so I wouldn't know what it was doing, and if I did use a light that might wake it up, and anyway, somebody might see the light and come to find out what I was doing. So I finally decided that what I had to do was try to pull it out some real bright morning when it was near to shore, just after the sun came up but before it was ready to come up to the surface on its own. That way, maybe it would still be only half turned-on again, and even if it was all the way awake, maybe it would just try to swim back out to the middle and start sunbathing a little early.

I bought some plastic rope, the kind you use to tie things on cars and trailers, and a heavy khaki sack from the Army-Navy surplus store to keep the duck dark in while I got it away from the lake and into the ten-gallon can. I'd cleaned the can out a long time ago, right after I got it from the station, and it had a lid on it, so I could shut the duck tight inside it where none of the light could get in to turn it on when I took it home.

I waited until one night when I saw it was down in the mud close enough to shore on my side of the lake, then hid the can in somebody's hedge about half a block up from the lake. I had about an inch of water in the can in case the duck needed it.

I went down to the lake a long time before the sun came up and waited for the sky to get pink and for things to get bright enough so I could see. Not very many cars drove by and nobody in any of them paid any attention to me, except for one police car but I had all my stuff hidden and they were both friends of my father's and already knew me, so it was all right. I told them I liked to come out and run around the lake and get some exercise and one of them said my father used to be just like me, which made me feel bad for a while even after they left.

The sun came up while I was talking to them and it was already pretty bright by the time they left so I got my stuff out and put all the bamboo sections of the fishing pole together and went after the duck.

It wasn't all that hard to get the noose around the lily pads and pull them in to shore but when I got them I saw that they just seemed to stretch all the way back to the part of the bottom they'd been floating over. I waited a moment before I touched the lily pads and the stems, then tried it. They seemed to be made of some sort of tough plastic, so I got all the stems together in my hands and started pulling on them. At first they were real easy to pull in, like that kind of clothesline that goes on a spring-reel and that you can stretch out a long way, but after a while I felt them grab, like when you're fishing and you finally reel in enough line to feel a big fish or a snag on it. I pulled and I could feel the duck on the other end. It was heavy and didn't want to come when I yanked but it didn't seem to be snagged and it wasn't fighting me like a fish or anything and when I quit pulling it just stayed where it was, so I knew it wasn't trying to get away or come after me. I tried pulling on the stems again and the same thing happened, so I kept pulling it in a little at a time, ready to let go and run if the duck started moving on its own.

A candy-red Porsche came by, going a lot faster than it was supposed to. I just stood still, pretending that all I was doing was looking out at the water. The Porsche went by without stopping but now I could see another car over on the other side of the lake and somebody on his bicycle going up the back way to the college, so I knew that everybody was starting to get up and go to work and I had to start dragging the duck in a lot faster, without stopping every few seconds to check it like I'd been doing.

Pretty soon I could see it and it wasn't a duck at all, it was more like a big piece of dead wood, a branch about three feet long and maybe a couple of inches thick, with four or five broken-off little branches sticking out of it. At first I thought it was just something I'd snagged and that when I got it in to shore I'd have to get the lily pad stems from wrapped around it but then I saw that each stem came out of the end of a different one of the broken-off branches.

As soon as I had the branch up out of the water and into the light it started to change. The ends started slowly humping in to the middle and the middle started to bulge out, but everything was happening real, real slow, like a slug creeping up the porch steps after it rains. I quick threw the sack over it to shut out the light but I could see it was still changing underneath until I got the lily pads in under the sack and out of the light too, and then it moved slower and slower until it stopped.

There wasn't anyone else around and the thing was still too long to get into the can, so I pulled the sack off it again. It started squeezing itself in some more and humping out all around the middle, still moving real slow, while I got the sack open and ready to throw over it again, but this time so I could push it inside the sack with the pole. I waited until it wasn't much bigger than a real duck, though it didn't look like a duck any more than it looked like a branch now, just a big lump of mud. I put the sack over it open and reached in underneath with the pole and wedged the pole under it so I could tip it back and make it fall into the sack, then pushed it back more and more until it was all the way inside the sack and I could tie the sack closed. I picked up the sack, making sure it didn't get too close to my body. The duck was just a big round lump in the sack and it didn't move at all. It wasn't too heavy either, maybe about twenty pounds, but that was still heavy enough to makc it a lot of work to get it up to the place where I had the can hid.

I got the can out of the hedge and put the bag in it, but even though it wasn't too big around to go in it was too long for me to put the top on it, just a little, maybe a couple of inches, but it was too late to try to open the sack and let in enough light to make the thing change some more, so I just left the lid there and carried the can the rest of the way home and put it in the toolshed behind the garage, under a bench, before I went back for the lid. Mother never used the toolshed, it was something Father'd built for himself back before they had me but sometimes the mess sergeant would make something out of wood for us back there, or work on something that needed fixing. He wasn't really a bad man, even though I hated him. So even though there were a lot of cobwebs and spiders there and it was real dusty and full of other junk the lights still worked and the shed was in good enough shape to keep the rain and the sunlight out. It didn't have any windows. If you went inside and closed the door before you turned the lights on nobody could see that they were turned on from the house.

When I went back to get the lid I decided to check back at the lake to see if I'd left anything there, but I hadn't, so I went back to the shed and put the lid by the can under the bench, then moved a broken black-and-white TV that was sitting in the far corner over in front of the can so that nobody could see the can unless they took the TV out from in front of it and so that even when the door was open the light from inside wouldn't touch the can. I'd been thinking about what I had to do for a long time and I had it all figured out, or most of it, anyway.

I even knew whose duck it was. James Patrick Dubic, the one I'd helped mother arrest and put away in prison. There couldn't be two people that hated ducks that

much, and in some of the clippings Mother'd saved for
me they talked about how smart he was and how good he
was with computers. I'd figured it out for sure that time
I'd seen *The Invisible Boy* on TV because I'd already
figured out that the duck had to be a robot or something
just pretending to look like a duck the way it was pretending to look like a lump of mud right now. I got out
my clippings just after I saw the movie so I could be sure
what James Patrick Dubic looked like and after that I'd
been watching all the people sitting on the benches and
walking around the lake, but he wasn't ever there, at least
not unless he'd changed an awful lot.

I locked the shed and left the duck there in its can until
Saturday night. That way if it had solar batteries maybe
they'd run down enough so that even if it wanted to hurt
me it wouldn't be able to. Also, if it tried to escape I
wouldn't be there when it tried and so it couldn't hurt
me.

Saturday night Mother had to work. I asked her before
she left for the station what'd happened to Dubic, if he
was still in prison or if they'd let him out or put him in a
mental hospital or anything. She said she didn't know
but she'd ask and try to find out for me if I wanted. I said
yes. It was still early when she drove away, about six-
thirty, so it wasn't nearly dark yet.

We'd all had dinner together and Mother'd wheeled
Father into the living room to watch the movies on the
cable TV chain so I didn't have anything to do except
watch them with Father until it got dark enough.

Around nine I went back to the shed. I had a flashlight,
so when I unlocked the door and pushed it open I shone
the light in through it before I went in to turn the real
light on, but the duck was still in its can behind the TV
set. I closed the door again and dragged the can out. It
was heavier than I'd remembered, maybe twenty-five or
thirty-five pounds. I pulled the bag out of the can and put
it down, then got between it and the door and opened the

door so I could run out of it and get away from the duck if it came after me. Then I turned the lights off and used the flashlight to see by when I dumped the duck out of the sack.

It was still just a big lump, though some of the mud was dry and falling off. It smelled like mud and like sewers. I poked at it with the wooden end of a hoe and it didn't do anything even when I poked it again harder, so I turned on the lights. I was right there by the door with my hand on the light switch waiting for it to do something but it didn't do anything, even when I poked it with the hoe again. I watched it for three or four hours but it never did anything. I was afraid I'd broken it somehow but if I hadn't maybe I'd be able to handle it safely at night with the lights on, which was good. I put the sack back over it and tipped it back into the sack with the hoe handle, then pushed the sack back under the bench behind the TV.

Mother was home all day the next day and she and Father had some of his old friends from back when he was on the Marina police force, back before they'd combined it with the fire department there, over for a barbecue. They made hamburgers and spareribs in the black metal cooker in the backyard, then sat around drinking beer out of cans and talking about what things'd been like before Father's accident and how good a cop he'd been. I couldn't get back into the toolshed with them there. Father and Mother seemed to be having a pretty good time, like they liked each other again. Mother had Father's shirt off so he could get a bit of a tan and one of the other men had his shirt off too. After a while I got really bored and uncomfortable so I went up to Beth's house. I hadn't seen her for a long time, not like I usually did, so I put my swimming suit on under my clothes and rode my bike up to her house but her brother had all his friends over to use the pool and her cousin was there too so she couldn't go away with me even though she didn't like any of them any more than I did. I went down to Thirty-one Flavors and got myself a double cone and a banana split before I went down to the wharf. I watched the tourists there for a while. It was a very nice day, all hot and clear, and there were two sea otters playing in the water. There was some sort of convention at the Doubletree Inn too, so there were too many people on the wharf and even though the organ-grinder had his monkey passing the tin cup and everything the tourists were all old and drunk and boring, worse than the golfers always were even. One of them threw a beer can at one of the sea otters but he missed. I told the traffic cop who was keeping them from driving out on the wharf when they weren't supposed to anyway, and he made the man leave.

After that I went over to the secret beach behind the Navy School that nobody's supposed to use and went swimming for a while. The water wasn't all that cold but it was still *pretty* cold, so when the sun started to go down I went back home. Mother and Father were still out back with their friends. Father had his shirt back on and he was starting to make nasty comments about Mother every now and then even though he still seemed to be having a pretty good time. I didn't understand everything he said but I understood most of it, and when I didn't understand something I could tell whether or not it was mean from the look on Mother's face. One of his friends didn't look very happy but the other one'd drunk as much as Father or maybe even more and he was all loud and happy. Mother was pretending she loved Father a lot and that the only reason he was saying all those awful things about her was because he wasn't grateful for all she did for him but I don't think anybody but Father and me noticed what she was saying.

After a while I asked her about Dubic but she said she hadn't had a chance to check up on him yet and she'd find out for me Monday.

Monday she didn't have to go to the station until late. I tried to tell her I was sick and couldn't go to school but she had a hangover and got really angry and hit me, she said she had enough sick people in the house without me trying to get away with things by pretending to be sick too when I wasn't, so I had to go anyway.

She wasn't home when I got back but she'd put Father's wheelchair by the window because there wasn't anything he wanted to watch on TV and that way he could watch the birds and the squirrels and the flowers in the backyard if he didn't feel like reading. I couldn't go back into the toolshed with him there so I put another magazine in his reader, then went down to the lake and watched the ducks for a while.

The next morning I got up before it was light out and went back to the shed. The hinges on the door were rusty and made some noise when I opened it but not enough to wake anybody up. I used the flashlight to make sure the bag with the duck in it was still under the bench before I closed the door behind me and turned on the lights, then I oiled the hinges before I got the duck out from under the bench. I turned the lights off again and used the flashlight to see by while I got it out of the sack. It still looked like it was wet, even though the mud on it was almost all dry on both sides when pieces of it fell off.

I wasn't sure whether it was safe to touch it or not even after I poked it with the hoe again and it still didn't do anything, but I already knew I had to learn more about how it worked if I was going to be able to make it do what I wanted, so I opened the door again. It was still dark outside. I got on the door side of the duck before I reached out and touched one of the spots where it was still coated with dry mud real quick.

It didn't do anything. I pushed it a little, to see if I could feel it react to me, but no motor started running inside it or anything. I pushed it again a little harder, still on one of the mud-covered spots, then touched it for just a second on one of the spots that looked like it was made out of wet muck. But it wasn't really wet at all, just a little cold and all smooth and slick and sort of greasy, like the bottoms of those nonstick frying pans when you just rinse them out for a few days without using detergent on them. And it still hadn't done anything.

I looked at it for a while, trying to see if I could tell any difference between the different parts of it, but it was still just a lump and the same everywhere. So I touched it again in a different place and then in still another place, but the third time I let my hand stay there touching it a lot longer, maybe almost a minute, before I took it away. Then I pushed it again, only a lot harder this time.

I sat down and looked at it again for a while, trying to get my courage up, then I picked it up real quick before I dropped it and ran back to the door to see what it did. But it didn't do anything and I was starting to get really afraid that I'd broken it somehow.

The sky was beginning to go pink and purple. I picked the lump up again and took it over to the door and put it down close enough so the sunlight coming through the doorway would hit it soon. The door opened into the shed so I couldn't put the lump right inside, it had to be back a bit so I could swing the door shut to keep it locked up inside if anything went wrong, so I had it maybe two feet back from the door. I tied a long piece of string to the door handle so I could stand outside away from the shed and pull the door shut without coming near the duck if I had to.

About half an hour after the sun finally came up all the way the light coming through the doorway started to hit the duck, and after about ten more minutes it started to change again the way it'd changed that other time, just after I pulled it out of the water, only even slower this time. It humped itself in tighter and tighter, just like it had when it'd been changing from a log into a lump, until it was almost the same size as a real duck, maybe just a little bigger, and sort of the shape of a duck, only it still didn't have a head or a tail or any wings or feathers or legs. While it was doing this all the dry mud on it cracked and fell off so the whole thing was wet-looking and glistening like it had just come out of the water. That took almost another hour and it was starting to get late so I pulled the door shut with the string and then locked it and hid the rope and went back inside the house.

Mother was already up and in the bathroom. I'd forgotten to close the curtains to keep anyone from seeing what I was doing out back and the bathroom had two big windows beside the skylight, but she hadn't noticed me or she would have come out to find out what I was doing. I put her coffee on for her, then got Father up and helped him into his wheelchair and took him to the bathroom while she made French toast for all of us for breakfast. He was really dirty for some reason so I had to clean the bathroom up a bit before I took my own shower and finished getting ready.

The phone rang while I was still in the shower. When I sat down to eat Mother told me she'd just gotten a phone call and that a lot of other cops had caught some sort of weird ten-day flu from a bunch of Australian wine growers here for a convention and that she was going to have to be filling in for all sorts of people and that everyone's hours were going to be messed up even worse than usual for a long time and she wasn't going to be able to come home very often for the next few weeks. I wasn't sure but I thought she was lying to us and that she had somewhere else she wanted to go for a while, maybe up to Lake Tahoe again with her mess sergeant. I asked her whether she'd found out anything about James Patrick Dubic for me yet and she said she'd forgotten again and that she was sorry but she was going to be too busy to check for me for a while now, and why was I so interested all of a sudden? I told her I'd found all the old newspaper clippings while I was cleaning my room and she seemed to think that answered her question because she didn't ask me any more about it.

Father said something about liberal judges and parole boards and how you sometimes had to exaggerate the truth a little because otherwise they'd ignore half of what a criminal'd really done and let him out when he was dangerous and should be kept in jail for a lot longer. Mother agreed with him and they talked about police work for a while. Then they talked a while about getting him a new TV, the kind with the videotape built into it, so he could record his favorite programs and movies and stuff that was on after he wanted to go to sleep, and we all thought that was a good idea even though Mother said we'd have to wait a while to get enough money to pay for it because she already owed too much right now.

She finished her coffee and we wheeled him into the living room in front of the TV, then I set up his reader so he could use it if he wanted to and made sure the switch to change from the TV to the reader was where he liked it on his shoulder and strapped on tight enough so it wouldn't slip back where he couldn't get at it if he nudged it too hard with his chin. I still had a little time before I had to go to school but I wanted to wait until dark before I opened the shed again so I could see if the duck had done any more changing or moving around in the dark after I'd shut the door. So what I did is I took the binoculars down to the lake and watched the ducks through them for a while to make sure there wasn't another robot duck there already to replace the one I'd taken, and at the same time I checked to make sure there wasn't anybody else down at the lake looking for the duck the same way I was, or anyone who looked like James Patrick Dubic. But there wasn't anybody else looking and there didn't seem to be anything special happening with the ducks on the lake, so I went to school. After school I checked again but there still wasn't anything worth looking at happening.

Father was asleep in his chair. I closed all the curtains so he couldn't see out to the backyard, then went back and tied my string to the shed door again and unlocked it and pushed it open.

The duck had changed in the dark this time, but just a little. It was still in almost the same place but something had started to push out where its neck and tail were going to be and it looked a little different where its wings were going to be. It was starting to look like a real duck or one of those wooden decoys, but all covered with mud. But it was too late in the day and the sun wasn't coming directly in through the door anymore so it didn't do any more changing.

I heard the telephone ringing and yanked the door to the shed shut by pulling on the string real hard but didn't have time to lock it before I ran back into the house. It was Mother, saying she wasn't going to be home that night or all the next day and asking me if I had everything I needed and if there was enough food in the refrigerator and freezer. I checked and told her there was and she said if I ran out of anything or needed help to come down to the station and one of her friends there would take care of it for me, she'd tell them I might be coming in so it would be all right. I said OK and she hung up.

I was really tired because I'd been getting up so early for so long so I set the alarm clock to wake me up in time to fix dinner for Father and took a nap. When I got up I made him macaroni and cheese with tuna fish in it then stayed up and watched television with him until it was time to put him to bed. He said it was a good thing I was superstrong for my age and not just tall and skinny when I was getting him into the tub, because even though he was still mainly skinny he was awful flabby and he'd be getting fat pretty soon, so moving him would be getting to be a lot of work before I was much older. I told him the exercise was good for me and anyway all I had to do was wheel his chair from one room to another every now and then and then help him in and out of the bath and anyway I was used to it. He said, thank you for saying that Julie, but I know how hard it is on you and your Mother with me like this, and then he started talking about how wonderful Mother had been before the accident, when she hadn't had to take care of him all the time, and that made me feel bad for him again and at the same time like Mother a little more, even though I knew that half the reason he was telling me all this was because even though he knew it was true he wanted me to tell him it wasn't so he could pretend to himself it wasn't his fault.

Wednesday morning when the sun came in through the door and hit the thing and its lily pads it finally finished changing all the way back into a duck. The head and the tail and the wings pushed their way out from inside until the duck was the right shape, even though it still didn't have any legs and was all smooth and brown, like one of those pottery ducks people use for sugar bowls.

It started reeling the lily pads in. The stems got shorter and shorter and at the same time the lily pads themselves were closing up like flowers that had been open going back to being buds, only they were even tighter than that, like rolled up pieces of paper, so that by the time the stems had been reeled all the way back into the duck they weren't any bigger around than the stems had been and they just followed them into the duck.

And while the duck had been reeling in the stems its skin had been changing. First all over its surface a lot of things like tiny doors had opened, only none of them were much bigger than the lead in a pencil and they were all over the surface, everywhere, so it was like the whole duck was a venetian blind that somebody had opened. Then the doors all closed again, but on the other side, so what had been on the back of them and hidden inside the duck before was now on the outside where you could see it and you could see that the duck had what looked like feathers again.

And then the orange legs came pushing out from the bottom of the duck and it started to try to swim. It wasn't trying to stand up or anything like a real duck on land, it was trying to swim like it thought it was underwater and had to get to the surface.

A few seconds later it stopped making swimming motions, either because it thought it had made it to the surface or because it had figured out it wasn't in the water. I couldn't tell which. But it still wasn't standing or lying like a duck on land, it had its feet sticking out backwards under it so it was tilted forward a bit with its tail in the air. That didn't seem to bother it, though, and it started preening itself like it always did after it came up out of the mud in the morning even though there wasn't any mud on it.

When it finished preening itself it looked all around just like a real duck deciding what direction it wanted to swim in, only it was still tilted forward like a wheelbarrow. It kept looking around for a long time and I wondered what it thought about being in the shed, if it knew there was anything wrong or what to do about it. Then it started swimming for the door, out into the light, only it wasn't using its wings to help it and it wasn't walking, just paddling its legs, but even so that pushed it slowly across the floor so that maybe ten minutes later it came to the doorsill and then it hopped over the sill just like a duck in the water hopping over something even though it went back to trying to swim as soon as it was outside in the backyard.

It looked around again as soon as it was out of the shed and then changed its direction, paddling across the grass to the center of the yard as far away from the fence and the shed and the house as it could get, with its chest still pointing down and its legs sticking out behind it and its tail up, so it looked more like it was trying to dig its way into the lawn than like it was walking. But it got to the center of the yard finally and stayed there, all stiff and fake-looking now that it was out of the water.

I was way back at the other end of the yard, maybe thirty feet away from it, but since the sun was shining bright I knew it wouldn't attack me if I got closer to it, so I came forward a bit, until I was maybe twenty feet away from it, and then a little more, until I was fifteen feet away from it, then ten, but I was afraid to get any closer right then and I went back to the toolshed and closed the door, then went in and got Father up and fixed his breakfast for him, then put him in the living room with the TV and his detective novel. I had him facing away from the window and I had the curtains closed anyway, so there was no way he could see what I was doing in the backyard.

I told him I wasn't feeling very well and didn't want to go to school today and he said, OK, if the school called just give him the phone and he'd say I was sick and he wouldn't tell Mother. It was the only thing he was really ever able to do for me and he did it whenever he could, even though Mother sometimes got real mad at him for it and yelled at him and even hit him.

It was still bright out so I went back out into the yard and tried coming close to the duck again. I came up behind it and got maybe ten feet away from it again but it still didn't seem to notice me, even when I circled around so I was beside it and then in front of it where a real duck would have been able to see me.

Then I thought about those old men and women you see with their metal detectors looking for money people've dropped on beaches so I went back into the shed and got the hoe out and came at the duck with the metal end, real slowly. I got a lot closer than fifteen feet, maybe even less than a foot away from it before it started to try to get away, and then I spent a while just chasing it around the yard, but always making sure I kept it out of the bright sunlight and away from the shade near the house and fence and under the trees, even though it looked so clumsy and pompous and stupid, even stupider than a real duck. When I finally quit chasing it it worked its way back into the middle of the yard.

Only that wasn't good enough because out in the lake I'd watched it go away from two or three rowboats made out of wood. So maybe it had two systems, some sort of metal detector and some sort of thing to keep it away from wood. (And a third system, too, to find the ducks and swans with.) I tried it with the wooden end of the hoe and it wouldn't do anything until I actually touched it with the wooden end of the hoe, and then it just tried to move a few feet away before it stopped, just far enough so that if the hoe'd been a branch the duck wouldn't have gotten snagged on it.

Maybe it had some sort of radar or sonar system to keep it from getting too close to big objects, like boats or piers. So I tried to use the metal end of the hoe to herd it close to the side of the fence that was still in the sun, but it wouldn't go close to the fence, when it was maybe ten feet away from it the duck would start to go off at an angle sideways so it never got any closer.

The phone rang. I ran inside and got it and took it into the living room and held it up to Father's ear and mouth without saying anything. It was the school, asking why I wasn't there. But we had an agreement, even though we'd never come right out and talked about it. He said I was sick, some sort of flu, that it probably wasn't serious but that even so I wouldn't be able to come in until at least tomorrow or maybe the day after and that, no, I hadn't been to a doctor and I wouldn't have a doctor's excuse because he was my father and it was his decision to make whether or not he let me go to school, he knew perfectly well what a flu was like and what you had to do to get better from one and he wasn't going to pay a doctor just to write me a note and say that there was a lot of that going around so not to worry, and, no, he wasn't going to write a note for me either, because my mother was away working for a few days and he happened to be paralyzed from the neck down, but if they wanted to send somebody out to make sure he really was my father and that he really was sitting in his wheelchair paralyzed they could go right ahead, but it would be easier if they just looked at their records or talked to someone who knew what he was talking about there at the school. The school said, No, we're sorry to have bothered you, Mr. Matson, to him and he had me hang up. I kissed him and went back out to the yard.

The duck was still out in the middle of the yard sunbathing. I wanted to push it into the shade from the house and see if it would attack me even if I was bigger than a swan and wasn't a bird at all. It wouldn't be very dangerous because as long as I stayed in the sunlight the duck would stop attacking as soon as it got back out into the sun with me. But I didn't want to be too close to it when it came at me in case it came at me a lot faster than it moved when it was trying to paddle around as if it was still in the water. So I took one of the pieces of the bamboo fishing rod and tied it to the handle of the hoe to make it long enough so I'd be further away from the duck when I herded it into the shade.

I pushed the duck as far away from me into the shade as I could with the metal end of the hoe, so it was maybe almost ten feet out of the direct sunlight before I stopped. That took almost ten minutes. Then I started to back away from it.

As soon as I took the hoe away it moved its head like it was looking for something then started coming at me, paddling as fast as it could and ripping up the lawn a little but even with the way it was kicking it was still just inching and sliding its way across the grass slower than I could have moved on my hands and knees. It wasn't trying to use its wings like I'd been pretty sure it wouldn't, it only used its wings when it made its other kind of attack, the one it did with the scissors that came out of its mouth when the sun was going down. I stayed just on the bright side of the shadow's edge but I moved away up towards the side fence so that I could watch the duck chase me some more. It was so slow and stupid-looking and I was in the sun, so I wasn't very worried. Besides, I wanted to see what it would try to do to me when it came time for it to try to dive under to grab me.

What it did was when I let it get about two or three feet away from me it stuck its head down under its body, pushing it in under its puffed-up chest which made it look even sillier because of the way its chest was already resting on the grass so that with its two legs sticking out behind it looked like some sort of crazy toy wheelbarrow. Then it kicked off with its legs like it was trying to dive straight down to the bottom of the lake but all that happened was that it fell back into the same sort of wheelbarrow position again. But it didn't even seem to notice it wasn't underwater, because then it pulled its head out from under its chest and stuck it straight at me and paddled as fast as it could at me until it was just almost to the edge of the shadow, then it suddenly arched its head and neck and body backwards and did something with its wings real fast so it fell over on its back. I moved away a little further down the shadow line so it could come after me without getting in the sun. Now that it was over on its back it was using its wings to try to swim at me like they were the oars of a rowboat and that was working a little better than the paddling had because the grass was very smooth there but even so the wings could sort of catch in it and slide the duck along. I stood where I was this time and when it got closer to me—it was about two feet away from me now, just before where the shadow ended—its legs moved away from each other and turned around sideways so its feet were facing each other like it wanted to clap them together. Big steel claws like meat hooks that must have been hidden somewhere in its hollow legs came out of its feet very fast and its belly opened up and something like a long rotary file and a drill and a buzzsaw all at the same time came out and started whirling so fast it was just a blur even though it didn't make any noise like a drill or a buzzsaw usually would.

The duck had finally gotten to just at the edge of the dividing line between the shadow and the sunlight and I knew that if it came any further it would be out in the sun and just go back to being a fake duck, so I used the bamboo stick that I'd tied to the hoe to turn it around facing the other way so I could see what it would do. But it just used one wing and not the other to turn itself around in a circle so it was coming at me again and this time I let it get itself out into the sunlight so it would turn itself off.

As soon as its head was out in the sun the claws went back into its feet and the drill-thing stopped turning and started to go back into its stomach. I got a better look at it this time, and it was all covered with little barbs like fish hooks and other little knives of all sorts that looked like they turned around on their own, not always in the same direction as the whole thing, but before I could get a better look at what it was like its stomach closed up again to where they should be so it was just a fake duck lying on its back again.

It couldn't seem to turn itself back over so I used the bamboo end of the hoe to tip it back into the right position.

I sat down in one of the lawn chairs and watched it struggle back to the center of the yard.

It was too slow and clumsy in the daytime to be any use if I just left it in the backyard, especially because it wouldn't come near metal and all but one of the lawn chairs had metal frames. I was sorry we didn't have a swimming pool and tried to think of a way I could get to use Beth's pool but I couldn't think of one that would be any good. But even though I couldn't see any way to make the duck work right except maybe just by throwing it on somebody it was still good to know that the duck would chase things and try to kill them even if they were people and not other birds.

But then I thought that that was just what the duck did in the daytime when it got cloudy and that it had a whole different way of attacking things at sunset, when it used its wings a bit and went a lot faster over the surface of the water to cut off the other ducks' heads. So maybe that would work. Only if it did work I didn't want to be there in the backyard with the duck when it attacked.

For a while I thought about getting a dog or a cat or something and putting it in the backyard with the duck to see what happened but the idea made me sick and I couldn't do it. Then I thought about going back down to El Estero Lake and catching another real duck but it would probably make a lot of noise when I was catching it unless I killed it, and if I got caught killing a duck what with the way everybody knew how I liked to go down to the lake and watch the ducks all the time everybody'd be suspicious of me and wonder how many other ducks I'd killed and maybe notice that there were a lot less ducks there on the lake than there usually were and think that I was crazy or evil, so that if someone got killed after that they'd be sure I did it.

But then I thought, it didn't have to be a real duck at all, not a live one, I had more than enough money to go down to the poultry shop in Monterey and buy myself one that was ready to cook, and I could probably even get one with the feathers and head and everything all on it. So I rode my bike down to the poultry shop, but they didn't have any ducks that weren't already plucked and the chickens were all plucked too, so I had to buy a goose, which cost a lot more than I wanted to spend. I got it anyway and they put it in a plastic bag for me and gave me a little sheet of paper with instructions for how to cook it even though I said it was for my mother.

I put it in the backyard, about five feet away from the duck so it wouldn't have to go too far to get it, then changed my mind and put it halfway across the yard, so I could see how fast the duck could go when it was after something.

It was pretty late but the sun wasn't down yet, so I went back inside and took care of father, then put some fresh clothes on him in case Mother was going to be coming home tonight even though she'd said she wouldn't, and then fixed us TV dinners. There was a movie on the cable channel, *Casablanca* with Humphrey Bogart and right after it *Shanghai Express* with Marlene Dietrich, and I would have liked to have seen both of them even though I'd seen *Casablanca* before, but it started right after dinner and I wasn't sure I'd have time to finish it before the sun went down. I tried to watch a little of it anyway with Father but I couldn't get interested in it at all so I went back into the kitchen where I could watch the backyard out the window just like I could've from the living room if I hadn't closed the curtains there so I could be sure Father wouldn't see anything.

But when the sun went down and the light went away until it was completely dark out, there wasn't even any moon, the duck didn't even try to do anything to the goose. It just turned back into a log and stuck its lily pads a little ways out of the ends of its broken-off branches. I went back into the living room in time to see the very end of *Casablanca* and all of *Shanghai Express*. *Shanghai Express* was pretty good, but not as good as *Casablanca* had been the time before.

I'd been refilling Father's drinking bottle with beer all day and he was pretty drunk by the time the movie was over but instead of getting sleepy the way he usually did he was wide awake and something in the movies had made him all angry and sad at the same time. It was really awful.

First he got angry at Mother and started yelling and telling me what a bitch she was, how she treated him like shit the way she did and even brought her mess sergeant home with her as if it didn't make any difference what Father thought and even told him that at least Don— that was the mess sergeant's name, but I didn't like to use it even though he asked me to because that would make it too much like he was my friend or an uncle or something —could help her with him when she had to get his wheelchair into the car to take him to the beach or somewhere else nice and that Don was a lot of help too with getting him in and out of the bathtub and cleaning him up, as if that wasn't worse, having to let his wife's lover clean him up when he'd dirtied himself because he couldn't get out of his wheelchair to go to the bathroom on his own and they were too busy in the bedroom to waste the time to come and help him. Like he was a baby and it was OK if they changed his diaper every day or two.

He'd been yelling for most of this, but then he got real sad again, and that was even worse, he started talking about what a good wife Mother'd been back when he could take care of her and when he'd been handsome and strong and everything Don was now only a lot better and how she would have been a perfect wife to him if only he hadn't had the accident and it wasn't her fault that he couldn't be a husband to her and even if she got angry at him a lot and had to find someone else to do all the things that it'd been his duty to do for her as a husband he couldn't blame her, because at least she hadn't divorced him or put him in a home or anything like that.

It went on and on and after a while he was crying, and then he was yelling again. His bottle was empty so I went and got him another one, only I put half a Librium in it like I'd sometimes seen Mother do when she wanted to make sure he got to sleep and after a little while he calmed down and went to sleep.

I went out in the backyard and put the log in its sack and put it in the shed. I didn't even bother to use the stick or anything this time, because I was sure it wouldn't do anything to me now that it was late enough at night so the light had been gone for a long time. I put the sack behind the TV set under the bench but I couldn't really think of what to do with the goose because it would probably rot if I just left it in the shack but if I put it in the freezer or the refrigerator Mother'd probably find it if she came home tomorrow and I couldn't think of any reason to tell her why there was a goose in the freezer.

Then I thought, what I'll tell her is I bought it with my savings because since she'd been away working all that time I wanted to cook it for her for a kind of celebration when she got home and I'd gotten all the directions for cooking it and everything, only they looked too hard. And if she asked me why I'd gotten a goose instead of something like a turkey I'd tell her it was because I'd never had a goose and I'd heard that they were something special that people had for Christmas in England and that I wanted this to be very special. She'd have to believe me even though it was a pretty silly story because she wouldn't be able to think of any other reason why I'd have a goose to put in the freezer. Unless I'd stolen it, and I had the receipt and the piece of paper with the instructions on it to show her and she could always check back with the man at the poultry store if she was really suspicious.

Then I put fresh sheets on Father's bed and got him out of his wheelchair and into it. It really *was* like he was a baby, only even though I was real strong for how big I was he was twice as heavy as I was and I almost dropped him like I'd done a few times before, but I didn't.

And anyway I was growing fast so it was getting easier all the time. I was taller than all but one or two of the other girls in my class, and I was real strong and muscular just like Mother was and like Father'd been in the pictures when he used to be on the Police Basketball Team. I was good at sports, too, especially gymnastics and swimming and soccer, but Mother said I'd have to start being careful about what I ate and about doing real exercises and not just playing around pretty soon if I didn't want to end up getting fat and flabby like Father, though she said that right now everything was OK and I was still just solid.

I still wasn't sleepy, even though it was pretty late. What with getting up early every morning and everything I'd gotten into the habit of not sleeping too much. I took a bath and washed my hair and tried to watch TV but there wasn't anything on worth watching, and I didn't feel like reading or anything like that, so I went and got another TV dinner out of the freezer and put it in the oven.

It was a fried chicken dinner and when I took the tin foil off at the end and saw it I thought, maybe that's how the duck figures out whether something's alive or not, because if it's alive it's got a temperature just like I do, 98.6, though it probably wasn't the same thing for birds. But even if it wasn't the same the duck had chased me just like it had chased the ducks and swans so that wouldn't make that much difference.

Unless the reason it hadn't tried to kill the goose was because the goose had just been lying still there on the grass and not moving at all. But some of the real ducks I'd seen the robot duck attack hadn't been moving, at least not so I could see, and part of the time my duck had been flopping across the lawn after me I'd just been standing still watching it, not moving at all. So if Mother still wasn't home tomorrow I'd put the goose in the microwave just before sunset and get it out in the yard all hot right when the sun went down to see if that would make the duck attack it.

Mother called in the next morning while I was cleaning up after breakfast to say she was going to be gone at least two more days because she had to take over liaison duty with the state police on an arson charge. I asked her if she'd had a chance to find out anything for me about James Patrick Dubic. She said, yes, he was still in prison, but even though his behavior there was very good and he was not only doing some sort of on-the-job-training program for some outside company that would look good to the parole board but had also volunteered for something called Aversion Therapy that was going to make it impossible for him to ever touch another bird again without getting sick and passing out, they *still* weren't going to let him out for at least three or four more years.

It wasn't quite eight in the morning yet but I could still hear what sounded like a party in the background, a lot of drunks and yelling and music and laughing, or maybe she was in a bar or a gambling casino in Lake Tahoe or Reno or Las Vegas or wherever she was. I could tell she wasn't anywhere close like she pretended she was because there was so much static on the line I could barely hear her.

She told me to go down and see one of her friends at the station after school, Desk Sergeant Crowder, and he'd have twenty-five dollars for what she called my "baby-sitting time." That made me really angry again, not that she was trying to bribe me to keep me on her side but that it was Sergeant Crowder who was covering up for what she was doing with the mess sergeant because even though he didn't come around to see us nearly as much anymore as he used to, he'd always been one of Father's best friends and Father thought he still was.

After Mother hung up I told Father that she wasn't going to be home for another two days but I didn't mention anything about Sergeant Crowder. He looked unhappy, more miserable and hopeless than angry for a minute, but then he grinned at me even though I could tell he was making himself do it and said that in that case maybe I'd better dial the school for him so he could tell them that even though I was starting to feel a little better he wanted to keep me home with him for two more days to be sure.

After the phone call I wheeled him into the living room and set everything up right for him and put a beer in his bottle, then I went back to the shed and got the duck. I didn't bother to be extra careful this time, I just picked up the sack and dumped the log out of it into the middle of the backyard, then made sure the backyard gate was locked. I waited until the log started to hump in on itself then went back inside and drew all the curtains and locked the back door, so that nobody who happened to come by would see the duck.

I played checkers and cards with father most of the morning—I moved all the checkers for him and we had a little rack set up so he could see the cards in his hand even when I couldn't that he used when his friends came over to play poker—and I let him win a lot, even though I was better than he was. I fixed him a hot lunch around noon and refilled his bottle with beer two or three times and cleaned him up a bit before I left him in the living room with a new Ed McBain mystery in his reader because the afternoon TV looked pretty boring.

Then I went down to the lake to watch the ducks for a while and think about my duck and what I was going to do with it, but also to keep a lookout and find out if there was anybody else there watching and trying to learn what'd happened to my duck. I didn't think there would be, not with Dubic still in prison, and there wasn't.

About four o'clock I rode my bike over to the station and got the money from Sergeant Crowder. One of the other cops, somebody I didn't know, came over just as if it was something he'd thought of doing on the spur of the moment and told me what a good job my mother was doing and how much she was sacrificing for her work and how they hoped that pretty soon she could get the kind of rest she needed and stay at home like she wanted. I said that it was OK for me, I had school and everything, but that Father got a little lonely sometimes and Sergeant Crowder said it'd been too long since he'd come by to see us and that he'd drop in on us as soon as he had a few hours free. I said that would be nice.

I got Father cleaned up before dinner, then put a whole Librium in his beer so I could cook the goose and everything without him smelling it or noticing I was doing anything strange. He fell asleep right at the table and I took him into his bedroom and put him to bed with plenty of time to get the goose cooked before sunset.

I waited until the sun was almost entirely down, then put the goose in the microwave and turned it on to get it really, really hot. All the feathers got singed and it smelled really awful when I took it out because I had to leave it in a little longer than I'd planned so that I didn't get it out in the yard too early, or it would have been too cold for the duck to attack it when the light went away. And I didn't want to risk putting it out there too late, because then the duck might attack *me,* and I didn't know how fast it could go on land when it was doing its scissors thing and not the thing where it came up from underneath the ducks like some sort of meatgrinder with claws.

I propped the goose's head up in position with tooth-picks and then ran out and put it down at least ten yards away from the duck, then ran as fast as I could back into the house and slammed the door.

The duck was already getting ready to attack the goose by the time I got turned around again with the door closed so I could watch it out the window. It had its neck stuck forward with its mouth wide open and it was doing its paddling thing and even though the way it was beating its wings wasn't quite enough to make it really fly it was still close enough so that the duck was sort of half-running and half-hopping across the lawn and it was going as fast as I could have run or maybe even faster until it got to the goose and then the scissors came out of its mouth and I was close enough this time to see the scissor blades were all jagged-edged like the saws butchers use before the duck cut the goose's head off.

The scissors went back into the duck's mouth and it closed its bill and did that thing it'd done before, when it'd tried to dive down through the ground to get at me, only this time after it paddled a little it just stopped and turned back into a log.

So I knew that all I had to do was get Mother out in the backyard away from any metal or the fences or the house when the sun went away and the duck would kill her. I could do it tomorrow night when she came home if I wanted to, or whenever I wanted to after that.

It made me feel good. I wrapped the goose in tin foil and put it back in the freezer in case I found another use for it, then put the log back in its sack and hid it back in the shed. I was real excited and I rode my bike all the way to Lover's Point and the Asilomar beaches in Pacific Grove because I felt so good and I was laughing to myself all the way there and back. Then I watched a late movie on TV, *Thoroughly Modern Millie,* and it was sort of stupid but fun anyway and I even laughed two or three times.

But the next morning Father woke me up yelling because I was late with his breakfast and he had a hangover and because I'd put him to sleep so early the night before all of yesterday's beer had still been in him and he'd wet his bed in the middle of the night and when he woke up and his bed was all sticky and wet and disgusting he had to yell and yell and yell to get me to wake up and come help him. He was really angry with me just the way he was always really angry with Mother, even after I cleaned him up and got him breakfast and set him up for the day in front of the TV with his reader.

And when he yelled at me again at lunch I realized something that I should've realized a long time before. He really *was* just like a big baby, and with Mother gone there'd be no one left to take care of him but me and pretty soon he'd hate me just the same way he hated Mother and I'd hate him just the same way Mother hated him. With maybe a little love left that would come back to the surface every now and then when we remembered what it'd been like before, but less and less until all that we had left was that we hated each other.

Only it wouldn't even be that, because they'd probably put me in a foster home and put him in some sort of nursing home, the one thing Mother'd promised never to do to him where she'd kept her promise, until I was old enough to go back to taking care of him. I'd have to get a job and pay for him along with me for the rest of his life, and I'd never be able to go away or get married or even have boyfriends or do anything because he'd be jealous of me the way he was of Mother even though he loved me.

He hated what he was and the only way he could stand hating himself like that was to take it out on somebody else. It wasn't his fault, he couldn't do anything about it, but that's what it was, he had to hate somebody and make them miserable and if it wasn't Mother it was going to be me.

I couldn't get away with just running off and leaving him, either, not with the new interstate runaway laws they'd been lecturing us about at school, at least not until I was fifteen or sixteen. Besides, I didn't have anywhere to run to, not yet, and no way to keep myself alive even if I got away.

Unless I killed Father first. He wouldn't mind, not really, not if he was drunk enough and I put two or three Librium in his beer so he wouldn't feel anything. He probably would've killed himself a long time ago, if he'd been able to and if his mother hadn't raised him a Catholic. I'd heard him tell Mother that a lot of times when he wanted her to really *know* how horrible she made him feel.

And then the duck would go back to being just a log again and I could hide it away until I was fifteen or sixteen before I used it to get Mother. Nobody'd ever guess what it was if I kept it hidden someplace dark.

Only what if when the other police came all they found were my footprints and they took the log in to examine it because maybe they found blood on it? If they didn't figure out what it really was they might blame me and then be sure it was me when I got Mother later, and if they did figure out what it was they wouldn't blame me but I wouldn't be able to use it again. And all they'd have to do was pick it up and they'd know it was too heavy to be a real log.

But what if they never found his body, he just disappeared, like those ducks that my duck pulled under out in the lake?

What did it do with their bodies? Why hadn't I ever found even a feather with a piece of skin attached to it?

The thing that came out of my duck's stomach looked like some sort of cross between a drill and a meatgrinder. Maybe it ground up their bodies so small there weren't any pieces left.

He wouldn't feel anything if there was enough Librium in his beer and he drank enough beer. Or if he did it wouldn't be much, not much worse than it was like for him every day just to be alive anyway.

And with him gone Mother wouldn't be angry with me all the time, wouldn't always be finding something else for me to do around the house so she could go get away from him. She might even go back to being more like she was before, the way he told me she'd been when she married him.

And if she didn't, I'd still have the duck. But I had to find out what happened to the bodies of the ducks my duck pulled under when it killed them.

Father was watching a football game turned up loud. I went into the living room, refilled his beer bottle.

The duck was still back in the shed. I went into the bathroom and checked. It was in the corner of the house, with big windows on each side and a skylight Father'd put in when he first bought the house. There'd be bright sunlight in it for the rest of the afternoon.

I opened the windows as wide as possible, so the glass wouldn't screen out any of the sunlight in case that made a difference like it did when you wanted to get a tan, then got the sack out of the shed and dumped the log out of it into the bathtub. It was a big, big bathtub, all long and deep, made out of that white stuff they use for sinks and bathtubs and toilet bowls. The only metal in it was the faucet and the drain plug.

Maybe forty-five minutes later the duck was floating at the far end of the tub. It didn't seem bothered at all by the walls around it. Maybe they were pushing the same on it from all four sides so it didn't have to try to go anywhere else.

I put the headless goose in the microwave until it got hot, then tossed it in the tub. I used the curtain hook to pull the curtain for the skylight, then quick went back out into the hall and closed the bathroom door. I ran out the back door and around and closed the shutters for both windows, not quite all the way because I didn't want the duck to think it was nighttime, but enough so there wasn't very much light coming in.

And my duck dipped its bill in the water like it was taking a drink, then dived down under the goose, grabbed it in its meathook-claws and used its meatgrinder drill to rip it into tiny, tiny pieces. It took about five minutes, and then the duck left what was left of the goose on the bottom of the tub like some sort of mud and went back to floating at the other end.

I opened the shutters wide to let the sun in, then got the hoe so I could hold the metal between me and the duck, even though I didn't think it would attack me with the sun shining on it. I went back in the bathroom and pulled back the skylight curtain with the curtain hook, then kept the duck at the far end of the tub with the hoe while I pulled the bathtub plug.

What was left of the goose drained out of the tub with the water, all except a few small fragments of bone. And when I picked them up they weren't at all hard and brittle like they should've been, they were all sort of soft and rubbery, like pieces of cauliflower. So the duck had to have something, some kind of poison or acid it used, to make sure that even the little pieces that were left dissolved.

But if it could do that I didn't know why it left the headless ducks floating on the surface of the water every night. Unless it was James Patrick Dubic's way of making sure that when he got out of jail he could come back to the park and watch his robot duck killing ducks for him even if what they'd done to him made it so he couldn't touch the ducks to kill them himself.

I ran the water down the drain for a few minutes. It didn't seem to be stopped up.

I went back into the living room. Father was still watching his football game. His bottle was empty. I emptied his urine bag, refilled the bottle with beer, added four Librium. He was still half-awake when he finished the bottle, though he was passing out fast, so I gave him three more Librium by telling them they were vitamins he was supposed to take. He was too groggy to wonder why I wanted him to take them.

I went back to the bathroom and filled the tub two-thirds full of water. With him in it it would be all the way full. Then I pushed his wheelchair into the bathroom and got him out of it into the tub the way I always did.

The duck stayed down at the other end of the tub, away from him.

I pulled the skylight curtains closed, went outside and shut the shutters. Not all the way, just enough to cut down the light like it was a cloudy day. I didn't look, just walked around the yard looking up at the sky, out at the fences, over them to the neighbor's houses, anywhere but at the bathroom windows.

Then I closed the shutters completely but I still didn't look in through them. I went back inside the house, turned off the television, turned it back on, walked around, finally opened the bathroom door and turned on the light so I could see what had happened.

The bottom of the tub was covered with red-brown mud. The log was half-buried in it.

I pulled the plug, watched the sludge drain out of the tub. I kept the water running a lot longer to make sure the drain wasn't going to get plugged up, then pushed the log under the running water so I could clean the last of the sludge off it. When it was clean I picked it up and put it in the sack again, then took the sack and hid it out under the floorboards of the shed.

I poured some Draino down the hole to make sure nothing got clogged up and washed the tub with cleanser, then put the wheelchair and the urine bottle and all of Father's clothes back in the living room and turned the TV on. There was another football game going, a replay of some sort of championship from a few years back.

I called up Beth and asked her if I could come over and go swimming with her for a while. She said yes. We swam for a while and then I said maybe it would be a good idea if we went back down to my house, I had some money back there and we could buy some ice cream or maybe go get some hamburgers at McDonald's, and anyway I still owed her for that time she'd bought me milk and given me half her sandwich.

So we rode our bikes back down to my house and when we found Father gone I called Sergeant Crowder and told him I was scared, Father was gone but his wheelchair was still there and I didn't know what had happened to him, whether they'd taken him to the hospital or somebody'd kidnapped him or what.

He said he'd send somebody right over.

Julie: 1991

That was three years ago. I'm fourteen now. A year after Father disappeared Mother married Don but even without Father to take care of she was as bad as ever, maybe even worse, and he divorced her less than a year later. The duck's still back under the shed and it still works—I took it out to check it a little over a week ago, when Mother was gone for a weekend somewhere, and it turned from a log back into a duck in the morning and then back from a duck into a log when it got dark out. So I can use it on Mother whenever I want. It would be better if I could wait two years but I don't think I can stand it that much longer. It might be better just to have them put me in a foster home for a year or two.

And anyway, I don't know if I can wait any longer at all, now. Three weeks ago Judge Hapgood disappeared and a week ago Thom Homart, the one that wrote those articles in the *RAG* that Dubic's lawyers sued them for, also disappeared. And The Forbidden City—the Chinese restaurant that changed their name from The Ivory Pagoda after they were convicted of buying sea gulls and cats from Dubic ten years ago—burned down and its owner died in the fire just last week.

I've been going down to the lake to feed the ducks almost every day now since Father disappeared. It's not so much that I've learned to like them or anything, though I guess I like them a lot better than I used to, but just that I wanted to be there watching in case another robot duck like my mallard ever appeared.

There's another one there now. A mallard, but a female this time, brown with black speckle-marks with bright blue on its sides—what the bird books call its mirror or speculum—and an orange and brown bill. It's been there almost a month. And every day now, for just a little over a month and a half, a skinny middle-aged man comes down to sit on a bench and watch the ducks. He comes down early in the morning and he never leaves until dark and he never, never feeds the ducks or swans or pigeons, even though he spends all day watching them.

Mother tells me that James Patrick Dubic was released from prison three months ago. So that has to be him, down there watching his robot killing the ducks he can't kill for himself anymore. I don't know what he thinks happened to his other robot.

And while he's sitting there on his bench watching the ducks, or maybe at night after he drives away, he's killing all the people who helped put him in jail. I don't know how, maybe with a robot person or taxicab or something else that works just like the ducks.

Mother's one of those people, so if he gets to her before I do he'll save me a lot of trouble and I won't have to worry about getting caught. And in a way it's a good thing to know that if I don't get her he'll get her for me for sure.

But the thing is, I'm another one of the people who helped put him in jail. Maybe even the main person, except for Mother, especially if you believe what all the newspaper articles they wrote about me said. And from the way the skinny man watches me sometimes when I'm feeding the ducks I'm sure he knows who I am and that he's watching me.

But he's too smart to try to get us all at the same time, at least not unless he's figured out enough different ways to kill us all so that nobody'll see the connection between all our deaths. So he's probably going to want to wait a while before he tries to get me or Mother. And I've still got his duck, and I've spent years now thinking about the best ways to use it.

So I think what I'm going to do is put a lot of the Librium I had after Father disappeared in Mother's whisky glass tonight if she's alone, or tomorrow night or the night after if she's not, so that she'll still be knocked out the next morning when it's light enough out for me to get her into the bathtub with the duck. Only this time it won't be like Father and I want to watch it all happen.

And then that same evening when the sun's going down and before Dubic has a chance to find out about Mother I'll take the duck down to the park and watch it jump on him and cut his head off with its scissors.

I've got it all figured out and I'm not really scared at all.

This time it's going to be fun.

Thomas Ligotti (b. 1959)

NOTES ON THE WRITING OF HORROR:
A STORY

Thomas Ligotti is the most startling and talented horror writer to emerge in recent years. Exclusively a short story writer thus far in his career, he published all of his early stories in semiprofessional and small press genre magazines for several years, remaining obscure. An American writer, his first trade collection of stories, *Songs of a Dead Dreamer* (1990), was published in England, the result of a gradually growing reputation among the avid genre readers. His second collection, *Grimscribe* (1991), was published at the end of 1991. Perhaps the most startling thing about his work, aside from the extraordinary stylistic sophistication (one is reminded of the polished prose and effects of Robert Aickman's strange stories), is his devotion to horror, which is positively Lovecraftian—as is his bent for theory and knowledge of the history of the literature. This present piece selected is his masterpiece to date. "Few other writers," says Ramsey Campbell, "could conceive a horror story in the form of notes on the writing of the genre, and I can't think of any other writer who could have brought it off." It is no less than an instructional essay on the writing of horror, transformed by stylistic magic and artful construction into a powerful work of fiction. Writing students I have taught have found it a revelation. It is included for your delight and instruction.

For much too long I have been promising to formulate my views on the writing of supernatural horror tales. Until now I just haven't had the time. Why not? I was too busy churning out the leetle darlings. But many people, for whatever reasons, would like to be writers of horror tales, I know this. Fortunately, the present moment is a convenient one for me to share my knowledge and experience regarding this special literary vocation. Well, I guess I'm ready as I'll ever be. Let's get it over with.

The way I plan to proceed is quite simple. First, I'm going to sketch out the basic plot, characters, and various other features of a short horror story. Next, I will offer suggestions on how these raw elements may be treated in a few of the major styles which horror writers have exploited over the years. Each style is different and has its own little tricks. This approach will serve as an aid in deciding which style is the right one and for whom. And if all goes well, the novitiate teller of terror tales will be saved much time and agony discovering such things for himself. We'll pause at certain spots along the way to examine specific details, make highly biased evaluations, submit general commentary on the philosophy of horror fiction, and so forth.

At this point it's only fair to state that the following sample story, or rather its rough outline form, is not one that appears in the published works of Gerald K. Riggers, nor will it ever appear. Frankly, for reasons we'll explore a little later, I just couldn't find a way to tell this one that really satisfied me. Such things happen. (Perhaps farther down the line we'll analyze these extreme cases of irreparable failure, perhaps not.) Nevertheless the unfinished state of this story does not preclude using it as a perfectly fit display model to demonstrate how horror writers do what they do. Good. Here it is, then, as told in my own words. A couple-three paragraphs, at most.

The Story

A thirtyish but still quite youthful man, let's name him Nathan, has a date with a girl whom he deeply wishes to impress. Toward this end, a minor role is to be played by an impressive new pair of trousers he intends to find and purchase. A few obstacles materialize along the way, petty but frustrating bad luck, before he finally manages to secure the exact trousers he needs and at an extremely fair price. They are exceptional in their tailoring, this is quite plain. So far, so good. Profoundly good, to be sure, since Nathan intensely believes that one's personal possessions should themselves possess a certain substance, a certain quality. For example, Nathan's winter overcoat is the same one his father wore for thirty winters; Nathan's wristwatch is the same one his grandfather wore going on four decades, in all seasons. For Nathan, peculiar essences inhere in certain items of apparel, not to mention certain other articles small and large, certain happenings in time and space, certain people, and certain notions. In Nathan's view, yes, every facet of one's life should shine with these essences which alone make things really real. What are they? Nathan, over a period of time, has narrowed the essential elements down to three: something magic, something timeless, something profound. Though the world around him is for the most part lacking in these special ingredients, he perceives his own life to contain them in fluctuating but usually acceptable quantities. His new trousers certainly do; and Nathan hopes, for the first time in his life, that a future romance—to be conducted with one Lorna McFickel—will too.

So far, so good. Luckwise. Until the night of Nathan's first date. Miss McFickel resides in a respectable suburb but, in relation to where Nathan lives, she is clear across one of the most dangerous sectors of the city. No problem: Nathan's ten-year-old car is in mint condition, top form. If he just keeps the doors locked and the windows rolled up, everything will be fine. Worst luck, broken bottles on a broken street, and a flat tire. Nathan curbs the car. He takes off his grandfather's watch and locks it in the glove compartment; he takes off his father's overcoat, folds it up neatly, and snuggles it into the shadows beneath the dashboard. As far as the trousers are concerned, he would simply have to exercise great care while attempting to change his flat tire in record time, and in a part of town known as Hope's Back Door. With any luck, the trousers would retain their triple traits of magicality, timelessness, and profundity. Now, all the while Nathan is fixing the tire, his legs feel stranger and stranger. He could have attributed this to the physical labor he was performing in a pair of trousers not exactly designed for such abuse, but he would have just been fooling himself. For Nathan remembers his legs feeling strange, though less noticeably so, when he first tried on the trousers at home. Strange how? Strange as in a little stiff, and even then some. A little funny. Nonsense, he's just nervous about his date with lovely Lorna McFickel.

To make matters worse, two kids are now standing by and watching Nathan change the tire, two kids who look like they recently popped up from a bottomless ash pit. Nathan tries to ignore them, but he succeeds a little too well in this. Unseen by him, one of the kids edges toward the car and opens the front door. Worst luck, Nathan forgot to lock it. The kid lays his hands on Nathan's father's coat, and then both kids disappear into a run-down apartment house.

Very quickly now. Nathan chases the kids into what turns out to be a condemned building, and he falls down the stairs leading to a lightless basement. It's not that the stairs were rotten, no. It *is* that Nathan's legs have finally given out; they just won't work anywhere. They are very stiff and feel funnier than ever. And not only his legs, but his entire body below the waist . . . except, for some reason, his ankles and feet. They're fine. For the problem is not with Nathan himself. It's with those pants of his. The following is why. A few days before Nathan purchased the pants, they were returned to the store for a cash refund. The woman returning them claimed that her husband didn't like the way they felt. She lied. Actually, her husband couldn't have cared less how the pants felt, since he'd collapsed from a long-standing heart ailment not long after trying them on. And with no one home to offer him aid, he died. It was only after he had lain several hours dead in those beautiful trousers that his unloving wife came home and, trying to salvage what she could from the tragedy, put her husband into a pair of old dungarees before making another move. Poor Nathan, of course, was not informed of his pants' sordid past. And when the kids see that he is lying helpless in the dust of that basement, they decide to take advantage of the situation and strip this man of his valuables . . . starting with those expensive-looking slacks and whatever treasures they may contain. But after they relieve a protesting, though paralyzed Nathan of his pants, they do not pursue their pillagery any further. Not after they see Nathan's legs, which are the putrid members of a man many days dead. With the lower half of Nathan rapidly rotting away, the upper must also die among the countless shadows of that condemned building. And mingled with the pain and madness of his untimely demise, Nathan abhors and grieves over the thought that, for a while anyway, Miss McFickel will think he has stood her up on the first date of what was supposed to be a long line of dates destined to evolve into a magic and timeless and profound affair of two hearts. . . .

Incidentally, this story was originally intended for publication under my perennial pen name, G.K. Riggers, and entitled: "Romance of a Dead Man."

The Styles

There is more than one way to write a horror story, so much one expects to be told at this point. And such a statement, true or false, is easily demonstrated. In this section we will examine what may be termed three primary techniques of terror. They are: the *realistic* technique, the *traditional Gothic* technique, and the *experimental* technique. Each serves its user in different ways and realizes different ends, there's no question about that. After a little soul-searching, the prospective horror writer may awaken to exactly what his ends are and arrive at the most efficient technique for handling them. Thus . . .

The realistic technique. Since the cracking dawn of consciousness, restless tongues have asked: is the world, and are its people, real? Yes, answers realistic fiction, but only when it is, and they are, normal. The supernatural, and all it represents, is profoundly abnormal, and therefore unreal. Few would argue with these conclusions. Fine. Now the highest aim of the realistic horror writer is to prove, in realistic terms, that the unreal is real. The question is, can this be done? The answer is, of course not: one would look silly attempting such a thing. Consequently the realistic horror writer, wielding the hollow proofs and premises of his art, must settle for merely *seeming* to smooth out the ultimate paradox. In order to achieve this effect, the supernatural realist must really know the normal world, and deeply take for granted its reality. (It helps if he himself is normal and real.) Only then can the unreal, the abnormal, the supernatural be smuggled in as a plain brown package marked Hope, Love, or Fortune Cookies, and postmarked: the Edge of the Unknown. And of the dear reader's seat. Ultimately, of course, the supernatural explanation of a given story depends entirely on some irrational principle which in the real, normal world looks

as awkward and stupid as a rosy-cheeked farmlad in a
den of reeking degenerates. (Amend this, possibly, to
rosy-cheeked degenerate . . . reeking farmlads.) Nevertheless, the hoax can be pulled off with varying degrees
of success, that much is obvious. Just remember to
assure the reader, at certain points in the tale and by way
of certain signals, that it's now all right to believe the
unbelievable. Here's how Nathan's story might be told
using the *realistic* technique. Fast forward.

Nathan is a normal and real character, sure. Perhaps
not as normal and real as he would like to be, but he does
have his sights set on just this goal. He might even be a
little too intent on it, though without passing beyond the
limits of the normal and the real. His fetish for things
"magic, timeless, and profound" may be somewhat
unusual, but certainly not abnormal, not unreal. (And to
make him a bit more real, one could supply his coat, his
car, and grandfather's wristwatch with specific brand
names, perhaps autobiographically borrowed from one's
own closet, garage, and wrist.) The triple epithet which
haunts Nathan's life—similar to the Latinical slogans on
family coats-of-arms—also haunts the text of the tale
like a song's refrain, possibly in italics as the submerged
chanting of Nathan's undermind, possibly not. (Try not
to be too artificial, one recalls this is realism.) Nathan
wants his romance with Lorna McFickel, along with
everything else he considers of value in existence, to be
magic, timeless, and the other thing. For, to Nathan,
these are attributes that are really normal and really real
in an existence ever threatening to go abnormal and
unreal on one, anyone, not just him.

Okay. Now Lorna McFickel represents all the virtues
of normalcy and reality. She could be played up in the
realistic version of the story as much more normal and
real than Nathan. Maybe Nathan is just a little neurotic,
maybe he needs normal and real things too much, I don't
know. Whatever, Nathan wants to win a normal, real

love, but he doesn't. He loses, even before he has a chance to play. He loses badly. Why? For the answer we can appeal to a very prominent theme in the story: Luck. Nathan is just unlucky. He had the misfortune to brush up against certain *outside* supernatural forces and they devastated him body and soul. But *how* did they devastate him, this is really what a supernatural horror story, even a realistic one, is all about.

Just how, amid all the realism of Nathan's life, does the supernatural sneak past Inspectors Normal and Real standing guard at the gate? Well, sometimes it goes in disguise. In realistic stories it is often seen impersonating two inseparable figures of impeccable reputation. I'm talking about Dr. Cause and Prof. Effect. Imitating the habits and mannerisms of these two, not to mention taking advantage of their past record of reliability, the supernatural can be accepted in the best of places, be unsuspiciously abandoned on almost any doorstep—not the bastard child of reality but its legitimized heir. Now in Nathan's story the source of the supernatural is somewhere inside those mysterious trousers. They are woven of some fabric which Nathan has never seen the like of; they have no labels to indicate their maker; there is something indefinably alluring in their make-up. When Nathan asks the salesman about them, we introduce our *first cause:* the trousers were made in a foreign land—South America, Eastern Europe, Southeast Asia —which fact clarifies many mysteries, while also making them even more mysterious. The realistic horror writer may also allude to well-worn instances of sartorial magic (enchanted slippers, invisible-making jackets), though one probably doesn't want the details of this tale to be overly explicit. Don't risk insulting your gentle reader.

At this point the alert student may ask: but even if the trousers are acknowledged as magic, why do they have the particular effect they eventually have, causing Nathan to rot away below the waist? To answer this question we need to introduce our *second cause:* the trousers were worn, for several hours, by a dead man. But these "facts" explain nothing, right? Of course they don't. However, they may seem to explain everything if they are revealed in the right manner. All one has to do is link up the first and second causes (there may even be more) within the scheme of a realistic narrative. For example, Nathan might find something in the trousers leading him to deduce that he is not their original owner. Perhaps he finds a winning lottery ticket of significant, though not too tempting, amount. (This also fits in nicely with the theme of luck.) Being a normally honest type of person, Nathan calls the clothes store, explains the situation, and they give him the name and phone number of the gentleman who originally put those pants on his charge account and, afterward, returned them. Nathan puts in the phone call and finds out that the pants were returned not by a man, but by a woman. The very same woman who explains to Nathan that since her husband has passed on, rest his soul, she could really use the modest winnings from that lottery ticket. By now Nathan's mind, and the reader's, is no longer on the lottery ticket at all, but on the revealed fact that Nathan is the owner and future wearer of a pair of pants once owned (and worn? it is interrogatively hinted) by a *dead man*. After a momentary bout with superstitious repellance, Nathan forgets all about the irregular background of his beautiful, almost new trousers. The reader, however, doesn't forget. And so when almost-real, almost-normal Nathan loses all hope of achieving full normalcy and reality, the reader knows why, and in more ways than one.

The *realistic* technique.

It's easy. Now try it yourself.

The traditional Gothic technique. Certain kinds of people, and *a fortiori* certain kinds of writers, have always experienced the world around them in the Gothic manner, I'm almost positive. Perhaps there was even some little stump of an apeman who witnessed prehistoric lightning as it parried with prehistoric blackness in a night without rain, and felt his soul rise and fall at the same time to behold this cosmic conflict. Perhaps such displays provided inspiration for those very first imaginings that were not born of the daily life of crude survival, who knows? Could this be why all our primal mythologies are Gothic? I only pose the question, you see. Perhaps the labyrinthine events of triple-volumed shockers passed, in abstract, through the brains of hairy, waddling things as they moved around in moon-trimmed shadows during their angular migrations across lunar landscapes of craggy rock or skeletal wastelands of jagged ice. These ones needed no convincing, for nothing needed to *seem* real to their little minds as long as it *felt* real to their blood. A gullible bunch of creatures, these. And to this day the fantastic, the unbelievable, remains potent and unchallenged by logic when it walks amid the gloom and grandeur of a Gothic world. So much goes without saying, really.

Therefore, the advantages of the *traditional Gothic* technique, even for the contemporary writer, are two. One, isolated supernatural incidents don't look as silly in a Gothic tale as they do in a realistic one, since the latter obeys the hard-knocking school of reality while the former recognizes only the University of Dreams. (Of course the entire Gothic tale itself may look silly to a given reader, but this is a matter of temperament, not technical execution.) Two, a Gothic tale gets under a reader's skin and stays there far more insistently than other kinds of stories. Of course it has to be done right, whatever you take the words *done right* to mean. Do they mean that Nathan has to function within the massive incarceration of a castle in the mysterious fifteenth century? No, but he may function within the massive incarceration of a castlelike skyscraper in the just-as-mysterious twentieth. Do they mean that Nathan must be a brooding Gothic hero and Miss McFickel an ethereal Gothic heroine? No, but it may mean an extra dose of obsessiveness in Nathan's psychology, and Miss McFickel may seem to him less the ideal of normalcy and reality than the pure Ideal itself. Contrary to the realistic story's allegiance to the normal and the real, the world of the Gothic tale is fundamentally unreal and abnormal, harboring essences which are magic, timeless, and profound in a way the realistic Nathan never dreamed. So, to rightly do a Gothic tale requires, let's be frank, that the author be a bit of a lunatic, at least while he's authoring, if not at all times. Hence, the well-known inflated rhetoric of the Gothic tale can be understood as more than an inflatable raft on which the imagination floats at its leisure upon the waves of bombast. It is actually the sails of the Gothic artist's soul filling up with the winds of ecstatic hysteria. And these winds just won't blow in a soul whose climate is controlled by central air-conditioning. So it's hard to tell someone how to write the Gothic tale, since one really has to be born to the task. Too bad. The most one can do is offer a pertinent example: a Gothic scene from "Romance of a Dead Man," translated from the original Italian of Geraldo Riggerini. This chapter is entitled "The Last Death of Nathan."

Through a partially shattered window, its surface streaked with a blue film of dust and age, the diluted glow of twilight seeped down onto the basement floor where Nathan lay without hope of mobility. In the dark you're not anywhere, he had thought as a child at each and every bedtime; and, in the bluish semiluminescence of that stone cellar, Nathan was truly not anywhere. He raised himself up on one elbow, squinting through tears of confusion into the filthy azure dimness. His grotesque posture resembled the half-anesthetized efforts of a patient who has been left alone for a moment while awaiting surgery, *anxiously looking around to see if he's simply been forgotten on that frigid operating table. If only his legs would move, if only that paralyzing pain would suddenly become cured. Where were those wretched doctors, he asked himself dreamily. Oh, there they were, standing behind the turquoise haze of the surgery lamps. "He's out of it, man," said one of them to his colleague. "We can take everything he's got on him." But after they removed Nathan's trousers, the operation was abruptly terminated and the patient abandoned in the blue shadows of silence. "Jesus, look at his legs, look," they had screamed. Oh, if only he could now scream like that, Nathan thought among all the fatal chaos of his other thoughts. If only he could scream loud enough to be heard by that girl, by way of apologizing for his permanent absence from their magic, timeless, and profound future, which was in fact as defunct as the two legs that now seemed to be glowing glaucous with putrefaction before his eyes. Couldn't he now emit such a scream, now that the tingling agony of his liquifying legs was beginning to spread upwards throughout his whole body and being? But no. It was impossible—to scream that loudly—though he did manage, in no time at all, to scream himself straight to death.*

The *traditional Gothic* technique.

It's easy. Now try it yourself.

The experimental technique. Every story, even a true one, wants to be told in only one single way by its writer, yes? So, really, there's no such thing as experimentalism in its trial-and-error sense. A story is not an experiment, an experiment is an experiment. True. The "experimental" writer, then, is simply following the story's commands to the best of his human ability. The writer is not the story, the story is the story. See? Sometimes this is very hard to accept, and sometimes too easy. On the one hand, there's the writer who can't face his fate: that the telling of a story has nothing at all to do with him; on the other hand, there's the one who faces it too well: that the telling of the story has nothing at all to do with him. Either way, literary experimentalism is simply the writer's imagination, or lack of it, and feeling, or absence of same, thrashing their chains around in the escape-proof dungeon of the words of the story. One writer is trying to get the whole breathing world into the two dimensions of his airless cell, while the other is adding layers of bricks to keep that world the hell out. But despite the most sincere efforts of each prisoner, the sentence remains the same: to stay exactly where they are, which is where the story is. It's a condition not unlike the world itself, except it doesn't hurt. It doesn't help either, but who cares?

The question we now must ask is: is Nathan's the kind of horror story that demands treatment outside the conventional realistic or Gothic techniques? Well, it may be, depending on whom this story occurred to. Since it occurred to me (and not too many days ago), and since I've pretty much given up on it, I guess there's no harm in giving this narrative screw another turn, even if it's in the wrong direction. Here's the way mad Dr. Riggers would experiment, blasphemously, with his man-made Nathanstein. The secret of life, my ugly Igors, is time . . . time . . . time.

The experimental version of this story could actually be told as two stories happening "simultaneously," each narrated in alternating sections which take place in parallel chronologies. One section begins with the death of Nathan and moves backward in time, while its counterpart story begins with the death of the original owner of the magic pants and moves forward. Needless to say, the facts in the case of Nathan must be juggled around so as to be comprehensible from the beginning, that is to say from the end. (Don't risk confusing your worthy readers.) The stories converge at the crossroads of the final section where the destinies of their characters also converge, this being the clothes store where Nathan purchases the fateful trousers. On his way into the store he bumps into a woman who is preoccupied with counting a handful of cash, this being the woman who has just returned the trousers.

"Excuse me," says Nathan.

"Look where you're going," says the woman at the same instant.

Of course at this point we have already seen where Nathan is going and, in a way too spooky to explain right now, so has he.

The *experimental* technique. It's easy, now try it yourself.

Another Style

All the styles we have just examined have been simplified for the purposes of instruction, haven't they? Each is a purified example of its kind, let's not kid ourselves. In the real world of horror fiction, however, the above three techniques often get entangled with one another in hopelessly mysterious ways, almost to the point where all previous talk about them is useless for all practical purposes. But an ulterior purpose, which I'm saving for later, may thus be better served. Before we get there, though, I'd like, briefly, to propose still another style.

The story of Nathan is one very close to my heart and I hope, in its basic trauma, to the hearts of many others. I wanted to write this horror tale in such a fashion that its readers would be distressed not by the personal, individual catastrophe of Nathan but by his very existence in a world, even a fictional one, where a catastrophe of this type and magnitude is possible. I wanted to employ a style that would conjure all the primordial powers of the universe independent of the conventional realities of the

Individual, Society, or Art. I aspired toward nothing less than a pure style without style, a style having nothing whatever to do with the normal or abnormal, a style magic, timeless, and profound . . . and one of great horror, the horror of a god. The characters of the story would be Death himself in the flesh, Desire in a new pair of pants, the pretty eyes of Desiderata and the hideous orbs of Loss. And linked hand-in-hand with these terrible powers would be the more terrible ones of Luck, Fate, and all the miscellaneous minions of Doom.

I couldn't do it, my friends. It's not easy, and I don't suggest that you try it yourself.

The Final Style

Dear horror writers of the future, I ask you: what is the style of horror? What is its tone, its *voice?* Is it that of an old storyteller, keeping eyes wide around the tribal campfire; is it that of a documentarian of current or historical happenings, reporting events heard-about and conversations overheard; is it even that of a yarn-spinning god who can see the unseeable and reveal, from viewpoint omniscient, the horrific hearts of man and monster? I have to say that it's none of these, sorry if it's taken so long.

To tell you the truth, I'm not sure myself what the voice of horror really is. But throughout my career of eavesdropping on the dead and the damned, I know I've heard it; and Gerry Riggers, you remember him, has tried to put it on paper. Most often it sounds to me very simply like a voice calling out in the middle of the night, a single voice with no particular qualities. Sometimes it's muffled, like the voice of a tiny insect crying for help from inside a sealed coffin; and other times the coffin shatters, like a brittle exoskeleton, and from within rises a piercing, crystal shriek that lacerates the midnight blackness. These are approximations, of course, but highly useful in pinning down the sound of the voice of horror, if one still wants to.

In other words, the proper style of horror is really that of the *personal confession,* and nothing but: manuscripts found in lonely places. While some may consider this the height of cornball melodrama, and I grant that it is, it is also the rawhead and bloody bones of true blue grue. It's especially true when the confessing narrator has something he must urgently get off his chest and labors beneath its nightmarish weight all the while he is telling the tale. Nothing could be more obvious, except perhaps that the tale teller, ideally, should himself be a writer of horror fiction by trade. That really is more obvious. Better. But how can the *confessional* technique be applied to the story we've been working with? Its hero isn't a horror writer, at least not that I can see. Clearly some adjustments have to be made.

As the reader may have noticed, Nathan's character can be altered to suit a variety of literary styles. He can lean toward the normal in one and the abnormal in another. He can be transformed from fully fleshed person to disembodied fictional abstraction. He can play any number of basic human and nonhuman roles, representing just about anything a writer could want. Mostly, though, I wanted Nathan, when I first conceived him and his ordeal, to represent none other than my real life self. For behind my pseudonymic mask of Gerald Karloff Riggers, I am no one if not Nathan Jeremy Stein.

So it's not too farfetched that in his story Nathan should be a horror writer, at least an aspiring one. Perhaps he dreams of achieving Gothic glory by writing tales that are nothing less than magic, timeless, and you know what. Perhaps he would sell his soul in order to accomplish this fear, I mean *feat.* But Nathan was not born to be a seller of his soul or anything else, that's why he became a horror writer rather than going into Dad's (and Grandad's) business. Nathan is, however, a buyer: a haunter of spectral marketplaces, a visitant of discount houses of unreality, a bargain hunter in the deepest basement of the unknown. And in some mysterious way, he comes to procure his dream of horror without even realizing what it is he's bought or with what he has bought it. Like the other Nathan, *this* Nathan eventually finds that what he's bought is not quite what he bargained for—a pig in a poke rather that a nice pair of pants. What? I'll explain.

In the confessional version of Nathan's horror story, the main character must be provided with something horrible to confess, something fitting to his persona as a die-hard horrorist. The solution is quite obvious, which doesn't prevent its also being freakish to the core. Nathan will confess that he's gone too far into FEAR. He's always had a predilection for this particular discipline, but now it's gotten out of hand, out of control, and out of this world.

The turning point in Nathan's biography of horror-seeking is, as in previous accounts, an aborted fling with Lorna McFickel. In the other versions of the story, the character known by this name is a personage of shifting significance, representing at turns the ultra-real or the super-ideal to her would-be romancer. The confessional version of "Romance of a Dead Man," however, gives her a new identity, namely that of Lorna McFickel herself, who lives across the hall from me in a Gothic castle of high-rise apartments, twin-towered and honeycombed with newly carpeted passageways. But otherwise there's not much difference between the female lead in the fictional story and her counterpart in the factual one. While the storybook Lorna will remember Nathan as the creep who spoiled her evening, who disappointed her—Real Lorna, Normal Lorna feels exactly the same way, or rather felt, since I doubt she even thinks about the one she called, and not without good reason, *the most digusting creature on the face of the earth.* And although this patent exaggeration was spoken in the heat of a very hot moment, I believe her attitude was basically sincere. Even so, I will never reveal the motivation for this outburst of hers, not even under the throbbing treat of torture. (I meant, of course, to write *threat.* Only a tricky trickle of the pen's ink, nothing more.) Such things as motivation are not important to this horror story anyway, not nearly as important as what happens to Nathan following Lorna's revelatory rejection.

For he now knows, as he never knew before, how weird he really is, how unlike everyone else, how abnormal and unreal fate has made him. He knows that supernatural influences have been governing his life all along, that he is subject only to the rule of demonic forces, which now want this expatriate from the red void back in their bony arms. In brief, Nathan should never have been born a human being, a truth he must accept. Hard. (The most painful words are "never again," or just plain "never!") And he knows that someday the demons will come for him.

The height of the crisis comes one evening when the horror writer's ego is at low ebb, possibly to ebb all the way back to the abyss. He has attempted to express his supernatural tragedy in a short horror story, his last, but he just can't reach a climax of suitable intensity and imagination, one that would do justice to the cosmic scale of his pain. He has failed to embody in words his semi-autobiographical sorrow, and all these games with protective names have only made it more painful. It hurts to hide his heart within pseudonyms of pseudonyms. Finally, the horror writer sits down at his desk and begins whining like a brat all over the manuscript of his unfinished story. This goes on for quite some time, until Nathan's sole desire is to seek a human oblivion in a human bed. Whatever its drawbacks, grief is a great sleeping draught to drug oneself into a noiseless, lightless paradise far from an agonizing universe. This is so.

Later on there comes a knocking at the door, an impatient rapping, really. Who is it? One must open it to find out.

"Here, you forgot these," a pretty girl said to me, flinging a woolly bundle into my arms. Just as she was about to walk away, she turned and scanned the features of my face a little more scrupulously. I have sometimes pretended to be other people, the odd Norman and even a Nathan or two, but I knew I couldn't get away with it anymore. Never again! "I'm sorry," she said. "I thought you were Norman. This is his apartment, right across and one down the hall from mine." She pointed to show me. "Who're you?"

"I'm a friend of Norman's," I answered.

"Oh, I guess I'm sorry then. Well, those're his pants I threw at you."

"Were you mending them or something?" I asked innocently, checking them as if looking for the scars of repair.

"No, he just didn't have time to put them back on the other night when I threw him out, you know what I mean? I'm moving out of this creepy dump just to get away from him, and you can tell him those words."

"Please come in from that drafty hallway and you can tell him yourself."

I smiled my smile and she, not unresponsively, smiled hers. I closed the door behind her.

"So, do you have a name?" she asked.

"Penzance," I replied. "Call me Pete."

"Well, at least you're not Harold Wackers, or whatever the name is on those lousy books of Norman's."

"I believe it's *Wickers*, H.J. Wickers."

"Anyway, you don't seem at all like Norman, or even someone who'd be a friend of his."

"I'm sure that was intended as a compliment, from

what I've gathered about you and Norm. Actually,
though, I too write books not unlike those of H.J.
Wickers. My apartment across town is being painted,
and Norman was kind enough to take me in, even loan
me his desk for a while." I manually indicated the
cluttered, weeped-upon object of my last remark. "In
fact, Norman and I sometimes collaborate under a
common pen-name, and right now we're working together on a manuscript." That was an eternity ago, but
somehow it seems like the seconds and minutes of those
days are still nipping at our heels. What tricks human
clocks can play, even on us who are no longer subject to
them! But it's a sort of reverse magic, I suppose, to
enshackle the timeless with grandaddy's wrist-grips of
time, just as it is the most negative of miracles to
smother unburdened spirits with the burdensome overcoat of matter.

"That's nice, I'm sure," she replied to what I said a few
statements back. "By the way. I'm Laura—"

"O'Finney," I finished. "Norman's spoken quite highly of you." I didn't mention that he had also spoken quite
lowly of her too.

"Where is the creep, anyway?" she inquired.

"He's sleeping." I answered, lifting a vague finger
toward the rear section of the apartment, where a shadowy indention led to bathrooms and bedrooms. "He's
had a hard night of writing."

The girl's face assumed a disgusted expression.

"Forget it," she said, heading for the door. Then she
turned and very slowly walked a little ways back toward
me. "Maybe we'll see each other again."

"Anything is possible," I assured her.

"Just do me a favor and keep Norman away from me,
if you don't mind."

"I think I can do that very easily. But you have to do
something for me."

"What?"

I leaned toward her very confidentially.

"Please die, Desiderata," I whispered in her ear, while gripping her neck with both hands, cutting short a scream along with her life. Then I really went to work.

"Wake up, Norman," I shouted a little later. I was standing at the foot of his bed, my hands positioned behind my back. "You were really dead to the world, you know that?"

A little drama took place on Norman's face in which surprise overcame sleepiness and both were vanquished by anxiety. He had been through a lot the past couple nights, struggling with our "Notes" and other things, and really needed his sleep. I hated to wake him up.

"Who? What do you want?" he said, quickly sitting up in bed.

"Never mind what I want. Right now we are concerned with what *you* want, you know what I mean? Remember what you told that girl the other night, remember what you wanted her to do that got her so upset?"

"If you don't get the hell out of here—"

"That's what *she* said too, remember? And then she said she wished she had *never met you*. And that was the line, wasn't it, that gave you the inspiration for our fictionalized adventure. Poor Nathan never had the chance you had. Oh yes, very fancy rigmarole with the enchanted trousers. Blame it all on some old bitch and her dead husband. Very realistic, I'm sure. When the real reason—"

"Get out of here!" he yelled. But he calmed down somewhat when he saw that ferocity in itself had no effect on me.

"What did you expect from that girl? You did tell her that you wanted to embrace, what was it? Oh yes, a headless woman. A headless woman, for heaven's sake, that's asking a lot. And you did want her to make herself look like one, at least for a little while. Well, I've got the answer to your prayers. How's this for headless?" I said, holding up the head from behind my back.

He didn't make a sound, though his two eyes screamed a thousand times louder than any single mouth. I tossed the long-haired and bloody noggin in his lap, but he threw the bedcovers over it and frantically pushed the whole business onto the floor with his feet.

"The rest of her is in the bathtub. Go see, if you want. I'll wait."

He didn't make a move or say a word for quite a few moments. But when he finally did speak, each syllable came out so calm and smooth, so free of the vibrations of fear, that I have to say it shook me up a bit.

"Whooo are you?" he asked as if he already knew.

"Do you really need to have a name, and would it even do any good? Should we call that disengaged head down there Laura or Lorna, or just plain Desiderata? And what, in heaven's name, should I call you—Norman or Nathan, Harold or Gerald?"

"I thought so," he said disgustedly. Then he began to speak in an eerily rational voice, but very rapidly. He did not even seem to be talking to anyone in particular. "Since the thing to which I am speaking," he said, "since this thing knows what only I could know, and since it tells me what only I could tell myself, I must therefore be completely alone in this room, or perhaps even dreaming. Yes, dreaming. Otherwise the diagnosis is insanity. Very true. Profoundly certain. Go away now, Mr. Madness. Go away, Dr. Dream. You made your point, now let me sleep. I'm through with you."

Then he lay his head down on the pillow and closed his eyes.

"Norman," I said. "Do you always go to bed with your trousers on?"

He opened his eyes and now noticed what he had been too deranged to notice before. He sat up again.

"Very good, Mr. Madness. These look like the real

thing. But that's not possible since Laura still has them, sorry about that. Funny, they won't come off. The imaginary zipper must be stuck. Gee, I guess I'm in trouble now. I'm a dead man if there ever was one, hoo. Always make sure you know what you're buying, that's what I say. Heaven help me, please. You never know what you might be getting into. Come off, damn you! Oh, what grief. Well, so when do I start to rot, Mr. Madness? Are you still there? What happened to the lights?"

The lights had gone out in the room and everything glowed with a bluish luminescence. Lightning began flashing outside the bedroom window, and thunder resounded through a rainless night. The moon shone through an opening in the clouds, a blood-red moon only the damned and the dead can see.

"Rot your way back to us, you freak of creation. Rot your way out of this world. Come home to a pain so great that it is bliss itself. You were born to be bones not flesh. Rot your way free of that skin of mere skin."

"Is this really happening to me? I mean, I'm doing my best, sir. It isn't easy, not at all. Horrible electricity down there. Horrible. Am I bathed in magic acid or something? Oh, it hurts, my love. Ah, ah, ah. It hurts so much. Never let it end. If I have to be like this, then never let me wake up, Dr. Dream. Can you do that, at least?"

I could feel my bony wings rising out of my back and saw them spread gloriously in the blue mirror before me. My eyes were now jewels, hard and radiant. My jaws were a cavern of dripping silver and through my veins ran rivers of putrescent gold. He was writhing on the bed like a wounded insect, making sounds like nothing in human memory. I swept him up and wrapped my sticky arms again and again around his trembling body. He was laughing like a child, the child of another world. And a great wrong was about to be rectified.

I signaled the windows to open onto the night, and, very slowly, they did. His infant's laughter had now turned to tears, but they would soon run dry, I knew this. At last we would be free of the earth. The windows opened wide over the city below and the profound blackness above welcomed us.

I had never tried this before. But when the time came, I found it all so easy.

SPINE-TINGLING
HORROR FROM TOR